Firefly & Wisp

www.fireflyandwispbooks.com
www.facebook.com/fireflyandwisp
www.twitter.com/fireflyandwisp

OENONE
AGATHA RAE

1st Edition Ebook (2013)

Firefly & Wisp Publishing, LLC

BISAC: Fiction / Fantasy / Epic

Library of Congress Control Number available upon request.

ISBN-13: 978-0615823492

ISBN-10: 0615823491

FIREFLY
& Wisp
BRINGING Fantasy TO REALITY

Firefly & Wisp Publishing
422 Myrtle Street,
Ravenna, OH 44266

Agatha Rae

"Oenone"

Acknowledgements

I would like to take this opportunity to thank my friends and family for helping me in creating this novel. First of all, to my dearest friend Agata Mioduszewska, who has given me so much support I cannot even describe. I am very grateful for your patience, for your advice and for your faith in me . Carrie Rae, thank you for all your help and for sharing your experience with me. You are the bravest person I know, and I admire you dearly. Ladies, this book is for you.

I would also like to thank my dear Uncle Leszek "Lex" Mazur as well as my friends Iwona Brauza, Magda Richert, and my fiancée Daniel Grabowski for giving me valuable hints and tips concerning the story.

A huge thank you to Danielle Zwissler and Firefly and Wisp Publishing, LLC for believing in me and allowing me to publish this book. Thank you for letting it all happen!

Special thanks to my Mom and Dad for keeping their fingers crossed for me and my work. I love you very much!

To Henry Cavill. Thank you for the enchantment and inspiration.

❧1❧

Everything is dark. She already discovered she had had a velvet scarf tied around her eyes. It is very gentle and does not allow her to see everything. She is lying on a comfortable yet quite cold mattress. She knows she is undressed, and she feels a pleasant breath of evening breeze caressing her body. Being aware of it all but does not make her uncomfortable.

Someone else is in the room. Very close to her. Deep down she knows it's him, she can smell his skin, recognize his breath. But why is it so dark? Why can't she see him? A gentle touch on her arm, shy, delicate, but firm, makes all her questions disappear. She does not care about anything else now. She feels her senses tightening up, her whole body waiting for more. His palm is stroking her neck, she can feel his lips on her ears, he's saying something, but what is it? She can't understand it, but she does not care about words. Not now. Now, words are useless. My God, how could a single touch deliver such pleasure?

An alarm clock.

Evy woke up suddenly, angry and frustrated. The alarm clock's irritating, high-pitched sound was penetrating her brain without any mercy, reminding her that she needed to get up and go to work. She got out of bed and opened the window. The refreshing smell of morning air filled her lungs. Evy took a deep breath and felt her organism lazily waking up. Her apartment's location was superb, being situated in Foxborough. It - a one-bedroom condo with a kitchen annex - was located on the 6th floor of one of the newer buildings in Boston, and she had a great view. She loved Boston; however she did not grow up there, but moved after college.

One of the best ways of relaxing for Evy was to make herself raspberry tea and sit in an old armchair on her balcony, listening to the sounds of a not-too-distant downtown area, and looking at its evening glow. The place was close enough to the city not to be late for work, but far enough to enjoy the better parts of life like waking up to the sounds of birds' singing and breathing fresh air instead of smog

Evy went to the kitchen, turned on the kettle and went to take a shower. It was Wednesday. She was about to begin another day of her life as a single woman. She never minded that. She had had some relationships, but all of them were a history. It had been a year and a half since she broke up with her last boyfriend. It wasn't anything spectacular; he got a job in a different city, and they both decided that a long-distance relationship was not an option for any of them. Maybe she would follow him, after all, they had been together for almost four years then; it was a relationship they both had invested emotions and time in, but she got very angry when he was pushing her into making a decision, and the worst thing of all was that he gave her an ultimatum: either you're coming with me, or we're done. No time to think things through. No time to make any decisions. Not to mention he did not tell her about the job until he had signed the contract. He knew she'd have doubts about moving out. A fait accompli. She was considering moving out, but at the same point she got promotion at work, a work she truly enjoyed and, oh well, it's been sixteen months since Pete and Evy broke up.

She reached for shampoo.

About six months ago Jeff appeared in her life. Well, not exactly in *her* life. He became a new Creative Manager in the publishing house she had been working for, WORDS. It was a breath of fresh air for the company. WORDS had been having certain financial difficulties lately; they needed new contracts and clients. Before taking his new position, Jeff helped to rescue a paper company and some minor candy manufacturer from going bankrupt, so everyone was counting on his creativity, sense of market and his gift of finding clients and sponsors. Quite soon it turned out he was an invaluable asset for WORDS. He introduced e-book and audiobook markets in the company, started looking for clients in fields unknown for their publishing house, and it looked like the darker days were getting over. Evy, apart from being impressed by Jeff's success, was truly intrigued by him. He was cute. She suspected he had never paid any attention to her, but it was okay. He was her boss after all. She loved flirting with him, but she did not have any hopes he would be interested in her. There was, however, something about Jeff that did not allow her to let him go mentally.

Jeff Richards was the sexiest man she had ever known. There was some kind of aura around him that would not permit her to take her mind off him. Of course he was handsome, but it was something more than that. His personality was amazing. He was so warm, friendly and helpful. He was charming; his smile was to die for. And he smelled perfect. Jeff had been filling her mind almost entirely for two or three months; however, apart from all his attractiveness, he was her boss, and he had never crossed that line, nor had he ever given her any sign he was interested in her privately. Evy did not want to spoil her relationship with him, so, not wanting to risk their professional contact, she had decided not to ask him out. The dreams she had been having about him, which were quite regular and intense, were satisfying, and, at least for now, she did not feel any need to deepen their contact. It was good to see him almost every day and she knew he felt good around her, which made him approachable. On the other hand, once the reasonable side of her would step aside, she knew under her skin, she wanted him badly.

Evy walked out from the bathroom, wrapped in a towel with wet hair sticking to her shoulders. She made herself coffee, and got a yogurt and muesli to prepare a breakfast. In about thirty minutes she was almost ready to go to work. She was wearing her favorite lavender shirt, a black jacket and skirt. Yes, she had to admit since Jeff started working at WORDS she started wearing skirts much more often. She also started wearing high-heeled shoes. Not very high, as she wasn't used to it, but anything above sports shoes level was already a success for her. She combed her long, deep-brown hair, sprinkled her neck with perfume, took her briefcase and left the apartment.

Oenone~Agatha Rae~

2

It was the first week of May and the air smelled of spring. The trees were getting decorated with shy, pale-green leaves and finally, after months of snow and rain, Evy had to wear sunglasses to see the street properly. She had a CD on, she was an audiophile, could not be anywhere without the music, classic rock bands favorably. Right now she was singing "Immigrant Song" along with Robert Plant, felt her blood pressure getting higher and she was becoming more energetic than after drinking the coffee in her apartment twenty minutes ago.

Evy parked her car, a fifteen-year-old 4Runner, which she loved (and secretly called Bob when no one could hear her) outside WORDS and walked into the building. She worked on the 9th floor of an office building on Franklin Street. She was a senior editor and it was a fantastic job for her. She had loved books since she was a child. Reading and writing where her elements. She had been finding her duties very gratifying; not only was she the first reader of a given book, very often a really good one, but also she had to look into some of the things a writer would include to check their correctness. It certainly helped her to expand the general knowledge. There weren't many people among her friends who would beat her during pub contests, she thought and smiled both with irony and lighthearted spirit. The elevator stopped, the door opened, and Evy entered her beloved environment. People hushing here and there, telephones ringing, lots of papers around. She loved it, she really did.

The whole office was an open space with desks. Everyone saw each other and Jeff, being a Creative Manager always had his office open; a symbolic sign telling he himself was open for ideas and suggestions; his way of saying he was there for them rather than the other way round; a gesture everyone appreciated and liked.

The editors' job was done mostly at home, at the office her task was to send emails to the authors with her corrections of their texts, answer to those who would not agree with her ideas, negotiate with them, help them accept the text in its new form and take part in staff meetings. Evy would not spend much time behind the desk, only four to five hours a day. She hated when authors would call to protest against her changes. They were always angry when her corrections were too visible. Their most common accusation was that they could no longer identify with the text, that they feel it was no longer theirs. It was true, sometimes the text, after Evy got her hands on it, did not resemble the original one too much, but people had problems understanding that spelling was important, or that some basic grammar was needed for books to be clearly understood. Of course such explanations would escalate the conflict as authors would want her to realize that despite writing so badly as she had put it, they somehow managed to get published, so maybe she was being too harsh. Yes, sir, yes, ma'am, you did get published because the *material* was good. Not the craft. Seriously, all books were published with *their* names on the covers and all the credits were given to *them*. She was invisible for a statistic reader. The readers would know who Evelyn Dax was only if they looked on the inside page of the cover, and who does that? People from the business, yes. But who else? The authors ought to be thankful for showing them some imperfections of their works. Next time it might help to avoid them, right? Well, apart from some grumpy authors (and they were truly a minority), Evy really liked her job. It was a wonderful combination of freelancing and a regular job.

She sat behind her desk, turned on her computer and was looking for her mug in the drawer when she heard Laura's voice from behind.

"Hi, Evy! How are you?" she asked cheerfully.

"Oh, hi, Laura! I'm good, how's it going?"

Laura was her best friend. They had known each other for over eight years now. They both started working for WORDS together. She was also an editor, but her life was entirely different than Evy's. Laura had been married to Bruce for ten years now. They were both great people, and Evy really liked hanging out with them. When he had a poker night with his friends, Laura would often invite Evy for a lady's pajamas night when they would eat ice-cream, watch "You've got mail", paint toenails and talk about life, job and boyfriends. Laura was really disappointed that Pete and Evy broke up. She knew about Evy's crush on Jeff and was pushing her into asking him out, doing *anything* really. Apart from as sweet a person as Laura was, she did have that little annoying attitude that a woman in her 30s ought to get a husband as soon as possible, so the news that Evy found Jeff attractive triggered all her enthusiasm and hope. She was really keeping her fingers crossed for them, even though Evy kept reminding her it was futile.

"Fine, fine—listen, did you hear we're having a meeting scheduled for today?"

"No, is there anything important to announce? I didn't get a memo."

"Jeff got us a new big client. We're going to publish books for students at the local university. Exclusively. For the next five years! The university decided it was cheaper for them to hire an outside publisher than to publish the books on their own."

"Wow, that's a big thing; that's great!"

"Yeah, I suppose Jeff wants to tell us about it. So, have you given a thought to my idea?"

"Oh, Laura, come on—"

"What? All I said was that you should really ask him out. Nothing fancy—
You really do not need to dress nicely or anything; just ask him out for a coffee after work. What's wrong with that?"

"Well, he's my boss, that's for starters. Also, I have no job-oriented excuse to ask him out."

"He's your boss, so what? You wouldn't do anything inappropriate. In Europe people ask their bosses out for a coffee all the time," Laura said and smiled cheekily.

"Yeah, I bet."

"They do! And it's getting more and more popular here! Just read some women magazines for once! It's normal to ask your boss out if you find him attractive. Check it out; it's in the newest issue of 'Goddess'."

"How many new sex positions are they recommending this time?"

"Seventy-eight. But they guarantee your man will be left wanting more."

"I am sure they will. You know what makes a man astonished in bed?" Evy asked, finally grabbing the mug and getting up from her seat to go into the kitchen.

"What?"

"When you wake up in the middle of the night and start doing push-ups. That's what makes a man *astonished*."

"Yeah, that, too. Actually, what you've described is mentioned here as position number fifty-four, called 'sex-ups'."

"You have got to be kidding me! Give me that magazine!" Evy said, putting the mug away as she took hold of *Goddess*. The moment she was looking through the list of contents, she glanced at Laura and they both laughed.

Laura was sweet, and she really wanted Evy's happiness, but the problem was Jeff and Evy were in a really unfortunate professional position. *Hey, does Goddess mention professional position?*

11

"So, do you still dream about him?" asked Laura when they were making themselves coffee in the kitchen.

"Laura, for the love of God!" Evy hushed her. She looked nervously around to make sure there was nobody in the vicinity. "Stop asking me those things at work! It's inappropriate. And yes, I do."

"How is it?"

"Crazy. And awesome. Look, Laura, the thing is I am really getting tired of this. I've been having the dreams quite regularly, basically since I met Jeff. And they really frustrate me because they make me realize that dreams are all I'm going to have."

"But it proves you want him."

"Of course I do! But you know what? I was listening to a CD when I was on my way here, a record I found behind the back seat of my car when I was cleaning it last week—a random one. I put it on and the very first song was 'You can't always get what you want' by The Rolling Stones. And I thought, that's it. That's what this situation is about."

"Well, then you must have listened to it quite inattentively, because it also says 'But if you try sometime you find, you get what you need'."

"Laura, I love you, but honestly, don't you have some editing to do?"

"Hey, ladies, listen up!" Ben, one of the junior editors, came to the kitchen. "Jeff is here, and we're having a meeting in the conference room in five minutes."

"We're coming!" said Laura and Evy simultaneously.

"He's here!" Laura giggled as she nudged Evy.

"Yeah…" whispered Evy both worried and excited.

3

Jeff Richards started his job at WORDS almost half a year ago. He had worked for other, smaller companies before, but he never had anything to do with books. His job was searching for clients and, once he had found them, making sure they felt good co-operating with his company. He was thirty-three years old, but quite impressively experienced. He had a great rapport with his clients; everyone knew that his secret weapon, apart from outstanding intuition, was that he was a very easy-going person, who easily broke the ice between people and thus had no problem with gaining new clients. It simply felt good working with Jeff. At WORDS he had become the Creative Manager, responsible for getting new clients and the development of the company, and he was about to announce to the staff that he had just signed a very lucrative contract with the association of academic teachers at a local university for a series of scientific books for students.

Jeff knew that Evy had had a crush on him and, to tell the truth, he was finding her quite attractive himself. She was the first person to reach out to him when he appeared in the office for the first time. He couldn't help but notice her beautiful smile and long, brown hair. As much as it surprised him, he quite often found himself wondering if she was dying her hair, or if its beautiful color was natural. And those legs…

These were his very first impressions of her, but quite quickly it turned out that Ms. Dax was simply a tremendously good worker. Not only was she a great editor, but everything she did, she did on schedule. She was also very creative and was a great help during staff meetings, when there was some marketing strategy to talk through.

Evy laughed a lot, and Jeff loved that about her. The sound of her laughter was so pure and soothing to listen to. Knowing that she liked him, he did allow himself to flirt with her from time to time. It was more of a teasing, but it gave him a tremendous satisfaction that they did have some delicate, sensual tension between them. But it wasn't just that. Quite soon, Jeff realized he really liked Evy. As a colleague, as a worker and as a woman. He loved sharing his ideas with her, when he was conducting a meeting, he loved it when she was there, because she always had great ideas and was very approachable. It wasn't long until Jeff spotted that every time he parked in the building's garage, he was, consciously or not, looking for her car, too. Every day he hoped she would come, because that would mean the day was going to be at least fine. It felt truly empty three months ago when she was sick and did not show up at work for over a week. Jeff guessed that was the time he had realized he might have been having deeper feelings for her.

About two months before he started the job at WORDS, he was going through a rough patch with Rachel. Rachel and he were getting ready to celebrate their fifth anniversary, but things had been going downhill for them for some time. They had argued countless times about getting married, starting a family. Jeff had always been skeptical about it, his parents divorced when he was seven. As children he and his sister Monica saw hideous fights between their parents, and then came the nightmare of an ugly and stressful divorce. Since then, both of them stopped believing in the institution of marriage, but Rachel, on the other hand, was very pushy about it. As if the fact they had been together for so long somehow indicated they ought to finally marry. Jeff had secretly admired Rachel for being so confident about him and their relationship. To tell the truth, he had not been sure for some time prior to the break up if he really loved her or if he was simply used to her. They had not been sleeping together for a while now. They did *share* a bed, but there was no passion between them. Either they had mechanical sex, or just did not care to even bother. Jeff knew that Rachel was punishing him in this way for his doubts and lack of engagement, but he never felt like succumbing to this physical blackmail as he had called it. It was not long before his job at WORDS started when they had finally broken up. No tears, anger, nothing. It was as if they were both expecting it for a while, and it seemed they both felt relieved it was finally over. The saddest part of it was that he wasn't even as surprised nor as enraged as he thought he should have been.

Soon after that he met Evy and it was such a breath of fresh air. She was everything Rachel wasn't. Evy seemed spontaneous, funny and fully aware of the impression she made on him. After a while he started having fantasies about her…quite often he was imagining them staying late at work, and making love on his desk. He had the whole scenario ready. He'd ask her to come and sign some papers and then their eyes would meet and the sparks would start flying. He could see him unbuttoning her shirt, while kissing her neck and putting his hands on her thighs …

The problem was that it was so early after breaking up with Rachel that he was afraid he'd treat Evy as a rebound girl, thus at first he did not want to start any new relationship until he was sure of his feelings. He also felt worried other women may want commitment, too, and he was just not into it. He was a long-lasting relationship guy, but he knew it was hard to explain to women he wasn't looking forward to any wedding declarations, it simply wasn't him. What was more, it wouldn't be easy to start a relationship with Evy because he was her superior. If he was even a bit wrong about her feelings toward him, he might face a sexual harassment lawsuit. And even if things would not become as serious as this, he still would risk ruining their professional relationship which was simply flawless. But he had to admit, Evy was very sexy and intriguing. He *really* liked her.

.

Oenone~Agatha Rae~

❧4❧

Laura Levinson was an easy-going, light-hearted and warm person. In love with her husband, absolutely fulfilled with her job, and totally committed to her best friend Evy. They had known each other for years, and they were definitely soulmates; they knew exactly what one of them thought, sharing their deepest secrets and communicating without words. Their friendship started naturally not more than a month after Evy had started working at WORDS. Laura had gone through Evy's breakup with Pete; she had been witnessing her best friend's crush on Jeff and, despite Evy's worries, was actually supporting her and keeping fingers crossed for her happiness.

When Pete left Evy, Laura felt a tiny sting of shame in her heart that Bruce and she had been happily married for years and Evy kept on going on a quite lonely break-up-rebound route at the same time. Laura knew that her friend was looking for and waiting for a relationship, that she was emotionally devastated after the break-up and simply wanted to have a man shoulder to put her head on while watching TV in the evening. At first Evy kept on dreaming about a knight in a shining armor, but she soon became more realistic, and Laura had to admit she, the more common-sensed Ev—certainly, it would spear possible her hurt and disappointment in the future. However, her fascination with Jeff was turning her back into the hopeless romantic, and that meant she was getting ready to sacrifice many aspects of her life just to be with him. She wanted it too much. Laura certainly did not like that; it made her best friend vulnerable, even gullible at times. Laura believed the sooner everything would become clear, the better chances were that Evy would regain her self-awareness, hence she encouraged Ev to make the first step. Not to mention she thought they would simply be good for each other and the chemistry between them was obvious.

Laura was thirty-eight years old, she was slim and tall and had absolutely wonderful, dense, red curly hair and pale skin. She had penetrating green eyes which knew how to smile coquettishly and warmly, but also had no problem piercing another person's soul whenever she was angry.

She had been with Bruce for almost twenty-two years now, ten of which as his wife. They'd been living in Reading, Massachusetts, on the outskirts of Boston. They met in high school where they had some classes together. During the very first two years they hated each other with Bruce thinking Laura was cold and mean and Laura thinking Bruce was simply an ignorant and, basically, a dick. They did get to spend quite a lot of time together because they had many common friends, but they would consequently avoid each other.

It wasn't until the last but one year in high school that all of their gang went camping during a spring break. They made a camp by the lake in the middle of the forest (it wasn't the most legal thing Laura had done in her life and looking at modern teenage horror movies, she kept thinking how irresponsible they all were then) and spent almost entire time swimming and sunbathing. One evening when they were all sitting by the bonfire, discussing the uncomfortable feeling of anxiety concerning their unknown futures after they graduate, Laura went away to go to her tent to get some anti-mosquito gel. Suddenly Bruce appeared behind her determined to confront her about their weird situation. She was angry at first, as he scared her appearing out of nowhere, and they started arguing, as always, when suddenly Bruce pulled her to him and kissed her passionately. She was stunned and outraged at first, but the sparkling feeling they shared once their lips touched simply overwhelmed her. It wasn't long before they both got inside of her tent, zipped the entrance and decided to end the strange animosity between them once and for all. It was the first time for both of them, it was chaotic and rapid, but they wanted it more than anything else at that moment. After half an hour they were lying on the pile of sleeping bags and laughing. Bruce told her he had had a crush on her for two years and she told him she felt that too but was too stubborn to make the first move. Bruce was too shy for it too, hence they both replaced their feelings with anger and frustration and that caused the misunderstanding. They went out from the tent to take a bath in a lake and by the time got back to the rest of their friends, some of them had already been sleeping. The few of them who were still up saw them holding hands when they were approaching and started applauding. Apparently, everyone was more aware of the feelings Bruce and Laura had for each other than the two of them. It wasn't after a week that Laura got nervous they should have used protection, but she did not get pregnant. Not then, not ever.

It all started that night and they survived college years apart from each other (the reunions were the sweetest things ever). After they both had graduated and she became an author of a column with advice of any kind in a new magazine for women (in those times it was impossible to simply google answers to all questions, so her job relied on a solid research) and Bruce opened his construction company, they decided it was the right time to get married. Then the magazine Laura worked for went bankrupt, she got an editor's position in WORDS, a medium-sized publishing house, and Bruce's company was simply in bloom.

Everything was going so fine that two years after their wedding, they decided to try and have a baby. Laura had never been too enthusiastic about it, but she thought that perhaps a woman was never *entirely* ready for having a baby and the whole maternity love would appear once the pregnancy was a fact, so she decided to give it a try. They tried for six months. Then they went through a series of tests, injections and the final verdict was that Bruce was infertile. It was a shock, they went through a rough patch, but it was mostly Bruce who was depressed. He kept telling her he was letting her down, and for her it really wasn't any *big* tragedy. Of course, she was stirred at first, but having a child was never her number one priority and, to tell the truth, it was kind of a relief she no longer needed to remember and think about contraception. She was truly surprised by how much Bruce was devastated, it turned out she had no idea how much he wanted to be a father. They'd undergone a therapy and, some months later, they were able to rebuild their marriage. Then she met Evy and everything started settling down again. She hadn't spoken about the infertility problem with anyone else apart from Bruce. She thought it was loyal, and being loyal to him was her priority. Laura was even willing to say that she was the one with a problem if anyone asked her, but nobody ever had, and now it'd been so long after the sad discovery, that, if asked, she would be tough enough to just say that it simply wasn't anybody's business.

Laura with her light-hearted personality had always been the last person to worry about anything and to cause any of her friends and family trouble. Hence, when she felt a small but distinct thickened area in her left breast when she was taking a shower the other night, she decided not to tell anyone about it , at least until she knew what to say. There was no need for some unnecessary worrying, was there?

The meeting started. Twenty people were sitting in a conference room waiting for their boss to come. Some of them were sipping mineral water from a container standing behind the doors of the conference room, others were busy talking with colleagues or scrolling their smartphones' screens. Evy was sitting with Laura in the third row, right next to the window. The sun was pouring inside and she was keeping her palm on the forehead to see everything clearly. Jeff walked into a room filled with his employees and he immediately spotted two things. One that everyone was visibly anticipating the news, and two that Evy was already in the room. It made him beam inside, he felt good that he was about to announce his success and she was there to witness it.

Jeff hung his jacket around the chair, put his attaché case aside and walked toward the people. He put his hands in his pockets, leaned against the desk and looked at the WORDS staff with a smirk on his face. "Ladies and gentlemen, we've got the contract with the university."

Everyone started applauding and clapping. This was the news they'd been waiting for for months. They had two other competitors and nothing was sure until the end. A contract with a university was a very lucrative bite. Not only had the institution had hundreds of workers who needed to publish books in order to boost and keep their scientific status, but also publishing textbooks assured years of reissuing, new editions and supplements. WORDS had just been contracted to be the official publisher for the university for next five years. It was wonderful news. People were cheering and congratulating Jeff. Evy and Laura were also applauding, although Evy was a bit distracted seeing Jeff smiling. He had a gorgeous smile. Also, she had a feeling he was peeking at her from time to time. Their eyes met few times, and it was pretty electric for Evy, she could feel her heartbeat increasing every time Jeff laid his sight on her. She was very proud of him, and at the same time the joy that was filling up her heart was mixing with the bitter reality that she would not be able to congratulate him in any unofficial way. Only handshakes, perhaps a friendly hug, nothing more.

Jeff was about to start his presentation to explain and inform the staff about all the work that was now ahead of them due to the contract. Evy, however, wasn't able to focus on anything apart from him. She was literally dreaming of him while being awake. When she saw him there, focused on his work, speaking to all of them so confidentially, joking and delivering his speech at ease, she was absolutely unable to concentrate on the essence of his presentation. Evy was slowly drifting into her fantasies, seeing her and Jeff on a romantic dinner. She saw them having a meal in an Italian restaurant (*Does he like Italian food?* She'd love to know that), going for a walk, holding hands and then passionately kissing on the backseat of his car somewhere in the middle of woods. All of it was so perfect.

"Evy, wake up, the meeting is over." Laura nudged her.

Evy looked around astounded by the sound of clapping and realized Jeff ended the meeting. She joined the others and also started applauding and then Jeff went out and left the conference room. It was a lunch break time, and everybody started gathering their things from desks, getting ready to go out and eat something.

"You were with him again, weren't you, Evy?" Laura asked.

"Um—what did I miss? Was there anything important?"

"No, only contract details, nothing the editors would be particularly interested in. All in all, we have a job secured for few years ahead, and that is the most crucial thing for me."

"Oh, yes, that *is* crucial. Wanna go for lunch?"

"You bet, I'm starving. Where are we going?"

"The Antonio's? I am craving for pizza."

"Meet me by the elevator in five minutes."

❧6❧

The Antonio's was one of the best places one might go to enjoy great food and atmosphere. Dark, heavy wooden chairs and tables were situated in a quiet room, lit only with some single dimmed and lazy lamps. The air was filled with the wonderful smell of herbs coming from the kitchen, and on each of the tables there was a candle burning and the whole place seemed to have been swaying to the sounds of John Lee Hooker music. It was a perfect place to go to with a bunch of friends on a Friday night to drink a gigantic glass of cold beer and enjoy live blues music. Looking at such places, one might have truly felt a sting of regret that smoking was no longer allowed here. It kind of deprived the place some piece of its soul. Although, it would be a shame to have ones clothes absorb the cigarette smell when you had to go back to work in about an hour and a half. Yes, The Antonio's was great. And the pizza was delicious. After all, it was voted Boston downtown's number one pizza place three years in a row.

Evy and Laura sat by their favorite table hidden in the corner of The Antonio's. It was the best area to sit because not only did one see the whole place, but also there was no speaker above the table, enabling to talk peacefully. It was also intimate as the table was quite far away from the other ones and instead of wooden chairs, it had very comfortable, red couch to sit on. When Evy and Laura took their seats, Evy for a split of a second wondered how many teenagers were sitting there kissing and going crazy between their meals and bills. Probably a lot. The place definitely asked for it.

After scanning the menu for few minutes, Eve ordered a Caesar salad and a small pizza capricciosa, with ham, mushrooms and double cheese, and a big portion of cold soda with ice and lemon. Laura decided to give spaghetti Bolognese a chance.

"And a diet soda, please," she told the waiter.

"Certainly," the waiter hid his notebook and a pen behind his belt and moved swiftly to the kitchen to report the order.

"I can't believe you drink that diet crap," said Evy teasing.

"Well, your portion of liquid sugar is like a daytime portion for at least three people, so go figure," answered Laura and winked.

23

"Well, yeah, but if you *wanna* drink that kind of stuff, at least do it properly." Evy laughed, "I only get nauseous whenever I drink anything diet."

"Ok, screw the diet soft drinks. How's the Jeff Situation going? We started talking about it this morning—"

"Well, there's nothing new. I have a crush on him, but he's got no interest in me, and he's my superior who just got the job quite recently and won't jeopardize his career for a fling with an editor."

A waiter brought cutlery and drinks.

"Look, Evy, it's been some months now, I know you're pining for him. And honestly, what do you have to lose? You work in the office only a few hours a week; it's not like you need to see him Monday to Friday from nine to five if something goes wrong."

"I know, but I'd hate myself if I made an attempt and he'd reject me, don't you get it? I'd be *so* humiliated—"

"Oh come on, what year do you think it is, 1894 or something? It's the 21st century, women *do* ask men out, and well, they *do* get rejected sometimes. The point is if you don't try, you will never know."

"Maybe," replied Evy and took a big sip of her soda. "The things is, though, I might have the courage to ask him out, but first, I'd need to know if he has any feelings for me."

"Are you blind? Or are you kidding me now?"

Their lunch was served. Evy took her fork and started digging it in the salad.

"Oh come on, Laura, let's drop the subject."

"No. I have known you for years, I see what you're going through. You like him *a lot*, and it's painful to see how you control yourself when he's around, how much you deny your feelings, only because of some office romance bullshit. Look, nobody told you to seduce him, just ask him out for a coffee, it's not exactly asking him to marry you."

"What did you mean when you asked me if I was blind?"

"That you either pretend you don't see the way he looks at you or you're blind."

Evy's eyes widened. It was so funny; she wanted to snort with laughter, but the pieces of lettuce in her mouth stopped her. She felt as if she was a fifteen-year-old schoolgirl giggling with excitement when her friend tells her an older boy she'd been fascinated with asked someone about her phone number.

"Get outta here."

"Evy, it's *obvious*. He looks at you when you're at your desk, he always looks for you in the conference room, and, frankly, I sometimes have a feeling he makes his announcement first of all for you, and then for the rest of the people." Laura poked her pasta with a fork and reached for a salt shaker.

"Well, maybe because he thinks I am distracted during the meetings—"

"Yeah, and we both know why that is."

"Well, so what do I do? I want to get to know him better, get to know him privately, but I am too much of a chicken and don't want to spoil either my or his career."

"Look, I told you, ask him for a coffee. It's so reserved and safe it's ridiculous. If he says no, you'll know you can let Mr. Richards go and you won't have anything to be ashamed of. And if he agrees, you'll spend a nice, not binding, hour talking with him about business."

"I still dream about him, you know? And there's more and more of it, I'm afraid that any contact with him might only trigger fantasies."

"Or cool them if he turns out to be an idiot. Evy, just do something. You keep telling me how much you want him and how much you're scared of even talking to him. Grow up, do something or this thing will eat you alive."

"If I had any certainty that this might work out, I'd be having my lunch with him, not you," said Evy and winked at Laura.

"Ouch," Laura replied and nodded her head in 'an this what I am dealing with' gesture.

They were quiet for some time when Laura finally said, "We've found a great place for summer holidays, Bruce and I, let me tell you—"

Oenone~Agatha Rae~

❧7❧

When Evy and Laura got back to WORDS, Jeff was in his office answering phone calls. He looked across the room, saw them walking in and was glad Evy was sitting opposite him, where he could easily see her. He wanted to get to know her better, but he needed a professional reason to do so, not to mention that Evy, as an editor, did not show up in the office too often. Inside his head there was, however, a plan to invite her to go for a two-day conference with him. It was a conference that was about to take place in a charming town in the mountains, organized by a local university for publishers and students. The students would present their ideas and manuscripts and the publishers would search for new talents. Jeff was seriously considering asking Evy to come with him, after all he was a manager and she was the best senior editor, so that it would not seem unprofessional to ask her to come. He knew that Evy was supposed to work late today. She would either come to the office three days a week to catch up some paper work, or twice and stay longer if she needed more time to work at home. Today, as he heard, Evy told Laura not to wait for her after work. It was perfect because Jeff really wanted to ask her about the conference when there was nobody around. He was worried that people could start gossiping about it and he did not want her to face any mean comments.

It was 5.30 and WORDS was finally getting empty. The last of the people were leaving to go home and Evy was sitting in front of her computer's screen, wearing glasses and wondering if she was using Martian language while corresponding with one of the authors. She had no idea how much simpler she could express herself to make him understand the mistakes he had written in his novel. The author was specifically irritating as he was rejecting any corrections she had made, and he was deeply disappointed that a woman was editing his book. The book was a psychological mishmash about how listening to ones penis' needs would make all the bigger problems in a man's life disappear. Evy was apparently not the most suitable person to check that kind of a text, and correcting mistakes in it was simply beyond author's comprehension.

Finally, tired and irritated, Evy decided to let it go and not worry about it until the next day. She logged out, turned the computer off, hid her glasses in a case and started packing her briefcase.

"Evy? May I ask you to come to my office?" Jeff asked.

Evy jumped in her chair; she thought she was alone. She stood up, and walked to Jeff's office. Evy had been there before, but she liked the place so much she could not deny herself the pleasure of scanning the room with curiosity every time she was there. It was very spacious and seemed really comfortable. There was a gigantic window with a spectacular view of the city. In the middle of the room there was a very big desk standing on a fluffy carpet. The whole office was painted in brown, beige and caramel colors. Opposite the desk there was a leather sofa and two armchairs surrounding a wooden coffee table. There were three massive bookshelves covering the walls. The whole office was cozy and seemed intimate. It must have been a great place to work.

"Please, have a seat," said Jeff, pointing to the sofa. "Would you like something to drink? I can offer you water, soda, something more powerful—"

"Water is fine," said Evy, a bit nervously. It was the first time she was alone with Jeff. Apart from them, there was nobody else on that floor and Evy was able to spend time with him without any interruption or other people coming into the office. She was getting drunk with the thrill of that situation, but she was also a bit worried she would say something dumb, or that she would be too approachable.

Jeff poured water into two glasses and came across the office. She put her glass on the coffee table and sat in the armchair. For him, it was a unique situation as well. It felt great seeing Evy in his office, sitting on a sofa, looking around the room. He glanced at her legs, her uncovered knees were very sexy, and the high heel shoes were shaping her feet and calf in an erotic way. He had to remind himself what the exact reason of inviting her here was.

"So, how's the *pricky* client?" Jeff asked and took a sip of cold water.

"The Penis Guy? Yeah, he's a pain in the ass. I am seriously thinking of asking Hank to take his book over from me. Not only is Mr. Clarks unbelievably impertinent, stubborn and convinced of his own infallibility, but now he thinks I am being sexist because I am criticizing a book for men. It's been over a month since I can't get anything done properly with that guy, I think I'm going to let him go."

"Do that. There's no point for you to get frustrated."

Evy smiled delicately and drank some water. They were silent for some time. Evy was admiring paintings on the walls and was wondering what the reason Jeff had called her. She was also getting stressed that her stiffness might be visible; she was trying very hard to act and talk normally, as if she would be here talking to any regular colleague. Yeah, a fifteen-year-old, for sure. Jeff on the other hand, was looking at Evy and was wondering how to ask her to go with him without causing any awkwardness. Also, he found himself unable to get his eyes off her hair. Finally, he cleared his throat, put the glass away and decided he would just ask her directly.

"Evy, I want to ask you something."

"Sure," Evy answered and felt truly intrigued. The moment he confessed, he had something he wanted to talk with her about, Evy's discomfort disappeared. She was now curious of what this whole meeting was about.

"As you know, the annual edition of Written Word, a conference organized by a college in Westville is coming."

"The conference for publishers and authors organized by Westville College in Colorado; yes, I know."

"Right. This year the board has delegated me to go there as the representative of WORDS and they are allowing me to take someone from the staff with me."

Evy felt her heart beating fast. *Me? Does he want me to go with him?*

"And I was wondering if you'd like to go with me."

For a second, Evy had no idea what to reply.

"Why me?" she finally asked.

"Well, because you're the senior editor," Jeff replied calmly.

"Oh, of course!" Evy said and laughed. She was both relieved and a bit disappointed. Apparently, it was supposed to be a strictly business trip. But maybe this is exactly what she needed? Business trip or not, it could be a perfect occasion to spend some time with Jeff privately, get to know him. This could be way better than Laura's idea for drinking coffee after work.

"When are we going?" asked Evy and drank some more water. It was getting slightly warmer. Just as she was.

Oenone~Agatha Rae~

~8~

Laura was in a waiting room. She was expecting to be admitted in about thirty minutes by an oncologist-gynecologist. She was reading some brochures left on a desk between artificial flowers in a vase and some magazines. Just like it always is at gynecologists, the leaflets were devoted to the newest contraception methods and information about menopause. Skimming the pile of brochures, Laura spotted one about breast cancer. She hesitated, but took it and started looking through it. It turned out to be a guide on prophylactics. Check your breasts regularly, once a month after menstruation, and always remember to ask your gynecologist to do it for you during your examination. Avoid smoking and drinking too much alcohol. Remember to live actively; a long walk every day is the minimum. If there have been cases of breast cancer among your family, remember you need to be extra cautious.

All of those points thrust Laura's heart. She couldn't remember when the last time was that she examined her breasts, not to mention the mammogram she was supposed to have every two years. She wasn't forty yet, but her sister, Kate, had a breast cancer at the age of twenty-seven and underwent mastectomy, so it clearly meant Laura was, statistically, in a bigger danger. She also counted it had been almost four years since she went to visit a gynecologist. Since Bruce was infertile, she no longer needed to take the pill, so she stopped going to the doctor regularly. It all looked hopeless. She put the brochure back on the table and was about to take a tissue out from her purse to dry her eyes, which were becoming wetter with every minute, when the doors opposite her chair opened and a gynecologist asked her gently to come in. Laura had a nasty feeling that once she had left this place, things would never be the same again.

Oenone~Agatha Rae~

❧9❧

They had already discussed the details of their trip and were having a good time together. Evy felt so relaxed she even took her shoes off and was touching the fluffy carpet with her bare feet. It felt nice, delicate and soft. Jeff took off his jacket and they were just sitting there, laughing and telling each other stories from their lives. When Evy looked at her watch, she was shocked to see that almost two hours had passed since she went in to Jeff's office. It was almost 7 p.m. now, and outside there was a wonderful view of a sunset covering the city with its bloody and orange glow. Evy put her shoes back on and started to buckle them up around her ankles. Jeff looked at her softly.

"You don't need to go yet."

"Thanks, but I still have about forty minutes of driving before I get home."

"No, really, Evy, you don't need to go yet." Jeff leaned closer, and touched her palm.

"Oh—no, I better go." Evy slipped her palm from his fingers and walked across the room to the glass door. Jeff got up and walked after her. "Let me open the door for you."

"Thank you." Evy was pleasantly surprised by his chivalrous behavior. Jeff opened the door slightly, and she made a step forward.

Jeff moved swiftly and whispered close to her ear, "Don't go, Evy, don't go—"

Her whole body shivered. Some part of her wanted to leave; she could literally hear an alarm in her head, a nasty, awful sound telling her to leave the place at once or she would be sorry. But that part of her was the sensible one. The sensible Evy had no chance to be heard , it was the sensual Evy that was waking up.

"Jeff, I don't think it's a good idea—"

"I guess we'll never know if we don't try—" he said hoarsely, whispering words directly into her ear. He closed the door and was now gently kissing her ear and neck.

"You know we're alone here, don't you?"

"Yes, I know", Evy replied and closed her eyes. She wouldn't resist him. Not anymore. She felt as if she was getting dizzy with him so close to her. He put his hands on her arms and gently took off her jacket. She leaned her head on him and allowed him to touch her. This was the moment she'd been dreaming of for months. He stroked her hips, started unzipping her skirt. She turned around and kissed him passionately. She did not care if anyone came in, if the professional obstacles that were between them were to be analyzed or not; she decided that this was what she wanted, nothing else. And she wanted it right there and then.

Jeff lifted her thighs and sat her on his desk. He leaned forward and started unbuttoning her shirt. She felt his warm body on her chest and lay down. Nothing mattered, only this moment.

❧10❧

Laura was sitting in the gynecologist's office stiff and stressed. The doctor, Tessa Green, was looking through her medical records. Laura had been, more-or-less, a regular patient of the clinic since Bruce and she started their hopeless battle to become parents. Even though their effort was futile, she liked the personal approach of the doctors working at Femina and decided to keep paying the monthly fee in case she needed any help in the future.

"Ms. Levinson, how long has it been since you were last examined?"

"Over four years ago," Laura said, holding her breath.

"Four years? You do realize that with breast cancer running in your family, you are more exposed to it, don't you?" Dr. Green replied; her voice showed traces of an unpleasant mixture of surprise and moralizing.

"Yes, I am aware of that, but here I am, scared and worried; so please, spare the bitter words." Laura said, surprised with the firmness of her voice. She wasn't being unpleasant. She was determined.

"'Of course… please prepare yourself in the changing room and enter the other room behind the partition. Call me when you're ready.'

Laura walked into the changing room, which was very small, but cozy with gentle, yellow wallpaper, a small night lamp on a tiny table and two coat hangers stuck on a wall. She closed the doors, switched the light on and started to undress herself. When she took her bra off, she touched her left breast carefully, hoping against any common sense that perhaps the thickness that did not allow her to sleep for the past two nights had somehow disappeared. It had not. Laura sighed, undressed herself entirely, put on the hospital-like pajamas and walked out from the changing room. A moment later, she stood in full view of expensive medical equipment, a room which had nothing in common with the dim lit and cozy changing room, a room which, she knew very well, would forever remind her of one of the most traumatic experiences she would most probably need to face in her life. She sat on a chair, lay down and leaned her back on its backrest. She closed her eyes, swallowed loudly, then took a deep breath and called the doctor.

Dr. Green was thorough and gentle. She kept informing Laura about everything she was doing. She took some samples from the Pap smear and asked her to stand up and undress herself from the top up. Tessa stood behind Laura and started examining her breasts. Her left hand stopped immediately once she felt the thickness. A series of questions started; when did Laura discover it, how did she discover it, did it hurt. The right breast was perfectly fine, but Laura saw the shadow of anxiety of Tessa's face when she finally told her patient to dress and to come to her office once she was done. Laura humbly walked back into the changing room, but she had major problems with putting on her clothes. Her hands were shaking, she had to take two deep breaths to button up her bra and then discovered she put her t-shirt on inside-out. Laura fixed it quickly and, with her heart beating so strongly she could hear the pounding inside of her head, she walked out of the changing room and sat on the chair by Dr. Green's desk.

"I won't lie to you, Laura, this doesn't look good."

"Oh—," Laura whispered. She cleared her throat then spoke, "What do you mean?"

"I mean that I don't like this thickening, and I am worried that it might cause us some trouble. We need to go through some tests to be sure what we're about to face."

"We?"

"Of course, I always stay beside my patients. If you're in trouble, we both are going to face it."

Laura felt the very first wave of tears coming into her eyes. She swallowed, hoping to stop the onslaught of more tears.

"What now?"

Tessa leaned on her armchair.

"Your pap smear was fine. I am worried about your left breast, but you already know something's wrong, and I know you're worried, too, otherwise you wouldn't have come. You will have to undergo a biopsy, so we know what is going on.'

Biopsy.

"All right. When will I know the results?"

"We still have our laboratory open, so if you want, I can take you for the biopsy now. The results should be back by Friday, Monday at the latest.

Laura's first reaction was to run away. She did not need any biopsy. She had a lovely life with her husband who was crazy about her, Evy who was like a sister, and her dog Spark who would always wake her up exactly fifteen minutes before the alarm clock so she would spend more time with him during a morning walk. She had all this—it was so comforting—she did not need any biopsy which would most likely tell her that this exact part of her life was over, or at least suspended. Because no matter what the result would be, the careless and fun life of Laura Levinson was over.

"Laura? Do you want to go today? Or do you want me to schedule a test for you for the next week?"

"No, I'll go. Where is it?"

Oenone~Agatha Rae~

The telephone rang. Evy opened her eyes and looked around. She was in her bedroom. She tried hard to remember what exactly happened the other night, and she realized she left Jeff's office once they settled the trip to Westville. Everything else was just a dream. Nothing happened. Again. Grumpy, she picked up the phone.

"What?!" She asked irritated. A long signal in her phone made her realize it was the entry phone that was making the noise. She got up, dressed in a wrapper and walked to the doors making angry and determined steps.

Damn buzzer. If that's the brochures people, I'll kill them! She thought and picked up the receiver.

"What is it?"

"You tell me, my dear," Laura replied. "It's 10:30 AM, we were supposed to see each other by the lake at nine. I hope you got yourself a good excuse for leading me up the garden path."

"Crap! I'm so so, sorry, Laura! Oh my God, come in!" Evy woke up in a second and pushed the button of the entry phone as strong as possible, as if it was to help Laura get to her apartment faster. She quickly tied up her hair and made the bed.

Laura knocked quite angrily. Evy had known her long enough to know that her friend simply hated being late herself, but also late-comers, late deliveries, getting up late, and basically everything that was late. They once joked that only reason she liked latte coffee was because it was lucky enough to have a double "T" in its name.

"Being late shows a total disrespect to the other person who is waiting for you. I even hate when my period is late."

"What, it also shows disrespect?"

"No, a period shows disrespect every time it happens, that's the nature of it. But when this is late, it's not disrespectful anymore. It's fucking annoying."

Evy opened the door and saw Laura waiting outside. She was both irritated and worried.

"Jesus, Evy, what happened? Are you sick?"

"No, not at all, you know it's my day off, so I wanted to spend some time in my pajamas."

"I know it's your day off, and let me just remind you I am having a day off, too, and our devious plan was to do some Nordic walking around the lake, specifically *because* we both have a day off."

"I know, and I'm sorry, please come on, I'll make you some coffee."

"Yeah, you better," replied Laura and walked into the apartment. She locked the door, took off her shoes and followed Evy to the kitchen. As Evy put some water on, she looked at her friend carefully.

"What happened? Why didn't you come? You're never late."

"I know, I guess I must have come back late yesterday...I mean I *came* back late yesterday, had my mind wrapped around other things, and forgot to turn the alarm clock on. I am sorry I got you worried."

"What other things?"

"Work stuff."

"Oh, honey, work stuff. You can say 'work stuff' to your mom, but not me. I know you stayed late in the office yesterday. And judging by your distraction, I believe you were not alone there, were you?"

Evy blushed and smiled. Even though Jeff did not want to let her out from his office only in her dream, he still asked her to join him in a conference. He asked *her*, not anyone else, although there are plenty of other editors among the staff and, deep down, Evy knew he invited her not because of her senior position. He wanted to spend time with her. It all made her soul levitate among the stars.

"No, Laura, I wasn't alone. Here's what happened."

Before the coffee was drank, Evy told Laura the whole story, about the chat in Jeff's office, his invitation and how wonderful it was to talk to him, and how she felt a connection between them.

"That's great, Evy!" Laura said and hugged her friend cordially. "I must say I am stunned. But not surprised. I've been telling you for some time now that Jeff likes you."

"I know, I still haven't asked him out for that coffee by the way."

"Well, when you go with him, you'll have plenty occasions to drink coffee together. I would say he's probably had a difficult decision to make about asking you to join him."

"Why?"

"First of all you could have said no. Even though I am positive that he knows you find him attractive –

"Oh, Laura, come on!" Evy laughed.

"What are you, fourteen?" Laura nudged her. "Adult people *know* certain things and they do not find them embarrassing —they find them normal. So, you could have said no, which would be tough for him. I mean, I'm sure he must have thought the whole thing through very carefully before asking you to join him."

"Due to our professional complications?"

"Of course. It was natural for him to invite an editor; it did not have to be you. And since you both flirt and exchange looks every time it is possible, he risked to invite you. He made the first step, Evy. You were unable to force yourself to ask him for a coffee, and he has just invited you for a weekend in a small, romantic town hidden in the mountains. Ev, it's great. I bet you'll both be checking your own boundaries and expectations all the time."

"I was wondering if I should accept the invitation."

"Well, it's his move, and his risk. He also has to take under consideration the fact that perhaps nothing will happen. It's a good thing that you have agreed. I can't wait to find out what happens."

Evy smiled and winked. Laura was thinking about telling her about her left breast's moody nature and about the biopsy she had done the previous day, but seeing how happy Evy was, she decided not to. If she was sick, and she was slowly taming that thought, there would be plenty of other moments to tell it to Ev, not now when she was waiting for such an important thing to happen. She only hoped Evy wouldn't notice how nervously she was glimpsing at her cell phone laying on the table right next to her coffee.

❧12❧

The conference was to take place the upcoming weekend. Jeff and Evy talked about it on Wednesday and, since Evy did not have any more office hours that week, she spent the rest of the week editing manuscripts at home. At least that was what she was trying to do, because her mind was constantly wrapping around Written Word. Obviously she felt excited about the trip and really curious about how things between her and Jeff would resolve. She wasn't counting on too much, but she did hope for a nice dinner or a drink. She basically hoped they'd get to spend some time together.

On Friday morning, Jeff and Evy met at the airport. They shook hands warmly and moved to check-in kiosks. They placed their luggage on the TSA conveyer belt and made their way toward TSA Screening. It was a pain to have to arrive this early, but you were never sure how long it would take you to get through security. As soon as they got their boarding passes, they got in line quickly. There was a swarm of travelers in line ahead of them.

Once they got closer to the scanners, each took a gray bin and began removing their shoes, and their jackets. They laid their carry-on bags on the slow moving belt along with the bins that held their laptops. One by one, they followed as others were cleared through to the terminal gates. Once they were done, Evy sloppily slipped her shoes back on and sat on a bench a few meters away to tie the laces. Jeff followed her and once their shoes were firmly placed on their feet, their belts on and their cell phones back into their pockets, they decided it was time to have a cup of coffee before departing.

They were soon sitting in an airport's café enjoying their espresso and latte and chatting while waiting for the flight. Jeff was so approachable and easy-going that he would make anyone feel comfortable in his presence. When they took their seats in the restaurant, they still had about an hour before the screens all around the airport would start flashing the information that they ought to move to the gates area. Their table was right next to a huge window, which served as a view point and tempted many people, both kids and adults, to stick glued to its glass to watch the planes landing and taking off. It surely was an impressive view.

"How do you feel about flying, Ev?" asked Jeff picking up his cup of espresso. Evy spotted how cute he looked gently blowing on his coffee before sipping it. It's ridiculous how such ordinary and normal things people do all the time without even paying attention to them, seem so eye-catching once a person you care about does it, isn't it? Oh and he called her Ev. A version of her name reserved only for friends and family. He must have heard Laura calling her like that it felt great.

"Oh, I have no problem with that. Perhaps not the best way to travel, but I don't freak out. You?"

"I'm ok. I do get nauseous when the plane lands and takes off, but it's ok. Short flights are totally bearable."

They spontaneously looked through the window as a Boeing 767 was rising towards the sun. Soon it was just a dot among the clouds and it finally disappeared entirely.

"So, how do you like working for WORDS?" asked Evy. Not knowing him well and not being sure where the border between his private and professional life was, she thought that work seemed like the best, neutral topic for them.

"Great! It's been really fruitful and the people I work with are fantastic. I am sorry if my answer seems cliché, but that's the truth. I really like working there," Jeff replied.

"That's good. I think WORDS has gotten new quality since you became our Creative Manager."

"Thank you, that's very kind." He smiled broadly.

"It's true; I am not just being polite. You're the first manager in two or three years who has started so many changes. And they all seem to be steering WORDS in a very good direction."

"Thank you, Evy, it's really nice to hear. Especially since I have never had any experience with managing a publishing house."

"Well, you're doing it really well," she replied and took another sip of her latte.

"Thanks, I'm trying." He smiled. "I'm really glad you were able to accompany me to Written Word. I have never been to such a conference; what exactly is going on there?"

"Well, there are book markets and symposia. We will get a program and choose what we find interesting for WORDS. There are authors presenting their books, and there are lunches with other publishers where you get to meet the competition. Generally speaking, it's two days of intense work, only it's outside the office."

"Well, I certainly hope we get some free time anyway. I hear Westville is nice."

"It is; it's very charming—hidden among the mountains—a small, but very friendly town."

"How many times have you been there?"

"Twice. The last time was two years ago. As you know, the managers are invited and they decide who goes with them. Last year Laura went with our previous Creative Manager."

"Were they successful?"

"Well, they managed to find some spruce beer, something I guess Westville is famous for, but it's hard to find it in shops at this time of year." Evy laughed.

"Ok, so, were they also successful professionally speaking?", asked Jeff smiling.

"Yeah, we signed three contracts with really good writers. They are supposed to provide us with twelve books all together in the next five years. Among them are a detective stories' author, a horror-gothic-erotica author, and a romance writer."

"Well yes, *that* I know, but have they been published anything yet? I know I should know this, but I haven't checked their results yet -"

"Yes, they have. *Crazy Days, Wilder Nights* and *Tears And Blood* have been published so far. We're still waiting for the crime novel, but the writer got stuck waiting for some ballistic research results. He says he won't go any further with the story until he gets them. He should receive them this month."

"Yeah, but why is it taking so long?"

"He had to pay for it himself, and such things aren't easy. We agreed to pay for publishing and promoting his book, not to financially support the background of the story."

"How many writers are you editing now?"

"Six. I have two pseudo-psychology how-to-do-something-books, one telling the readers how to lose weight and think positively while doing so, the other is the Penis Guy you know. I also have two romances on the way, one is medieval, so it's a pulp full of inquisition, sex and church, the other one is very sex-in-the-city kind of stuff. And then there is one historical novel, really good one, by the way, and a novel of manners."

"You work a lot."

"I like it, I don't mind."

"Doesn't it affect your private life? That is if - if you don't mind me asking -"

"My private and my professional lives have mixed - long time ago. I work at home most of the time, after all, my best friend is my co-worker, and I don't have too big needs as far as my private life is concerned."

"You're single?" Jeff asked this question very spontaneously, but felt a bit stupid the moment he heard himself saying it. If his previous question seemed too private, then this was simply inappropriate.

"Yes, I am. But, I mean, you know, it hasn't always been like that."

"Yeah. Sorry for asking. That was dumb of me."

"No, it's ok," Evy replied and took a mug with almost finished latte in her hands. She was surprised he asked her that. Apparently he *was* interested in her after all. Why else would he want to know?

"I've been thinking about WORDS lately, and the things you are telling me now only confirm my fear," Jeff said after few seconds. "There's no precise publishing genre."

"You're right, there isn't, but I don't think there has ever been. At least not since I work there?"

"Exactly, you just told me you're working on psychological books, medieval romance and a book of manners. I think that WORDS need to have a specific profile, something that would make us more visible and categorize us."

"You just got us a contract with a university. It's something we've never done before."

"I know, but we need the money. You know very well the situation of WORDS is not perfect. However, I am thinking of reshaping it so we would be a publishing house devoted to one, two, *maximum* three genres of literature. One of them might be a university publisher, the other might be crime fiction, and the other, for example, fantasy. I mean, I think it's a good idea to use Written Word as the first step in making such changes, you know? I believe it might be smart to look for promising writers in those particular areas. To avoid the mish-mash."

"I've never thought that we are publishing mish-mash."

"Oh, we are. And I think there's too big competition on the market to publish everything we get our hands on. I mean the company has been doing so since the beginning, so for almost forty years. It was fine at first, but the market has changed and, as you can see, the results are not exactly peachy."

"I don't think anyone in the company has ever come up with such an idea," Evy replied surprised. But it seemed that Jeff was right. That might have been the thing stopping the company from achieving a really significant success. That might have been what was causing the unstable financial situation.

"Well, I am a *creative* Creative Manager, aren't I?" Jeff smiled.

"Yeah, you are," Evy said and she really meant it. "I'd love to talk more about it. Come on, Jeff, they're calling us to the gate."

"Ok, we're going." Jeff took the last gulp of his espresso and stood up.

This trip is going to be great, Evy thought. Jeff thought exactly the same. And that it felt really good to be around her.

Oenone~Agatha Rae~

❧13❧

Laura was in a supermarket walking around the vegetable department thinking about what to prepare for dinner when her cell phone rang. She looked at the display, and a chill ran down her spine. It was Femina. She pushed the answer button.

"Hello?"

"Good afternoon; am I speaking to Laura Levinson?'

"Yes, this is she."

"Ms. Levinson, my name is Shawna Henderson and I'm Dr. Green's PA—Physician's Assistant. I'm calling to inform you that Dr. Green has received your biopsy report. She would like to know if it is possible for you to come to the office sometime this afternoon?"

"Can't you just tell me what the result is, please?"

"I am very sorry, Ms. Levinson, under the law, only Dr. Green is allowed to disclose test results. She's seeing a patient right now, but does have an opening at 2:15; do you think you could make it here by then?"

"But it's my result. *My* result." Laura felt she was getting very hot and angry. She understood the HIPPA rules, although at this point, they felt terribly inhuman. It was difficult to wait a moment longer!

"I know, and once again I am very sorry," said Shawna in a calm and soothing voice. "I understand your frustration, and I'm so sorry I can't tell you more. If 2:15 won't work for you, give me a time and I'll see what I can do to get you in as soon as I can."

Laura looked at her watch. It was 1:30.

"I'll be there at 2:15."

"Thank you, Ms. Levinson. Goodbye."

Laura was standing with a cell phone in one hand and a head of lettuce in the other. She looked left and then right; she could feel her heart pounding. Mechanically, she put the phone back into her handbag and put the lettuce away. After few deep breaths, she took the phone out again and called Bruce.

"Honey, order a pizza today if you're hungry, I have to take care of certain things after work. I will be home later. Ok. No, nothing happened, why would you even think that?" She bit her lip and hoped Bruce did not sense her emotions. "I'll tell you what it's all about once I am back. All right. Love you!"

Then she called Colin, a secretary at WORDS and informed him she wouldn't be back after lunch break. He said, he'd see her next week and wished her a nice weekend. She walked out of the supermarket and promised herself she would be strong.

❧14❧

On the plane it turned out that Evy and Jeff were sitting in completely different aisles. There were 5 rows of seats between them. Evy was surprised at first, but Jeff explained that Colin managed to book the very last seats on the plane. He wasn't sure if he was even going to the conference until only a few days before.

Luckily, the flight was a little under two hours and Evy had a book and an mp3 player with her. She got her music player filled with her beloved The Tea Party's music from her carryon and sat comfortably by the window. Next to her sat a man in his forties, a German guy who, as it turned out, did not understand a word in English. Evy wasn't the kind of person to integrate with co-passengers on trains or planes anyway, so it was a great opportunity for her to listen to some fine music and, from time to time, to drown in her own thoughts. On the right, in an opposite aisle, five rows to the front, there was Jeff sitting by the passage. He had a book in his hands, but Evy could not see the title nor the author. She saw him ordering water with ice and lemon and a chocolate-coated wafer. She had a sandwich, some peanuts and soda with lemon. She was thinking about this whole trip, wondering what was going to happen. Jeff was obviously focused on work and it was clearly his priority for the upcoming days in Westville. Actually, Evy was also curious about it, too. Written Word was a great opportunity to get familiar with really well-talented and aspiring authors, grateful for any interest, full of fresh ideas and creativity. She was also looking forward to seeing the town. It reminded her of Whistler, a town hidden in the mountains in British Columbia.

The conference was to begin with an inaugurating dinner for the publishers at 6pm, three hours after their arrival. Saturday was going to be very busy with symposia and markets. The whole conference was to finish with a lecture given by the university's dean on Sunday after lunch. Evy was wondering if there was going to be any time for her and Jeff to spend together, apart from work. The plan for Evy for the upcoming weekend was to do what she was going there for, namely to find aspiring and promising authors, and enjoy the fact she would spend some time with her manager. She put her headphones on and pushed play. The Tea Party's "Angels" filled her brain with sheer pleasure and, nodding to the music, she allowed her thoughts to drift.

Jeff was a bit disappointed by the fact he wasn't sitting next to Evy, but, actually, they were lucky to get the tickets on the same plane. He was looking forward to the trip. Being a newbie in a publishing business, it was the very first time he was going to see a writers and publishers conference, so, naturally, he was curious to see what it all looked like and if they were to find any new talents. He certainly hoped so. There was no doubt in his mind that with WORDS publishing *everything* it made the publishing house was disappearing in the whole flood of new books releases. The publishing houses which were big enough and had their market position firm and stable, were able to publish all genres but WORDS needed to have a trademark, something they would be known for, to be easier to find by the readers, and, frankly, to spend less money on printing and publishing all there was. He did push the company forward, introducing the world of Internet and audio books as forms of selling their products, but it only made them up-to-date; it wasn't anything to push them forward, to excel the competition. There was potential, and there was a really good personnel working there, and he was given a lot of credit once he got the job and he felt it was a matter of his responsibility, and ambition, to make WORDS jump from a rather small and mediocre publishing house to one that would truly matter on the market. Not even local, but, who knows, perhaps national. He hadn't talked to the board about his idea of profiling yet, but he was more than sure the idea was good and worth of pursuing. He needed the upcoming conference to see the publishing reality from the inside. It was a whole new world for him, and yes, he knew what the marketing strategy was, he knew how to help business and prevent, or even save, it from bankruptcy, but the publishing market was a virgin territory for him. Jeff was excited and curious about the event. He was also very glad Evy was there with him.

The delicate sound of the fasten-seat-belt sign turning off woke Jeff up, who had no idea when he started dozing. He blinked his eyes few times and looked at the small signalizing devices above the seat in front of him. The no-smoking sign was still on, but the seatbelt one was dark. He realized it was not a mishear. He looked at his hips and discovered his belt was fastened. Jeff looked to his right and there was a chubby teenage boy sleeping calmly. He looked over his shoulder and saw Evy waving to him from her seat. She nodded her head friendly and it was clear she fastened up his seatbelt. He waved her back and got up to get his hand baggage from the above-seats storage. She did the same and they smiled at each other again. Some minutes later, after countless mini-steps in an overcrowded aisle, they finally left the plane and took a deep breath of Westville air.

"I assume it was you who fastened my seatbelt?" Jeff asked smiling.

"Guilty as charged," Evy replied and smiled back at him.

"Why did you do that? A flight attendant could have woken me up."

"Yeah, but the idea was *not* to wake you up. You told me you feel nauseous when a plane takes off and lands. I wanted you to have a pleasant landing."

"Thank you." Jeff smiled.

"Come on, let's take a cab."

Oenone~Agatha Rae~

☙15☙

They checked in to a pretty nice hotel called The Panorama and Evy immediately liked the cozy feel of it. It was a three-star hotel with a wooden restaurant and a foyer with purple ornaments. The building wasn't too big, it had six floors and the walls were decorated by pictures of nearby lakes and mountain peaks. They showed their IDs, their bookings were checked, the concierge handed them their keys and they headed for their rooms. He took the stairs, she decided to give an elevator a chance and to their surprise, not only did they meet on the same floor but it turned out their rooms were right next to each other. After the awkward exchange of "who knew" facial expressions, they opened their doors and ... to each other's amazement, it was a suite, one big room with a thin wall and double doors separating them. There was an awkward silence during which he and Evy stared at each other through the open doors between their rooms which, as if it all wasn't enough, were open. It was clear nobody wanted to be the first one to close them, but it was also obvious they both felt a bit uncomfortable with the situation.

"I – I hope you don't snore," Evy finally joked and they both laughed a bit nervously.

"Oh, you bet I do, I feel sorry for you already!"

Ok, now I won't be able to talk in my sleep. Everyone who had ever shared a room with her reminded her of that little quirk of hers.

"I had *no* idea that we would be in a suite," Jeff said and put his right palm on his chest in I-swear-to-God-it's-not-my-fault gesture. "I'm sorry, Evy, please don't think it was my idea or plan or anything. Apparently, the hotel was full once Collin made the booking."

"Err, yeah, no, no worries. We're adults. I think we can handle it, besides, we won't be spending too much time in the room...rooms anyway. The conference will pretty much kill all of our free time."

"Sounds good," Jeff replied.

"See you there." Evy closed the door, which was now the only obstacle between their beds. Is that how she saw it? An obstacle between their beds? Well, Mrs. Dax, time to take a shower. A cold one.

She heard Jeff unzipping his suitcase and then his steps when he was walking around his part of the room. He was whistling and turned on the TV. Then there was silence, and she heard water pouring from a shower in his bathroom. At least there were two bathrooms. Evy realized none of them said anything about changing rooms. Perhaps deep down, both of them were content with the way things were playing out. A minute later, she went inside her own bathroom, and was thinking about what she got herself into while waiting for the water to become warm enough to wash her hair.

☙16☙

"Stage two breast cancer is not the worst diagnosis, Laura, although I realize you must feel terrified," Tessa said. Stage two, as Laura learned, was cured with the removal of the changed tissue, but first she would need to undergo chemotherapy, and depending on the results of the treatment, she would either have her whole breast or only part of it removed. Because she *would* have some part of her body removed, as, starting from stages two and up, there was a higher chance for reoccurrence. Stage one could be cured using chemotherapy or radiation, but Laura's situation was more serious, although apparently not hopeless.

"If I had mammogram done regularly, would I have been diagnosed at stage 1?" She knew exactly what Tessa was saying, but she was also trying very hard not to burst into tears. It felt like she was watching her life outside her body, at a distance, like a spectator. Laura still could not fully understand what was happening to her. She could not believe that at the beginning of the week she was planning how to spend her summer leave with Bruce, and now, on Friday she was talking to a doctor about chemotherapy, a lumpectomy or mastectomy. How the fuck had this all happened?

"Perhaps, yes. But now there's no point in thinking about it. It won't change anything," Tessa replied. She took Laura's hand and sighed. "Laura, listen to me. I know this is shocking. I know you feel lost and you probably are wondering why this is happening to you. But trust me, you've made the best decision to come here the moment you felt something was wrong. You haven't denied it, you've decided to seek help immediately and that decision will save your life; I am *sure* of it. You are a strong woman, I can tell that, and I know we will beat this cancer. But we need to take action. Are you ready for it?"

She was looking straight into Laura's eyes, which was calming and kind of soothing. Suddenly, for a second, Laura was almost sure she could beat it.

"I am. What do we do now?"

Tessa told Laura she was going to be admitted to the clinic as a cancer patient on Monday with the first dose of drugs given to her that very day. She was going to be treated with neoadjuvant chemotherapy which is supposed to reduce the tumor so that maybe the surgery won't be needed. She would most probably feel nauseous and weak after the first portions, but Tessa thought it was very likely that she would retain at least the majority of her left breast.

Twenty minutes later, Laura was walking out from the clinic. She felt dazed and confused, which immediately made her think of Ev, a Led Zeppelin fan, and she smiled bitterly. She walked to a vending machine standing in the hallway next to the door, dropped some coins inside of it and pushed water button. A small plastic bottle appeared on the bottom of the machine making a rattle noise. She picked it up, opened it and walked out from Femina. She took a sip of cold, refreshing water, felt it dropping down her body, cooling it from the inside, sat on marble stairs, put the bottle aside, covered her face in her hands and started crying. She was crying for over half an hour, hot tears were burning her cheeks. She felt their salty taste on her lips, but simply couldn't stop. She was crying out her fear and her misery. And the worst was still to come; she had to tell Bruce; it would terrify him and the last she would ever want was to make him unhappy. Laura sobbed loudly, embraced her bent knees with her arms and kept on weeping.

Evy dried her hair, put on her t-shirt that read "Limited edition" and black jeans. She decided to wear sports shoes, although she did have a pair of sexy high-heels in her suitcase, but she was keeping them for a special, perhaps a more private occasion. She gave her hair a quick brush, put on some lip gloss and left her room.

Jeff heard her leaving and decided he was ready to go as well. He was planning to suggest her a late lunch in the center and was hoping for a walk afterwards before the conference would begin.

Evy was already in the lobby, sitting on a sofa and reading a local newspaper when he joined her. She looked fresh and girlish and Jeff was truly amused by the sign on her t-shirt. He found it hard not to agree with it. She looked at him and smiled. He looked dashing wearing a Henley and jeans. She realized she had never seen him in a casual outfit before.

"Would you like me to show you the town?"

"Sure. How about having some lunch later? Do you know any nice restaurants in the area?" he replied.

"As a matter of fact I do. Great idea, but, just to be clear, I pay for myself."

"Ok, however I'm the one who signs your checks, so I don't see any difference if you pay for yourself or if I pay for your lunch," Jeff replied, winked and put on sunglasses.

"Ok then, you're paying."

"Yes, ma'am."

***

The place looked fantastic. It was a small, campus town, charming and beautifully hidden among the mountains with slopes covered with thick woods and capped with snow. There was also a huge artificially made pond with clear, sparkling water, with a pier so long its end reached the exact middle of it. The center of Westville had a European feeling; it had an open air market situated in a pedestrian zone, full of cafes, pubs and restaurants with tables either outside or hidden in the basements, which seemed to be a wonderful concept during hot days. A romantic fountain in the middle of the market added even more charm to the place. The town had some galleries and many small shops selling typical memorabilia such as key chains with Westville's emblem, t-shirts with some nonsense and cliché taglines like "Good Girls go to Heaven, Bad Girls go to Westville" or 10 reasons why it is worth to visit the town and umbrellas or pencils with Westville logo on it. Evy and Jeff were walking around, talking a bit about their jobs and discussing the possible restructuring of WORDS. About an hour later, Jeff decided it was high time for them to eat something and the two chose a small restaurant with tables located near the fountain. They ordered their food and some ice teas and sat comfortably in their chairs, enjoying the early afternoon. Evy felt relaxed and she was no longer worried about any unprofessional behavior or conversations; Jeff's easy-going attitude could melt any tension.

"Ok, so we've talked about job, we've talked about authors, how about talking about each other?" Jeff asked smiling friendly.

"Ok, tell me something about you, I'm listening," Evy replied and winked.

"Well, I'm 33 years old, I have no pets, although I love dogs, I spend too much time watching bad movies and too little reading good books—"

"What do you mean *bad* movies?"

"I mean like really, *really* bad. I love all the crappy classics out there, Ed Wood's stuff, *Robomonster, Doctor of Doom, The Killer Shrews*, you name it. You must think I'm insane." He laughed.

"On the contrary! Every time there is a festival of the worst movies in the world, I always buy the whole pass ticket! I mean, where else will a person see such classics as *Glen or Glenda*! I am a huge fan of classic so-bad-they're-good movies!"

"You're joking! You like the cinematography catastrophes as well?" he asked in disbelief, smiling cordially.

"I've got the entire Ed Wood collection," she added.

"So at least you understand me and do not give me an eye-roll like most people do when they find out I like those crappy films."

"Nah, I really like those movies. It's wonderful that those people were able to pursue their dreams of becoming actors and directors and literally *nothing* on earth could have stopped them. I mean the message is really uplifting. Did you know that there's actually an Ed Wood Church? Their religion is Woodism and they preach that, by watching his films, one might learn to live a happy, positive life."

"No way!"

"I swear!" Evy laughed. "Besides, you have to admit that potters hanging from a fishing pole imitating flying sources do have some charm."

"Oh, no doubt."

"So, what else is there about you, Jeff?"

A waitress brought them their food. Jeff put a napkin on his knees and put the cutlery in his hands.

"I love classic rock."

"Black Sabbath with Ozzy or without?"

"Oh, with, absolutely!"

Evy laughed as she took a bite of her salad.

"What about you?" Jeff asked.

"I have a 15-year-old 4Runner which I love dearly and I think I'd become very depressed if I ever had to sell the car. I also like classic rock, currently my theme song is 'Somebody to Love'."

"Bieber?" Jeff winked.

"Yeah, Bieber," she replied. "God, no, no. Not even Queen. Jefferson Airplane. I basically love all rock music from the 60s and the 70s, but my favorite band ever is The Tea Party. Apart from the old crap movies, I am addicted to science-fiction stuff from the 80s, especially the first *Robocop*, the first *Alien*, and the first *Tron*."

"Oh yeah, the sequels were terrible. But, you must admit, *Tron Legacy* had a remarkable soundtrack."

"Totally. But yeah, the first one was better. Very imaginative in the times without green screens or CGI. What else, I have an older brother, Sam, who almost never calls and I had a dog for 13 years until she died last year which I haven't entirely come to terms with yet. Her name was Bertha."

"Why don't you have a regular contact with your brother?"

"It just happened like that. He lives in a different city, he moved there to college, and decided to settle there. He lives with his fiancée who doesn't like me too much, perhaps that's the reason. We usually call each other on our birthdays and we meet at my parents' place during Christmas. Do you have any siblings?"

"I had a sister, Monica. She died in a car accident nine years ago."

"Oh my God, I'm so sorry to hear that!"

"Thanks. The fucker who did that was completely drunk and drove into people who were crossing the street. He later said he hadn't noticed the lights were red for him. He killed three people, including Monica."

He paused for a minute. Evy was completely taken aback by this confession. She thought they were still on the level of talking about some harmless miscellaneous facts, but apparently Jeff felt he could tell her something personal.

"How did you handle it?"

"It was very tough. My whole family, and, of course particularly my parents and me, were devastated. I guess, in a way, we still are. My mom was so traumatized she underwent therapy and was struggling with depression for three years. I guess such things never let you go entirely."

"No, of course not."

There was a moment of silence during which they were eating.

"So, we are having an intro conference in an hour and a half." He said and looked at his watch.

"Yes, the university's authorities will introduce the potential future writers and poets. The history of Written Word is going to be summarized, it always is, and the schedule for tomorrow presented. I don't think it's going to take more than an hour. Usually it never does."

"Ok then, so, let's go back to the hotel, what'd you say?"

"Sure."

Jeff paid for their checks and then they headed back to the hotel. It was only about thirty minutes away. While they were on their way, they discovered they liked similar books, sushi, and that they had no idea what the whole fuss about *Star Wars* was.

✿18✿

Bruce was coming home late that evening. He was quite content when Laura called him and told him to order takeout because it turned out he had to stay a bit late at work. He decided to grab some Chinese food for both of them, bought a bottle of wine and was driving back home, thinking that his wife had been apparently going through something difficult. He had known her for almost twenty years, and he knew exactly when things were wrong, but he also knew there was no point in asking her about it. She wouldn't tell. He knew he had to wait, because sooner or later, when the burden would become unbearable, she would talk to him and explain what was bringing her down. Still, it had never been comfortable knowing the person he loved the most felt miserable and knowing it was impossible to do anything about it—a very frustrating feeling. He took the last turn to their house and, with a pleasant surprise, he saw the light on the porch. Great, Laura was home! He parked on the driveway (Laura always parked in the garage) and walked into the house. Spark, their beloved mutt adopted from a shelter three years ago, immediately ran to him and after few cuddles and hugs, Bruce let him out into the backyard.

There was a complete silence and darkness in the house, which Bruce found surprising. He put his jacket on a coat hanger, took his shoes off, unbuttoned the sleeves in his shirt and started rolling them towards his elbows. Bruce turned on the light in the corridor, headed towards the kitchen and saw Laura sitting on a chair in its darkest corner, lit only by a dim light of their ventilation hood's bulbs. She was holding a glass with some whiskey and ice in it. Bruce immediately knew something was really wrong, Laura normally never drank anything stronger than beer or wine, unless she was very stressed and needed something to relax and sleep better. He stopped in the doorway and leaned on a doorframe.

"Laura, what is it?" he asked softly.

She sighed heavily and rubbed her forehead. "I have a breast cancer. Stage two. I am starting chemotherapy on Monday," she replied automatically and took a sip of alcohol.

Bruce was stunned. The feeling of total horror and hundreds of questions filled his mind; his heart immediately started beating faster. He felt an unbelievably unpleasant chill down his spine as he instantly recalled Kate's drama. God, how many times had he asked, *pleaded*, Laura to take care of herself.

"Oh my God, Honey—when did you find out?"

"I discovered the tumor, I mean then I had no idea it was a tumor, on Monday. And here we are, it's Friday night and I am bracing myself to face cancer."

"Why didn't you say anything?" he asked her, knowing already what the answer would be.

"Why would I say anything since I had no idea what it was? I am telling you *now*. I have a fucking cancer," she said bitterly, struggling with herself not to sob again.

Bruce had no idea what to say, what to do. He walked in further and turned the light on.

"Don't!" she shouted, but it was too late. She hid her face in her palms, and Bruce, petrified, realized how scared she was, how depressed.

There she was, curled up on a chair, shaking her head with disbelief, shivering all over. He had never seen her so terrified. Slowly, he walked up to her, gently touched her hands and kissed her palms so that they would uncover the face. She resisted at first, but the smoothening feeling finally made her give up and she looked at him. Her face was swollen from tears; her eyes were very narrow and red. She must have been sitting there in darkness for quite some time as she was blinking nervously; she needed a moment to get used to the light.

This was his Laura. The woman who had no fear to crush any spider that was running around the home. The woman who won an amateur off-road race in their city, driving her Wrangler, charging through the mud flats, hills and holes. The woman who knocked down a bully in high school who was trying to terrorize her into giving him her pocket money. There she was, miserable, petrified and looking at him, her only hope. He knew she was waiting for him to fix everything, to help her. He felt his heart shrinking from compassion and sympathy. He knew, immediately, he would do whatever it took to support her, get her, them both, through this. He held her in his arms and they were both clinging, him on his knees and her sitting on the chair.

"Oh, Honey; we'll get through this, baby. We'll just stand up and fight—we'll fight!" he whispered.

"This is my fault, Bruce! I was scared this *might* happen, so I stuck my head in the sand and pretended it would never be my problem. I should have taken better care of myself," she replied surprisingly calm. His touch truly soothed.

"Oh, Honey—", he said softly, kissed her cheek and neither of them wanted to move.

Oenone~Agatha Rae~

❧19❧

Jeff impressed Evy; that much was obvious. He was no longer just the handsome guy who was able to sweep her off her feet just by smiling at her; he was becoming a friend. It was a true pleasure talking to him. He was a gentleman, a ladies first kind of guy.. He was witty, charming. What was more, Jeff could listen. Not hear, but *listen*. He paid attention to everything she said, he asked questions, and he was truly interested in what she had to say.

Evy simply felt good in his presence. She was amazed by how many things they shared; music, films, he understood her attachment to Bob. A thought sweet, but most probably too impertinent to be taken seriously, appeared in her head that perhaps Jeff was her soulmate. It was crazy, especially after only a few hours of knowing him better, but Laura would always tell her that Bruce was undoubtedly her soulmate and that she knew that almost instantly, and how one would just *feel* such things. Perhaps Evy was spending too much time with them, admiring and yearning for such love, too, and thus she was expecting heaven-knows-what. She thought about the afternoon they had just spent and was getting ready for the opening conference. After putting on some makeup, a bit more visible than the lunch date, and changing into more formal, smart clothes, she combed her hair, letting it cover her shoulders freely and spritzed perfume on her neck and wrists. She packed a notebook and a pen in her hand bag and was ready to go to the conference.

Jeff changed into more formal clothing and couldn't help but think of the lunch date he had earlier with Evy. She was very enchanting, there was no doubt about it, and it felt good to be around her. Yesterday he wouldn't imagine that his senior editor loved the crappiest films ever and loved to sing The Doors' "Peace Frog" at the top of her voice when she was in her car. Bob. That was hilarious, because he had his beloved car, too, an 11-year-old Corolla, he named it Hank. Jeff had no idea how many people were out there naming their cars, but the fact that him and Ev were among them was pretty funny. Hank got stolen when his owner was on one of his first dates with Rachel. Maybe he could have rescued him; they did not leave Hank too far away from the beach where they went for a picnic, but, let's face it, at that particular moment, Jeff was more interested in getting into Rachel's cleavage than in Hank.

He really liked the fact that Evy had a rather informal style of being. Rachel was far tenser, both in the terms of behavior and clothes. And food! Evy ordered a whole steak with potatoes, salad and lemonade! It was hard to believe, since dating Rachel. Lunches with his ex were disastrous; she would check the calories' index on a bottle of water! Evy felt simply normal. And that was great; he felt he was becoming enchanted with her. At the same time, he realized he spent literally one afternoon with Evy and had already compared her to Rachel twice. Even though he and Rachel had split up almost six months ago, he still felt hurt that he had invested five years of his life in the relationship and it all fell apart so peacefully, as if they had no motivation to fight for it. Of course, both of them were to blame for that, but still. Five years was a lot of time; apparently it was only natural that he was subconsciously comparing Evy and Rachel. Although he and Evy weren't a couple. And she wouldn't be, because that would seriously complicate their work relationship. No, he wouldn't even think of jeopardizing his career for a fling that might be nice, but might well end unpleasantly in the future. He hated the idea of mixing private life and business, it was one of his rules, to never let happen. He had seen how it ended for some of his friends who either started a relationship with their colleagues, or, what was even worse, started a company with their wives or boyfriends, and now not only were they single, but had no companies or careers as well. Nothing like the inability to communicate after a relationship breakdown.

Cynical? Yes. But honest. He finished changing his clothes and left to meet up with Evy at the conference which was held in the auditorium of the university.

❧20❧

The auditorium was gigantic, and there was a lot of left over room. Each seat had a piece of paper with the name of publishing houses' representatives invited to the Written Word, and there were only a little more than half of the chairs assigned. The whole room was decorated with Written Word logos and in front of the audience there was a microphone, some chairs and a podium for the university's officials to host the event. Jeff walked into the room and spotted Evy sitting down in their company's assigned seats. She waved at him, and he nodded and walked toward her. He took his seat and they both waited for the ceremony to begin. The guests were coming, and soon all the chairs were taken. Evy and Jeff did not speak to each other; they only observed the auditorium becoming more and more crowded. At 6 p.m., the University's dean, professors, staff and guests showed up and took their seats. The dean stepped on a podium and delivered a welcoming speech.

"Good afternoon, ladies and gentlemen. I am Andrew Nicholson, and I am the dean of Westville College. We are more than glad to welcome you to the annual Written Word conference organized by our university for the 12th time."

Everybody started clapping. When they stopped, the dean continued.

"This year we are going to introduce you to over 120 aspiring authors and writers, both from our department of drama and creative writing as well as from other colleges and universities around the country. Among them are fiction literature writers, poets, authors of photographic anthologies, guidebooks, and those hoping to launch a variety of magazines. All of them are looking for that special publisher that will help them do it. We kindly encourage you, dear and honorable guests, to give all of them a chance to grip their dreams and to have their talents, creativity and hard work appreciated. Throughout its twelve-year-long history, Written Word has helped to discover over 100 authors. Among the writers who have been spotted at our conference, we have Sue Beckett, the author of a highly acclaimed detective stories series, John Anders, who is now one of the most popular national poets, his latest volume 'Time Trapped Under Ice' was recently nominated to a prestigious Golden Pen award. We must not forget about writers Michael Fiedler, the author of a series of historical novels, Tracy Lagan whose immensely successful romantic novels can melt every reader's heart, and, of course, Tom Dancy, whose spy and political thrillers have already been adapted for screen three times. All these authors have taken their first steps here at Written Word and we are very proud of them and feel like godfathers of their success. In fact, Mr. Dancy is here with us tonight—"

The audience started clapping. Dancy got up from his chair situated behind the dean and bowed graciously.

"— and he will share his experience with us in a minute."

"Wow, I had no idea Dancy and Beckett started here! They're fantastic! I love their stories, especially Beckett's," Jeff told Evy. Evy had already known about all those successes as they had been repeated here for years now. Written Word clearly needed some fresh blood, as their trophy authors were becoming a bit dusty.

"Ladies and Gentlemen, please welcome Tom Dancy!"

The dean stepped down from his podium, shook hands with Dancy and the writer stepped closer to microphone, bending it a bit. He buttoned up his jacket and, when the audience stopped clapping, he started his speech.

"I was picked by The Black Publishing House here, during the 4th Written Word. What drew their attention was a fledgling story that would become my debut novel, namely 'The Eye of the Hawk'. It was eight years ago, and since then I have been blessed enough to publish four other novels for The Black House. As a person who has experienced the gift of being able to form my words into books and allow the readers to enjoy my work and share my imagination with me, I cannot express how grateful I am to Westville University's teaching staff, especially Professor Altman, for having faith in me, for all their support and encouragement and finding me good enough to include on the 2005 Written Word Author's List."

Neither Jeff nor Evy were listening to Dancy's lecture carefully. It was pretty pompous and cliché. Instead, they started leafing through brochures introducing the aspiring authors and pointing to each other the ones they both found interesting. She made a few funny remarks on the titles of their book-prototypes, but Jeff only smiled faintly and did not reply. It was obviously working time, Evy thought. They were sitting in this auditorium and that was an official beginning of the real reason behind their coming to Westville. Evy liked that, but on the other hand, she felt a bit disappointed. The afternoon they had spent together made her think they crossed some strict professional borders. Jeff, however, seemed to have been quite determined to distinguish professional and private parts of his life. She was wondering if they would get to speak to each other again the same way they did only two hours before, but she understood that now it was not the time for it.

Tom finished his speech, earned some applause and the dean stepped back on the podium.

"With hope that you, my dear publishers, find what you're looking for, here at the Written Word and with an immense belief that there are numerous writers waiting to be discovered and appreciated, I hereby announce the 12th Written Word open!"

The dean got up and bowed to the audience; people again began clapping. Everyone started leaving the auditorium and Evy asked Jeff, "How about getting a drink in The Panorama's restaurant and look through the brochures carefully so we know who to stalk tomorrow?"

"Good idea," he replied.

Oenone~Agatha Rae~

❧21❧

Bruce and Laura had no idea how long they had been sitting in the kitchen. After some time, they looked at each other and without words they kissed deeply and went to the bedroom. They made love passionately and roughly, as if they feared that it would be the last. They needed the closeness to relieve the tension and wash away at least part of the distress and drama they were about to face. When their passion was still pulsing inside their bodies, tired and sweaty they lay down and hugged each other.

"We'll be fine, Laura. We'll be fine, you'll see," he whispered.

Laura, although scared, believed him.

Oenone~Agatha Rae~

❧22❦

The restaurant was cozy and quite intimate with dimmed light and fluffy red coverings on the chairs and tables. Each table had a small candle burning and easy listening music sounded through the speakers. Jeff and Evy sat at one of the tables next to a wall. She ordered a mojito, while he preferred a whiskey on ice. They both opened the brochures. Slipping off her heels, she leaned back in her seat. She raked her fingers through her hair and rolled her neck to each side, letting it flow freely on her shoulders. Jeff was observing her discreetly and smiled.

"So, I was thinking about choosing authors representing concrete genres."

"Yeah, like you said. Have you discussed it with the management, though? Do they know about this strategy?"

"Not exactly. No, I did not tell them. It's a fresh idea, and I'd like to see how it works first."

"Okay, so basically we're limiting our search to what kind of writers exactly?'

"I was thinking fantasy, crime and detective novels and some scientific for the general public things. What do you think?"

"Maybe. Those things do seem to be very popular nowadays."

"Exactly. And we really need to have a breakthrough. I am even thinking of making a subdivision of WORDS and transferring the academic contracts there so we can focus only on the more commercial and popular genres. Because we do need the academic contract, and I'm really glad we got it, but it makes our editors stuck with a lot of niche work. I mean, it's more about the prestige, not the money. Money is in the mainstream literature."

"Yeah, I know what you mean, but we've already signed the deal with the university, right?"

"Yes, but we can always make an annex to the contract and, if we don't change any conditions, and we won't, I don't think the university would change its mind. They know that we still have a far better potential in distributing their books and publications than if they were to do it by themselves."

"All right. So, who do we want to catch tomorrow?"

"Let's do it like this. Take a closer look at the fantasy and detective novels' parts of the brochure and pick up some authors you find interesting and promising. Please make sure to have some plan B as well, because if we find something interesting there, it's pretty obvious others will also. And if someone's faster than us, we need to have an alternative. We cannot come back to WORDS empty handed."

"Okay, so I understand you're going to take a look at science for the general public?"

"Precisely so. I want to take a closer look at some books on popular culture, on history, on linguistics and literature, and one on tantric sex."

"Tantric sex?"

"Yeah, sex always sells well," he answered and they both had a laugh. Evy unintentionally touched his calf with her foot. He looked at her amused and she nervously withdrew her leg. She looked down at her drink and took a big sip through a straw.

"Sorry," she murmured,

"It's all right," he replied and smiled. He had to admit, the unexpected touch was quite electrifying.

"So, what time do we start tomorrow?" she asked, still blushing a bit.

"The writer's market starts at 9 am, so perhaps we should meet at breakfast at 8.30?"

"Good, let's do this," she said, then finished her drink and put her shoes back on her feet.

"Ok, I'll be going back to my room. You're coming?" he said. She looked at him and, amused, had no idea what to answer.

"I mean—you know, are you coming to your room, just like I am going back to mine—that, that did not sound well," he said and laughed a bit nervously. He looked embarrassed.

"No, not at all," she admitted. Her eyes were cordially laughing, and finally she smiled.

"Yeah." He smiled, too.

"Yes, I am coming," she said and stood up.

They called the elevator and it came down very quickly. They entered its narrow space. Jeff hit "5". Soon the doors closed behind them and Evy realized that for the very first time since they got to Westville, she was totally alone with him. She stood a little bit behind him and observed, wondering how the hell she got so lucky to spend the weekend with him.

She closed her eyes and gently scented his cologne, which had a delicate but very masculine and sensual fragrance. Suddenly, Evy felt the urge to hug him, just wrap her arms around him and never let go. She just wanted to feel close to him.

He was very much aware of the tension between them and even though they both could have pretended that they just liked each other professionally, it was clear they crossed a certain line. Jeff somehow felt that they might cross it even further during the weekend. He was sure they both wanted it. He felt a glow of her body's warmth on his shoulder, and for a split of second he saw himself turning around and kissing her slowly, passionately. It wouldn't be right, though. This would not be the way he would want it. They were both a bit tipsy and tired, maybe that was only it.

The elevator stopped and they silently went to their rooms, exchanging goodnights as they were closing their doors. Evy took off her clothes and went to the bathroom to take a shower. For a crazy second she had a feeling Jeff wanted to walk in to her room—that he was standing behind the wall, listening to what she was doing. Nothing happened though, and she closed the door to the bathroom.

Jeff, at the same time, was considering knocking on her door and perhaps inviting her to his part of the room for a drink or two, but he quickly let go of the idea. He knew above any doubt that something *did* awaken in him at the restaurant table, but rushing anything wouldn't be a good idea. And what if his intuition was wrong? What if she did not want to cross that certain line? However, God help him, if they lived three, four floors higher, if he would have had more time, he truly might have kissed her in that elevator. Maybe it would be better to take the stairs next time.

Oenone~Agatha Rae~

☙23☙

Evy woke up at 6.55, five minutes before the alarm clock got into its panic mode. Knowing she would not sleep anymore, she turned it off and was laying in her bed wondering what the day would bring. Before going to bed yesterday, Evy examined the writers from her part of the brochure and circled those of them who seemed interesting enough to talk with and tosee what kind of potential writers they were. She had seven names on her A list and five on B.

Evy got up, washed her face and opened the window. She made herself some tea and sat on the window sill appreciating the view of the mountains and the nearby boardwalk. She comfortably leaned on the window casing and allowed a chill but pleasant morning breeze to delicately touch her face and disperse her hair. She gave herself into the moment, relaxing before the truly insane day began.

At the same time, Laura woke up and walked out of the bedroom leaving Bruce in bed. She walked barefoot on their fluffy creamy rug and then on wooden floor in the corridor. Quietly, she walked into the kitchen and put a kettle on, put two spoons of coffee into a mug and walked out on the terrace. She took a deep breath and closed her eyes. The morning breeze, so fresh and innocent was gently waking up every cell in her body. She heard an electronic beep informing her that the water had boiled; a minute later, she poured it into the cup.

Having taken her coffee, she walked on the terrace again, sat on a rattan chair, moved another one closer to stretch her legs on it, sipped the hot liquid and put the mug away on a table standing nearby. Laura closed her eyes again and was listening to the world surrounding her, the world which, just like her, was lazily waking up in this typical way that only weekend mornings can do. Everything was really peaceful. Her house was situated on a hill, so she had a wonderful view of Boston's skyline in a far distance, and mornings were usually busy as all the neighborhood would be heading toward the city center to get to work. But not today. Today's morning was just perfect. Quiet, peaceful, soothing. She took another sip, opened her eyes and for the very first time this week, she thought she would not give up. Not that easily at least. She wasn't a quitter. The truth was, her situation could have been worse, much worse. That, however, absolutely no longer mattered. What mattered now was everything she was about to do from this moment forward. Tessa had laid it out and now it was time for Laura to start analyzing everything.

The tumor wasn't as big as it could have been. The suspicion was that it was stage two, but it may very well be proven that fewer lymph nodes were involved. That could mean a lumpectomy. If she needed a mastectomy, it could be done on a much smaller scale and the reconstruction would be accomplished easily. Tessa had explained to her that nowadays, they performed the reconstructive surgery immediately after the mastectomy—without the patient even leaving the operating room!

It was indeed possible that she would never have to look in a mirror and feel as if she'd been mutilated; that she was somehow only partially a woman. And they would use her own tissue to rebuild her breast, which meant she would finally have that liposuction she had always dreamt of but never had the courage to decide on. *Win-win*, she thought, smiled bitterly and sighed.

It all did not sound that bad, considering she avoided the doctors for the past few years. It could have looked far, far worse. She smiled, drank a bit of coffee again and decided it was time to call Evy. Now that Laura knew what was going on and she had a plan on how to react to this, she felt it was the moment to let her best friend know about the upcoming battle. She got up from the chair, walked into the kitchen, took the phone and dialed Evy's number.

At the same time Evy was sitting on a small sofa in her room and picked up her cell phone from her purse. She searched for Laura in the contact list and to push "call" button. She had a rather simple, hand-folded phone, nothing fancy. She was very skeptical towards the new smartphones, glittering with awesomeness and fanciness, because she couldn't imagine having a phone that would display aaaaabrgskzay on its screen every time she wanted to send a text message. Maybe it was her who was imperfect and had problems with the touchable keyboard, but she had a great connection, so to speak, with traditional phones and had no need to change them for a NASA-like technology that checks emails (any notebook does that), allows you to listen to music (my mp3 player does that), has GPS inside (my GPS device is in my car, no need for another one), and probably can scan an area around you in the search of aliens and radiation. To her amazement, the phone was actually ringing (she forgot to change it from "silent" to "general" mode after the inauguration of the conference), so she pushed the small green button and answered.

"Hi Laura, you won't believe it, but I was just about to call you, I was reaching for my phone when you called," she welcomed her friend cheerfully.

"Hi, Ev," Laura answered. Evy immediately had a feeling Laura's voice seemed burned out, depressed. "How's the conference?"

"It's good; a lot of things are happening."

"I bet. Do you have any authors you found interesting?"

"Yes, twelve actually."

"That's not too much; how many authors have been listed in the roster?"

"One hundred and twenty."

"And you have only twelve you find interesting? Is it that bad this year?"

"No, no, it's just that Jeff has some new ideas for the company and wanted me to narrow my search only to some genres."

"Oh, that sounds interesting; I hope he knows what he's doing. How is he anyway?"

"Fine."

"Come on, Ev, you know what I'm talking about!" Laura said in her typical tease mode.

"It turns out we have *a lot* of things in common. He's really sweet, but I don't think he's interested in anything apart from professional stuff."

'Well, I hope you didn't expect a hot romance this weekend. It's great you're having an opportunity to get to know each other, but I do believe such things need more time, you know?"

"Oh, I know. But that doesn't change the fact I waxed very thoroughly before we got here," Evy said and they both laughed.

"Listen, Evy, I need to tell you something—"

"Oh, Laura, I'd love to hear that, but I was on my way for breakfast. Jeff and I are supposed to meet in the canteen and start our hunt for authors afterwards. I just wanted to tell you 'hi'. You know how busy the second day of Written Word is."

Laura was silent for a moment, Evy had a feeling her friend was somehow baffled. After few seconds, she answered, "Sure, no problem. Will I be able to catch you in the evening?"

"You bet! Sorry, Laura, you know I am."

"I know, no problem. Have a good one!

"And you have a gorgeous weekend. Bye, Honey!"

"Bye."

Ev hung up. Laura looked at the phone and smiled. She couldn't expect Evy to focus on her problems now; she was too busy with work and too excited about Jeff. But it did sting a bit. Nah, it was simply selfish. If Evy knew what was going on, she would at least hear her out, not to mention she would consider coming back earlier and see her.

Bruce touched her shoulder. Laura got scared at first and she jumped. Then she turned around and saw him standing next to her wearing a wrapper and carrying a mug of coffee in his hand.

"Sorry," he said. "Good morning, Honey," he said softly and bent to kiss her lips. She kissed him back.

"Good morning. I need to tell you something."

"Yes?"

"I am not giving up."

"Atta girl."

⁂24⁂

Jeff got up at 8, took a quick shower, dressed and went to the restaurant. He did not occupy his mind with Evy anymore; it was a new day, full of duties and he did not want to think about what would have been or what could have been. He felt quite stressed. He had fished certain names from the brochure and he was very determined to get those writers. He was about to change the whole profile of the publishing house he worked for and the truth was he had not discussed it with his superiors.

Jeff had felt for some time now that WORDS needed to be a profiled publisher, and their income, turnover and the whole marketing situation only proved his theory. He had carefully scanned the books published by them that had the best following and the results seemed clear—fantasy, science for public knowledge and crime stories. In his opinion there was no need to blow their budget in publishing romances, cookery books or photo albums since hardly anyone had ever bought them. The reason behind it was simple—such books weren't bought not because they weren't interesting, it was rather because there were other publishing houses with a reputation of being faithful to these genres for years, and they were their readers' number one source for such books. It was honestly very surprising that the management of WORDS had never commissioned any of such studies before. For Jeff it was the very first thing to do once he got the job. Not to sound too impertinent, but they really needed his help, especially if the board seemed to be clearly short-sighted. He only hoped that management would accept his decision.

He entered the restaurant, scanned the area and realized Evy wasn't there yet. He walked towards the smorgasbord, put some vegetables and hot sausages on his plate, got some black coffee and sat by the table. He was in the middle of his meal when Evy appeared. She walked to the buffet, put some mini pancakes on the plate, poured maple syrup on them and walked to his table.

"Good morning." Evy smiled.

"Hi, and how was your night?" he replied, got up and moved the chair opposite to his to make a space for her to sit.

"Good, I was fast asleep," she replied and sat. "Shit, I forgot coffee—"
She was getting up when Jeff told her he would bring it for her.
"I like when my coffee is Beastie-Boys style," she said.
He looked at her surprised, not sure what she meant.
"I like my sugar with coffee and cream," she cited a verse from "Intergalactic".
"Oh! I prefer it Ella Fitzgerald style."
This time she wasn't sure what he was talking about.
"Black coffee since the blues caught my eyes—" he sang quietly. Evy laughed and started eating her pancakes. Jeff soon got back with her daily portion of caffeine. Mornings were usually the only time in a day that Evy would drink coffee.
"How was your night?" she asked.
"Awful."
"Oh, why is that?"
"Someone behind the wall was snoring like crazy," he said.

"You got me, no alibi, I'm afraid," she said.
"It was fine." He smiled. "Seriously though, the beds are comfortable, the neighborhood is quiet and I had absolutely no problems with sleeping."
"Me neither. So, what about the writers hunt? Do you have a list?"
"Yeah, I do. I have thirteen authors on my A list and ten on B. You?"
"My! That's a lot! I only have seven for A and five for B!"
"Should be enough. At least I hope so. Perhaps I have too many names, maybe I'm being unrealistic. Please remember it's my first time here."
"Well, I think it's good to have so many names to choose from. Now I'm thinking I might have circled not enough of them."
"We'll see what happens, but I will be satisfied if we get back to WORDS with at least eight potential authors."
"Ok then." Evy wiped her lips with a serviette and finished her coffee. "Let's boot and rally."
"All right. We'll see how it goes. I'll see you during lunch. Good luck," Jeff replied, got up and walked out. She did the same some minutes afterwards.

❧25❧

The hall where all the stalls were was gigantic. The one hundred and twenty writers were gathered in the room, each of them displaying their books. They were divided into genres which made looking for them much easier for the publishers. The writers who got the university support, received special scholarships from the authority to publish a small amount of their books, to use them later on for publicity. Most of them would usually decide to use the copies during Written Word, but the majority of them would send the already written books to the publishers and wait for their answers, just to double their chances. There was a clatter in the hall, dozens of people were walking around the stalls, talking to the writers, there were business cards exchanging, leafing through books and a lot of convincing, promising and assuring.

Evy stepped into the hall and started looking for her literary categories. The genres were divided into colors. The ones for her were purple (fantasy) and green (detective stories). Having decided to check out the fantasy authors first, she entered a small purple corridor made of pieces of material hanging between the stalls' ceilings. There were about twenty authors in there and Evy started looking for the ones she had circled in the brochure. She had five of them on list A and two on list B. Mark Johnson was the first one.

He had written a novel about a witcher, a male witch-like character in Slavic mythology, bringing up and training a young boy so that later on they could face evil dragons attacking a small village. The author stated the whole story was to be a trilogy at least, and Evy was intrigued enough to ask him some questions about the details of the plot and the possible upcoming parts of the story. The first chapter which was included in a bulletin all the editors and publishers received during the opening ceremony, was quite interesting, and Mark's writing skills were really impressive. They exchanged their business cards, she promised him WORDS would invite him for an interview later on during the week and he agreed to sign on to her list as willing to co-operate. All the publishers had to think of the contracts they were to propose to their future writers quite swiftly because it was obvious that once one of them found a new author interesting it was just a matter of time for the others to like him, too.

She moved on to other stalls and after two and a half hours later she had six fantasy authors booked, so to speak, for further talks in the publishing house's office. Apart from Mark she exchanged telephone numbers with authors of a wizard saga, a story about fairies and one about fire-eaters. Evy was becoming quite tired and decided to go for a short coffee break. She was vaguely wondering how Jeff was doing. Also, for a minute she recalled the weird, unnatural for Laura pitch of her voice when they were talking. Evy knew deep down something was possibly wrong and she promised herself to call her friend in the evening. She bought a latte to go with double espresso, sprinkled it with cinnamon and moved on to the green section. *Hello, psycho murders, embezzlers and thieves. Evelyn Dax is coming to get you!*

Jeff was into scientific for the general public genre. That was a red color. It was one of the least crowded areas of the hall. He was interested in guidebooks and any kinds of science analyzes. He was hoping to be more successful, but it turned out his impressive list of overall twenty-three names was drastically shortened by the reality check—most of the authors he was interested in were already booked, and apparently were promised some truly rewarding contracts since they did not want to talk to anyone else. Jeff managed to book authors of survival know-how, a book on Romanticism in Poland, a culinary guidebook concerning South-East Asia, and a book on dog psychology. He had seven authors in his hand and he really hoped Evy did better. They needed at least eight authors interested in their offer to meet with them and discuss all the details necessary to sign contracts, otherwise their whole escapade would be useless and, Jeff would not be able to defend his new strategy during the next corporate meeting.

Evy and Jeff saw each other during a lunch break. They sat together at the table and discussed their progresses over a bowl of vegetable soup and a Caesar salad. They wished each other good luck and left the canteen. Jeff proposed a dinner after the long day and before they departed, they agreed to meet at 7pm, at the same restaurant they had had lunch the day before.

Overall they spent seven hours on talking, reading, exchanging business cards, negotiating and sketching possible contracts. Evy ended her part of the searching for new authors at 5 pm and she was more than happy to go back to her room. She kicked the shoes off her feet, combed her hair with her fingers and started unbuttoning her shirt. The nightstand clock displayed 5.15. Ok, she still had about an hour before she was going out. She decided to take a shower and search for some fresh clothes in her suitcase. Evy took off the shirt, threw it on the bed right next to the skirt and opened the closet doors. She wore a crème-beige dress, one of her favorite ones. It was very soft, shoulder-strapped, knee-long, girly and classy. She threw things out of her purse to pack them into a smaller one and she looked at her phone. For a minute, she felt she wanted to call Laura, but she looked at the clock again and decided she didn't have time.

Jeff got back about 6 pm. He wasn't very happy about his results and was getting worried his new strategy would not please his supervisors. However, he made a resolution not to think about it this evening. The official reason of his coming to Westville was over, tomorrow at 11 there was only a closing ceremony and lunch for all guests and they had plane tickets for a flight at 4 pm. Now was the time he could and wanted to focus on Evy. His plan for tonight was to spend a pleasant evening, eat something delicious, drink some good wine and talk. Maybe, just maybe, he considered spending the upcoming night together, but the thought, although present, was hidden very deeply in his heart and he would never have said it out loud even to himself standing alone in his room. He got a white shirt and black, causal jacket, decided it would fit royal blue jeans and he went to the bathroom to refresh himself.

Oenone~Agatha Rae~

❧26❧

Laura and Bruce went for a walk. The evening was wonderful, warm, a bit windy and it encouraged to leave home. The Levinsons spent the entire day lying in bed, watching TV and reading books. They were so busy doing that, they forgot to eat anything; so the plan was to go for a walk and drop by some pizzeria for an unhealthy, fat, double-cheese, double-pepperoni pizza with a few cold beers. They were sitting at home with their phones and the Internet off, talking, laughing, cherishing their probably last careless weekend, for many weeks or months ahead and embracing for what was to come. Laura decided she would pack her bag to the clinic on Monday and the weekend was only for them, for nobody else. After their morning coffee on the terrace, they walked back to the house, went to the bedroom with a bunch of magazines and some DVDs. How many movies had they promised themselves they would watch and never had time? Today they had all the time in the world. They caught up with some weekly papers, had wonderful lunch made of dry fruit, Honey and almonds, watched *Little Miss Sunshine* and decided to go out for a walk. They chose not to take the car, just to stroll lazily here and there along the streets of their neighborhood. It was wonderful to rediscover the pleasure of pacing around, savoring the smell of the trees, grass wet by sprinklers, to have it all in the reach of ones' hands and to enjoy the feelings of being free; free from rush, from the buzz of the world. It was all simply delicious. When they finally made it to the pizzeria, they made their order and talked about very casual things while drinking beer and waiting for their food.

"So, I told Sam she should think-through her decision to to have a year gap thoroughly, because it might turn out she won't be interested in coming back to college anymore," Bruce said. Sam was his 20-year-old niece who was still in her rebellious years, had pink hair and about 17 ideas per minute concerning what to do you with her life.

"Let it go, Bruce," Laura said and rubbed his forearm in comforting gesture. "Nobody can change her mind; you know what she's like. If her parents cannot persuade her to stay at college, nobody will. You know it's all about spending time with Jim, don't you?" She took a sip from her bottle.

"Yeah, I'm just surprised, a 20-year-old still thinks and behaves as a 16-year-old," Bruce replied and sighed.

"I would be more surprised if she behaved as a 40-year-old. Come on, Bruce, don't you remember what it was like to be a kid?"

"I guess I am forgetting."

"She says she wants to travel to Europe. It might be a really valuable experience for her."

"So, why wouldn't she go during summer? Why does it have to be the whole year? Her parents have been working their asses off to save money for her education. And she is willing to throw it all away, now, when she's already halfway through the whole thing. Why is she doing it?"

"Because she wants to spend more time with Jim. He's 26, he's older, more responsible and they've been together for two years. And he's fascinated with Europe; you know he goes to different countries every summer. He might show her around some wonderful places."

"But the studies—"

"Bruce. The studies are not the most important thing in life. Trust me."

They were enjoying their pizzas which were simply delicious. The entire evening was wonderful; when they got back home, they watched some television and fell asleep afterwards hoping not to dream about what was coming. Laura only hoped she wasn't too obvious in checking to see if Evy called. She didn't want to upset Bruce.

☙27☙

It was a beautiful and warm late-spring evening. Evy got to the restaurant at about 7.15 and saw Jeff waiting for her. He picked up a table outside, which was wonderfully lit by lanterns and separated from other ones by some wood and plant decorations. It all felt charming and intimate. There was a candle burning gently in the middle of their table and the menus were already lying there waiting to be opened. Jeff saw Evy and was stunned. She looked beautiful. He hoped he was careful enough not to let her know he was simply devouring her with his eyes. Her hair was tied into a loose bun with single strands gently laying on her naked shoulders, wonderful legs visible so well from underneath her knee-long dress, the gentle neck ornamented with a very delicate silver chain. Her make-up perfectly underscoring the breath-taking greenness of her eyes. She was magnificent. She was dreamlike. Stunning.

"How are you, Jeff?" she asked, pleasantly embarrassed by the way he looked at her. She knew exactly what impression she'd just made on him and enjoyed every bit of it. He got up and moved a chair a bit to help her sit and sat down opposite to her.

"Great, it's a wonderful evening," he replied. "I hope you're hungry, I know I am. I haven't eaten anything since lunch."

"Me neither."

"I am so sorry, but I haven't had a chance to ask yet, and although I promised myself I wasn't going to talk about work during the dinner—"

"Six fantasy novels and three detective stories. You?" she asked, not the least surprised by his question.

"Seven! We needed at least ten and we have sixteen! That's a fantastic result!"

"High five!" She laughed and spontaneously reached out her hand. Both palms touched without hesitation.

"Looks like we're making a good team, Ev," he said smiling.

"Oh, no doubt," she replied.

"Good evening. My name is Michael and I will be serving you tonight."
He smiled friendly and added," May I offer you a glass of our own semi-dry red wine for a start?"

Jeff looked at Evy who nodded.

"Of course, that's a great idea," he said.

"Fantastic. May I take your order?"

"Oh, we haven't decided yet," Jeff replied.

"No problem, sir. Take your time," Michael replied and went back into the kitchen only to come back few seconds later with two glasses and a bottle of wine. He put the glasses on the table, opened the bottle and poured the liquor and left them.

"May I say you look wonderful, Evy?" Jeff said softly, looking straight into her eyes. All of a sudden his gaze made her feel a bit shy. She looked down blushing a bit. God only knew how many times she had imagined hearing those words from him, but now that it had finally happened, she had no idea how to react. She felt her heart beating faster from the excitement, and she was sure she blushed a bit. He felt a bit confused; he had never thought such a delicate compliment would make her feel visibly troubled, but he found it cute.

"Ok, I think I know what I'll order. You?"

"I think I know as well." He closed the menu and sat more comfortably.

Michael came back, took their orders and asked how they liked the wine. They enjoyed it a lot and Jeff asked for the whole bottle. Evy decided to try prawn soup and grilled salmon with a vinaigrette salad, Jeff's choices were red peppers filled with meat as a starter and roasted chicken bits in mushroom sauce. Michael noted everything down and left them.

"To success," Jeff proposed a toast and lifted his glass.

"To success!" Evy replied, and they clinked their glasses.

"So, how do you like Westville?" Evy asked.

"It's wonderful, it's charming and brings back a lot of memories from my childhood," Jeff replied looking around the area.

"You mean you used to come here as a child?"

"No, but such small towns, hidden in the mountains, usually have quite a specific atmosphere. And that is what I meant. My parents, Monica and I would go skiing every year to a place like this. I am sure Westville blooms in winter."

"Oh, no doubt. I also like it a lot. It reminds me of Whistler in Canada."

"In British Columbia?"

"Yes. I am Canadian, in case you didn't know. My parents still live in Vancouver. We would go to Whistler every winter."

"Of course I know you're Canadian. I've been to Toronto twice, but unfortunately, I haven't had a chance to see any other parts of Canada."

"Well, if you ever feel like you'd like to, let me know, I may show you around."

"Deal." Jeff smiled and reached for her hand to shake in agreement. "My grandmother on my father's side was Polish, so I have some European blood in my veins. When did you move to the States?"

"I got here for college, and then it sort of happened. I got my first post-college work here and I just settled. I'm thinking of going back to Canada, actually."

"You are?" Jeff asked surprised. Was it Evy's mishearing or was there a shade of disappointment in his voice?

"Well, yeah, I've been thinking about it for some years now, so no worries, it won't happen too quickly." Evy laughed. "It's just that I was quite lucky here. I got the job, then I had a boyfriend, so it looked as if I was about to settle down here. The relationship did not last too long, but while it was happening I began settling in Boston, rented the apartment, started working for WORDS. Then there was Pete, and it looked really serious. We'd been together for some years, I was trying to convince him to move to Canada, but he never wanted to hear anything about it. It's quite ironic, because he left me about a year ago to take a job in Detroit."

"Changing a city is not *exactly* the same as changing a country."

"Or perhaps I wasn't enough of a girlfriend for him to reconsider his decision," Evy said quite bitterly. She was surprised hearing her own voice, because she was sure she had let Pete out of her life for good. Was it still uneasy for her to think about him? Did she still feel the grudge against him for leaving her? Ridiculous.

Michael brought them their food and they spent several minutes in silence eating.

"So, are you going to let me try your salmon, or do I have to beg you?" Jeff asked; his eyes were laughing.

"Beg me!" Evy replied and put a piece of fish into her mouth pretending to be cruel.

"I will, but only if you allow me to taste your chicken."

"You have my word on it!"

"Well then." Evy poked some piece of her salmon with her fork, "Here you go." She reached the fork to him. He leaned over and tasted the fish.

"Splendid. It really is," he said and gave her some chicken. She tasted it and admitted the food was wonderful.

They spent the rest of their dinner talking about their lives. Jeff told Evy about Rachel, how their relationship burned out, and he admitted he still was not able to imagine himself as being committed "till death do us apart". Evy, on the other hand, told him the story of her and Pete. Marriage never came up as an option for them, after the four years they dated, they never even lived together, only casually slept in one another's apartments. They discussed their childhoods, college years, and their previous professional experiences. It was a great evening.

Three hours and two and a half bottles of wine later, they were strolling by the lake and were heading toward a pier situated by the pond. The night was beautiful, the sky was cloudless and there were thousands of stars looking down on them. They were having a wonderful time, laughing, perhaps even a bit too loud, and telling each other anecdotes and stories. When they were walking along the narrow beach, heading toward the wooden pier, Evy took off her shoes and allowed the water to gently lick at her feet. She felt relaxed and because she was a bit tipsy, she was laughing loudly and reacting quite spontaneously to whatever Jeff was saying. He enjoyed her company a lot, and there were a few times he actually thought he would kiss her. He was absolutely sure that moment was coming, and that he would not be able to resist it any longer. She was perfect. Her body, her mind, her personality; it all created an irresistible combination. Jeff felt he had less and less arguments against their affair. He knew she wanted it, and it did light his desire. It was obvious they felt a bind between them, that there was a powerful force drawing them toward each other. They walked along the pier and stood at the very end, looking at the endless sky.

"When I was a kid I used to dream of getting a telescope, so I could gaze into the stars," Jeff said.

"You wanted to be an astronaut?"

"No, I just wanted to be closer to the stars, to observe them, watch them carefully. The universe is so beautiful, so mysterious; so many things are yet to be explored. It leaves a huge, gigantic space for the imagination."

"Let me guess, you were a huge fan of The X-Files?" Evy smiled.

"Yeah, but show me anyone in the 90's who wasn't?" he replied.

They were standing at the end of the pier, leaning on the fence. Below them there was a still surface of the pond, so flawless it almost looked like a mirror.

"So, can you recognize any of the constellations?" Evy asked.

"Sure, can't you?"

"No." She smiled. "Show me; the sky is clear, and I bet there are a lot of them visible now."

"Okay, come here." He gently pulled her to him. She was standing so close to him now, she was leaning on him. He could smell her hair and feel the warmth of her body on his chest. He put his one hand on her shoulder and pointed the other one to the sky.

"Look, follow my index finger," he said.

"All right, where shall I look?"

"You see those two, very bright stars? One above the other?"

"Where exactly?"

"Exactly where I am pointing. Can you see it?" He slightly moved up and down his finger to make it easier for her to see what he was showing.

"Yes! I can! Okay, so, what is it?"

"Well, now that you can see those stars, look a bit up and you'll see two more, one to the left and one to the right. See them?"

Evy was looking very hard, but she wasn't sure if she saw what she was supposed to. Jeff spotted that and stood exactly behind her. Now he had two arms free and he started showing her the stars again.

"Look, these two we've already found, right?"

"Yes."

"Now look a bit above them and you'll see two brighter? Stars, one to the left, one to the right." He spread his arms and pointed his fingers to the sky. "Can you see them?"

"Oh! Yes, *now* I can! So, what is this constellation?"

"It's Zeus' Slingshot," Jeff said and turned his head a bit to hide his laugh.

"A what?" she asked.

"It's Zeus' Slingshot. Haven't you ever heard of it?"

"No—as a matter of fact, I haven't," she replied and looked at him. "Oh," she said when their eyes met and they both started laughing.

"I'm sorry," Jeff said. "I hardly know any constellations." He kept laughing.

"That was a good one," she replied. "I thought that since you liked gazing at stars, you kind of knew what you were looking at."

"A bit yes, but not too much."

They stood there for a moment without saying anything, just looking at the wonderful surroundings.

"I'm cold," Evy finally said.

Jeff took off his jacket and wrapped it around her arms. He embraced her and rubbed her arms to warm her. At that point Evy looked into his eyes and he kissed her. First it was gentle, shy, as if he was making sure she wanted it, too. When she didn't resist, he turned her around, pulled her to him and kissed her passionately. After a long, wonderful moment, they looked at each other, twin gazes of desire.

"Maybe, we'll go back to the hotel?" she said as she licked her lips.

"Great idea," he replied.

They got back to the hotel, walked to Jeff's room, embracing and kissing and fell on his bed. His hands reached up to her shoulder straps and his lips were caressing her neck. At one point he stopped and looked at her. He brushed her hair off her cheek and forehead and their eyes met.

"Evy, I can't promise you anything," he said, a bit sadly, but firmly.

"Just love me tonight," she whispered heavily and closed her eyes.

His scent on her skin was something unspeakable for her. She had been dreaming about this moment for months. She allowed him to undress her, and soon she was unbuttoning his shirt, kissing him.

❧28❧

Jeff woke up first. He rubbed his face with his palm, looked at his cell lying on a night table. It was few minutes past 7 o'clock. He turned around and watched Evy's sleeping form beside him. So they did it. He did it. They spent the night together. His head was filled with contradictory thoughts. As much as he wanted it all to happen, as much as he was hoping for it for the past few months, he couldn't shake the feeling that he had made a mistake. He was afraid Evy would now hope for a relationship, and he certainly did not want that. He didn't want a commitment. Sure, she was a beautiful, fascinating woman, but when he said he couldn't promise her anything, that much was true. He had to cool them both, and he was completely aware he would have to act like a total son-of-a-bitch. Jeff could only hope that when the emotions would finally fall, they would still work together. *Damn it, Jeff, you knew it would complicate everything.*

Evy woke up and looked around. She glanced to her left and saw Jeff's jacket hanging on the chair beside the bed. She smiled, looked to her right and realized she was alone in bed and that Jeff was taking a shower. Evy leaned on two pillows. She forgot to call Laura yesterday, but there was no doubt that Laura would understand. After all, something wonderful happened last night, a reason Laura was keeping her fingers crossed. So Laura wouldn't be mad at Evy for not returning her call. Evy looked at Jeff's watch on the night table. 7.30. They still had few hours before the closing ceremony and the farewell lunch. She had a few ideas on how they could occupy their time until then. Evy smiled again and waited for Jeff to come out from the bathroom. The whole situation was surreal. Finally, after all these months, she experienced the real Jeff and not just a dream.

He walked out a few minutes later, smiling.

"You're up."

"Yeah, when did you wake up?"

"About thirty minutes ago," he lied.

"Oh, okay. So, we still have some time, right?"

"Yes," he answered, looked away and started dressing. His tone was different, off.

"I can wait for you so we can come down for breakfast together," he said.

"I thought we might order breakfast through room service." She smiled and winked. He smiled back at her and walked toward the bed.

"Evy," he said and sat at the edge of the bed, took her hand and looked into her eyes.

"Do you remember what I told you when we got back to the hotel?"

"Yes, you said you couldn't promise me anything," she said and felt a gigantic pile of sadness coming up toward her throat. She gulped.

"I meant it, Evy. I'm so sorry if you were counting on anything else. I know I'm sounding like a total asshole now," he said with visible remorse in his voice and lowered his gaze. At this point, he couldn't stand the eye-contact between them.

"You are, actually, but I know I agreed on something last night. I just had no idea it would last this short."

"Look, you are an amazing person, you're sexy, talented, funny—"

Evy felt a single tear falling down her cheek. Damn it, she did not want to him to see her cry; it was purely humiliating.

"Please don't cry," he said softly and wiped the tear with his thumb. "The thing is, Evy, you're looking for a stable relationship and I cannot give you that."

"How do you know what I am looking for?"

"You told me things about Pete, last night, so I can tell. He hurt you mostly because you had certain expectations, and you wanted to be in a firm and stable relationship. I am a person who wants to avoid it, that is why my relationship fell apart. I cannot promise you I would be your boyfriend—that I would change."

"But you and Rachel spent years together."

"True, but we split up when she started pushing me into marrying her."

"Oh my God, Jeff, are you paranoid? We spent one night together and you're telling me you don't want to get married?" she replied irritated.

"No, no, of course not. I am just telling you that I am not looking for a commitment. I won't lie to you, I was waiting for this night, hoping for months it would happen, and it was special, wonderful. But I don't want you to think that I am treating it as a beginning of something serious."

"So—so, I was a one-night stand?"

"No, God, of course not! Ev, please don't get me wrong... I wanted this so, so much." He kissed her forehead like a brother kisses his sister.

Evy sobbed uncontrollably. "Please, Evy, please do not let anything change between us." He couldn't believe he actually said it. He felt like a total weasel.

"But everything *has* changed, Jeff," she said weeping silently.

"Evy, I do not want to create the illusion that we could be a long-lasting couple, because it has never been so in my case. My break-up with Rachel made it clear to me that I do not want to get myself into serious relationships. I am immature, I know, and I'm sorry. Also, we work together; an office romance is not the best solution for any couple."

"You're right, but there is one thing you're missing."

"What's that?"

"I don't feel like starting a relationship either. Not one that goes nowhere, Jeff. I don't want it. I don't want to invest my emotions, to invest in a relationship that, in the end, goes nowhere. So, I appreciate your honesty and I think it really *is* better for us to be friends only." That was definitely not what she thought she'd say to Jeff the morning after they had spent the night together, but Evy was being completely honest. She was aware of the sexual tension between them, and did not regret sleeping with him; she wanted it as much as he did, but if this was how he saw things, then it would be a total waste of her energy to try to build something out of nothing.

He kissed her palms and looked into her eyes. "Thank you, Evy, and I am very sorry that I've disappointed you."

"I want to eat my breakfast alone, if you don't mind."

"Not at all, I understand."

He kissed her on her forehead, which she had no idea how to interpret as pitiful or as apologetic, and went out from the room. Evy looked around one more time, processing everything that had happened and burst out crying. She sobbed in the pillows, not sure if her sadness was triggered by her feeling stupid, humiliated or by being so gullible. Evy couldn't accuse Jeff of lying to her; he was straight about everything, and he did not do anything against her will. They both felt the attraction, but they had different expectations. They needed this night, both of them, but it would be a mistake to count on anything more to happen and it was a feeling that simply pierced her heart. When Evy felt she was calming down, she got up, dressed and left Jeff's room. Because the doors they shared were closed, she had to go out into the hallway to get back to her own room from the outside. She went to the bathroom and looked at herself in the mirror. Her hair was a mess, her make-up was weepy, she had her favorite cocktail dress unzipped and her eyes were all red and swollen after crying. This wasn't exactly what she had in mind after spending the night with Jeff.

Evy took out her cell phone from her purse, searched Laura's contact number and pressed the dial button.

☙ 29 ☙

Laura woke up and looked at a window in the bedroom. The rays of sun caressed her cheeks, gently waking her up. She lazily opened one eye, then the other one, stretched and smiled. The morning felt peaceful. She turned around and saw Bruce covered in his quilt. She called it "the Pharaoh position". He would cover himself up very tightly, not to let the air get through, having only his head outside the cocoon. Lying there, covered like that, he looked like a mummy in a sarcophagus. That was the reason they always had two quilts on their bed. She smiled again, and started uncovering him. He opened his eyes, yawned and embraced her with one arm when she lay her head on his chest. Bruce covered her with his quilt and they were both laying there listening to morning silence. They had no idea what time it was, but hearing each other's heart beats allowed them to ignore the world.

"What if I lose my breast?" Laura whispered.

Bruce opened his eyes, embraced her even more and said.

"Don't think like that."

"Yeah, but I can't. I am really afraid of that. I am going to be mutilated if it happens."

"There are surgeries that allow breasts to be reconstructed, you know that," he replied peacefully.

"But it won't be the same."

"If losing your breast would mean saving your life and health, then I don't think the choice is difficult."

"You mean you wouldn't mind?"

Bruce opened his eyes; he was completely awake at this point. He gently moved Laura and sat on the bed.

"What are you talking about, Laura?"

She sat as well, looked at him a bit embarrassed, swept her hair behind her ear and looked down.

"You know, I'm afraid I won't be attractive to you anymore if I lose my breast," she said quietly.

He put his hand on her chin and forced her to look at him.

"Don't you *ever* talk like that! Don't you ever *think* like that! Do you really think I've been finding you attractive for the past twenty years because you have two breasts?"

Perhaps he wanted it to sound funny, but it came out rather serious, and she could tell she hurt his feelings.

"Laura, for God's sake, I love you. You, your mind, your personality and your soul. Your health is the most important thing to me. I couldn't care less about your physical appearance; I just want you to be here with me, smiling like you always do, safe and sound. That's all that matters to me."

Laura embraced him tightly.

"Honey, that is the last thing on your list to worry about." He kissed her ear like he always did when he wanted to cheer her up.

"I'm going to look awful. Bald, pale, sick," she wept.

"Can you remember how many times I held your hair after a night of drinking?"

"No." She smiled.

"Well, me neither. And do you remember when I had to clip your toenails when you had that cast after you twisted your ankle?"

"Yeah—"

"My point is, don't worry, we'll manage. As long as there's your health and life at the end of the road, I am willing to do anything it takes. Taking care of you and seeing you getting better will be the best thing for me." He kissed her again.

She was grateful to have Bruce in her life. She loved him so much. If there was anyone in the world she would die for it was him. He was her soul mate, her partner, her lover, a person that allowed her to be who she was; he understood her and accepted her entirely.

"Come on, Laura, let's have a coffee on the terrace, shall we? It looks like it's another beautiful morning," he said and kissed her cheeks and eyelids.

"Ok," she replied and got out from bed. When she reached the bedroom doors, she turned around and smiled.

"And I don't drink that much!"

"No, *that* much you don't," he said and winked. She picked up the pillow from the nearest armchair and threw it at him. They laughed. Laura's cell phone rang.

"Ok, I'll make the coffee; you go ahead and pick it up," Bruce said when he was looking for his slippers.

❧30❧

Laura looked at her cell and knew it was Evy calling. After mouthing that it was Evy on the line, Laura left Bruce inside while she went out to the porch.

'Hello?" she said.

"Laura! Hi! What's up with the serious tone?"

"Evy, hi, so good to hear you!" Laura was truly happy. They had experienced longer breaks from seeing each other than two days, but because of what was going on in Laura's life, the lack of her best friend around her was very painful.

"Laura, I slept with Jeff," Evy said and there was complete silence for few seconds.

"Oh—" Laura had no idea what to say. From the tone of Evy's voice she didn't seem as if she had been on cloud nine. "When did it happen?"

"Yesterday. We went for a dinner, perhaps we drunk a bit too much, went for a walk and it sort of happened that we got back to the hotel together."

"Evy, I can tell you're not exactly happy. Are you regretting this?"

"I don't know," Evy mumbled sadly. "Today he told me there's no chance for any potential relationship between us and he basically left me alone in his room."

"Ouch, that's harsh. I'm so sorry. I never thought Jeff was a guy who would sleep with a woman and kick her out of his bed few hours later."

"Well, he did tell me yesterday I shouldn't expect anything, that he wasn't looking for any stable relationship, but still, it hurts."

"So now what?"

"I agree with Jeff that we both needed it. I think it was tension and curiosity on both sides, and I don't really regret it; I was just hoping for something more than one fling."

"When are you coming back?"

"We have a plane at 4, so I will be back at 7."

"Will you have time to see me today then?"

"I don't know, Laura; I think I'll see you in the office. I'm not in a mood to see anybody."

"Evy, you're a grown-up person; please remember that."

"How do you mean?"

"I mean that if he told you he wasn't interested in a long-term relationship and you still decided to sleep with him, then you need to get a grip."

"Bye and gone?"

"Yes, exactly."

"Thanks that's exactly what I needed to hear."

Suddenly Evy's problems seemed irrelevant and irritating for Laura. She *wanted* to sleep with Jeff; she'd been *dreaming* about it, and now when they finally did, she was upset he wasn't preparing an engagement ring for her? Was she *that* unrealistic?

"Evy, come on. Look, maybe things will change, maybe he'll think it through, maybe not. If not, then at least you got what you've been dreaming about for a long time."

"Maybe. Yeah, I guess you're right."

"Aren't you going to ask me how I'm doing?"

"Ok, Laura, how are you doing in your perfect, married life?" asked Evy rather contemptuously. Perhaps she wanted to sound funny, perhaps she wanted to be mean, but it definitely hurt.

"I have breast cancer. I was diagnosed on Friday, and I'm going to undergo chemotherapy. I'm starting tomorrow. I'm sorry, Evy; I am not the best listener today, but there's a bigger picture than your will-he-won't-he relationship with Jeff. You slept with him, fine, you're an adult, and you make your own decisions. I am sorry you feel hurt, but from what you've been telling me, he was honest with you from the beginning. Too bad; I'm sorry there's probably no perspective for you two to have three kids and a house in the suburbs, but please, stop making him the center of your world. There are more important things."

There was a complete silence. If everything was normal, Laura would probably call Jeff an asshole; she would buy a gigantic portion of ice-cream and take Evy shopping. But at this point, she couldn't give a damn about Evy's problems with the Creative Manager. Six months she's heard about that man. Enough. Now she wanted Evy's attention on her for a change.

"Laura, what are you saying?" Evy replied shocked.

"I'm saying I am sick and that it's serious. Now excuse me, but I need to go back to my perfect, married life, while I still have one," Laura said harshly and hung up.

Evy was standing in her room looking at her cell phone with disbelief.

Oenone~Agatha Rae~

❧31❧

"Oh my God," she whispered. In one instant the bitter aftertaste of the night before disappeared and Evy knew immediately what she had to do. She picked up her things, packed her suitcases and rushed to the bathroom to take a shower. Fifteen minutes later, she was ready to leave The Panorama. Evy decided to find Jeff before she would depart and tell him not to wait for her during the closing ceremonies and lunch. She closed the doors of her room firmly, went to the elevator, left her suitcase by the reception desk and then walked to the dining area to find him. He was finishing his breakfast.

"Jeff, listen," she said.

"What's the matter?" he asked, seeing she was visibly stirred.

"I need to go. I need to leave Westville as soon as possible and get home."

"What happened?" he asked surprised. Was it because of him?

Evy hesitated. She wasn't sure if Laura had told anyone about the cancer, nor did she have any idea who ought to know about it, so she decided not to say anything to Jeff.

"My friend is very sick, and I need to see her," she said quickly.

"How are you going to get back now? Can't you wait until 4 pm?"

"A receptionist checked the trains for me. If I leave now, I will catch one at 11. I should be home by 4 pm."

'Ok, sure, no problem.'

"All right; bye." She was about to leave when he grabbed her by the hand.

"Evy, when will I see you again?"

She looked at him, irritated. *Oh yeah, I still work for him, don't I?*

"I'm at work on Wednesday," she replied and left the room.

She took her suitcase and went outside to catch a taxi. Half an hour later, she was on a train. Laura's remark about Evy being so occupied by Jeff felt very uncomfortable. She should have called her yesterday; she *felt* something was wrong, but decided to spend a nice evening with the Creative Manager than to talk with her friend. If she had known about

Laura's situation sooner, she would have left Westville yesterday evening and came to her today. Evy felt very guilty, but then again how was she supposed to know the situation was that serious? She was absolutely fine only few days ago! And the whole situation with Jeff turned out to be one big mess. Heaven only knew what their future co-operation would look like now that they had slept together. Would all this have an impact on their professional life? Undoubtedly. Would she let him go after that night? She had no idea.

Laura came into the kitchen. Two cups of hot, strong, black as night, coffees were standing on the table luring her with aromatic steam levitating lazily above their edges. She picked one of them up and inhaled the fragrance deeply. How wonderful. Just smelling the coffee helped calm her nerves.

"Did you tell her?" Bruce asked. He got up from his chair, came closer and stood behind Laura embracing her. He put his chin on her shoulder.

"Yeah, I did, but that wasn't a nice conversation."

"I can imagine."

"No, it wasn't nice in the sense that I was quite unpleasant to her. Something happened in her life the other night, something she had been waiting for for a long time, and I treated her problems as something trivial. It was selfish, and I feel quite embarrassed actually. But it did seem so, I don't know, shallow, not important to me. I guess a week ago I'd be stirred by what she told me, but today I only got mad she had such stupid things on her mind."

"Maybe you got jealous of the irrelevance of her problems in comparison to what you're going through?"

"I think that's exactly what happened." Laura turned around and looked at Bruce. "I think I owe her an apology."

"She'll understand," he said and kissed her softly on the forehead.

"I know. I'm feeling pretty dumb now," she answered and kissed her back.

"Come on, let's go to the bedroom and have our coffees there, shall we? The weather is getting worse."

"All right."

They went to the bedroom, lay on the bed and watched TV for some time. After two hours, when all the Sunday morning shows were over, Laura texted Evy.

I'm sorry.

After two minutes a reply came.

I love you.

❧32❧

Evy arrived at the Boston South Station at 4, but since she had to take the taxi to pick up Bob from the airport parking lot, she arrived home at 5:30 pm. She opened the door of her apartment, left her suitcase in a hallway and was already on her way out to Laura's. The weather got worse, the sky was overcast, a lot of very thick, dark and dreadfully-looking clouds were hanging above the city, moving lazily due south. It seemed there was going to be heavy showers in a few minutes, perhaps even a storm. Normally, under such circumstances, Evy would put on "Thunderstruck" by AC/DC in her player (tacky or not, it did not matter), it always seemed like a perfect supplement for such weather, but this time she did not even think about it. From her apartment to Laura's home there was about 40 minutes of driving and she was focused on getting there as soon as possible. In the rear mirror she saw a lightening tearing the sky in half. For a moment she thought about Jeff and if his plane would land safely, or perhaps it was delayed and he was still in Westville.

She parked her car on a sidewalk near Laura's home and ran towards it just as drops of rain started falling down from the sky, slowly and heavily, like little bombs. She knocked on the door, Spark started barking and Bruce opened it.

"Hi, Evy!" he said warmly. "Come in."

She stepped inside and hugged him cordially. He reciprocated the gesture.

"How are you doing?"

"Not too bad. It's Laura that you should be asking the question."

"I know, I know, where is she?"

"On the terrace."

"Ok, I'm going to talk to her, all right?"

"Of course, would you like some tea or coffee?"

"Tea."

She walked upstairs, looked through the window and saw Laura sitting on a bench under a huge garden umbrella. She was sitting there with her eyes closed. Evy opened the doors and swiftly walked outside. Laura heard her and looked at her with joy on her face. She stood up and they embraced each other. Evy had no idea when she started crying and Laura was stroking her head, comforting her. It was a bit embarrassing, because it would seem more natural if it all happened the other way round, but it was the moment that Evy realized entirely what was happening, and a wave of fear for Laura, mixed with her own frustration and regret, made the tears appear on her face spontaneously. After few minutes when Evy pulled herself together, they sat on the bench. Bruce brought them both teas and left them to talk peacefully.

"I am so, so sorry, Laura," Evy said sobbing.

"Me, too." It was painful to see her best friend in such a mess.

Raindrops were banging on the top of the umbrella. The air became colder but it was refreshing and pleasant. For few seconds they were just sitting together, drinking their teas.

"So, what's going on, Laura. Tell me everything."

Laura told her about the cancer, about the test results and how her life turned upside down within a week. She told her she was about to be admitted to the clinic for the first chemotherapy the following day in the afternoon.

"How are you holding up?"

"Well, the worst thing is that I don't know what to expect. I am determined to beat the cancer, but I am scared of the treatment. I am supposed to see my doctor before the therapy begins and she will tell me what the whole party is going to be like."

"Laura, I'm sorry I was so focused on my stupid problems instead of listening to you."

"How were you supposed to know something was wrong? It all happened within a week, *I'm* still confused about it."

"Is there anything I can do for you? Can I help you somehow? Because I will do whatever I can."

"I want to have my hair cut tomorrow morning. And I'd love you to come with me."

"Why would you like to do that?"

"I have long hair, I was told that the shorter the hair is, the lighter it is and might fall out at least a bit later. Besides, I was thinking about changing my hairstyle for some time now," she added smiling.

Evy touched Laura's hand.

"Of course I'll go with you."

The rain became a bit lighter and a pleasant delicate thunder tore the sky.

Oenone~Agatha Rae~

"So, what about Jeff, what exactly happened in Westville?"

Evy told her about the conference, their dinner and that they went to bed together. She told her about Jeff's distance and how he told her not to expect anything.

"He was straight, you need to appreciate it."

"I know, but I must admit, I was hoping he'd change his mind after that night we spent together."

"Personally, I think it's the upcoming days that will be meaningful, not what he said in the hotel. In the morning he repeated his philosophy, but he might think it all through and when you see him at WORDS next time, it is possible his attitude might change."

"You think so?"

Sure I do. However, it is also nothing might happen, and that's possible, too. You need to take that option into consideration as well. Look, Evy, just enjoy it. You spent a great night with the great guy, your fantasies had come true. Enjoy it and think about it like that: the man you've been dreaming of couldn't resist sleeping with you, after you had spent only two days together. He got the chance to meet you a bit, on a more private basis, and I'm sure he must have found you very attractive both physically and mentally."

"Yeah, I guess you're right."

"I *know* I am. And if he doesn't want to be with you after all, screw him, oh, wait, you already have." Laura winked and they both laughed.

"Well, we'll see what happens. I am just afraid that if he doesn't consider us being together, I might be heart-broken."

"You'll get over it." Laura kissed Evy's forehead and they looked at the sky. The storm finished and the sky was clearing up. A huge rainbow embracing two ends of the world appeared. It was gigantic, like a portal to a different dimension.

"You'll be fine, Laura," said Evy looking at it.

"I hope so."

Oenone~Agatha Rae~

❧33❧

Evy got back home around midnight. Being broken into pieces, she was unable to focus on anything at home and couldn't find herself any place in her apartment. She took off her clothes, to take a hot shower. When she was naked she looked at herself in the mirror in the hallway, the same one she would always glance at before going out anywhere to make sure her clothes would fit. She was looking good. She touched her breasts trying to remember when was the last time she went to see a doctor to have them examined. She couldn't recall it, and promised herself to do it the upcoming week. Evy liked her body, felt good looking at herself. She was given a figure that did not need any extra attention to be impeccable. After last night with Jeff she felt even more attractive and appreciated. The truth, no matter if sad or not, was that most women needed men's attention to feel good about themselves.

Evy had always felt good about herself, being with a man would only boost this feeling, but it had never been necessary. She forgot, however, that a body might turn against its owner and that health was not eternal. It was a gift that ought to be cherished, nurtured and appreciated. She went to the bathroom, took a shower, covered herself with a cozy terry robe afterwards and went to the kitchen to make herself some lime tea. It was something that would always calm her and allow her to sleep better. She opened her kitchen window and with a cup of tea, sat on the window sill and was now looking at the city glow. Beautifully lit Zakim Bridge was majestically hanging above the Charles River. Boston was asleep, getting ready for a new day and a new week. Evy was supposed to meet Laura at the hairdresser's at 11:00 a.m. She hit upon a certain idea while drying herself after the shower. She was determined to help Laura get through her illness and was sure that, at least for now, her friend was her priority, not Jeff. A sting of sadness pinched her heart when she thought about him. It looked like her story with him was over and she wasn't sure if keeping him at the distance, and being delusional at the same time, as she was only two days ago, was actually a better solution than knowing what it felt like to be with him and that she was going to pine for. After all, that night was amazing; Jeff was a great lover, perfectly sensing her needs, her tempo and her expectations. And he kept eye-contact with her the entire time, which simply drove her insane with passion. She felt like the queen of the night with him and there was painful about knowing it all happened just once. Evy sighed, looked at the city again, took the last sip of her tea and felt she was getting tired and ready to sleep. She closed the window, put the cup into the sink and was heading toward the bedroom when she spotted in the corner of her eye a red light blinking on her phone. A voice message. She pushed the button and heard Jeff's voice.

"Hi, Evy, it's Jeff. I see you're not at home, and I couldn't connect with your cell phone—"

Shit, she had turned it off on the train when she wanted to have a nap on her way to Boston and forgot to switch it on.

"—so, I hope you got home safe and sound. Just wanted to tell you I had great time with you at the conference and that I am really sorry I disappointed you that badly. I hope you don't hate me—I think we did a great job in Westville and I hope your friend is fine. I am looking forward to seeing you on Wednesday and—um let me know if you're ok, all right?"

There was a pause and he said, "Good night, Evy."

Damn you, Jeff. She went to the bedroom, lay in bed and turned the light off. It was 2:30, but she had a feeling that there would be no sleep.

❧34❧

Laura woke up at eight. Bruce wasn't in bed, but she heard him in the kitchen downstairs. She sat on the bed and looked around the bedroom. For a second she felt a pain in her chest at the thought of being a different Laura Levinson than her normal self, before chemo. No matter what was about to happen, no matter how the treatment would go, and if she beat the cancer, that part of her life was over. She got rid of the tearful feeling that clung around her throat and got out of bed, put on her gown and walked downstairs.

Bruce was preparing breakfast, the smell of toast and strong tea filling up the kitchen, wrapping around Laura like a warm blanket. Inhaling the sweet smell, she smiled and kissed Bruce's ear from behind when he was standing by the work surface, cutting vegetables.

"Good morning." Laura smiled.

"Hi, honey," he replied, turned around and kissed her cheek. "When did you wake up?"

"Five minutes ago," she said and took a slice of her favorite green pepper. She loved the crunchy sound it made, and it was without a doubt the tastiest pepper she had ever tasted. Bruce, however, would always claim it tasted like peas.

"Well, you could have given me half an hour more, so I could welcome you in the kitchen with some royal breakfast."

"Yeah, I see what you mean, but no worries, you've swept me off my feet anyway."

"Don't I always?" He winked.

"Of course," she replied and kissed him.

"So, when do you plan to—prepare?"

"In the afternoon. I need to be at the clinic at six. Tessa will explain everything to me, and I will have some tests done before the chemo starts."

"What time exactly are you having your first dose today?"

"Yes, but late in the evening."

"Will it be alright if I went with you to talk to Tessa?"

"Bruce, I will need you to be there with me the whole time, *including* the conversation with Tessa."

"I will be there. Don't worry about it."

"It's just that I thought you'd need to go to work today."

"There is no way that I would let you do this alone, even if you didn't want me there, I'd be there…waiting for you in the building. Besides, Family and Medical Leave Act," he replied. 'I've already taken care of it."

He put the toast and vegetables on the table and invited Laura to sit down. When she did, he looked at her, bent over and kissed her gently.

"We'll be fine. We'll make it through this, I promise you, honey," he said softly.

"I believe you." And she honestly did. She was scared, but determined to win this battle.

"So, what are you going to do until going to Femina?"

"I'm having an appointment at the hairdresser's at 11."

Bruce looked at her a bit surprised.

"I want to have my hair cut. So that it's less painful once it starts to fall out," she said stirring her tea.

"Good idea," he replied and opened up a morning newspaper he had taken from their doormat.

"I'm going to spend some time with Evy today; after the hairdresser, I want to ask her if she would help me pack."

"Sure. I will go to work today to pass my duties and I will be back at 5. Then we'll go to the clinic."

Can't wait, Laura thought and started putting mozzarella on her toast.

❧35❧

She had been waiting for Evy for over twenty minutes now. The salon they would always go to was "Kristy's" in the downtown area. Their typical ritual included the hairdresser, coffee and shopping. Those days were all about gossiping, talking about sex, enjoying all possible sales in the area and eating everything consisting of chocolate, fat and sugar. Sometimes they would go to the movies for some stereotypical romantic comedy where they would sit at the very back and comment on most of the scenes, laughing loudly at their absurdities. No men were allowed to distract them, no matter if it was Bruce or Pete. Laura hoped the tradition would never die. No, she *knew* the tradition would never die. Today she had time only for the hairdresser part, and the circumstances were, well, different, but she was very glad Evy was coming with her. It had the feeling of their ritual, and Evy would provide the comfort Laura needed. But where was she?

Laura's cell phone rang. She looked at the display and saw Evy's picture on it.

"Where are you? I'm waiting in front of the Kristy's."

"I'm so sorry, Laura, I'm stuck in an awful traffic jam; I think there must have been some accident or something. Listen, start without me, or you'll lose your appointment. I'll be there as soon as I can. I'm sorry!"

"It's ok, I understand. Ok, I'll see you later."

Laura was a bit disappointed, but who could predict such a scenario. She stepped into the salon, and was asked to take a seat in front of a huge mirror. Her hairdresser was Jim, a guy who was able to make magic with scissors, combs and hairspray. He was also a very good listener. Laura and Evy would update all possible celebrity gossips with him and he would always offer them the best possible coffee with milk. Today Jim wasn't at work, but then again the purpose of this visit was entirely different than usual, so maybe it was good.

Laura sat comfortably, asked for coffee and was waiting for the hairdresser, Brooke to come to her.

"How are you doing?" asked Evy out of nowhere, Laura turned around and instinctively looked at the entrance door. But there was no one there.

"I'm here!" Evy giggled. Laura looked to her right and saw Evy on the chair next to her having her hair cut short.

"Oh my God, Evy what are you doing?" Laura asked stunned.

"I figured I could use a new style of my own as well." Evy smiled.

Laura was stunned and touched. She loved her very much. Evy reached out to her and they were sitting there on their chairs holding hands tightly, assuring they were both there for each other.

When Laura looked into the mirror after Brooke had finished her work, she felt a lump in her throat. She had always had long hair, not waist-long, but always covering half of her back. She had always taken good care of it, and considered it to be one of the most important aspects of her look and personality. Seeing herself like that for the first time in her life was shocking, not only because she looked entirely different than the way she had always been used to, but also because it was the very first vivid and tangible proof that she was about to face the battle for her life.

And that the battle would start really soon.

Laura beat the tears coming to her eyes and reminded herself of her own thoughts she had on the terrace two days ago: *it was not the end of the world. Just hold on, and you'll make it.*

She felt a strong grip on her shoulder and looked up. Evy was standing behind her and looking into the mirror as well.

"Well, well, well, aren't we cute?" She laughed. The truth was they both looked really nice in their new hairstyles. Instinctively they raked their hair, and Evy was about to turn around to get her purse when Laura grabbed her hand.

"Will you help me pack for the clinic?"

"Of course I will."

~36~

J eff was checking his phone more often than he wanted. He left Evy a message the night before, and he had no idea if she wanted anything to do with him, or if she simply decided that his message did not require an immediate reply. He felt pretty bad about what happened in Westville. Of course he kept telling to himself he was honest with Evy when he warned her not to count on a relationship, but his behavior still made him a total dick. All the talk when she woke up, it was true, and he honestly meant it, but after some time, when he was on his plane back to Boston, he couldn't help but wonder if he had made the right decision. Evy was entirely different than the women he used to hang out and sleep with. She was a woman he needed to *win*. Jeff was sure she wouldn't have slept with him if it wasn't for that weekend when they got to talk and know each other better. The truth was, she intrigued him and the night they spent together felt deeper than just sex. After he had split up with Rachel, he slept with few women; all of them were one-night stands, because it fit his philosophy of not-engaging. He found Evy attractive almost immediately when he met her at WORDS, and because of the professional line he really did not want to cross, he had time to get to know her better. Frankly speaking, that was the reason that he felt pretty bad about leaving her like that on Sunday. There were so many things about her that just dazed him. Her scent was something he simply could not take out of his head, just thinking about it made him almost dizzy. And never before had he seen such eyes. Green, expressive, bright and very emotional. There were times, moments he felt he could drown in them. Maybe he made the decision to end the relationship, before it even started, too rashly.

It was Monday and he was just coming back from lunch break. At 3:00 p.m. he was to meet the board to report the results of Written Word. Apart from introducing new potential authors, he was also about to confront his new vision of the publishing house with the management of WORDS. He was nervous before that meeting; he wasn't sure the board would understand his ideas, and he knew he would need to explain why he had decided to search for new authors on the basis of his not-yet-accepted-concept.

Laura wasn't at work today and Jeff immediately guessed it was her who was sick that Evy had to see immediately. He was worried; he valued her professionalism and liked Laura privately; she was one of the nicest people in the office. It occurred to him that he was worried about Laura not only because she was sick, but also because he knew that her problem would also be Evy's drama. And he did not want to see Evy suffering. When he entered the conference room, though, he immediately pushed away that thought—it was time to focus on the meeting.

⁓36⁓

Laura was carefully packing her bag. She was to spend a week in Femina and, if her medical condition was satisfactory, she could be released for few days to go home. She packed her pajamas, a toothbrush, two books she promised herself she would read but never had the time to actually do it, her mp3 player and a cell charger. She prepared the list with Evy and now, as Laura was zipping her bag, they sat on the couch.

"I'm scared, Ev," Laura said.

"I know, and it's completely natural," Evy replied and hugged her friend.

"I'm supposed to be at the clinic at 6 p.m., it's 3. Ev, would you be upset if I went with Bruce only?"

"Of course not! But I *will* be upset if you don't inform me about how you feel and how the treatment is going."

"I'll keep you posted, I promise." She kissed Evy on her cheek.

They hugged again and were sitting there in the living room in silence.

"Evy, live a normal life, whatever happens, all right?" Laura finally said.

"What do you mean?" asked Evy stunned.

"I mean that I want you to pursue your happiness, your life, no matter what happens with me. I have Bruce to be with me when I need him; I don't want you to let go of your daily life because I am sick."

"Jesus, Laura, don't talk like that, it's creepy."

"No, it isn't. I'm just saying." She took Evy's hand. "I will call you whenever I need anything. But please live your life."

They embraced dearly and Evy hid her face in Laura's shoulder.

"Would you like something to eat?" Laura asked her gently after few minutes.

"Sure." Evy wiped her eyes.

***

The meeting in WORDS conference room started at 3 p.m. sharp. The five board members were already waiting in the room. The chairman was David Garbinsky, the initial founder. He was a very kind-hearted and friendly man, who personally pushed Jeff's hiring. Two other board members included Ted Gardner and Jake Pinett, who never liked Richards and his coming to WORDS triggered a series of conflicts between them and David about it. Garbinsky took Anna Larson's and Dean Allen's side, the two other members who supported Richard's candidature, which was how he got his job. And his enemies. Whenever there was anything new, innovative that he wanted to push, he always had problems with Gardner and Pinett. E-books—nonsense, it's a fashion that will disappear sooner than we think. Internet bookshop—idiotic, people want to touch and smell the book, thumb through pages before buying it. The collaboration with the university—nobody reads stuff published by professors, it's too niche. Truthfully, if it hadn't been for Garbinsky, Jeff's situation at WORDS would have been difficult, if not in fact hopeless. Actually, Jeff simply wouldn't work there at all if it hadn't been for David. His situation was always two votes for, two against him and it was always Garbinsky who would save his ass. Jeff certainly counted on the formula to work that time as well.

When he got to the conference room they had all already been there. He took a deep breath and walked in, hoping he looked confident, but in fact he was really nervous. If David didn't like his idea, his days at WORDS could be over.

Everyone got up as he walked in, he shook hands with everybody and Donna, Garbinsky's secretary asked him if he wanted some coffee. He asked for some cold water and a few seconds later they all were alone, looking at each other.

"So, Jeff, how was the Written Word conference?" asked David. "Everything you imagine it to be?"

"I thought it was great. A search for fresh blood, unlike something like watching America's Got Talent and waiting for some writers to finally show up, we can just go to Westville and sniff out some really promising people who want, like and know how to write."

"Splendid! Well, we can't wait to see what you've got for us." David smiled.

Jeff got his flash drive out from the pocket and inserted it into a laptop connected with a digital projector. Once everything was ready, he opened the file "Written Word 2012" and three catalogs were displayed: "Fantasy", "Detective Stories" and "Scientific for the general public". Jeff quickly skimmed his audience and saw that David was vividly interested, but The Mutant Force, as he liked to call the Pinett and the Gardner team remained visibly indifferent because, obviously, there was nothing Jeff could do to make them interested. Their faces would always reflect disappointment or disapproval whenever Richards was around. Normally he wouldn't care, but this time he felt he would love to throw them out of the window. He could almost *see* them falling down—*Horrible Bosses* style.

"I know that in the past, the representatives of WORDS would go to Westville's conference and pick up basically all the writers that would only be willing to co-operate with us—"

"With WORDS, you mean?" Ted asked and cleared his throat.

"Yes, why?"

"Well, this was your first conference, so you cannot reference to the previous ones and what the publishing house had accomplished then and use the word "us". It's inappropriate."

Jake smiled sarcastically, but Jeff did not miss his drift.

"You are absolutely right, Ted, thank you for that valuable comment. So, to clarify, so far my ideas as a Creative Manager have been quite successful. Our sales have risen over 15% in the last quarter, mostly due to the introduction of the e-books and the internet shop, the collaboration with the university will open totally new perspectives."

"It's been a good time for us, no doubt," David said amiably.

"It sure has. So, as Ted was kind enough to mention, this year's Written Word was the first Westville conference that I participated in. And a few days before my departure, I'd decided to change the formula that WORDS had always followed and instead of offering a contract to absolutely anyone, I thought about narrowing our publishing profile."

Jeff paused for a moment and looked at his audience. There was silence in the room, but everyone seemed fairly intrigued.

"I have spoken to the staff and have done a very thorough research in terms of what kind of books we sell the most, and which genres are less popular. It turned out that the three categories which you can see on the screen are, in fact, our most popular and most successful ones. So this year, Ms. Dax and I decided to search for the best, the most promising authors of these particular genres."

He started opening files and discussing all of the authors that he and Evy had found attractive. The introduction of the writers took about half an hour. Each of the potential new bestselling authors was presented with the information about their achievements, the plan of their work and the concepts of their books and stories. When the last author was introduced,

Jeff finished his presentation and looked at the board. Nobody said anything for a moment and finally David spoke.

"Sixteen authors? Only three categories?" He was obviously surprised.

"Yes, David."

"You do realize that every year we had about thirty new writers after Written Word?" Ted asked quite harshly.

"We did? Sorry, Ted, not really. Last year we signed only three contracts; that would assure us twelve publications in the upcoming years, so it wasn't that impressive, check your facts. However, this year is finally the time to make changes. I want to propose dividing WORDS into two branches. One for fantasy, detective stories and scientific for general public, and the other, smaller one, specifically created for universities and colleges."

"In the time of recession, you've decided to make such revolutions and to limit our potential? Are you insane?" Jake said quite aggressively. Jeff did not care about him too much, because he had always been against any of his ideas, but he *was* watching David and waiting for his reaction.

"In the time of recession we cannot allow ourselves to waste money on publishing books that people won't buy. If our readers choose detective stories, fantasy and scientific for the general public from our repertoire, and apparently believe these are the genres we truly are good at, then it's about time to grow up and stop having so many irons in the fire."

"I'm sorry, I'm sorry, have we ever been at the verge of bankruptcy?" asked Ted.

"I have no idea where you got that idea from, Ted, but truthfully, would you really like to wait and do nothing just to see this happen?" Jeff replied angrily.

"This is outrageous! You have been hired to help this company, not to take it down!" Jake said. "Who the hell do you think you are, Richards? Coming here without any experience in publishing business, pretending like you know shit and turning everything upside-down without consulting anyone?!"

"Jake, calm down. There's no need to talk like that," David said firmly. He looked at Jeff and leaned back in his chair. Then he looked to his left side at Larson and Allen. "What do you think?"

"Jeff, why didn't you convey your ideas to us beforehand?" asked Anna.

"I did not want to risk your saying no."

"It's not your company, Jeff, *we* hired *you*, remember?" Jake said.

"Oh, I remember, but perhaps you might consider my idea as a really good one since I am ready to jeopardize my career for it."

"And what about that division, to create another publishing house for university releases?" asked David.

"Yeah, do you think it's a good idea to start a new company during the recession?" asked Allen.

"This is a specific market. Look, most of the colleges and universities publish the works of their scientists, of any kind. No matter if it's Biology, Economy, Medicine or Language Science. Most of the science workers who want to be successful in their fields are bound to publish. It's a matter or prestige. However, books and scientific works published through universities' publishing houses are usually not known outside the academic environment. I have spoken to several smaller colleges and private universities in the state, also interested in signing contracts with us, which hope that publishing their work in a more commercial format could make it more popular and will be a great opportunity to earn more money for their other purposes."

"Great, we're supposed to have them in tow during the economic crisis." Ted sighed.

"Yeah, and earn some money while doing it," Anna replied.

"It's all innovative," David said. 'But risky.'

"I know, but I am more than sure it's worth it," Jeff replied.

"Jeff, leave us for few minutes, will you?"

"Of course." Jeff left the conference room and went to the coffee machine in the hall. He got himself a cup of hot espresso and sat on the sofa. He was nervous. The meeting did not go the way he wanted. David was far more reserved than he was expecting and for the first time, Jeff was really worried his career might be at stake. Ted and Jake only waited for a moment when David would finally have some doubts; they won't let it go easily.

Twenty minutes later, Donna asked him to go back to the room. All members of the board were vividly stirred. David looked at Jeff and showed him a chair asking him mutely to sit down. Jeff took a seat and Garbinsky cut to the chase.

"Jeff, I have always defended you and your ideas."

"I know David, and you know I have always been grateful for that."

"Yes, but this has gone a bit too far this time. During the conference you made a very important decision about our company and did not consult with us first. This is not your company, Jeff, and I am very sorry and disappointed that I need to remind you of that."

Jeff did not say a word, he gulped and scanned all the members of the company. Looking at Ted's and Jake's faces, he had a feeling not all was lost, though.

"It's been a hard decision, but based on the successful decisions you've made so far, we're willing to give you another chance."

Jeff's face beamed.

"David, you won't regret it!"

"Well, we hope so, because we're giving you six months to prove you're right," Ted said.

"Excuse me?"

"He's right. After a tough discussion, we've decided to give you an ultimatum. You have half a year to prove your ideas are good. In that time we expect you to start the branch for university and scientific press and to continue working for WORDS," said David quite coldly.

"Six months? How will I be able to publish so many books within such short time?"

"I'm sure you as Creative Manager will be creative enough to figure it all out," Jake added with a smirk on his face. The son-of-a-bitch was enjoying the hell out of this. "Publish at least five Written Word authors and start creating the university publishing house."

"Alone?"

"Of course not," David said. "Creating a small branch should not strain us too much, you'll get the financial help as far as printing and hiring an office are concerned, but it's going to be your job only to promote it all and make it profitable as soon as possible. You can also ask some of our editors, not more than two though, to work for you on the scientific publications. WORDS will pay them salaries for the next six months."

Jeff had no idea what to say. This wasn't exactly giving him a chance, this was humiliation. The timeline he was being given was simply ridiculous.

"David—" he started but was immediately interrupted.

"Jeff, stop. We cannot allow you to be that independent. We needed your help as a Creative Manager, but it's a long way to go before making such serious decisions on your own," said Anna kindly but firmly.

"I know, but you want me to achieve the unachievable."

"Aren't you the brightest Creative Manager in the great state of Massachusetts?" asked Jake viciously. He enjoyed every single word of it.

"Jeff, six months. That's all we can do for you," David summed up the meeting. Jeff couldn't tell by the look in his eyes if Garbinsky was more disappointed by him or embarrassed by the outcome of the board discussion. He seemed even apologetic that the situation was somehow beyond his control.

Jeff left the room. He needed some fresh air.

Oenone~Agatha Rae~

⁓37⁓

Laura and Bruce got to Femina at 5:40 p.m. Having been admitted to the clinic, they were waiting at Tessa's office to be instructed by Dr. Green on what to expect once the treatment began. They were sitting by her desk, on two comfortable chairs holding each other's hands in a grip, looking blindly through the window in front of them. They were completely silent. Tessa walked into the office at 6 p.m. sharp. Laura and Bruce stood, Tessa shook hands with him and hugged Laura. When they all took their seats, Tessa finally spoke.

"How are you, Laura?"

"I'm not too bad, actually," Laura replied fully convinced of what she was saying. She felt good, calm. At least now.

"Laura, I'm here to explain to you what is going to happen a few hours from now and during the following days and weeks."

"We're listening," Bruce said and gripped Laura's palm firmly.

Tessa softly described to both of them what Laura was going to get through once the first chemotherapy started.

Three hours later Laura already had an IV port below her collarbone. She was lying in a small, comfortable and quite intimate room. There was a TV on the wall and she had her own bathroom. The walls had a warm, yellow color and the bed covering smelled fresh. Laura was looking at a poison entering her body, drop by drop hoping it would save her. The hanging bag seemed drastically unpleasant and excessive. She knew it wasn't going to hurt while going in, but, that she was going to feel sick later on. It all did not matter as long as it served its purpose. She closed her eyes and started analyzing what Dr. Green had told her.

Tessa said that her treatment would last six months during which she would have one chemo session per two weeks. She couldn't be fully ready for what was about to happen to her body. The whole conversation was not to prepare her, but to warn her, and make sure she wouldn't feel entirely lost during the process.

First of all, Tessa praised Laura for shortening her hair. *Long hair is far more prone to fall out faster due to its weight.* She said Laura would lose all her hair. She should also have a silk pillow to sleep on, as it's delicate for the hair and doesn't rub it away. Losing all her hair meant, apart from what was on her head, that every single hair on her body would fall off. Pubic hair, eyebrows, eyelashes, hairs in her nose—all of it. In some cases, the hair gets thinner only, but Laura was going to go through an aggressive treatment. Losing all hair meant that Laura would suffer from constant runny nose, something called "chemo-drip" and she would need to wash her eyes with saline solution once every few hours.

Why hair loss? Because chemotherapy attacks small cells, and that's what most cancers are made of. Unfortunately, hair cells are small as well and the drugs do not differentiate between them, so they all die or at least suffer severely. However, it might happen that the fingernails might improve.

Great, a break from shaving legs and armpits, Laura thought and smiled sadly. And she might finally have the Brazilian waxing she had always wanted to have done, but was always too shy and chicken to actually decide on it. Who knew, it might be a completely new experience for her and Bruce once that whole shit was over.

How long until it all fell out? Could be a matter of weeks before it all falls out entirely. Or days. It's really very individual. However, single hair will start falling out quite soon.

Would it itch when it will be growing back? Like crazy.

Here's a card of one of the best wig manufacturer in the city. You will be surprised to see how great you're going to look.

Losing the hair might mean you'd like to sleep with a scarf or handkerchief on your head. You'll feel much colder as you'll lose a lot of heat through your head.

The drop in platelet count and white cells are the most risky of the results of chemo. The more depressed your natural immune system is, the harder it is for the body to fight off infection, colds, the flu…. If your white blood cells and platelets drop too low, you might need hospitalization to be put into protective isolation. This would mean that anyone entering the room must be gowned, gloved and masked to ensure you're not exposed to anything. Should it happen, you would be given medications to induce the bone marrow to produce more cells faster. If your white cells don't drop too drastically, we will let you go home between chemos. You won't need to be here all the time; it all depends on your test results.

Would I have other side effects besides the hair loss?

Most probably you would be sick; your senses may turn upside down. The smells you'd liked so far might become unbearable. It could be *temporary, but might stay this way forever. I had a patient who had worn the same perfume most of her life, and was unable to stand it during and after her treatment. Your taste might change. You could be oversensitive about spicy or salty food. It could induce feeling nauseous.*

What could you eat? If it happens that you sustain your appetite, then you might consider baby food for a while. It's delicate and lacks any irritating spices. And think about organic food, it has no preservatives, so it's also something that your exhausted organism might handle better. You would need to drink lots of fluids, though, in order to get the toxins out of your body as fast as possible. You'd need to focus on water and so called "clear" fluids. If you can see through the liquid, it's clear. So water, apple juice, fruit popsicles, it's all fine. Forget about coffee, orange or tomato juices, they are prone to cause heartburns and intensify nausea.

Those thoughts were running through Laura's head, she was trying to put them in order, but they seemed very chaotic. She felt flooded with information, but it gave her a sense of being prepared, at least theoretically. However, if half of the things that Tessa had told her were about to come true, Laura was heading toward the Gates of Hell.

Outside her room Bruce was sitting on a chair. He was holding a cup of coffee in his hands. *Half-full,* he thought and smiled. He bought it an hour ago, but managed to drink only some of it. Now it was cold, and it had lost its smell and taste completely. He was looking blindly at the floor. *How the fuck had all this happened? Laura was given the drugs about an hour ago.* He was there at the beginning, holding her hand, but a few minutes later, she asked him to give her some time alone. She wanted to focus on everything Tessa had told them in the office, and she felt she might want to take a nap. He kissed her forehead and went out, promising he would be just outside.

Bruce thought that he should be update Evy and took his cell phone out of his pocket. He searched for her phone number and pushed the send button. She answered almost immediately.

"How is she doing?"

"They are giving her the first dose of drugs now. She asked me to wait outside for some time; I think she wanted to take a nap."

"How are you?"

Bruce paused for a moment. All the things he heard from Tessa and the view of his wife having needles in her body made him feel weak and powerless. When troubles are theoretical, they seem easy to handle. The perspective changes a bit once you face the reality. He was glad Laura had

131

asked him to wait outside; he thought she might have felt upset with the look on his face. He did not see himself in the mirror, but right now he felt he might have looked at least ten years older.

Bruce told Evy more or less about what they had learned from Tessa.

"She's going to go through hell, Ev," he said and Evy had a feeling he sobbed at that particular moment. She was quiet, had no idea what to say, so she thought the best way for her would be to let him do the talking.

"I don't understand it," Bruce said.

"What do you mean?"

"I mean, she knew she should have paid attention to that stuff. For Christ's sake, Kate lost her breast when she was only 27. It was supposed to be a wake-up call. How could Laura ignore her health like that, allowing the cancer to attack her?"

"Bruce, she was scared. She did not want to know."

"But it was so irresponsible," he said quietly.

"She was running away from the perspective of being sick."

"I know, I know, I keep telling it to myself as well. But look where it got her."

After a moment of silence, he abruptly said he had to hang up. They exchanged byes and Evy was more than sure he went to cry alone.

❧38❧

Jeff was home. He lived in Back Bay, on the fifth floor in one of Boston's classic brownstones. He had a spacious, one-bedroom apartment. The interior was pretty dark with heavy wooden floors and green walls, which looked more like a pub. The place was decorated with muted light, and the brightest place was the kitchen, which was modern and minimalistic.

The living room was full of CD stands and his walls were decorated with framed posters of his favorite movies. A huge, 52 inch TV graced one of the walls, and among the furniture there were a leather sofa, an armchair in the middle of the room and a small party fridge for refreshments and beer in the corner. There was no balcony, only a big window with a very wide sill where he was sitting now sipping whiskey from a glass. He was very angry, and he needed some time in a complete silence to clear his thoughts.

He had set his phone to vibrate and was now leaning against the window. He was given six months. Six months! In order to get that many books published in such short time, they would need to work on each of them simultaneously. He would need to have the books out in approximately three months so that they would start earning money to prove his new vision of WORDS would work. It meant that all five editors working at the publishing house would need to sit down as soon as possible, by the end of the week preferably, and begin working on the new books. However, one of his best editors was currently fighting cancer and who knew when or if she was going to return to work. His second best editor was actively involved in Laura's illness and probably did not want to have anything to do with him, and his other three were swamped to say the least. What was even worse was that some of his writers hadn't finished their books yet. Peachy. Just fucking peachy.

Oh, and somehow he had to start the new publishing house! It did not matter that it would be a smaller, niche, what mattered was that he would need to focus on advertising and getting new clients. In order to get it all started, he had to create a business plan. It had to be accepted by the board if he wanted to get money.

Accepted by the board.

Fantastic.

He had about three weeks to do it if he wanted to meet the deadline. He was sure the ultimatum was Ted's and Jake's idea, but he knew he lost David's trust when he had made the decision to narrow the scope by himself. He expected he would be in trouble, but hoped he could talk the board into it. Now here he was sitting on a window sill, drinking a second whiskey and trying to think of any ways of making the next six months bearable. He needed a plan and at this point his mind was blank.

What made him even angrier, was that he couldn't stop thinking of Evy. He had a nasty feeling that he'd made a serious mistake on Sunday morning and it kept haunting him. Jeff felt he wanted to repeat that night they had spent together, but he knew it was unlikely a possibility. He was wondering why Evy hadn't simply slapped him when he was telling her all that nonsense about his not-getting-engaged attitude. That was something for one-night stands. Evy was different. He knew so much about her, things he couldn't care less to know about his previous lovers. And the sex was entirely different. It wasn't just lust, it wasn't mechanical, it was emotional, and he felt *connected* with her, he cared for her comfort and satisfaction. Jeff valued her, felt good in her company, and yet he had decided to lump her into that nonsense.

Now he needed her help and was worried she might refuse to put his problem on the top of her list. She had other authors to edit, and she would need to work twice as much, if not more, to take care of them and Jeff's new writers. *Why would she?* Of course, he was the manager, he could just tell her do it, but then at the very least he'd put himself right in the middle of a sexual harassment lawsuit and the worst would be having to say goodbye to any chance of them ever getting closer again. *See Jeff? This is exactly why you shouldn't have mixed life and work. Damn it.*

He took another sip of whiskey and felt the burning taste as it moved down his throat. Suddenly his cell phone started vibrating. He looked at his watch and realized it was pretty late for any phone conversations, as it was 11:15 p.m. He looked at the display of his phone and was shocked to see it was Evy calling.

"Hello?" he answered.

"Hi, Jeff, got a minute?"

"Yeah, what's happening?"

"Are you home?"

"I am."

"Are you alone?"

"Yes—" He could tell by the tone of her voice that she was depressed. He knew it must have had something to do with Laura.

"Ok, see you in a minute."

"What? Um. Okay." Immediately there was a loud buzz of an entry phone. Jeff put the phone away, walked toward the door and pushed the entry-access button. He glanced at his living room; it was fairly clean. Next he looked at his bedroom—decent. There was a knock on the door. He opened it and saw Evy standing in the hallway.

"Hi," he said stunned.

"Hi, Jeff. Look, I know I'm probably the last person you'd expect to see, but I need to talk to someone."

He looked at her and smiled warmly. He opened the door wide and made a welcoming gesture.

"Please, come in, Evy. May I make you some tea?"

"Yeah, that would be great, you know I love tea," Evy replied, smiled and walked inside. She took off her shoes and followed Jeff to the kitchen. Discreetly, she looked around the apartment and her impression was that it was cozy and elegant. Jeff put the kettle on and took two cups from the cupboard. He put them down and turned around to look at Evy. She was sitting behind the table, looking at him, a bit amused and a bit shy at the same time.

"Nice apartment," she said.

"It's all right. I've been living here for half a year and certain things have not been finished yet, but I like it a lot. Nice hair."

"Oh, thank you." She laughed and combed it with her fingers. She kept forgetting her hair was much shorter now. "I haven't had such short hair since I was a kid."

"It suits you," Jeff said nicely and he meant it.

The water had boiled and Jeff poured it into mugs.

"Come on, let's go to the living room."

"How about tea bags?" asked Evy.

"Oh yeah, sorry." He laughed and put the bags into the mugs.

He handed her a mug and they left the kitchen.

She was following him, gliding slightly on a gorgeous parquet floor. They both sat on the sofa in front of a heavy, wooden coffee table, Evy curled her legs.

"Wow, you've got quite a collection," she said looking at his CD stands.

"Six hundred and Forty five."

"No way!"

He smiled. "Evy, I've been thinking about what happened yesterday—"

"Jeff, I'm really not here to try to convince you to anything," she said firmly.

"I know. But I feel awful after what I had said to you."

"And you should," she admitted entirely seriously. "Look, you were honest with me, there's no need to go back there." She waved her hand in "let's not go there" gesture.

"Yeah…" He drank some tea. "How's Laura?"

She looked at him a bit surprised and put her mug on the coffee table.

"She's scared. But she's determined to fight." She looked at him. "I'm sorry, Jeff, for coming here at this hour, unannounced—"

"Well, you did call."

"Yeah, I did, I'm not that bad… The thing is… that I am quite bad at making friends. My world, maybe it's my work, maybe it's other circumstances, has always been quite empty when it comes to people. I've always been satisfied having one or two close friends; I've never had the desire to be the most social person in the area. And as much as I like it, in moments like this I feel it has certain drawbacks."

He was listening to her attentively and suddenly he felt closer to her, it was hard to describe.

"Since I moved to Boston it has always been Laura and my boyfriends, mostly Pete because my relationship with him was the longest one I've ever had. I've never needed anyone else. But now I am single, and my dear Laura is struggling with a really nasty and devious disease and while she's in a clinic having needles attached to her body, I find myself all alone and craving somebody to talk to. And I know you're my boss, I know we've spent a quite awkward weekend together, but I got to know you better during last days, and it turns out you're the only person I can come and comfortably share my thoughts with. And I really need that."

He was touched. He had never heard anyone telling him he was needed to comfort someone, nor had anyone ever confessed to having a special, intimate connection with him that would help to pass traumatic moments. Who was she? What was going on here? It all felt warm, it felt good, but he was a stranger in a strange land in this situation. What was he supposed to do now? Hold her hand? Hug her? Ask her if she wanted some more tea?

"So, what's Laura's prognosis?" he finally asked.

"She has breast cancer stage two, which is not the worst case scenario. There are four stages. But she needs to undergo treatment and she might lose her breast, or at least a part of it."

"How are you coping with it?"

"I'm scared for her, but I'm going to support her no matter what happens."

"Great, it's great to have such friends."

They were sitting in silence and drinking their teas.

"I told David about the Westville strategy."

"Oh! You did! What did he say?"

"I met with the whole board today, actually."

Jeff told Evy what happened during the meeting, about the ultimatum he was given and how enraged and utterly terrified he was that he might not fulfill his plan and lose his job. She was listening to him attentively. When he finished, she put her hand on his shoulder.

"Jeff, I will help you."

He looked at her surprised. "I thought you might not want to do that because of what happened two days ago."

"First of all, three days ago, it's ten past midnight." She smiled. "Secondly, Jeff, don't worry about that weekend. We're both grown-ups and it's not like you broke my heart. I admit, I was hoping for something more, but I understand where you're coming from."

She was being sincere. Laura's problems made her redefine her thoughts, focus on entirely different things and all her problems circulating around Jeff had, at least for now, vanished.

"I want to help you because I want us to remain friends, and since you're in trouble then I will gladly help you. You can start sending me your new authors' manuscripts on Wednesday, ok?"

"Ok. You have no idea how glad I am—"

"Did you expect me to be vengeful? Oh please. Besides, you're my boss. Technically, I have to do what you say, but I'd rather do it as your friend. And if it helps you keep your job, which I strongly believe you're great at, I'm happy to do it."

"Thank you, Evy," he said with deep appreciation in his voice.

"So, what do you listen to?" She walked toward the CD stands.

"The usual stuff. New Kids on the Block, David Guetta, Justin Bieber. Nothing fancy," he answered and Evy burst out laughing. They spent about half an hour going through his CDs. He felt great knowing she was so impressed by his collection. He was also proud of it.

"Well, I need to go, it's super late. Sorry for coming here like that, but it helped me a lot."

"Please, come by whenever you feel you want to," he said genuinely.

"Tempting idea, I won't lie." She put the mug on the table and walked toward the doors. She was putting her shoes when he cleared his throat.

"Will I see you at work tomorrow?"

"No, I'm coming in on Wednesday."

"Ok, I'll see you then."

"Jeff? Can we forget about what happened? It will make me feel much more comfortable around you. I think it would be good for—for both of us."

He looked at her for a minute. He knew what she meant; however deep down it kind of hurt his feelings. What was he expecting after what he had told her? He blew it. He couldn't expect anything else from her right now.

"Sure, I - I understand."

"Thanks. See you!"

He closed the door behind her and leaned on it. No, he did not want to forget about what happened. When Evy was speaking to him he realized that Rachel had never needed his comfort, nor had she ever resisted the temptation to judge him when he made mistakes. Jeff was pretty sure she would have told him that if he was foolish enough to make such decision without anyone's permission, then it was only his problem. Evy did not criticize him, but offered her help instantly and told him he was good at what he was doing. No, he did not want to forget about their night. He had a plan to think about it regularly and cherish it. As much as it scared him, he realized he was falling in love. And he managed to screw it all before it even started. But if she needed the space now, if she felt too hurt, or perhaps too offended by his earlier attitude, he would stand by her as a friend and co-worker and hope that perhaps one day she might allow him to get closer to her again.

Lying in her bed, Evy was thinking about her little tea party with Jeff and felt two tears falling down her cheeks. She turned on the right side and nestled her face in the pillow. The sense of guilt and a bitter feeling of loss were intertwining within her heart. She felt like the worst friend in the world because her Laura was suffering in a clinic at that moment and all she was able to think of was Jeff and how badly she wanted and needed him. She never wanted to forget the night they had spent together, but Sunday morning was so painful and humiliating to her she had promised herself not to allow Jeff to ever touch her again. However, Evy did not want to lose him either, so in her head being friends and good co-workers was the best solution she could think of.

Tired, she closed her eyes and fell asleep.

Oenone~Agatha Rae~

❧39❧

Tuesday was, by far, the worst day in Laura's life. She was horribly weak, felt nauseous and vomited all day. She experienced nerves tingling and the loss of touch in her fingers, a situation that was to be temporary but, nonetheless, it was quite disturbing. She felt tired and irritated. Everything would fall from her hands due to the loss of touch; Laura was unable to get a good grip around objects she was given, mugs or bottles of water. She felt sick, weak and annoyed. Bruce was there for her all the time making sure Laura was as comfortable as it was possible under the circumstances.

Evy called her to find out how she was feeling. Laura told her she felt like shit which wasn't even remotely true, as she felt much, much worse. Tessa came to see her three times during the day and told her and Bruce that Laura did not seem to have any abnormal side effects apart from the typical and expected ones. She gave her some anti-nausea drugs and in the evening when the sickness began to feel bearable, Laura and Bruce turned the TV on and watched an episode of "30 Rock". They had a pretty good time and Laura managed to forget about her battle at least for some time. Later, she kissed Bruce goodnight and was given a sedative so she could rest calmly. Her husband went to his sister, Sam's mother, to take Spark home and update Irene on Laura's health condition.

Evy finished editing one of the books and decided to go to the theater. She hated going to the movies alone, but there was nobody to go with and she felt she was unable to stay home all day. It was quite a chilly evening. Summer wasn't there yet, obviously, so there was no sense in going for a walk, hence her idea wrapped around watching a film. Evy decided to see a comedy which turned out to be a good choice; she had a good time laughing and eating a gigantic cardboard bucket of popcorn and it gave her a lot of positive vibes and energy.

Later, she got back to Bob, put on The Doors' "Morrison Hotel" and spent an hour driving around the city singing along with Jim. City at night from the perspective of streets, traffic and neon lights was what Evy would always find very relaxing. It was already past midnight when she got back home, took a long, hot bath and drank a mojito while lying in the foam. For a minute she had a feeling that everything was going to be fine, Laura would beat the cancer and Jeff would love her one day. There was no reasonable explanation for that, but she was sure it all would turn out exactly that way. She felt the familiar warmth within her body coming from the inside. Evy put her glass aside and allowed her mind to disappear in the world of shameless fantasies that did not require anything else but herself and Jeff.

❧40❧

Four days after the first chemotherapy session, Laura was at home taking shower. The feeling in her fingers had come back and she was even regaining a delicate appetite. Her weak stomach did not tolerate anything apart from applesauce, some organic baby food and water, but it felt good to eat something without any nauseous consequences afterwards. She had lost some weight, nothing alarming, but her belly seemed sunken. Laura basically looked like a victim of some nasty stomach flu.

The previous morning she found a few dozen hairs on her pillow. She looked at it horrified and touched her head delicately not wanting the rest of it to fall out. She could feel small bald spots in few places. It wasn't a tragedy, but it was a signal; she had to get used to the fact that soon she was going to lose her hair.

She showed it all to Bruce who seemed distressed at first, but simply hugged Laura and kissed her forehead. She hugged him back and had no idea when she started crying on his shoulder. It did not last long, just a few tears and sobs, a sign of disappointment, frustration and regret. She quickly pulled herself together and put a scarf on her head when she was sitting on the terrace.

Laura hadn't gone out anywhere since she came from the clinic. First of all, it wasn't advisable as her immune system was very much weakened and more prone to catch a cold. Secondly, she simply did not feel like seeing anyone. The only person visiting them was Evy. She told Laura about Jeff's problems and Laura aptly responded that he had only himself to blame and added she would eagerly help the moment she could focus her attention on anything other than not-vomiting.

Laura noticed all the changes with both amazement and puzzlement. When she opened the fridge yesterday afternoon for the very first time, the smell of prawns she used to love almost made her throw up. She couldn't stand it. Bruce threw them away. She also couldn't stand Bruce's cologne, exactly the same she loved only a week ago and had given him for his birthday. Bruce stopped using it without a word. Last night was the first night she actually slept well and wasn't just lying down trying not to focus on the achy stomach and muscles. She remembered a saying describing people who would feel sick as "looking like death warmed over" and it made her laugh. It sounded so ironic now. She couldn't laugh too much, though, it made her belly hurt.

Laura reached for a shampoo on the shelf behind her and noticed a clump of hair on her shoulder. This time it was alarming. She also noticed that the constant temperature of water she was always using seemed far too hot for her now. Her scalp was simply burning. She turned the water off and slowly, gently moved her fingers across her head. Her palm was full of hair.

Suddenly she was afraid of getting out of the shower cabin and confronting her image in the mirror. She cried a few more tears, took a deep breath, reached for a towel and, having covered her body, got out of the shower. After wiping the mirror with her hand, she saw herself and that time couldn't stop crying. She was almost entirely bald. Some weak, single hairs were still clinging to her skin, but overall it looked miserable. She was able to see most of her scalp clearly. She touched her head gently; she was stroking it for some time, feeling the skin under her fingers for the first time in her life. It was shocking. Suddenly she heard knocking on the bathroom door.

"Laura? Are you all right?" asked Bruce worried.

She wanted to answer, but she couldn't. Her voice was trapped inside her throat and she was unable to release it. Bruce knocked on the door once again, this time more firmly.

"Laura!"

At that moment she screamed at the top of her lungs. That scream contained all she'd been holding inside; anger, pain, fear, terror, frustration. Bruce entered the bathroom and hugged her very strongly. She was swaying in his arms, weak and hopeless, crying and holding him as if he was the last remaining evidence of her sanity. He looked at her, first in the mirror, then he looked down at her with tears in his eyes.

"We'll get through this, Laura, do you hear me? It will all go away, it's just temporary, please remember! I promise you we'll get through this," he was whispering straight into her ear and this seemed to calm her down a little bit. When her panic attack was weakening, she opened her eyes and looked at him.

"Why did you come? I didn't call you."

"No, but it's been an hour since you went the bathroom. I got worried that maybe you fainted or lost your balance and needed help."

Shortly thereafter, they sat on the sofa in the living room. Laura was sitting on Bruce's lap, leaning on into him and swaying gently. She had a towel on her head, the only thing that allowed her to leave the bathroom.

"Honey, this is it. Nothing worse is going to happen to you. You've lost your hair, so what, it will grow back. From this moment on, everything can be only better."

"I look awful," she sobbed.

"You look beautiful." He kissed her. "Don't ever think differently. Your body is fighting that damn cancer, and is winning, I am sure of it. Please, just hold on. All this will pass, and you won't even notice when you're going to ask me to look for a hairband because you lost it again."

"I'm scared."

"Don't be. I am here for you."

"Will you always be here?"

Bruce looked deep into her eyes and said with conviction, "I'm not going anywhere."

Oenone~Agatha Rae~

❧41❧

Seven weeks had passed. Evy and Jeff were working very hard on his projects. Evy's previous authors were given to the less experienced editors and she had edited four new authors for Jeff. She was swamped, but her mind was filled with work which was allowing her to have her thoughts occupied by something other than Laura's treatment. Jeff was organizing the new academic publishing house, which he called OMNIBUS. All the paper work had already been done, he was waiting for few more confirmations and signatures, but it was only a matter of time before OMNIBUS would start functioning independently. He had hired two new editors, was in the middle of renegotiating new contracts with printing houses and was working on an advertising campaign to draw more clients.

Being entirely focused on the company's issues, neither Jeff nor Evy had the time or will to discuss any non-professional topics. They had been eating lunches together, but during those moments she was telling him about the authors she had been editing, and he was updating her on OMNIBUS stuff. They felt they had become a team and they both enjoyed it, but they were entirely focused on work and career. For Jeff it was all about surviving in WORDS, and for Evy it was the pleasant experience of creating something and it felt good that Jeff was consulting most of his decisions with her.

In the meantime Laura had undergone three chemotherapies. She was completely bald and most of the time she felt as if she was having a flu. Substantial problems with regulating her body's temperature had appeared; she was either too cold or too hot. At night she either put an extra blanket on her quilt, or slept only in her underwear. She had an almost constant runny nose and by this point even her eyelashes had fallen off. Laura wore a wig whenever she was outside and at home she work handkerchiefs on her head. Bruce kept telling her he didn't mind her being bald, but Laura felt much more comfortable when she kept her head covered. She stopped using perfumes as its scent would make her nauseous and used only cosmetics for babies now.

The smell of fumes drove her insane and she felt like vomiting every time she smelled them, so Laura stopped driving. She was very reluctant into going anywhere by car unless Bruce would promise to turn the A/C off so that no smells from the outside would appear in the car.

Because of her stomach being so touchy, Bruce stopped cooking and was trying to eat out as to not irritate her. The numbness in her fingers would come back from time to time and then she needed his help in doing such basic things as drinking from a mug or a bottle. She felt pretty bad about all this because her sickness did not revolve around her only, but interrupted his life as well; there, however, was nothing else they could do.

Evy was now visiting her much less often since she was very busy with Jeff's projects, although she would always come to Laura whenever she was back from the clinic and they had a regular phone contact. Laura was always waiting for those visits and calls because she was finding everything that was going on at work very curious and all the stories from there were truly entertaining.

Laura felt like a total mess. She underwent tests that showed the treatment hadn't infected her tumor too much yet. Tessa kept telling her she was at the very beginning of the road to recovery, but Laura was miserable. She felt useless due to her inability to work. She wasn't even able to work from home yet. She wasn't able to recognize herself in the mirror and it was becoming unbearable to feel nauseous almost every time she smelled or tasted something. Laura was unable to imagine going through all this for next months and she felt that either something would finally help her really fast, or she would lose her spirit and determination, discouraged by the lack of results and control over her own body.

During one of the stays in the clinic she came across a brochure about natural methods of treatment. She never believed in such things like the healing power of herbs. Of course mint tea could calm a stormy stomach but, let's not kid ourselves; a brewed combination of different kinds of grass could cure cancer. She glanced at the leaflet, but never gave it a second thought until her third session at Femina. That was the first moment when she felt irritated and tired of her condition. Laura took one brochure from the table in the waiting room and when she felt a bit better after the chemo session, she took it out of a drawer near her bed and looked carefully through it.

It was about a woman named Alyssa. She described herself as a fortune-teller, an herbalist, a Shaman and a source of comfort, support and positive energy for everyone who needed it. It sounded tacky and the whole design of the brochure was corny with some ancient Egyptian and Celtic symbols, but somehow, Laura was unable to explain it, the content of it felt oddly soothing. "Desperate times call for desperate measures," she sighed and shook her head with disbelief. About three months ago, which felt like *eternity* ago, Laura would never believe that she would take such things seriously, that she would even consider searching for this kind of help. She was about to tear the brochure and throw it into the garbage can when she looked at her IV stand. Was this the way she wanted her life to look like for the next months? And who says she would defeat the cancer anyway? Perhaps that was the scenario of the rest of her life? However long it would be anyway. She was lying weak in bed, feeling pain all over her body, hairless, cold, and scared. Perhaps a month ago she would simply ignore the brochure, but the Laura who was diagnosed and the Laura who was there in the clinic were entirely different people. The new Laura decided not to throw away the brochure, but instead, she put it inside her handbag which she kept on a chair next to her bed. Who knows, it might become handy one day. After all, a little bit of hope and herbal tea wouldn't hurt anyone, right? And besides, this was the only brochure that was distributed in the clinic, maybe it meant the doctors did not see Alyssa's work as charlatanism, maybe she was indeed helping their patients? Perhaps the hospital approved her work?

One day when Bruce was out, she made herself some chamomile tea, took out Alyssa's brochure and sat by the computer. She hesitated for a minute and Googled "Alyssa Sadler, Shaman". She clicked search and, in a blink of an eye, she saw dozens of pages related to Alyssa. The woman seemed quite popular, there were many forums where people posted about her, and there was also her official webpage. First, Laura decided to check the boards, because, obviously, Alyssa's website wouldn't say anything negative about her. She was shocked. Everyone praised the woman. It seemed that Alyssa had helped many people. There were patients cured of cancers of all kinds, Parkinson diseases, Alzheimer, Tourette syndrome, cerebral palsy, disabilities, and migraines. There was a user named Oliver_73 who swore that Alyssa's single touch released him from the horror of headaches which he had been experiencing two—three times a week and which had turned his life into hell. Kinky_Sense_of_Humor was assuring everyone that drinking Alyssa's teas and her therapy cured him of alcoholism, that he had never drank a single drop of liquor since he met her eight years ago. Among many other people there seemed to have been people of all different ages and problems. One lady claimed she was 76

149

and she had had an advanced Alzheimer and, again, Alyssa's touch cured her. Laura looked through about seventeen different websites, read more or less 70 pages of posts overall and was really confused. Of course, one could say placebo, perhaps hypnosis, could help, sure. But so many people? Could it be possible that all of them were lying for some kind of profit just to help Alyssa gain patients? Laura was fighting with her in-born skepticism. She found it extremely hard to believe all those people, but the part of her that desperately wanted her life to be normal again, the part that hated herself whenever she looked into the mirror, *that* part pushed her to enter Alyssa's website.

Laura clicked on the link and it was pure magic. The website was glamorous. Emerald background, delicate, chill-out music, it was all soothing and relaxing. The green color brought an immediate association with peace and calm. Alyssa's picture was nowhere to be found; there was however an about me bookmark, which Laura, clicked. The note was very pared-down.

THERE IS ONLY ONE REASON WHY YOU ARE HERE: YOU ARE SUFFERING AND SEEKING COMFORT. ALLOW ME TO SOOTH YOU; ALLOW ME TO USE MY GIFT, MY POWER, TO HELP YOU. ALLOW ME TO HEAL YOUR SPIRIT, TO BRING PEACE TO YOUR MIND. MY NAME IS ALYSSA, I HAVE THE POWER THAT CAN MAKE ALL YOUR PAIN GO AWAY, THAT CAN HELP YOU MAKE YOUR DREAMS COME TRUE. OPEN YOUR EYES, MIND AND SOUL AND ALLOW ME TO CHANGE YOUR LIFE.

It all sounded fabulous, but Laura couldn't tell if she was convinced or not. It all sounded too good to be true. She had always been a skeptical person, she had never been religious and her illness had not made her change those views. So far at least. Alyssa's website seemed very tempting, but Laura felt deep down that the sensible part of her soul had not been convinced. She added the website to her favorites and went to the kitchen to prepare herself another portion of tea.

Laura passed a big mirror in the hallway, the one she used to use to see if the shoes fit the dress and the one in front of which Bruce and she had made love many times, turned back and looked at herself carefully. She gently took the scarf off from her head and for the first time faced herself in day light. It was high time to confront the reality. She put the mug on the floor and undressed. She looked really bad; pale, skinny, hairless, with grey shadows around her eyes. No eye brows caused the lack of any facial expressiveness. The lower part of her body, with no pubic hair and such thin legs that the outline of her knees was visible, looked as if it belonged to a little girl rather than a grown-up woman. The upper part, on the other hand, seemed to have belonged to an elderly person with sunken stomach and breasts and colorless skin. In complete silence, Laura dressed up again, went to the kitchen and put the kettle on. When her tea was ready, she came back to the study, this time avoiding the slightest glance at the mirror, and clicked on Alyssa's website. She searched for the contact information and found the phone number. Laura took her cell phone and hesitated for a minute. What was she doing? Some months ago she would knock herself on the head at the very thought of seeking supernatural help to solve her problems. Right now she saw nothing crazy about it. After all, it could not get any worse, right?

She dialed the number on the website and a woman answered.

"Good morning, Laura, it's Alyssa Sadler speaking, how can I help you?"

Laura was totally surprised she actually got through so quickly and, apparently, it was the Alyssa speaking to her, not some assistant, or a secretary. And how, for the love of God, did that woman know who was calling?!

"Um, yes, hello. My name is Laura Levinson, I am calling—"

"You need help, I can tell."

Laura was totally taken aback.

"Well, yes, I mean I wouldn't be calling if I didn't."

"Of course, how can I help you, Laura?"

"I found your brochure at the Femina clinic and I've looked through your website."

"I'm glad you've reached me, Laura."

"Me, too," she answered and she meant it. It was very awkward, very surprising; but somehow, she felt that Alyssa was a very good and helpful person. Laura had no idea how she was able to feel it after a few seconds of the telephone conversation, but deep down, something inside her was thrilled that she was talking to Alyssa. Her voice seemed calm and very soothing and all of Laura's doubts had vanished. She actually felt agog at meeting her.

"I was wondering if perhaps you have a moment to see me and, hopefully, help me."

"Of course, I have time for everyone who is in trouble."

When making the appointment, Laura made sure to check Bruce's schedule to know when he would be away from home. She did not want to

151

tell him about the idea; it still seemed pretty dumb for her. She decided not to let him know about it until she knew whether it helped or not. Looking at his planner, she realized he had a dentist appointment the following day. It turned out Alyssa was available at the same time and they had arranged a meeting at 4:00 p.m. When Laura hung up, she was beaming. Deep down she knew it was irrational to put her trust into someone who claimed she could heal people's spirits, but for the first time since the diagnosis, she felt as if life was returning to her veins. She was thrilled.

❧42❧

When Bruce got home, and he noticed immediately that Laura was different. She was smiling, and was listening to one of her favorite CDs, "Super 80's compilation". "Everything She Wants" by Wham was filling up the whole home and Laura asked him to dance with her. It was one of her favorite records of all time and she simply adored George Michael. While they were dancing, they both recalled what a great time they had when they went to see him live during his tour in 2008 when he played in Boston. She only managed to dance during the first verse and a bit of the chorus, but she was vividly happy when she laid on the sofa to rest. He was joyous to see her in such a good mood, and asked her about the source of it, but she only kissed him passionately and assured him she was getting better.

Laura also called Evy and asked her if she could come over in the evening. Bruce was going out for a poker night with his friends, something Laura actually encouraged a lot. She ensured him she was feeling much better and she insisted on him living a normal life. He already ate most of his meals out as not to irritate her with smells, he still had over six weeks of FMLA left so he was not going to work and he practically was not seeing anyone. When she heard about the poker session idea, she was thrilled and kept pushing him to go. If not for the sake of his own pleasure then for the sake of her own conscience as she couldn't stand all the sacrifices she had been causing him. Not exactly convinced he finally agreed to go, but promised her to be back before 11:00 p.m. Evy confirmed she would come and Laura couldn't wait to tell her about Alyssa.

In the evening, Evy came. Laura opened the door, gave her a big hug and invited her in. Evy took her shoes off and followed her friend to the kitchen.

"So, Ev, tell me what's going on, how's OMNIBUS doing?"

"Well, we finally got all the needed permissions so OMNIBUS officially exists. Jeff is now negotiating with the building's administrator to rent us three rooms on the floor below WORDS, so we can physically keep our new creation separated from them. Jeff is trying to negotiate a better rate for that because we're already renting the whole floor as WORDS. We'll see."

"Does it have to be the same building?"

"It'd be very convenient."

"I have noticed that you kept saying 'our' and 'we'." Laura winked.

"Yeah, well, we're becoming partners in crime." She took a glass and poured some water in it. "With David's permission, Jeff has moved me away from all other projects and I am editing only his books now. He hired two more editors to work at WORDS, who got my previous books to work with and—" Evy stopped suddenly.

"And my books, right?" Laura asked.

"Yes."

"It's okay, I understand that work cannot wait for me, and I do not feel good enough to do it now."

Evy did not say anything and only sipped the water.

"I really get it, no worries. It's possible I might be better soon, so perhaps you could ask Jeff if I might be useful to help you."

"Of course, no doubt! Although, you're the senior editor, you're the only editor more experienced than I am at WORDS, I suppose Jeff would prefer you to help the juniors rather—"

"Or he'd just prefer to spend some time with you only." Laura smiled.

"I highly doubt it; nothing's been going on between us apart from work issues. It's been almost three months since Written Word; I think we both have other priorities now."

"Maybe. Maybe not."

"Say, what do you mean that you might be better soon? Do you have new test results?"

"No, but it's possible I've found something better. Come on, let's go to the bedroom, I need to lay down."

They went upstairs and both lay on the bed. It seemed like a typical girl talk atmosphere. Teas in mugs, lying on the bed, bare feet, Laura on her belly, Evy on her side. It was almost unimaginable they would be talking about the cancer and a Shaman. They ought to be talking about men, sex and the latest episodes of favorite shows. Laura told Evy everything. How she came across Alyssa's brochures, how she was skeptical at first, but decided to give it a try after the horror she had faced in the bathroom, how she felt the whole traditional treatment is ruining her and how optimistic she felt when she spoke to Alyssa. She had no doubt that the woman must have had some kind of a gift; she couldn't explain it properly, but there was something in her voice that gave her hope. Evy was listening to it all very carefully. At first, she thought Laura was joking, but the more her friend was telling her about her plans for the next day, the more obvious it was that she was seriously considering looking for some kind of supernatural help. She was just lying on the bed, drinking her mint tea and waiting for Laura to finish her story.

"What do you think?" she asked.

"I'm shocked," Evy replied honestly. "I would have never expected you to even consider such an option."

"I would have never expected myself to have cancer," Laura replied firmly. The lack of Evy's immediate and spontaneous enthusiasm hurt her feelings a bit. "What am I supposed to say? Desperate times call for desperate measures."

"But I hope you're not thinking about quitting the traditional treatment, are you?"

"No, of course not! I would have to be an idiot to even consider it! I mean we're talking about a Shaman, Evy! I really know what it sounds like. I want her to help me get through the chemotherapy—I don't want her to *cure* me." Laura realized at that very moment when she had said those words out loud for the first time that yes! Yes, she'd *love* Alyssa to cure her. She would love the perspective of never going to the clinic again, she would love to comb her hair, she would love to have sex with Bruce and feel feminine and attractive again while doing it, she would love to drive the car again and eat her favorite food. But most of all, she would love to have the perspective of a long and healthy life ahead of her.

"Okay, okay, I'm just saying. Look, Laura." Evy sat on the bed. "I want you to be healthy more than anything. If you feel this woman can help you, if you're convinced it's a good idea to go to see her, then I'm all for it." She took Laura's hand. "I don't know if that is Alyssa's power working on you already, but I know I haven't seen you so relaxed and smiling for a couple of months. And if that is the effect that woman would have on you, so be it. I love it already." She kissed Laura's forehead.

"Thank you, Evy." Laura also sat on the bed and hugged her best friend tight. "You know it means a lot to me, your support and care."

"And you mean the world to me. Even if it's some damn placebo effect, if it's supposed to help you, I'm all for it. I just don't understand why wouldn't you tell Bruce about it?"

"I want to surprise him. Since I spoke to Alyssa I have been really light-spirited, and he saw it. He knew immediately I was better. If that woman is to help me, I want to handle it myself so I could come to my husband and whisper in his ear, baby, I'm fine. Just like you promised."

"But if Alyssa's treatment would require visiting her regularly, what alibi will you have to sneak out of home?"

"I'll think of something. Evy, I just want that shit off me. That's all I can think of."

"Who knows, if that woman helps you, I might ask her for some advice myself."

"How do you mean?"

"Well, if she can cure a sick body, I wonder if she can cure a sick soul."

She looked at Laura for few seconds.

"Oh my God, you're still into him, Evs."

"I am. Pathetic, right?" Evy laughed.

"Oh, Honey! I thought you got over it."

"I am focused on our professional relationship, but I know the only reason I am not thinking about him day and night is because I'm so involved in creating OMNIBUS and helping him out with profiling WORDS."

"And you're doing it with him, hence your need for his company is somehow fulfilled."

"Exactly. I know, I should have forgotten about him after that weekend in Westville, but that evening I spent at his place, talking and sharing, I felt like we were soul mates, you know? And that meeting only convinced me that we could be a great couple. Even though now I know it's not going to work out, I am still into him. I feel like a teenager, really."

"Evy, if there's any lesson that can be taken from what I have been going through is that you should never give up. Life's too short to resign from your desires, expectations, needs and dreams. No matter how cliché it sounds."

"I know, and I totally get it. Perhaps I'll try to get closer to him once again when the whole pandemonium is over. I mean, we are pretty good friends now; he trusts my opinion, we share ideas and it's all very involving and creative. We see each other every day, eat lunches together, and call each other constantly. I have a feeling he's planning on making me his number two; he's told me many times I am wasting my organizational skills and creativity, that editing is reproductive and I am too inventive to sit all day surrounded by books and checking the spelling."

"He's right. I am the reproductive type."

"Oh, come on."

"No, seriously! I am an editor because I like not having stiff working hours. I like reading and it makes me feel independent and comfortable. And the money's good. But *you* always have so many ideas, how to organize things, you like creating, making up events, planning. I hate all those things. I like the fact that I don't need to come up with stories, that my job is to read and check them, but not to create them."

Evy smiled. It was true. Being in the center of the commotion felt great, and she liked it. Being in the center of commotion with Jeff felt even better.

"He's my weakness, Laura."

"I know. I also believe you are his. Just give him some time; this whole circus won't last forever. When the atmosphere gets calmer, and after all the hard work you do together, he might seriously change his mind about you."

"Sounds great!" Evy laughed, "I'll drink to that!" They picked up their mugs and drank.

They heard a noise down stairs.

"Bruce is that you?" Laura shouted.

"Yeah, hi!"

"Hi, Bruce!" Evy shouted.

"Hi, Evy!"

"Honey, how was the game?"

They heard Bruce walking upstairs. He stood in the bedroom door and leaned on the frame.

"Yeah, about that. I've lost our home and cars. We've got two days to move out," he said very seriously, scratching his chin.

"That was the last poker night in your life." Laura laughed.

"What?! I thought you'd be happy! You keep saying you want to move to a smaller house, and I am giving you a chance and now you're threatening me?" Bruce crooned, pretending he was hurt.

"Couldn't you have bet your mother, too?"

"I heard that!" he replied from the hall.

Now they all were laughing.

Oenone~Agatha Rae~

❧43❧

It turned out that Bruce, apart from a dentist appointment, was also meeting a client later, so Laura thought she had about two, maybe even three hours to see Alyssa.

They were supposed to meet at 4 p.m. Laura dressed up officially and put wig on her head. She was worried she might feel sick during the ride to downtown so she called a taxi. A few minutes before 11, she got out of a cab near Archstone Avenir, on Canal Street, Boston's luxurious and impressive apartment suite. She found the correct number and pushed an entry phone's button with "Soul and Body Therapy" sign. Nobody answered, but the doors opened almost immediately. Laura walked inside and called the elevator. The apartment she was looking for was situated on the fifth floor. Having no idea what to expect, if she was about to meet a cheater, a con person, or if she was really going to get help, she felt quite uneasy. Full of doubts but determined to give it all a try, she knocked on the door. She was curious of Alyssa. Would she use a crystal bowl like in old cartoons? Would she see her future in tea dregs?

Laura waited for a moment, which seemed endless, and was already considering leaving when the door finally opened. A young woman, in her thirties greeted her with a smile. She had unusually green eyes and very long, impressively thick brown hair. Looking at her, Laura instinctively touched her wig. Alyssa did not look like a Shaman at all. Dressed up nicely in smart, office-like clothes, she looked like someone ready to go to work and spend the next eight hours as a bank manager answering phone calls, receiving and sending e-mails and occasionally firing someone. There was no doubt Laura just met a very self-confident woman, who at least according to the first impression, seemed nice.

"You must be Laura; hi, I'm Alyssa. Come in," she said in a friendly voice. Encouraged, Laura stepped into the apartment. In the hallway, which was wide and quite long, everything was white, only the carpet was grey. There were huge pictures in heavy wooden frames hanging on the walls—all of them showed some winter sceneries with huts hidden among the pine trees, covered with snow, with grey smoke coming out of the chimney, or mountain hills stretching high, trying to reach the morning sun. The whole apartment was very clean; there were no odd smells, which Laura was grateful for. On the right there was a spacious kitchen combined with a dining room, with white cupboards and grey tiles on the floor. There was a huge glass chandelier hanging above a perfectly white kitchen table, and the only thing that was disturbing the coloristic of the place was a bowl full of oranges and lemon on the table. On the left there was a long, wide corridor with two doors; one leading to the bathroom, the other to the bedroom. The whole place made an impression as if it wasn't an apartment that a person lives, eats, drinks and makes a mess in; it rather felt as if it was a museum. Not a single crumble was anywhere to be found, no dirty post-coffee mugs, no open magazines or books. There was a radio in the kitchen and the sound of Lou Reed's "Walk on a Wild Side", one of Laura's favorite songs, was discreetly pouring out from its speakers, which helped her to relax. And candles. Dozens of candles everywhere, placed along the hall walls. All of them were white, tall and thick, but none of them were burning. Alyssa was looking at Laura with a mixture of curiosity and amusement.

"I know, it probably looks a bit odd with that white color everywhere."

"Well, I've never seen an apartment designed like this. It seems very spacious and peaceful."

"That was the idea. White is not distracting. It's a symbol of calmness, goodness and purity. It helps me focus, it gives me positive energy."

"It looks really beautiful, very cohesive."

"Thank you. Can I invite you upstairs? This is where my study is."

It wasn't until that moment that Laura spotted small, wooden, round stairs behind the entry door. The stairs were in a completely different style, they seemed old, a bit neglected. *What an unusual apartment*, she thought.

"Oh, of course."

"Would you like something to drink? I have chamomile tea."

"Oh, that's great! I love chamomile tea." Laura looked at Alyssa. Was it a coincidence? Or perhaps she *knew* that this was Laura's favorite tea? And those eyes, God, Laura felt as if the woman was reading inside of her soul with those wildly intensive green irises.

"Ok, please, have a seat in the study and I'll be there in a minute."

Laura walked up and heard an electric kettle working in the kitchen. So, the woman did use some kitchen appliances after all. Perhaps everything was so perfectly cleaned for that meeting?

The study was no longer white. Apparently Alyssa did not need to concentrate in the there. There was a massive, round, oak table in the middle of the room with two chairs standing opposite to each other. The chairs were also oak, but had white cushions on them. Laura looked around. *Well, no pentagrams or dead animals, that's good.* The room was cozy. Apart from the table and chairs, there was a book case and in the corner of the room and an old fashioned lamp with a shade. The study seemed old-fashioned. Maybe that was the inspiration for this particular room, or perhaps it still needed to be settled. It was quite empty, but café latte walls made it really nice and Laura had to admit she felt pretty good there.

"Here's your tea," said Alyssa walking upstairs. She put a cup on the table and sat on one of the chairs. She made a gesture, inviting Laura to sit on the other one and put her cup next to her hand.

"Thank you."

"So, Laura, how can I help you?"

"I am having health problems. Serious ones. It's a completely new situation for me, because before that I have never had anything more serious than the flu. Of course, the problems I am facing now are partially my fault, because I neglected to examine myself properly—" Laura had no idea what she was saying. She was stressed, her heart was pounding. She just wanted to say she had cancer, but it all became very overwhelming and she found it hard to focus on specific information. Her thoughts and words were chaotic, and Laura felt as if her brain was put upside down and shaken so that all the information would fall out from it without any particular order.

Alyssa grabbed her hand, gently, but firmly and looked at her. Their eyes met and for a second, and Laura had a feeling the Shaman's eyes were becoming even greener.

"Laura, it's okay, calm down," she said soothingly. "There's no need to be nervous. If you don't feel comfortable talking about your problem, I can look inside of you and I will know what you're suffering from."

Laura was stunned. The moment Alyssa grabbed her hand, she felt such serenity it was remarkable. Her heartbeat got normal, her thoughts became clear.

"I am suffering from breast cancer. Stage two. I have been undergoing chemotherapy for the last two months, but it's been having a very bad influence on me. I think I am experiencing most of the possible side effects, if not all of them." She took off her wig. "I feel depressed, I am

161

losing touch with the reality, and I walk around the home and cry almost every time I see myself in the mirror. I feel my femininity is gone, I am finding it more and more difficult to think positively and I am afraid that if this state lasts until the end of the therapy, which should be four months from now, I won't have any will or motivation to keep fighting for my life." Laura was struggling to stop the tears coming to her eyes.

Alyssa did not say anything; she was only looking at Laura. Her eyes were full of compassion and understanding and for a minute Laura thought that perhaps *that* was her gift that would help people; she knew how to listen to others, and that comprehension she was capable of was probably the thing that cured the souls and spirits of those who needed attention.

"Laura, I am so, so sorry for what you're going through," she finally said, "but I also admire you for the determination you have inside of you. The determination that allowed you to fight and now has brought you to me."

"Can you really help me? Because, I know my time hasn't come yet."

"I've already started helping you."

"You have?"

"Because of me you left home, got here leaving your asylum for the first time in weeks. Pretty good for a start, isn't it?" Alyssa smiled.

Laura smiled, too. She had never thought of that in this way. Yes, she was right.

"Laura, you have every right to be scared. You also have every right to seek help and this is exactly what you're doing. Do you believe that I can help you?"

"I want to believe, that's for sure."

"If you believe, I will be able to do it."

"What will I have to do for you to help me? How much will I have to pay?"

"Money is not the most important thing here. In fact, I never take any money before the treatment is over. I want you to focus on your health and we'll talk about the money later on."

"But on the average, how much does it cost to be healthy? I need to know what to expect."

"My usual rate is ten grand. Do you think that's a lot?"

"No Shaman has ever helped me yet, I have no idea what the average price is. But it sounds reasonable. For the promise of health."

"I think so, too." Alyssa smiled. "Laura, you may find my treatment weird, perhaps even unpleasant, but trust me, I have cured far worse cases of cancers than yours."

"Will I need to stop my regular chemotherapy?"

"No, not at all. I just don't think you'll need many more sessions. How many days are left until your next procedure?"

"Nine."

"And how many times do you think you might come here during those nine days?"

"How often *can* I come?"

"Every day."

"How many sessions do you suggest I take?"

"Enough to cure you."

This all sounded sublime. Laura was getting very excited and full of hope; she was ready to start, to begin the sessions with Alyssa right there and then. The vision of no more chemos, no more vomiting, hair coming back, appetite coming back, driving a car, work! Dear God, yes, how she wanted to be healthy again. Ten thousand dollars? Ridiculous money for the promise of coming back to life!

"When can I start?"

"We can start now if you have time."

"Oh my God, yes!"

Alyssa smiled, got up from her chair, and stood behind Laura.

"You need to trust me."

"I trust you."

"I can sense you're scared. Don't be. Your coming back to life is about to begin."

Alyssa put her hands on Laura's head, covering her forehead with her palms and asked Laura to close her eyes. The moment she did so, she felt a strike of energy going through her body. It felt like a weak electric shock, but wasn't unpleasant. Laura felt warmth being distributed through her veins, to her core, and accumulating in her left breast. At the same time she experienced a wave of tranquility filling her up from the inside. She had a feeling her legs and arms were becoming numb, and her heart beat was now very slow. At one point she felt the urge to go to sleep; she was sure she would simply take a nap right there, at that very moment, and slip from the chair she was sitting on. A few seconds after Alyssa had touched her head, Laura started feeling pricking in her left breast, in the exact place where her tumor was located. It wasn't particularly pleasant, but it wasn't disturbing either. All this time she *knew*, she understood that something good was happening. Gradually everything stopped; Alyssa took her hands from Laura's forehead and told her gently to open her eyes. Laura looked around, feeling as if she was awakened from a deep dream.

"How do you feel?" Alyssa asked. She was now standing somewhere in front of her. Laura opened her eyes and saw her washing her hands in a tiny water basin in the corner of the room. She hadn't spotted the basin before when she entered the room.

"Confused," Laura replied and it was exactly how she felt. She had no idea what had just happened.

"That's normal." Alyssa dried her hands.

"Why are you washing your hands?"

"I don't want to have all this nasty energy I have just taken out from you on my hands. I always do that."

"You mean you can feel it on your hands?"

"Of course. It feels like having hands covered with heavy, iron gloves. It's pretty unpleasant."

"And you use regular soap to wash it away?"

"Yes, funny, isn't it?" Alyssa laughed. "So, Laura, again, how are you?" she asked one more time and got back to the table.

"I feel—lighter. I feel—I feel better. Oh my God!" Laura took a deep breath.

Alyssa smiled. "We've began something really extraordinary, Laura. I have good news—your cancer hasn't attached to you yet. You've started chemotherapy soon enough to effectively get rid of it. It's also not a severe case. Laura, you're going to be fine. The chemotherapy would have been sufficient to deal with it, but I understand your feeling of frustration, so we will get rid of it sooner than in a traditional way."

Laura couldn't believe what she just heard. It felt so good to hear all those things. She looked at the watch and was stunned to realize she had been there only 40 minutes.

"I could have sworn I've been here much, much longer."

"That's normal; the sessions usually mess up people's sense of time."

"Okay, so I will be going then. When will I see the first results of the sessions?"

"Well, I think you are already feeling it. I think it's a matter of days before you start seeing the difference. I've wiped out an impressive amount of cancer from your body."

"This is simply unbelievable. I am so glad I've found you I can't even describe it," Laura said and her eyes became glazed. She reached her hand toward Alyssa, who grabbed her palm and covered it with hers in a very delicate, protective and tender gesture.

"Laura, everyone deserves help. I believe it was your destiny to find me and I believe it is my destiny to heal you," she said and smiled.

When Laura was on the street twenty minutes later, she was passing a hot-dog stand and realized the smell of food was no longer irritating. In fact, the smell was wonderful, delicious. Without any hesitation, Laura bought herself one and ate it with an appetite. It was a sheer bliss. That hot dog was by far the best thing she'd ever eaten, if not the direct sense of speaking, then definitely in symbolical one. She calmed down her euphoria and admitted, with more common sense, that it was the best thing she'd eaten in the last *two months*. She thought of making dinner in the evening and telling Bruce everything that has happened today. But first, she decided to eat another hot-dog.

Oenone~Agatha Rae~

When Bruce got home, the smell of stew filled his home. It was one of his favorite dishes that Laura would make and he was totally shocked when he saw his wife in the kitchen cooking, stirring and seasoning. He quietly walked to her, and looked at Laura. He was more than thrilled to see her in such a light mood and, apparently, her appetite must have come back, which was great news, unexpected at this point, but great. Only two days ago she looked miserable and was vividly depressed. She must have gotten some great test results; that had to be the reason. Laura turned around, saw him and beamed.

"Hi, honey!" she said, and came closer to kiss him. "How was your day?"

"It was all right," he answered and kissed her back. "I see your day must have been *fantastic*!"

"It was; it really was. I'm almost done with the stew. I've set the table in the living room, would you like to go there and wait for me a few minutes?"

"Sure." Bruce still did not understand what was happening. "Do you need any help?"

"No, I'm fine, don't worry. I am just great!" She smiled and got back to the kitchen.

Bruce looked at her again, totally confused, and went to the living room. He was stunned with what he saw there. The table was beautifully set with lavender napkins, elegant plates and two green candles burning lazily in the middle of it. There were big, shiny wine glasses next to the plates, and Laura set out their finest tableware. There was already a bowl with salad. He stepped closer and was amazed to see it was Laura's favorite shrimp salad with peaches, iceberg lettuce and Tabasco. All the things she was unable to stand within the last two months. Bruce had no idea what to think. For a second, a horrible thought pierced his mind that perhaps Laura's prognoses were bad and she had decided to quit the treatment and that was why her appetite was coming back. It was such a terrifying thought that he literally felt a chill going down his spine.

"Sit by the table, honey, I am coming in a minute!" he heard Laura's cheerful voice.

If she got alarming test results, she wouldn't be so optimistic.

She took her apron off, turned off the light in the kitchen and walked into the living room, wearing his favorite black, cocktail dress. This was the first time she wore it in months. She looked beautiful; the candle light exposed her smiling face and her glowing cheeks. She was wearing delicate make-up and, for the first time in two months, her eyes were cheerful. He stood up and moved a chair to help her sit. He sat opposite of her and watched her putting salad on her plate. When she spotted his gaze she stopped and looked at him.

"What?"

"Well, I can't stop looking at you," he said.

"Because I am eating again?"

"No, because you washed the floors," he replied a bit irritated and a bit amused. He was getting tired of this weird situation, he had no idea what was happening and he did not know what to think about it.

"Well, I'll tell you everything; just put some salad on your plate. I really want and *need* to enjoy this meal."

They started eating. For a minute, apart from the rattling sound of the cutlery, there was a total silence in the living room.

"You look wonderful," he said.

"Thank you," she replied, "I feel wonderful, too."

"Which makes me super happy, but, honey, what happened?'"

She took a sip of wine and looked at him very seriously.

"Promise me you won't interrupt me when I tell you what happened. Because it might seem crazy, silly, or both for you."

He put his fork away, looked at her seriously and said, "I'm all ears."

She swallowed her bite of garlic bread, drank some wine again and looked at him. She knew how skeptical he was, how he hated any extraordinary phenomena, all the talk about divine intervention, spirits, being superstitious. Bruce was "here and now" kind of a person. Laura was like that, too. Until today. She told him everything about how she found Alyssa, about what her apartment and the whole session looked like, about her appetite that came back practically immediately and how great she had been feeling since the meeting. Bruce was listening to her very attentively. He did not say a thing and, as he promised, allowed her to finish. He was observing her happiness and was under a huge impression of her faith in Alyssa's power.

"And even though I know it sounds crazy, but, I mean, look at us. We're having a normal dinner, which I prepared. I can eat, I can cook, and I can *smell* food again. I have no idea what's happening, but whatever that woman was doing, apparently, it's working."

He was looking at her for a moment, still not saying anything.

"Bruce, say something," she said finally beseechingly.

Bruce took a deep breath. "I don't know, Laura. I have no idea what to think. On one hand, I am so, *so* happy for you," he said and put his palm on his chest in assuring gesture, "It's wonderful you're feeling better. But I am afraid it might be only placebo, that it could be some kind of psychological—"

"Manipulation?"

"Trick."

"Bruce, but it's working."

"Honey, I know, I can see that. I am just worried it might not last long."

"Bruce, I am alive. For the first time since the diagnosis; I feel I am alive again. Please, trust me." Laura felt hurt because here she was laughing, optimistic, her self-esteem was coming back and she did not want to hear anything about doubts, suspicion, manipulation or tricks. That was not what she was expecting. She was convinced, to the core of her being that meeting Alyssa was probably the best thing that had ever happened to her and she was truly disappointed with Bruce's reaction.

"I can see you're better, Laura, and I am thrilled. And if you feel you can trust that woman; if you're really sure of it, then please, remember, I will support you. Always. But I cannot imagine a situation that you would quit your mainstream, your *official* treatment just because Alyssa promised to cure you. I simply won't allow it!" He was angry, but not at Laura. He was fully aware he was overreacting, but he was simply panicking. The two feelings, fear and happiness, were mixing in his heart and mind and he had no idea which of those two he ought to have listened. He was terrified Laura might have done something stupid, and yet was thrilled to see she was feeling better.

"Bruce, I am not even *considering* quitting my treatment. But Alyssa might help me get through it and, who knows, maybe because of her help, it might end sooner than we both thought it would."

"Honey," he stood up from the table and walked towards her. He knelt by her chair and looked at her, "I know you've been suffering a lot, but it's been only two months, people have been treated much longer before

169

they got to feel better. Maybe you're just being impatient? What if that woman is using you and your fear and the need of normal life?" He knew he was breaking her heart. Bruce felt awful, stripping her of her fresh hopes and enthusiasm, so he took her hand and, looked at her and said softly, "I appreciate your appetite's coming back, but I need more proof to be sure you're making a good decision to put your life and health in the hands of a Shaman, or a healer, or a goddamn fortune-teller, whoever she is."

Laura said nothing, but, looking at him, she reached to her wig and slowly took it off.

"Oh my God—, Bruce whispered. There were thousands of dark points on his wife's head. Thousands of hairs slowly and shyly growing back. And it wasn't until just then that Bruce had spotted Laura's eyebrows and eyelashes. He was speechless. He touched her head delicately, hugged her and felt he was about to cry.

⨣44⨤

When Laura woke up the next morning, she looked at Bruce sleeping next to her. She knew where he was coming from in his fears and doubts. She knew he wanted her happiness above everything, but he was scared her eagerness to be healthy might have messed with her mind. Laura knew it all seemed too simple, but everything that had been happening to her body now was a proof that Alyssa's powers were working. They had a fantastic meal yesterday, she wasn't nauseous at all, and later on they made love and she felt only the warmth of passion going through her body, no hurt, no sore muscles, no dizziness. She felt sexy, attractive and loved. Unconditionally. She hugged Bruce, kissed him on his cheek and got up to make coffee. It seemed so natural to do it. On her way to the kitchen she saw herself in the mirror and, stunned, she had to come back to look at her reflection. She was shocked. She had short hair all over her head. About an inch long, dense, healthy, dark hair. Laura touched her head gently, as if worried the hair would fall out again, or disappear. She couldn't believe it.

When the water was boiling, she took her cell phone and called Alyssa.

"Hi, Laura, I've been waiting for your call. How are you feeling?"

Laura told her everything that was happening to her. By the end of their conversation they had arranged a meeting for the afternoon.

Oenone~Agatha Rae~

❧45❧

Evy got to OMNIBUS at about 11:00 a.m. Jeff spotted her and called her. She left her handbag and briefcase and went to him. Once she entered his office, she saw a very impressive pile of packages arranged neatly next to a wall. There were about thirty of them, cardboard boxes wrapped in grey paper with courier sticks on them along with the OMNIBUS address. Behind her she heard a cork exploding and she saw Jeff with a bottle of champagne in his hands and a smile of satisfaction on his face.

"There they are, Ev. Four out of eight books are already printed and ready for distribution. What is more, our scientific projects are being distributed right now."

"Oh my God!" She smiled. "Wonderful!"

"The packages you see are the promotional copies we will be sending to reviewers, book magazines, and giving away as contests' awards. The rest of them are already being on their ways to both scientific and general bookstores in the whole state of Massachusetts."

"What, now?"

"Yeah, now. The first vans loaded with our new books are on their way to deliver them as we speak. I think that calls for a little celebration, what do you think?"

"I think you're right." She grinned and took the glass that Jeff was handing to her. He poured champagne in each of the glasses and they raised them to the success of the company.

"I got you another book I've edited," she said. "It's on my computer, ready to be sent to the printing house."

"Splendid. You know what, Ev?"

"What?"

"I think we're going to make it. I really do."

She smiled. She had the same feeling, but did not want to say anything until six months would have passed. Maybe she was superstitious, but she believed that announcing success before the deadline would only bring bad luck.

"And I think," Jeff continued, "that it would not have been possible if it wasn't for your help and engagement. Thank you, Evy."

"Oh, no problem; I loved the idea of creating the new publishing."

"Me, too, and I think we're making a great team."

"I think so, too."

"If everything goes well, and OMNIBUS turns out to be successful, I would like you to be in charge of it."

"Me?" She was stunned. "I have never had a managerial position before; I'm not sure if I can handle it."

"Of course you can. I am under a huge impression of your creativity and organizational skills. I cannot imagine anybody else to be in charge here."

"That's very sweet and thank you for having such faith in me. But let's wait with all the decisions until we actually *know* we're successful."

"Of course, no problem." He drank some champagne. "I cannot wait to see the board members' faces when we meet them the day after tomorrow, and show them everything we have achieved so far."

"Their jaws will drop, no doubt about it."

"Of course, and I cannot even tell you how much I will enjoy that moment. Have you already prepared the presentation?"

"Of course, yes, it's all ready, I have it on my flash drive."

"Great."

Evy's cell phone rang. She took it out of her purse and saw it was Laura calling.

"Hi, Laura, what's up?"

"Do you think it would be possible for you to eat lunch with me? At my home?"

"Lunch? Are you sure?"

"Absolutely."

"Ok then. Are you feeling better?"

"Oh yes. Much, much better. Can't wait to see you," said Laura cheerfully.

"I'll be at your place in about an hour, okay?"

"Sounds great; see you!"

Evy looked at Jeff. "It's Laura. She wants to have lunch with me. She says she's feeling better."

"That's great news. Sure, go ahead, just come back around 3:00 p.m., there are certain things I need to discuss with you, things concerning an advertising campaign."

"Of course. See you, Jeff!" She put her glass on his desk and left his office.

❧46❧

The day was simply beautiful. It was already July and the weather was fantastic. It was sunny and the wind was very pleasant. Evy was on her way to Laura, wondering what was going on. She seemed truly light-hearted on the phone; it had been months since she heard Laura sound so optimistic. Evy was sure Laura must have gotten some great test results. That had to be it.

She parked Bob and cheerfully walked toward Laura's home, smiling and anticipating the good news. She rang the doorbell and Laura opened the doors, beaming.

"Wow, Laura, you look amazing! This wig suits you!" exclaimed Evy and walked inside and hugged her friend.

"It's not a wig, Ev," Laura said.

"What do you mean?" For a second she thought Laura had had a hair transplant, but she quickly dropped that idea, because as far as she knew, people can have only their *own* hair transplanted, and well, Laura ...

"It's my real hair. It's growing back!"

"WHAT?" Evy couldn't believe it! She walked around Laura, looking at her head all the time. "Can I touch it?"

"Of course!"

Evy touched Laura's head very gently.

"Oh my God! It grew back so fast! It's unbelievable! But you haven't finished the treatment yet, have you?"

"No, not yet. Hey, would you like some caprese salad for lunch?"

"Sure," Evy replied surprised. "You can eat again?"

"Yes! And I love it! Come on!" They went to the kitchen. She opened the fridge and took out tomatoes, sweet basil, buffalo mozzarella and olive oil from the cabinet.

"Will you help me prepare it?" Laura asked, smiling at Evy.

"...yes," she replied and took a knife. When they were cutting the ingredients, Evy was looking at Laura trying to understand what was happening. Here she was preparing food with Laura, a situation that would not be imaginable only few days ago. Apparently, Laura no longer needed

175

the wigs. Was Evy that busy with OMNIBUS that she hadn't noticed all those changes?

"Laura, what is going on?" she finally asked.

Laura looked at her and smiled. "I went to see Alyssa. All those changes are her work."

"No way! The hair? And the appetite? It's all Alyssa?" Evy put down her knife as she was worried she might cut herself. That was stunning! "Tell me what happened yesterday! Tell me *exactly* what happened!"

"I will, but we need to prepare the salad first. My appetite now is insatiable!"

An hour later they were drinking lemonade and lying on sofas on the terrace, enjoying the sun and allowing it to gently caress their faces.

"I still cannot believe it! I *cannot* believe you went there and it is all working out so swiftly. And so well! I am so, so happy for you, Laura!"

"Thank you. I know, I find it all hard to believe myself, but here I am," she said smiling.

"Are you going to quit the chemotherapy now?"

"No, I am going to have another session next week."

"How are going to explain all those changes to Tessa?"

"I'm going to tell her the truth."

"The truth? That you went to a Shaman?"

"Yes. After all, I found Alyssa's brochures in the clinic, right? I am sure Tessa must have heard about her."

"Have you wondered how your tumor might have reacted after the session?"

"Yes, I am going to ask Tessa to perform new tests. But, you know what?"

"What?"

"I think the tumor is smaller. I checked it this morning." Laura smiled and bit her lower lip.

"Shut up! When are you going to see Alyssa again?"

"Today in the afternoon. This time Bruce is taking me."

"Say, do you think—do you think she might help me with my problems?"

"What problems?"

"Well, Jeff-oriented ones. Do you think she might help me with this?"

"Well, she does say she can cure both body *and* soul. A heart is, after all, a part of both, right?"

"I guess so. You know, I miss the way Jeff had been looking at me before we slept together. I miss the flirting, I miss the tension."

"You miss sex, Evy."

"True. And I especially miss sex with Jeff." She laughed.

"Was it that good?"

"It was terrific; are you kidding me? I still have chills when I think about it!"

"Okay, that must be the most ecological air condition ever," Laura said as she laughed and Evy nudged her.

"Will you give me her phone number?"

"Of course, Evy. If you're sure this is the kind of help you need. And the way you want to handle it."

"Won't hurt to try, will it?"

Oenone~Agatha Rae~

~47~

That afternoon Laura went to see Alyssa again. She asked Bruce to wait outside, as she had this feeling that her sessions with the Shaman were kind of intimate; she did not want to be distracted by anybody's presence. Alyssa was waiting for her and, once again, invited her to the tiny study upstairs.

"I can see my powers are working," she said when they were both sitting by the table.

"Oh my God, yes, it's unbelievable. I've regained my appetite, but the biggest change is this," she said as she pointed to her hair. "I can't believe it, Alyssa, it's a miracle!"

Alyssa smiled warmly seeing Laura's hair. For a second, Laura had a strange feeling that it was Alyssa's body that was smiling, but not her eyes. Her eyes seemed empty.

"I am so glad everything is working out so well. How is your soul?"

"My soul? Oh, I can't remember anyone ever asking me such question." Laura laughed. "Seriously?"

"Of course." Alyssa stood up and walked to her. She stopped just behind her, in exactly the same way as the day before, and touched her head. She started soothingly stroking her hair and Laura closed her eyes succumbing to the touch. "Nobody usually asks this, because hardly anyone is interested in people's souls. People are so focused on their bodies and appearances nowadays that they neglect their spiritual side. And it's our spirits that make us special, unique, they are what make us original, what animate us. How did you feel when you found out about the cancer?"

"I felt empty, lost, scared and depressed."

"Exactly; it was your soul crying. It wasn't the body. The body can stand a lot of pain; you've experienced it. You've had needles in your body, you felt sick, sore and pained. But the body is strong, it will allow nasty things happen to it, just for the promise of health and peace. The soul is different. It's the cry of your soul that led you to me; it was your soul being miserable that made you want my help. Your body was exhausted, but it did not want to give up. Your soul, however, shouted

STOP!

Laura had never thought of it like that. Perhaps Alyssa was right. The truth was that, after yesterday's session, her body was still weakened and miserable, but she had been so happy, so light-hearted that she no longer cared about being too skinny or having dark shadows around her eyes. The soul feeling better made her whole organism feel better. It was *amazing*.

"So, Laura, how is your soul?"

"It's getting better," she replied honestly.

"I know. I can see it in your eyes. Eyes are amazing, you know? They can never fool anyone looking into them. They are the window, the mirror of one's soul. And I saw your eyes smiling to me once you got here. I knew right away you were feeling better. Remember, Laura. Eyes. They will tell you everything you need to know."

Was it Laura's feeling or were Alyssa's hands a bit colder now? It seemed as if the whole room was suddenly a bit chilly. For a second Laura wanted to open her eyes, but felt like she wasn't allowed to do it. Alyssa bent over and whispered strictly to her ear, "Do you want me to cure you, Laura?"

"Totally?" She asked and her voice seemed weak, as if she was talking in her sleep.

"Yes, I *can* do that," Alyssa was whispering so quietly that Laura was no longer sure if she was actually saying anything. "I can make it all go away. But there is a price to pay."

"Cure me, Alyssa. The money doesn't count."

Alyssa put her hand on Laura's left breast and Laura felt that it was becoming hot, so hot it was almost burning. Her first reaction was to move away, but Alyssa was holding her very strongly. The warmth was unbearable and Laura started crying.

"Cry, Laura, cry it all out, get rid of it!" Alyssa told her straight to her ear.

"It hurts!" Laura shouted, but felt she was unable to move and she still couldn't open her eyes. "Alyssa, stop, it's excruciating!"

"I know, but it's the disease; it's the poison that had made you miserable. It doesn't want to let you go, but I'll *force* it to leave you!"

Now Laura's whole body was burning. She was screaming and howling, unable to free herself from Alyssa's incredibly strong grip. The moment she felt she was going to faint, everything stopped. The temperature of her body got normal, Alyssa let her go, and told her gently to open her eyes. Laura was finally able to do it. She opened them slowly, and for the first time felt her face wet from tears and sweat. She was breathing heavily and looked up at Alyssa who was smiling calmly. Her eyes were unbelievably green this time; it wasn't a natural color. It was a color that somehow made Laura uncomfortable.

"It's ok, Laura. It's gone," said Alyssa and walked to the corner of the room to wash her hands.

"What is gone?"

"Your cancer. The heat you felt was the cancer desperately holding to your body when I was getting rid of it."

"Oh my God!" Laura was still shocked. "But it wasn't just the breast, it was the whole body that was burning."

"Yes, first it was the cancer, then I took away all the poisons you were given in the hospital. Your body is free. You have no diseases and no toxins in it."

Laura was speechless. She instinctively touched her breast, the same way as people touch their bruises to see if they were gone—it was painful but necessary. She had a feeling the tumor was *gone*.

"So, that's it?"

"Yes. I told you yesterday that your cancer was not serious and that it hadn't attached to you yet."

"And it's gone? It's really gone?"

"It is. You felt it leaving your body, didn't you?"

"Oh my God. What am I going to tell Tessa?"

"Who?"

"Tessa. She's my doctor. How am I going to explain to her I no longer need chemotherapy?"

"You just had your cancer chased out of your life and you're worried what you're going to tell the doctors?" Alyssa laughed.

Laura was still a bit confused. Perhaps telling Tessa straight away was the best method. And yes, it did seem odd she was worrying about that. Who cared about Tessa's reaction? She was healthy, it was the only thing that mattered!

"When should I give you the money?"

"I'll let you know."

"Oh my God, I am so, so grateful, you have no idea—"

"I think I have.", the Shaman replied smiling mysteriously.

"Alyssa, there is one thing I need to ask you. My friend was wondering if you could help her."

"What is her problem?"

181

"She is unhappily in love."

Alyssa looked at her and frowned for a minute and then smiled. "Finally someone who wants to cure the soul. Of course, tell her to come to me. I will be waiting for her tomorrow at lunch time."

"Fantastic. Oh my, I feel so light, so *light*, I feel dizzy."

"It's normal, your body is coming back to its previous, pre-cancer condition. You see, cancer was feeding from you. Every disease that each person has is like a parasite. It sucks your life energy, it weakens your body, and it makes your soul miserable. The longer a person's body lives with it, the more the disease becomes attached and doesn't want to fight it anymore. It usually wreaks havoc on it. Like I said, your cancer wasn't that strong yet, but every day you can hear stories of people dying because of it—these are examples of bodies that got used to the parasite. They got used to and did not want to fight it any longer."

Laura sat quietly for few seconds looking all this time at Alyssa. Finally she got up, took her purse and started walking downstairs. Before she got out from the apartment she looked at Alyssa once again.

"Thank you so much; you have no idea how happy I am."

"I am always glad whenever I have a chance to use my gift to help someone."

"I will tell Evy to call you."

"She doesn't need to call me, tell her to come to me, tomorrow at lunch."

"All right. And, Alyssa—may I just say that you have truly extraordinary eyes. I've never seen eyes like yours."

The moment Laura said it, she spotted Alyssa's eyes becoming greener again.

"Thank you, that's very kind. My mother had the same, it must be genetic." She smiled.

"Really beautiful. Well then, good-bye," Laura said and, overwhelmed by emotions, she wanted to hug Alyssa, but she moved aside.

"I'm sorry. My body is full of toxins now, I don't want you to touch me, and it's a pretty nasty feeling touching me after such powerful session.'

"The soap didn't help?"

"No, only a bit. After such difficult session, I need to take a bath to feel clean again."

When Laura walked out of the building and was heading toward the car, she texted Evy.

I am cured. Your appointment is tomorrow at lunch.

Oenone~Agatha Rae~

After few seconds a reply came.

Jesus Christ….

Laura saw Bruce coming out of a café with two cardboard mugs in his hands, heading toward the car.

"Bruce!" Laura shouted. He looked at her and saw his wife running to him. She embraced him so hard and so unexpectedly, he dropped the coffees and embraced her, too.

"It's over, Bruce. I am fine."

Oenone~Agatha Rae~

❧48❧

Evy got Laura's message and had to read it five times to actually believe it. It was a miracle. It had to be! Who was that Alyssa? What kind of power did she have? It was intriguing and Evy had to admit she was getting really excited about the perspective of meeting her the next day. She got home from office, took off her shoes and made herself a drink. She mixed whiskey with coke, added a slice of lemon and a lot of ice, sat on the couch and called Laura. Laura told her all the details of her meeting with Alyssa, and Evy was simply stunned. And, since, apparently, the nightmare was over, both her and Bruce were considering going away for few days if her tests turned out to be negative.

Isn't it funny that from a hospital perspective what is negative is actually positive and the other way round? Evy assured Laura a million times she would go see Alyssa and that she was insanely happy to hear about her coming back to health. They also made a deal to see each other the next day so that Evy could tell her about her experience with the Shaman. Finally, after about an hour, they hung up and Evy made herself another drink. She switched the TV on and watched an old classic comedy, *Party* with Peter Sellers. She had some good laughs, and around midnight she went to sleep, unaware that this was one of the last ordinary nights she was about to spend in the upcoming weeks.

Oenone~Agatha Rae~

~49~

Tessa was waiting for Laura in her office. Laura called her the previous evening telling she needed to see her as soon as possible. Doctor Green wanted to see her anyway to inform her it was time to discuss the surgery. They arranged to have a meeting in the morning and now it was 9:00 a.m. and Tessa was waiting for her. Five minutes later, Laura came in. The moment she saw her, Green knew something was different. Her patient was vibrant, and she was walking toward her, smiling and waving in her direction. Tessa waved her back and was trying to comprehend what was happening. Was this the same Laura Levinson that left Femina about ten days ago miserable and weakened after another chemotherapy? For a second, Tessa felt a twinge of sorrow in her heart because she was about to ruin Laura's good mood by letting her know her breast, most probably, would not be rescued. The newest test results showed the tumor was almost intact by the chemotherapy and Tessa's hopes that it might shrink were now gone. When Laura came in, she asked her to take a seat and if she wanted something to drink.

"If you have some cold water that would be great; it's very hot today," Laura replied and sat comfortably in a chair. Tessa gave her a glass of water and ice and sat next to her.

"How are you feeling, Laura?"

"Actually, I am great! I am really, *really* good." Laura smiled.

"Yes, I can see that you're in a good mood and that's great."

"It is. And I regained my appetite."

"You did?" Doctor Green asked confused.

"Yes, to tell the truth, I have been having the time of my life since yesterday."

"You have?" Tessa was completely taken aback. Laura seemed to be an entirely different person. When she was leaving the clinic a few days ago, she was depressed and discouraged and Tessa was truly worried she might give up. Now it was a new Laura sitting next to her. She was relaxed and comfortable and she seemed not to worry at all. There was some kind of positive aura around her. She looked—she looked healthy.

"Laura, I am so sorry I have to spoil your—"

"No, no, Tessa, you won't spoil anything. I'm healthy. The cancer is gone."

"What do you mean *it's gone?*" Now Tessa felt worried and irritated. What was Laura talking about?

"I know you may not believe me, but I am cured. During my last chemotherapy I found, here in the clinic, brochures of a Shaman named Alyssa—"

"What? Who?"

"Alyssa. I am sure you must have seen them, the brochures. I figured the clinic approves her work since it allowed them to be distributed here."

"I have never seen any *Shaman* brochures in the clinic! Do you have one with you, can you show it to me?"

"Yes." Laura felt a bit disorientated. She reached inside her purse and showed Tessa Alyssa's leaflet. Tessa took it from her and looked at it carefully for about a minute, reading attentively what was written there.

"Laura, I hope you did not believe that woman, I hope—"

"I did. I went to see her this week."

There was a moment of complete silence. Tessa looked at the brochure again, looked at Laura and leaned on the chair.

"So—what happened when you went there?"

"I've seen her twice. She cured me; she told me she took the cancer away from me."

"And you believed her?"

"I do, but I want you to perform tests that would prove I am healthy."

"Laura, I have no idea what to say. Look, your recent test results show that the cancer does not succumb to the treatment and I was about to tell you that you need to have your breast removed."

Laura was looking at Tessa terrified.

"You told me there was a big chance that I would keep my breast and that if there was any surgery to be taken into consideration, I would have only part of it removed. And now, after more than two months of this ordeal you're telling me I might lose it?"

"I am so sorry, but the tests show that the cancer is resistant to treatment."

"Well then, in that case, I am glad I found Alyssa. The woman saved my life."

"Laura—"

"No. No, Tessa. I want you to perform tests on me, and I want you to confirm that the cancer is gone. I am not stupid. I did not go to a healer to refuse the regular treatment, but before you set a surgery date for me I want you to check if there really is no improvement."

"Laura—"

"I mean it, Tessa. Look." Laura took off her wig.

"Oh my God!" Tessa exclaimed. She reached out her hand and touched Laura's head. "How is that possible?"

"It's Alyssa. The hair started growing back after my first visit two days ago. I also started eating properly after that. Yesterday we had another meeting and she told me she got rid of the cancer once and for all."

"And what did those sessions look like? Did you have to drink some herbs and dance around a bonfire?"

"No, and I do not appreciate the sarcasm, Tessa. Not once did I say that I wanted to quit the treatment. I came here to ask you for tests, because I don't want to have any doubts,", Laura said harshly. She understood Tessa's doubts, but the sarcastic tone of her voice made her angry.

"You're right, and I'm sorry," Tessa said more calmly. "The hair—it's amazing—it's unbelievable. But I don't want you to have false hopes."

"You think's it's a placebo, don't you?"

"I am worried it might be."

"Yeah, the hair definitely looks like an illusion. You talk like my husband, and I get it, you're both worried about me. Do the tests, Tessa, then we'll both know if Alyssa was a swindler."

"Even if she wasn't, I believe it was highly irresponsible of you to go and see her in the first place."

"But, provided she was honest, I am healthy and I will live. Now excuse me, I need to go. Let me know when I can come for tests." Laura was very irritated. Tessa was looking at her as if she was a lunatic—a gullible and desperate person seeking some paranormal help to resolve her problems. Laura knew her story would seem unbelievable for most of the people, especially for a doctor who had been taught all her life to be reasonable. However, Laura *was* a reasonable and skeptical person, too, and because she was able to swallow her prejudice she was now enjoying life again. She got up, coldly shook hands with Tessa, who was visibly flabbergasted, and left the office. She wanted to go to the nearest styling salon and spend some money on hair mousse, hairspray and some hair gel, because she wanted to have some fun styling her new hairdo at home.

Tessa was looking at her patient leaving her office and had no idea what to say nor what to think.

❧50❧

Around 1:30 p.m., Evy parked Bob in front of Alyssa's building. She got out of the car, hid her sunglasses in her purse and closed the door. When she was walking toward the staircase, she looked around the area and was stunned to see how beautiful and posh it was. Apparently there were a lot of troubled people who were seeking help. When Evy found Alyssa's name on the buzzer, she pushed the button and the doors opened immediately. She walked inside, called the elevator and after few seconds, knocked on Alyssa's doors. The Shaman opened them and smiled cordially.

"Hi, you must be Evy, I'm Alyssa. Come in."

"Hi." Evy smiled and stepped into the apartment. She immediately noticed Alyssa's incredibly green eyes; Laura was right, they were spectacular. Evy discreetly looked around and was shocked, because the interior looked nothing like the way Laura had described it to her. The walls were red, there was a shaggy carpet on the floor, which was very red and dark, its color immediately triggered bloody associations. There were pictures in the hallway, in wooden frames just as Laura had told her, but instead of rustic winter landscapes they showed female and male nudes, very sensual and very classy. The kitchen was decorated in brown shades, but on the ceiling there was an impressive red chandelier which most probably made the kitchen flood in a dimmed red light in the evenings. The only thing that seemed exactly the same as Laura had described were countless candles put all around the apartment, but they were brown and red, not a single one was white. Also none of them were burning.

"Would you like something to drink?" Alyssa asked.

"Sure. I'd love some tea. Do you have Earl Grey?"

"I'll make some; could you please wait a moment in the study?"

"And where is that?"

"Upstairs, behind you."

Evy turned around and saw the stairs. She walked up and found herself in the room. It looked exactly the same as Laura had described, Evy found nothing surprising there. Soon Alyssa came with a cup of tea, put it on the table and sat opposite her.

"You have a very impressive apartment", Evy said sipping her tea.

"Thank you; I love it very much. I'm very proud of it."

"I must say, though, that it looks totally different than what Laura was describing."

Alyssa's eyes became vividly greener, which Evy found fascinating.

"Yes, well, Laura was looking for tranquility and needed meek and mellow surroundings. I know you're coming to me with an entirely different problem," she answered. "You've come here looking for passion."

Evy looked at her a bit disoriented.

"How do you know? Laura must have told you about me."

"She hasn't mentioned that, but I can see in your eyes that you want a certain man."

"Yes, yes I do."

"Tell me about him. And tell me why he is worthy of your attention."

Evy told Alyssa everything about Jeff. About her crush, about Westville, about their co-operation at work and how she has longed for him almost every day and how she believed he would never want her the way she hoped.

"I just want to know if it's possible for us to be together, and if not, I would love it if you could get him off my thoughts, off my mind."

Alyssa was listening carefully to Evy's story. When she finished, the Shaman leaned on the table toward her guest.

"What do you want me to do, Evy? I am not a fortune teller, I don't have any cards or magic stones to tell you if that man is worthy of your pursuit. I cannot tell you if you are going to be together or not."

"I know, but you are supposed to heal souls, and my soul is in a pretty bad condition now because of this whole mess."

"I know, I can tell."

"So what can you do for me?"

Alyssa leaned back on her chair, and was looking at Evy, not saying anything, which made Evy quite uneasy.

"So, you would like me to manipulate his feelings?" she finally asked.

"No! Not at all! Look, if we can't be together, could you just please erase him from my mind, from my heart so that I am finally free after all these months?"

"You know, I can bring his passion to you."

Evy looked at her intrigued.

"How?"

"Doesn't matter how, but I can make him want you."

"Will he *love* me?"

"I can't do that. You see passion and sex are primal instincts. Something that is very basic and very powerful, but it has got nothing to do with emotions. The emotional aspect of sex is something pretty new and fresh if we take humankind into consideration. The primal function of sex is prolonging the species. For thousands of years there has been nothing emotional or romantic about it. Therefore, I can control *that*. I *cannot*, however, control feelings, that is something far more advanced in a human structure and the person has to consciously make a decision if he or she loves someone or not."

"So, you can help me sleep with him, but cannot guarantee he will love me, is that right?"

"Yes, something like that. But, you know, once there is satisfaction on the sexual basis, it is possible there might be a chance for the deeper feelings to appear."

Evy was experiencing a stream of thoughts in her head. Laura came here because she was severely sick, it was even possible she would have died if it wasn't for Alyssa's help. Evy, on the other hand, she wanted Jeff with every cell of her body, but her situation was not life-threatening, maybe reaching out for such solutions was too much? Well yes, but that was something that she had been dreaming of for months, and the Westville weekend only made her realize how much she wanted him. And besides, Alyssa said she didn't have the power to control his emotions, thus it wouldn't be very much of a manipulation. Especially since he *did* find her attractive not so long ago. So, perhaps, her idea was worthy to think through. And maybe their possible relationship needed exactly that—a little push?

"Would I be doing something morally doubtful?"

"You want him, Evy?"

"Yes!"

"Well then, you won't be messing up with his head, nor with his heart. You only want to be satisfied and feel his closeness. I don't think it's morally doubtful. I think you deserve it. From what you've told me, he seems to be limited by his professionalism, but he certainly wants you. Let's help him get to you; let's help him to knock down the barrier that does not allow him to pursue you. You know, there are thousands of people sleeping together without any official commitment."

"Friends with benefits," Evy said quietly.

"Exactly."

193

Evy drank some of her tea and said nothing for some time.

"How much will it cost me?"

"First let's see if it works, then we will talk."

"But when should I pay, then? I prefer to be prepared."

"When you'll see that it works."

"When will you be able to well—do your... it?"

"Bring me a thing that belongs to him. Something small, a pen, or a button."

"What for?"

" I need to feel his energy to help you."

"A pen can carry someone's energy?"

"Not someone's but its owner's. When could you bring me such an object?"

"How about today?"

"That's fine. I'll be waiting."

Alyssa smiled and Evy could have sworn her eyes were becoming greener again. About twenty minutes later, Evy was back in her car. Her head and heart were pounding, she could not believe what was happening. Was she actually going to do it? Was she actually going to use the Shaman's powers that she had no idea even existed only three days ago to allow her to be with Jeff? She was excited, curious and anxious. She needed to get to his office.

<h1 style="text-align:center">❧51❧</h1>

OMNIBUS' floor was ready and Jeff had already moved all the things he needed to his second office. He tried to spend more or less the same amount of time in either of the places, but he was becoming more and more engaged in project *Ultimatum* as he sometimes sarcastically called OMNIBUS. Evy got to WORDS' office about twenty minutes after leaving Alyssa's apartment, hoping for two things: one, that Jeff would be downstairs, and two: that he hadn't managed to move all his things there yet.

All the way there she was asking herself the question "what she was doing and if it was worth it"? In case number one the answer was always "I have no idea", and in case number two it was "Who knows?" She did believe Alyssa had some kind of power. It wasn't only what was happening with Laura, Evy definitely *felt* something when she was at her place. It was hard to explain, it was even difficult to name it, but Evy could sense some kind of strange energy in Alyssa's presence. Maybe it was because of those eyes. Evy had never seen such color; emerald, light, seemed so pure, *transparent* even, and it freaked her out a bit that the eyes changed in color. Every time it happened, Evy felt uncomfortable, maybe even a bit scared. Who was that woman? *What* was that woman? A demon? An angel? A single thought concerning approaching a non-human being made her queasy. Evy had to admit that, obviously, Laura had had an entirely different problem, much more serious than the desire to shag her boss, but then again, after all, Alyssa did not refuse. If it was truly questionable whether Evy should allow her to do it, Alyssa would have refused. *Helping* people, not messing up their lives was her business, right? And besides, if she *was* a supernatural being, what would she need money for? No, she was most probably some kind of a master of manipulation, and all that "energy" talk was simply an alibi for her actions. She did, however, help Laura. *How would you explain that, Ev?*

All those thoughts kept running through her head, and she really had no idea what to do; should she really ask for Alyssa's help or come to terms with the fact that Jeff was not interested in her?

195

Evy parked the car, turned the engine off and sighed. Did she want him that badly? *Yes.* Was it messing up with his mind? Not necessarily if there was still some of that desire left in him? She would just re-awaken it, right? Besides, it wouldn't work forever. In the worst case scenario she would have the perspective of spending some nice time with him and *that* couldn't hurt anybody. *Ok, here we go.*

"Evy!" she heard Paul calling her. Paul was one of the new editors Jeff had hired who was given Evy's previous books to edit.

"Hi, Paul," she answered. She was quite upset she saw him. It was almost 3.30 p.m., and Jeff wasn't at work anymore, neither in WORDS or OMNIBUS. Evy knew that he had a meeting with an advertising agency, and most of the staff was already on their way home. She was hoping to be alone, go to Jeff's office unspotted and take his pen or handkerchief to bring to Alyssa.

"What are you doing here, I thought you had the day off?" Paul asked.

"I do, but I needed to get something from my desk—what are *you* doing here? I thought everyone would have been gone by now."

"I'm almost finished; I only have some telephones to make."

"Oh, okay."

"So, how's OMNIBUS doing?"

"Good, I guess. Jeff is focused on advertising it right now. We're publishing new books in the upcoming weeks."

"Great, great!"

They were standing there in silence.

"So, how about doing those phone calls, Paul?" she said as politely as she could.

"Yeah, okay. See you," he answered, a bit offended she was so obviously getting rid of him. "Bye."

"Bye, Paul."

Paul got back to his desk which, luckily, was hidden in the corner of the whole office and Evy went to sit by hers. After few seconds she could hear him talking on the phone. She had no idea what to do; she didn't feel that she could just go inside Jeff's office and take something from it; the absurdity of the idea was paralyzing her; she was afraid the new editor would see her, so her idea was to turn on her computer and wait until Paul would go.

She put her glasses on and logged on to the Intranet. It had been ages since she checked the WORDS forum. Evy hardly ever used that system, but now it looked like a good idea to kill some time. To her amazement she saw a topic entitled "New Creative Manager?" Intrigued, she clicked on it and saw a post by a Guest who wrote that OMNIBUS would be the end of Jeff Richards. The person claimed that the new project was in fact a set up prepared by Jake Pinett to end Jeff's career in the publishing house and both he and Ted Gardner pushed the six-month deadline by threatening to sell their shares, 37%, to the competition. Evy was reading this without any surprise, *everyone* knew Ted and Jake hated Jeff and would do *a lot* to get rid of him from the company. The post ended with a question if anyone knew anything about this case.

Evy scrolled down the screen and was in awe to see that the topic got 34 replies. That was definitely a record on the board which, normally, was so dull and un-alive that the people at WORDS would joke the forum would start generating its own post in order to survive. She opened the first reply and was shocked to see what was written there. The user called X claimed he knew about Jake sabotaging Jeff's effort to popularize his new publishing house. At first Evy could not believe that. After all, she knew, from Jeff, that everything he had been doing to promote the company was doing great. However, as she skimmed the thread, she realized there were some people claiming that Jeff was being set up and that Pinett was lobbying against him. Apparently Richards was to learn about the hard way. Quite soon.

"Oh my God," Evy whispered. She wondered if Jeff saw it and, if he did, if he had any clue as to who the people posting there were. If he had the slightest idea what the rumors around the company were. She suspected he might have not known, as he would have told her about it. Her first thought was to call Jeff and inform him about the forum posts so he could read it all by himself, but she recalled the reason why she was in the office and looked at her watch. It was almost 5 p.m. She wondered if Paul was still there.

"Bye, Ev!" she suddenly heard him.

"See you, Paul!" Evy replied, relieved he was finally going out.

"Will you close the doors?"

"Yes, I've got it!" she replied.

"Bye!" he said again and was gone.

Evy went to the doors and closed them from the inside. She hesitated one last time and finally went to Jeff's office and looked around, wondering what she could take so that he wouldn't spot it missing. At first she thought about one of the books from his bookcase, but she was worried that perhaps he never used them, maybe they were only there as a decoration. She looked at the desk again and spotted a pen lying on it. It wasn't hidden among other writing items, so it was possible he recently used it. Evy took a tissue (snorting with laughter when doing so) delicately picked it up and put it into a sandwich box she had in her purse. She felt ridiculous doing it, sneaking like that and being careful touching his things not to shake his energy off (did Alyssa say anything about shaking energy off? Or was she just being extra-cautious?). She put it all to her purse and left WORDS. Ten minutes later she was on her way back to see Alyssa.

W hen she arrived at her place, Alyssa opened the door and smiled at her warmly.

"Do you have something that belongs to him?"

"Yes, I have a pen he's been using," Evy replied and walked inside the apartment.

"Great, give it to me then and I'll make a use of it."

Evy handed Alyssa the pen. The Shaman took it carefully, went to the kitchen and placed it on a small wooden tray. She looked at Evy, a bit surprised she was still in her apartment.

"All right, Evy, thank you, I will take care of it now."

"So, you don't need me at this stage?"

"No, I'll do everything myself, don't worry. The pen will do. I can clearly feel his energy on it. He is a handsome man, very much focused on his career. But I can also tell you're not indifferent to him."

"How will I know if it's working?"

"Oh, you *will* know. Soon," Alyssa replied and Evy saw her eyes becoming greener again.

"When exactly?"

"Perhaps even tonight."

"Oh my God! Will he come to me?" Alyssa looked at her, her eyes were normal now. If they could ever *be* normal of course.

"Just wait for the magic to begin." Alyssa smiled, her eyes remained still.

Oenone~Agatha Rae~

❧53❧

At 6.00 p.m. Tessa called Laura. She informed her that her tests had been scheduled for 8:00 a.m. next morning. She would have blood tests, an ultrasound and an X-ray. She asked her to come on an empty stomach and, at the end of the conversation, she once again underscored how important it was for Laura not to abandon the conventional medicine at least until it had been proven she was really healthy. Laura assured Tessa she had no intention of giving up the treatment without firm evidence that she was okay. When they finished their conversation, Bruce and Laura went out to the movies. This time Laura was driving.

Oenone~Agatha Rae~

❧54❧

Evy came back home quite late, just before 7:00 p.m. The whole day seemed pretty crazy and unreal. She was glad she had decided to come back to the office and bring Alyssa that pen. Although Evy did not exactly believe anything would happen (but had to admit, she was *expecting* something to happen), she was under such a huge impression of Alyssa, she wanted to give her words a chance. If she had waited a day or two and had more time to think things through, she, most probably, would have changed her mind and never gotten that pen. But there she was, she trusted a Shaman (a Shaman!) to help her get Jeff's attention. Evy kept thinking about Alyssa's eyes. They felt empty, absent. There was no chance to read anything about her by looking into them. And the way they changed their color was simply freaky. The disturbing image of Alyssa's eyes kept reappearing in Evy's head again and again. She had a feeling that she would think about those eyes many, many times in the near future. And what was up with that interior? Laura had described it as peaceful, serene even, but from her point of view, it seemed full of sex and passion. How would Alyssa be able to so drastically redecorate as big apartment as hers in such a short period of time? She wasn't a human, she couldn't be. And again, the queasy feeling came.

When Evy got back home, she took a shower, dressed up in her favorite terry robe and put on Enigma's CD. She took a notebook with a manuscript of the latest book that was in OMNIBUS interest to her bedroom, lay on the bed, poured herself some wine and started editing. After a few minutes she was so much focused on her work that she hadn't realized when the air in her living room became a bit colder. When Evy finally felt the chill, she got up, a bit irritated, and closed the windows in the whole apartment. She was a bit surprised the evening was as cool as the day was pretty hot, perhaps a storm was coming. She got back to the bedroom and to work. This time, however, she wasn't able to focus. She couldn't explain it, but the air felt different. It seemed she could smell something sweet, something that made her dizzy. It was…jasmine. "Principles of Lust" started, one of Evy's favorite Enigma's tracks. She had always considered it to be one of the most erotic songs, however, when she suddenly felt a wave of arousal covering up all her body, she was completely taken aback. It felt so unexpected, but so powerful, that the only thing left to do was to succumb to it. Lying on the bed, Evy closed her eyes and while listening to the music, she started untying her robe, slowly removing it from her arms. The feeling of terry sliding down her skin was truly blissful.

In truly unexplainable way, Evy was becoming drunk of desire. She put away the notebook leaned back down, turned her head and, screamed. Jeff was there! How was that possible! He was naked and was lying on her bed, next to her. He smiled, leaned closer to her and touched her lips with his thumb, not once taking his gaze off her eyes. The moment she felt his touch, Evy immediately calmed down and started enjoying their closeness. She had no idea how or when he got to her apartment, but she no longer cared about it. It was him; she recognized his scent and his touch. The memories of their night in Westville immediately came back. He undressed her gently and when he was doing it, he was whispering in her ear. He told her how much he had missed her, how much he wanted her. She succumbed to the moment entirely.

> *"The principles of lust... Are easy to understand*
> *Do what you feel... Feel until the end*
> *The principles of lust... Are burnt in your mind*
> *Do what you want... Do it until you find love..."*

***

At the same time, Jeff woke up in his bed because he felt a chill in his apartment. He looked at the window in his bedroom which was closed, and got up. He searched for a blanket, came back to bed, put the blanket on the quilt and fell asleep soon after.

***

Evy woke up to the sound of the alarm clock. She lazily opened her eyes, turned her head to find her lover, but she was alone. Alone in bed, alone at home. She sat on the bed and looked around flabbergasted. Her bed was stirred, the sheets were in huge mess. She was undressed, but found her robe on the floor. What had really happened? Was he really there? The memories of the passionate night were very blurry. It all seemed very unreal now in the daylight. Maybe it never really happened? But it felt so real, so how was that possible?

Oenone~Agatha Rae~

Confused, Evy went to the bathroom and discovered a purple and red sign on her neck, indicating a very passionate kiss. Now, it wasn't exactly possible for her to do it herself, was it? *But how did Jeff get in here last night?* She did not remember any doorbell, nor couldn't she recall him leaving. *God, what happened?* The water started pouring on her and she closed her eyes...

Evy left the bathroom half an hour later and went to the kitchen. She passed the bedroom on her way there and once again looked at her bed, still in mess, a silent witness of the passionate night. Evy spent a few seconds there and went to the kitchen. She passed a mirror in the hallway, looked at her own reflection and spotted even more red and purple signs on her skin. They were on her neck, under her right collar bone and on her left breast, just above the nipple.

And on her stomach.

That must have been a really intense night, however the more time had passed, the less Evy remembered about it. Now it was more of a feeling rather than a physical experience. It was all very strange, very confusing.

Evy went to the kitchen, got some milk from the fridge and poured it into the bowl with cereal and muesli. She was stirring it lazily with a spoon when a telephone rang. She picked it up and jumped when she heard Jeff's voice:

"Evy, where the hell are you?" he shouted at her irritated.

"What?"

"What do you mean 'what'?! I am asking where you are!"

"I'm—at home." She was shocked by the tone of his voice. He had never spoken to her like that.

"Do you remember what day it is?"

"It's Friday...Oh my God! Shit! I'm so sorry, Jeff, how much time do I have?"

"The meeting starts in twenty minutes. You better be here," he said and hung up.

On this day Jeff and Evy had a meeting scheduled with the board. They were supposed to update them about the WORDS new profile and OMNIBUS development. Jeff and Evy had prepared for this meeting the whole week, completing all new contracts, gathering statistics and invoices. Jeff was very tense, and he knew that he would be mercilessly attacked by Ted and Jake and that any problem or mistake he would report would be used against him. Evy kept assuring him the meeting would go fine, and now she completely forgot about it! She put the cereal aside and ran to the bedroom to change her clothes. Minute after minute she felt even more panicked. Evy had no idea how all of this was possible; she knew how important that meeting was, for Christ's sake! She quickly put on a long-sleeved shirt, some elegant pants and shoes, she combed her hair, took her briefcase and left her home.

❧55❧

Laura was in Femina dressing. She just had an ultrasound. The doctor that was performing the test had been analyzing the image on his monitor very thoroughly, pressing the transducer to her breast. He was closing up the image and moving the array very slowly around the area where the cancer had been located. He had even called another doctor to consult the examination. The cancer was gone. Gone! Blood tests results were still anticipated, but since the tumor was physically gone, they were only formality. After Laura finished dressing, she said goodbye to the stunned doctors, and went to see Tessa, who was waiting in her office.

Tessa was sitting in her chair, and beaconed Laura to come in. She got up, walked toward her patient and embraced her strongly. Laura hugged her back, surprised by Tessa's reaction.

"I know the test results, Laura. You *are* healthy," she said.

The relief Laura felt at that moment was nothing to be compared with. She knew, deep down, that Alyssa had cured her, but there was a shadow of doubt, that perhaps it was placebo, that perhaps it was only her wishful thinking, that maybe Alyssa *did* manipulate her. Now, however, it was all clear. She was fine. She was healthy. She was going to live.

Laura smiled widely, and felt few tears of joy falling down her cheeks, she hugged Tessa and said "I told you".

"I don't understand that, Laura. As much as I am glad you're fine, I must admit I have no idea what happened, nor *how* it happened. Please tell me something more about that Shaman of yours."

Laura told Tessa everything. How she found Alyssa's brochure, how she was hesitating whether to call her or not, how she finally went to see her and what the sessions were like. She finished her story with all the side effects of chemotherapy disappearing, about her appetite, hair growing back, about the joy that started filling her soul the minute she walked out from Alyssa's apartment. Tessa was listening to Laura's story very carefully and attentively. She was asking about specific details, about concrete reactions.

"My scientific nature finds it difficult to believe that a Shaman, or a magician, whatever you want to call Alyssa, cured you. I *do* believe that she helped you, I don't know how, perhaps she activated certain areas of your psyche that beat the cancer. I don't know, I *really* have no idea."

"The funny thing is that I have always been skeptical. I am not a believer nor have I ever been a religious person, but I was desperate. I was scared, my body's reaction to the chemotherapy outgrew me, and I felt as if life was slipping through my fingers. I was sinking, sinking in my own despair."

"I know; *that* part I understand, more than you know."

"How come?"

"I've been there, Laura. Ten years ago I had breast cancer myself. I had two of my breasts removed."

"Oh my God, Tessa."

"It's okay, the reconstruction was very successful. That experience helped me build empathy with my patients. I really know what women go through when they hear the diagnosis. And I know that sometimes people are not strong enough to face it all, that they sometimes panic and look for help elsewhere; they search for God, they start taking drugs, drink some suspicious herbs, they completely change their lifestyle, blaming rush and unhealthy food for their problems. Sometimes they give up and sell their properties to travel and experience some aspects of life they have always dreamed of. And sometimes they visit fortune tellers to hear what they need to hear, that everything would be fine, that somehow, miraculously, everything would end up well. There is a very small percentage of the patients who face the diagnosis and the horror of treatment trusting only doctors and their ways of helping them."

"Did you search for other help than chemotherapy?"

"No. I have always been a very practical and skeptical person." Tessa looked down and added very quietly, "Perhaps that is why I had lost two breasts."

Laura took Tessa's hand. She felt truly sorry for her.

"Laura, listen. I know all the tests are fine, and I hope the danger is gone, but please, *please promise* me you will regularly check up your health. Once a year is a must."

"I promise."

"Take care of yourself."

"I will."

They stood up, hugged each other again and Laura left Tessa's office. She was pretty stirred with Tessa's story, and felt sorry for her that perhaps her skepticism was a reason she was now mutilated. But Laura was healthy. She went outside the clinic and that thought made her laugh out loud, from the top of her lungs. She was fine! The danger was gone! She took her cell phone out and called Bruce. When she told him the wonderful news, he proposed going for a vacation. Laura said it was a wonderful idea and they decided to surf the Internet in the evening in search for a perfect place to celebrate her victory. *Their* victory.

Laura was about to put her cell phone back in her purse when a text message appeared on its screen. It was Alyssa. The message included a bank account and information that Laura was to send the money for the treatment within 3 days.

Now that is what I call perfect timing. Laura smiled. She decided to go to the bank and pay the money right away. She did not want to start her new life with a debt on her mind.

Oenone~Agatha Rae~

56

Evy entered WORDS twenty minutes late. She ran to the board room where everyone was already waiting for her. Once she walked to the room, she saw all the board members sitting behind the table and Jeff standing in front of the projector where a graphic display showed OMNIBUS' progress.

"I'm so sorry I am late, the traffic jam was horrible," she said while taking her seat. She nervously combed her hair with her palm and looked at David who smiled and made a "don't worry" gesture, which was comforting. Then Evy looked at Jeff who was visibly angry. She immediately lowered her sight and felt her heart pounding. It felt terrible knowing she disappointed him. She knew how much he was stressed before that meeting, and how hard he was getting ready for it. This was, by far, the worst moment she could fail him.

When Jeff spotted Evy walking into the room, he felt a peculiar mixture of anger and relief in his gut. He did not feel too good today, he hadn't slept well, and he blamed the stress of the meeting for it, but he was also convinced he was catching a cold, so he was in a pretty bad mood. Evy coming late only made him grumpier. And he couldn't help but notice a very irritating smirk on Jake's face.

"So, as you can see, OMNIBUS is doing well, our numbers are promising, we are having more and more authors who are interested in publishing their books—"

"Correct me if I'm wrong, Jeff, but shouldn't it be that a *publishing house* wants to publish someone, and not the other way round?" Jake asked.

"Jake, for God's sake," David sighed.

"Every big publishing house has the right to choose among the aspiring authors, just like WORDS does, however, OMNIBUS is a completely new project, we're not exactly swamped by writers yet and we need to accept any promising material that fulfills our requirements. Feel corrected, Jake."

"I must admit, Jeff, that you and Evy have done a great job. It's only been four months and you have managed to find and publish five academic books; you're having an advertising campaign underway, it's all very impressive," Anna said.

"Do you already have contracts with the printing house, or are you still negotiating?" Ted asked.

"So far we have published on the basis of a contract annex—"

"A contract WORDS had previously signed with them, right?"

"Yes, Ted. We had an annex that would allow us to print out five books, each in the amount of 20,000 copies."

"But you have already published the five books."

"Correct again. We are already negotiating our own contract with them, we should sign it next week."

"When will OMNIBUS be able to be an independent company?"

"What do you mean *independent*?" Evy asked. "OMNIBUS is a branch of WORDS."

"A branch with its own manager and editor."

"Yes, with a manager that also works for WORDS and one editor."

"Yes, exactly, this decision cost us quite a lot, and we needed to employ two new editors because you had chosen to co-operate with Jeff."

"I wanted Evy to work with me, because I know she is a professional editor, an experienced one and I needed her to help me with her knowledge and reliability. The new editors would have needed to be employed anyway because Laura Levinson is sick and cannot work actively now."

"How about that profile change of WORDS?" Dean asked.

"Yes, well, we have already published three authors, but changing the profile of such a big publishing house is going to take time," Jeff replied.

"Exactly, it simply takes more time; I mean we still have thousands of our books on the shelves in hundreds of stores," Evy said.

"Evy, could you now tell us how many books you are editing and when will they be released? Is there any, at least preliminary, scheduled?"

"Of course."

She opened her briefcase and, horrified, spotted she had left her flashdrive at home! She had a multimedia presentation of all the writers she had already edited, all those that had already been published and those whose works she was editing now. It was all pretty impressive, and it was supposed to prove that OMNIBUS had a potential and that it was growing and getting stronger. It was supposed to shut Jake's and Ted's mouths about it. But the flashdrive was peacefully lying on her desk, as she was about to pack it after finishing editing yesterday evening. Well yes, but then she got quite busy. Damn it. She looked at Jeff. He was furious.

Twenty minutes later, the meeting was over. Evy confessed she did not have the flashdrive, but she was able to introduce all the authors, the published and the upcoming ones. David was quite pleased, but, naturally, Ted made a comment that OMNIBUS' success was a doubtful project because if the main editor could not keep an eye on such a small thing as flashdrive, then it was hard to expect such big undertaking as a publishing house to work well. David only eye-rolled and asked Evy to proceed with her presentation. When the meeting was over, Garbinsky shook Jeff's and Evy's hands, congratulated them on their hard work, and encouraged them to keep going. He told them to proceed with their project and invited them for a meeting two months from now to see how everything was doing. Ted and Jake were obviously disappointed; they were surely counting on Jeff's failure.

"I'm so sorry, Jeff," said Evy when they left the room. He was leaning on a vending machine, looking at her emotionlessly.

"Everything ended well, that's important. David gave us his blessing, prolonged our existence. I just cannot believe you were late. *Today*. Evy, you're *never* late. And that flashdrive. What happened?"

"I-I overslept," she said avoiding his sight. She felt unbelievably guilty. She failed him, because of some dumb fantasy. She acted irresponsibly as a partner. It was awful.

"Can I make it up to you? Maybe I could ask you out for lunch?"

He looked at her, quite sadly. Perhaps because he did not feel too good, or because Evy failed him, maybe both, but he felt he did not want to spend too much time with her. He wanted to be left alone for a while.

"It's okay, Ev. I'm fine," he said rubbing his neck. He felt tired. "The presentation was fine, we made it, that's what is important. I can't eat lunch with you today. I—I don't want to. I'm sorry." He felt quite bad saying it, but, that was the truth. He did not want to spend time with her. It was the very first time in months that he did not want to spend time with Evy. Jeff was surprised by his own feelings.

"All right then. I just hope we're still friends?" she asked, wanting it to sound like a joke, but it did not work like that.

"Of course we are, I just have other plans for lunch today. It's okay, Ev." He lifted her chin, forcing her to look at him. "We're fine. You've done a good job. I know I can count on you."

She smiled sadly.

***

213

Jake and Ted were in a social room drinking coffee and discussing the meeting that had just ended. Jake closed the door and started talking to Ted quietly.

"I'm telling you, it's over; Jeff is over."

"Did we just get back from the same meeting, Jake?"

"Yes, but let's just say that Jeff is, how to put it, not exactly informed about certain things."

"What do you mean?"

"I mean that I am pretty sure he won't re-negotiate a contract with the printing house."

Ted looked at Jake suspiciously. He put his cup away and walked toward him.

"What are you talking about?"

"That printing house he wants to continue to work with? They're not going to greet him with open arms, I can tell you that."

"But he's already printed some books there."

"Because that was as a part of *our* contract with them. He only made an appendix to the contract, and gave them our money. But you heard what he said, that it's time to renegotiate the contract, this time it's going to be OMNIBUS to pay for all this."

"But he is still going to have WORDS' financial back-up."

"But the printing house doesn't need to know about it."

Jake couldn't help but smirk.

'What are you planning?'

"I'm not sure yet," Jake lied. "But I'm counting on your help, of course."

"Jake, what has he done to you?"

"Who?"

"Larry King, damn it. Who are we talking about here?"

"I just don't like him."

"Because *you* did not get the job?"

"Precisely because of that. Also because he is a total prick who comes here out of nowhere, does nothing apart from sucking up to David, and *I* think there is no better way of telling him to get fucking lost if not by letting him know he's not Boston's manager of the year."

"Questioning Jeff's input in the company is insane, Jake. You know it as well as I do. It's personal for you, and that's it. There's nothing else that can motivate you against him. He's a good manager."

"If you like him so much, you can always take David's side, but remember I know few things about you, things you wouldn't want anyone else to know around here."

Ted's face stiffened. He loosened his tie a bit and swallowed loudly.

"That's just low."

"Is it? Let me put it like this. You *need* me to keep your little secret, but of course, perhaps you no longer feel uncomfortable about it, if that is the case, I can go ahead and let everybody know who Ted Gardner *really* is. So, it's your choice. You can start supporting David but then say good-bye to your position on the board. Or, who knows, maybe even your entire career."

"You son of a bitch. You do realize people are talking about the conflict between you and Jeff?"

"Let them talk, I don't care." He took the final sip of his coffee, put the mug on a counter and looked at Ted. "Do you?"

Ted did not reply, but turned around to make sure nobody was walking in to room and took a step toward Jake.

"It was one time, damn it. One time. You can't use it against me."

"Oh yes, I can." Jake smiled viciously and walked out of the room.

Oenone~Agatha Rae~

57

Jeff was sitting in a restaurant. It felt strange being there without Evy; he couldn't recall the last time they did not spend lunch together. It had been months, that's for sure. He was lazily poking his salmon with a fork, and hopelessly trying to silence all the thoughts that had been running through his head for some time now.

The meeting went quite well. It could have been less improvised (damn it, Ev), but it wasn't bad. He still had David's support and was able to sustain his interest in the new ideas. He did not care about The Mutant Force too much; he knew that as long as he had Garbinsky on his side, Jake's and Ted's dreams of ending his career at WORDS had no chance to come true. He knew Jake's ambition was to mess up his career, he was also aware that Pinett was hoping for his position and, evidently, had a tough time coming to terms with the fact he hadn't gotten it. But what was Ted's problem? Jeff had had few occasions to talk to him, and he never got the impression that Gardner hated him or had any personal agenda against him. To tell the truth, Ted seemed like a nice guy. They had couple of drinks during the WORDS Christmas party last year, and they exchanged some interesting and funny observations about hockey. Jeff was pretty sure that if it wasn't for Jake's influence, he would not have had Ted against him. Apparently, Jake had had some serious arguments. Pinett was a weasel; everyone at WORDS was aware of it. He practically hated everybody, he was always against any new ideas in the company, and it was hard to tell if he was actually working *for* them or *against* them, like a classic saboteur. If he was working at all, because he was more famous for wild, drug-flavored weekend parties at his home than taking care of anything concerning WORDS. As far as Jeff knew, everyone detested him.

Jeff's head was now occupied with Evy. He was actually surprised by how much her coming late struck him. She knew how much he cared for this meeting, and how he needed her to help him. She was the one person who knew everything that was happening both in OMNIBUS and WORDS, a person he trusted and, felt good around. More self-confident. Having such a wonderful, devoted, smart and disciplined assistant would be a pure treasure for everyone who would be responsible for any business. The fact that it was Evy, made it unspeakably better.

Throughout the months they had been working so closely together, Jeff only made sure he cared about her. He still had trouble calling it love, most probably because they had been so busy starting up OMNIBUS, that they were unable to find any private moment to meet and talk. They had lunches together, during which they would exchange information about who managed to take care of what, and Evy would tell him if she had finished editing another book or not. So far, however, they had not been on any dates, nor had they even exchanged any non-professional e-mails, faxes, or information. The truth was, he was planning to ask her out, once everything was settled and he wanted to ask her to become a manager of OMNIBUS. When he thought of her, an certain uncomfortable feeling pierced his heart. He remembered how angry he was at her for not showing up at the meeting on time. And then, the same wave of anger when it turned out she did not bring the pen drive. He had never felt like that toward her before. Of course, until that time, she had never failed him, but he was still surprised by the intensity of the feeling. It wasn't even such a big deal; they managed to present their work and convince David they knew what they were doing, so, really, nothing bad happened. Maybe he was just being super grumpy because of the cold he believed he was getting. He felt cold and had a pretty nasty headache in the middle of the night. However, all the symptoms were gone as swiftly and rapidly as they had appeared, so maybe he was just looking for an excuse to justify his behavior.

Jeff finished his lunch and was on his way to his car when his cell phone rang. He looked at the screen and was quite surprised to see John Abram's phone number. He was the manager of MODENA's Boston branch, a printing house that co-worked with WORDS and OMNIBUS.

"Hi, John, what's up?"

"Hi, Jeff. Listen, um, how are you?"

He was tense. Jeff did not like the sound of his voice. *Something's wrong.*

"I'm good."

"Great. Listen, we're having a problem. With the contract."

"What do you mean? Is something missing in the papers?"

"No, the papers are fine, but it all doesn't look good. Do you think you might be able to come to me today?"

"Of course. When?"

"As soon as possible."

\approx58\sim

"You're going to Okanagan Valley for a week? Seriously?", Evy was beaming. That afternoon, she came to see Laura. She was sitting down happily on the deckchairs on the terrace, enjoying a wonderful early afternoon. They were celebrating her tests' results with a bottle of semi-sweet wine and shrimps fried in herbs. The weather was marvelous; it was a warm, but a bit windy day, one of those that make you take your shoes off and walk bare feet on grass.

"Yeah, we've chosen Okanagan, because – a) I want to honor my dear Canadian friend—"

"Oh, come on!" Evy laughed.

"What! Seriously!" Laura laughed as well.

"And B?"

"B—because we found a wonderful resort there. Plus, it's not too far away."

"Yeah, I reckon five hours by plane."

"Which we both know is not a big deal." Laura smiled.

"True." Evy smiled, too. She put her glass away and stretched on her deckchair. She closed her eyes and enjoyed the delicate breeze playing tricks with her loosened hair. Suddenly, a friskier blow of wind, lifted her skirt, and Evy immediately recalled the previous night. Laura was sitting next to her, sipping her wine and looking ahead at the alley.

"So, when are you going?"

"Tomorrow. Tomorrow morning."

"Wow, I can see you really put things into action."

"Yeah, we're very determined to leave all this mess we've experienced behind."

"You have no idea how happy I am you're okay," Evy said and reached her hand to hold Laura's palm.

"Thank you, Ev." Laura smiled. "Oh, you haven't told me how Alyssa was. You went to see her yesterday, right? What is your impression?"

"Yes. She's strange."

"Oh yeah, she is, all right. I didn't mind it, though."

"I know, neither did I, but I did not feel too comfortable around her. Have you noticed her eyes?"

"Amazing, aren't they? Incredible."

"I would say mesmerizing and, well, disturbing. Especially when they change color."

"I found them rather remarkable actually, you know *fascinating*. So, will she help you? "

"Well, Alyssa told me that what I want from her is pretty close to manipulation. She also assured me she could not influence Jeff on the level of emotions. She can only make him want me in a physical sense."

"Why?"

"Emotions reach too deep into a person's psyche. Sexual drive is more ferocious, more basic, which makes it easier to control."

"It makes sense. So, have you noticed any change in Jeff's behavior? Is he even more shaggable now?" Laura laughed.

"Well, today he wanted to kill me, but I don't think it was because of the uncontrolled desire toward me."

"Can't blame him. He was counting on you."

"I know, and I felt pretty stupid. And guilty. I still do."

"Yeah, why were you late anyway? You're usually very cautious about such things, you're very organized."

Evy looked at her and was wondering if she should tell Laura about what had happened at night. After all it was a bit embarrassing and she was not even sure what it was exactly.

"You see, something happened at night and that was the reason I overslept and forgot the pen drive when I was rushing to work."

"What happened?" asked Laura intrigued, but a bit amused. She was pouring herself a second glass of wine.

"Truthfully, I have no idea. All I know is that it was intense, dirty, completely overpowering, and I still don't know if I was alone at home last night or not."

"Evs, I think I ought to put your glass away. You clearly drink too much." Laura laughed. "Well, after such an introduction you might as well tell me what happened?"

Evy sat on her deckchair, took her sunglasses off and looked at her friend quite seriously. Laura immediately felt she wasn't joking and assured her she was all ears. Evy told her how she felt Jeff's presence and that it was so intense she could have sworn he was there in her bed. She told her how confused, dizzy and powerless she felt, and how she succumbed to everything that was happening.

"I am telling you, Laura. This was by far the best sex in my life. Too bad I have no idea what exactly was happening nor if it was even real. On the other hand, maybe that is why it was so good." She laughed nervously.

"Do you think it's Alyssa's influence on Jeff?"

"I am sure of it. There were no emotions, we did not talk to each other, did not look into each other's eyes and every attempt I made to understand what was going on was futile, it was pure lust, pure…fuck. When I woke up, my bedroom was one big mess. What's frustrating is that I *know* last night was incredible, but, seriously, I cannot recall any details. I only know it was great, but it's all on the level of senses. I can recall his hands and lips on my skin, I can hear him breathing in my head, but it's all blank. I am not sure how to explain this."

"I cannot imagine how you were able to talk to him today having all those things in your head."

"Well, we did not talk too much because first, he was furious at me and later I proposed conciliatory lunch and he refused. Guess he was still hurt."

"So, what do you think will happen now? Would you like such a night to repeat?"

"Of course!" Evy laughed. "How would I not like it?"

"Well, because you know, apparently it's not exactly Jeff you slept with last night. Looks to me like an, I don't know, intensified fantasy."

"I know. Maybe he feels it, too, you know? Maybe this is Alyssa's way of pulling him to me?" Evy said.

"You think he had the fantasy as well?"

"Who knows? It's possible."

"I guess. Well then, for the wonderful, dirty, wet and unforgettable nights!" Laura raised her glass and Evy did the same. "Perhaps it's not good to analyze everything, maybe it's good to follow one's instinct. That's what I did and it cured me."

Evy nodded lost in her thoughts. "So, you're going for a week?"

"Ten days! We want to spend some unforgettable time in Okanagan Valley, visit vineyards, Vancouver, Victoria—"

"Beware of the Ogopogo monster!"

"Ogo-what?"

"A monster living in Okanagan Lake." Evy explained pretending to have claws.

"What, a Canadian version of Loch Ness?"

"Yeah, sort of." Evy laughed. "Looks like a pretty intense holiday."

221

"We just want to leave all the troubles behind."
"It's going to be fabulous, I am sure of it."
"There's no chance for it to be different." Laura smiled.

Jeff parked his car in front of MODENA. He unfastened his seatbelt and hesitated for a minute before getting out of the car. He had no idea what was wrong. He had double-checked all the papers before proposing anything to the printing house, they had known him since he started working for WORDS and he had an opinion of an honest and reliable contractor. He played basketball with John Abram every Wednesday evening for the past five months and, until that particular day he was convinced that OMNIBUS and MODENA co-operation would be smooth and non-problematic. Shaking his head with disbelief and sensing trouble, Jeff got out of his car and walked to the printing house. He stepped into the building, turned left to the receptionist, took off his sunglasses and spoke to a woman sitting behind an impressively big desk.

"Hi, my name's Jeff Richards. I was called here to meet John Abram. Could you let him know I'm here?"

"Certainly," she responded and called a proper extension number.

"Mr. Abram is expecting you in his office," she told Jeff after a moment.

"Thank you."

Jeff called the elevator and arrived at the second floor. He came to room 212 and knocked on the door.

"Come in!" said John and Jeff walked inside.

"Jeff, hi, so glad you could make it so quickly!"

"Hi, John," Richards replied and shook his hand. John invited him to sit down and asked if he wanted something to drink.

"Some water maybe. Cold."

"Sure." John walked toward a small fridge in the corner of his office and took out a bottle of mineral water.

"So, what happened, John?" asked Jeff, intrigued and worried at the same time.

John poured the water into glass, added some cubes of ice in it and turned around. He gave Jeff the glass and sat by his desk.

"We're having a problem with the contract."

"What do you mean, what's wrong?"

"We got a phone call from one of the employees of WORDS who claimed that OMNIBUS may not have a proper cash flow to sign a contract with us.'

"What?" Jeff exclaimed.

"I know, we found it shocking, too, but the uncertainty has already been sown."

Jeff grabbed the glass of water and drank a few gulps. He needed to cool down; he was worried he might lose it. *What the fuck was going on?!*

"Who called?" he asked quite aggressively.

"We don't know."

"So how do you know it was someone from WORDS?"

"The person told us."

"Just like that? And you *believed*?"

"All I can tell you is that the person who called let us know WORDS will no longer financially support OMNIBUS, and that means your financial flow might be quite slip. Uncertain. And MODENA doesn't want to make uncertain deals."

Jeff drank some water again. His thoughts were running inside his head with the speed of light.

"John, are you telling me MODENA will not sign a contract with OMNIBUS? Do you know we're having three books edited as we speak and we want all of them to be printed by MODENA? Come on, John, we *have* the clients! And we need promotion, we need flyers, posters, billboards, and we want all of this from you!"

"Look, Jeff. I hear you, all right? But the decision is not mine. I called you to come here because I wanted to let you know that the board is having doubts and that perhaps, just in case, you ought to search for another printing house."

"At this stage? John, do you know what you are telling me?"

"I know, I know, and am sorry, but I thought you should know."

There was a very awkward and uncomfortable silence in the room. Jeff got up from his armchair and holding a glass in his hand, he walked toward the window, looking at the parking lot. "When did that person call?"

"Today in the morning."

"Was it a man or a woman?"

"I can't tell you that."

"John, come on."

John looked at Jeff uneasily. He felt terrible. Jeff was his friend and he really wanted him to be successful with the new publishing business.

However, he knew the MODENA board would restrain from making any decisions until they investigated Jeff's situation. To tell the truth, he was quite sure that in the end they would reject Richards' offer. The fact he was giving away a tip about the printing house's doubts was all he could do for Jeff right now. And all he *wanted* to do for him, frankly speaking.

"It was a man, but that's all I can tell you."

Jake.

"Who did he talk to?"

"Look, Jeff, all this, it, it doesn't mean we will reject your offer. We just need to consider it more carefully."

"You know I don't have time to wait."

"Listen, you should simply get a bank loan, hire us for the money you'll get."

"I already did, I got a bank loan, with WORDS, the chairman's support, for renting another floor in the building and the ad campaign."

"Take it as OMNIBUS."

"Another one? In this economic situation? You must be joking."

"I'm sorry, Jeff, but I thought you should know what was going on. I mean it gives you the advantage."

"What advantage?"

"You can start looking for other printing houses quicker before", he paused.

"Before you officially reject OMNIBUS' offer?"

"Well, yes."

"So it's settled already?"

"What am I supposed to tell you?" John was starting to get upset. "The person calling made it clear your new company is on the edge of bankruptcy, that you won't get Garbinsky's blessing again, which means he won't feed you with his capital any longer. What are you expecting? It is obvious we will need to check out what is happening, we're talking about the possibility of losing a lot of money."

"But it's a sabotage, John! I need to have those books printed in two months! We've passed the whole procedure with constructing the deals, do you have any idea how long it will take me with a completely new partner?'"

"What would you do if the situation was reversed? Would you trust me because I say I am reliable, or check my numbers before signing anything?"

Jeff went quiet. Of course he would check. He knew that, he fully understood MODENA's point of view. He only felt bitterly disappointed and frustrated that that prick Jake would play *that* dirty. Jeff had no doubt it was him who was standing behind all this mess.

"Do I still have any chance to sign the contract with you?"

John looked at him, visibly uncomfortable.

"I'm not sure," he said. "I don't think so," he added quietly avoiding Richards' sight.

Jeff put the glass on the desk. He rubbed his forehead, he felt headache approaching. *Shit.*

"Okay, John, I appreciate your warning." He reached his hand and John, visibly relieved, shook it.

He's either glad I am not pushing the subject or that I'm leaving. Or both.

"I really wanted you to know about all this as soon as possible. Jeff, for the record, I know it's all a scam, I know you wouldn't propose any co-operation if anything was to be wrong."

"For the record, but off the record, am I right?" Jeff smiled bitterly. John did not reply.

"I really feel bad about all this," he finally said.

"Me, too, John. Me, too. See you," Jeff replied sadly and went out of the office.

❧60❧

Later in the evening Laura was packing her bags when she heard Bruce coming home.

"Hi, honey!"

"Hi!" he replied breathless. He just got back from his evening jog. In the evenings, three or four times a week he would run at least 6 miles. It kept him in shape and was a wonderful way of washing away the stress accumulated during the day. He neglected this habit when Laura was sick, because usually in the evening her mood would get worse and he did not want to leave her alone at home. However, since she was getting better, Bruce decided to resume his regular training and started jogging again. He was surprised how swiftly he had lost his physical condition; he kept feeling extremely tired after each jog, so tired he sometimes had problems breathing. He had a nasty feeling of weight in his chest and it wasn't until at least half an hour break when he would start to feel good again. This time however, he felt really weak and for the first time a thought pierced his head that, perhaps, it wasn't only him being unfit that was to be blamed. Hearing Laura's joyful voice upstairs he quickly pushed the distracting thoughts away.

"How was the run?"

"Pretty good."

"You came back quite quickly."

"I did not run the whole distance." He was quietly walking toward the downstairs bathroom.

"Why not? What happened?"

"I will tell you in a minute."

He closed the doors and turned the water on. Bruce washed his face and looked at himself in the mirror. He did not like his reflection at all; he was quite pale and looked suspiciously tired. He reached for a towel and dried his face, sat at the edge of the tub and was waiting until the moment of weakness was gone. Bruce knew he had to explain to Laura why he came back so soon, but telling her he did not feel right was the last thing he wanted to do. Not now. Not this week. This trip was to celebrate her becoming healthy again, it was about them enjoying their carefree holidays. Apparently, he took a too long break from jogging and that was the result.

When he felt he was fine again, he took a quick shower and walked upstairs to his wife. Laura was zipping up her suitcase when he stood up behind her, put his hands on her hips and kissed her neck.

"I came back so quickly, because I couldn't wait to spend the night with you," he whispered in her ear and kissed its.

"Really?" she asked, smiled and closed her eyes. She leaned her head on his shoulder and allowed him to unbutton her shirt.

"Of course, after all, during the next week we are going to be so busy I am afraid we won't have time for any fun," he continued and put his hands underneath it.

"I'm so glad you thought about it, because I was worrying about that, too."

They spent the rest of that evening making love on the floor of their bedroom. Bruce's worries almost vanished.

ॐ61ॐ

Evy was sitting in her living room and reading a book, this time for pleasure, not for professional reasons. She had a glass of Porto on her coffee table, and was comfortably sitting on a folding armchair, focusing on the book she was reading, relishing the mellow taste of wine in her mouth. It was Thomas Mann's first novel, "The Budenbrooks". A two-volume German story that would take its readers to the fascinating era of the turn of the 19th and 20th century. She was totally absorbed with it. There was peace and quiet around her; no music, no radio, and complete silence. There was a sound of thunder heard tearing the sky somewhere in the distance, but Evy barely paid attention to it.

She reached for the glass and, to her amazement, it was gone. Unwillingly, she looked on the floor, convinced she must have knocked it over, but there was no broken glass nor spilled wine on the carpet. She put the book aside and looked around the room. She felt her heart pounding. She wasn't alone, it suddenly became obvious; however she couldn't *see* anyone. Despite the bizarre situation, Evy, quite unexpectedly, realized she wasn't scared, nor disturbed. To tell the truth she was waiting for that visit; hoping it would happen. And jasmine. She felt it again. Out of nowhere, intense. Overwhelming.

"Jeff?" she whispered. Nobody answered. It was something unexplainable, but in spite of feeling uneasy, she was becoming aroused. Yes, she wanted him, yes she was waiting for him, and yes she loved the other night, and was hoping for another feast of senses. But where was he? Suddenly, she felt a drop of wine falling gently down her neck. It was falling lazily, caressing first the area behind her ear, then a curve around her cartoid, and timidly flowing down her cleavage. It was as if the drop was teasing her. It was very gentle, but it set her body on fire. This was it, he was here. Another drop followed, it was a bit tingling, but truly electrifying. It was also on its way down to her cleavage, but it was intercepted by lips. Jeff gently licked it from Evy's neck, his tongue went up, and he was now caressing her ear. He was kneeling behind her armchair.

"Did you miss me?" he whispered. His voice was harsh and low-pitched. Evy watered her lips to say something, but could not find any words, so she simply exposed her neck and looked at him. She felt another drop, lurking down her neck to her cleavage. He followed this one as well. This time he caught it much lower. Jeff started unbuttoning her shirt and took it off her shoulders, exposing her black bra. He put his fingers under its straps and touched her skin.

"How did you get in here?" she murmured.

"It does not matter, Evy," he whispered.

She licked her lips and leaned her head backwards. Jeff was now scenting her skin and kissing her neck.

"Nothing matters now, only you and me."

❧62❧

Evy woke up feeling sun rays caressing her cheek. She slowly opened her eyes and spotted she hadn't pulled down the roller-blind. She rubbed her neck and looked up. She was in her bedroom, but she couldn't recall how she got there. She was covered with a quilt and completely naked. Evy looked at the clock; 5.30 am.

"Jesus," she whispered and realized she was thirsty.

Evy turned on the other side. Jeff wasn't there. She was alone. Was this how it was going to be? She would spend crazy, sensual, amazing nights with him but he would be gone before the alarm clock would start waking her up? Was he a goddamn vampire, or something? Evy spotted a pinkish stain on her carpet. Surprised, she took a closer look and realized there was an empty bottle of wine lying on the floor, her glass was standing right next to it. And it wasn't the Porto she was drinking earlier, it was another bottle. Looked like the wine was pretty important last night. Too bad she couldn't remember any of it... She stood the bottle up correctly and sat on the bed. The bedroom was a total mess. Her cosmetics were left on the dressing table as some were scattered all over the floor, the mirror on the wall was moved, and a small lamp on the night table was on the floor. Apparently they had pretty ferocious sex. Evy looked at her body and was expecting to see lots of bruises and scratches, but she was perfectly fine. She got out from the bed, pulled down the roller-blind and went to the kitchen to drink some water. It was funny, she felt as if she was having a hangover; thirsty, confused, and sensing headache pulsing stronger and stronger under her skull. Evy took out a bottle of mineral water from her fridge and drank few gulps. She swallowed some painkillers, opened the window in the kitchen and looked outside. There was a complete silence, after all it wasn't even 6 o'clock yet and it was a lazy Saturday morning. After a few minutes, Evy came back to her bedroom, again looked around stunned and decided she still needed some sleep.

***

Jeff was sure he was getting sick. He felt cold almost the entire night. Around 1 a.m. he woke up and realized he was shivering. It was irritating

231

because he fell asleep not more than an hour earlier, unable to relax after the MODENA news, and now he felt cold all over his body. Angry, he got up, closed the window in his bedroom and went to his wardrobe. He took a blanket and went back to bed. The solution did not help, though, and twenty minutes later Jeff got up again, covered himself with the blanket and went to the kitchen to make himself some hot milk. His grandmother would always give him hot milk with honey to warm him up during cold winter evenings. It always helped. While he was waiting for milk to get warm, he searched his apartment, looking for possible sources of the unpleasant chill. He found nothing suspicious, and he started thinking he was really getting the flu, it was as simple as that. What was really strange was that the cold was appearing as waves. It was very intense only to disappear few minutes later.

Since he was awake, Jeff started again thinking about the unexpected situation he had been faced with. Apart from the fact he had no idea why Jake would do what he had done, he had to decide what to do next. The most natural thing would be to confront Jake about this whole mess and force him (but how?) to undo the harm he had done. No, the most natural thing would be to beat the shit out of him, Jeff thought and smiled. The image of teaching Pinett a lesson was simply delightful. Who knew, perhaps one day he might even do it, heaven knew the son of a bitch deserved it. The most important thing for now would be, however, to analyze what was the better thing to do: getting Jake and, perhaps, saving the contract with MODENA, or looking for a new job, perhaps in a different publishing house. The first solution was definitely tempting, but the second one seemed more pragmatic. At least now. At almost 2 a.m. Jeff felt another wave of cold penetrating his body, tightened the blanket around him and checked the milk. It was now hot, so he poured it into a mug and added two spoons of honey to it. He stirred it and drank all of it. It felt wonderful. He came back to bed and hoped he could get some sleep.

***

Jeff woke up around 10 a.m. He felt great. He hadn't had the shivers again that night and the milk and honey drink helped him fall asleep. He stretched, and turned on the left side toward the window. Sunlight was curiously lurking into his bedroom. He opened the blinds and allowed the light to fill up the room. He looked at his watch and discovered he slept for over eight hours. He felt rested and full of energy. And now he knew it. No dickhead like Jake would ruin everything he had worked for for months by one idiotic phone call. Nope. He was going to get him. And the idea on how to do that was slowly appearing in his head.

❧63❧

After breakfast, Jeff started looking for Neil Jackson's business card. Neil had been working in the paper industry for twelve years. He and Jeff met when Richards was working as a manager of a small designer company four years ago. They were preparing signs, logos and watermarks that were to be printed on all possible surfaces and that, at one point, brought Neil and Jeff together. Neil needed some unique drawings for a limited edition of stationery and chose Jeff's company to do it. They both got on well with each other and after a few business lunches and basketballs games, they were pretty good friends, Neil moved to New York two years ago and now their contact was less intense. Jeff thought about him under such circumstances because he hoped Neil's experience in paper and publishing businesses would somehow bring him closer to reveal Jake's scam. Neil knew a lot of people, people who might have turned out to be helpful.

He found the card and took out his cell phone, prepared himself a strong espresso and sat on the sofa in the living room. He stretched his legs on the coffee table and pushed the dial button. Neil wasn't answering, but Jeff was okay with it; he remembered his friend had a habit of turning off his cell during the weekends. Richards had always thought it was a very healthy thing to do. At the same point Jeff thought he would spend the weekend not worrying about the Printing Gate as there was nothing he could do about it during the next two days. Also, he had a premonition everything would resolve itself. He couldn't explain it, but he almost felt, *physically* felt, Jake's despair once he was done with him. He smirked. He loved the idea.

Jeff thought that since he did not have any ideas for the weekend, he might try to ask Evy out for a coffee. After all, she must have felt really bad after the meeting, and since everything seemed to be under control, he wanted to cheer her up and let her know he was no longer angry with her. He searched her number on his cell and called.

Evy was up. She was feeling much better, the headache was gone, and she was making a shopping list when her phone called. She looked at the screen and was quite surprised to see what it displayed. Would he now always call her after their bizarre late-night meetings? She hesitated for a second, but finally picked the phone up.

"Hello?"

"Hi, Evy!" Jeff said warmly. Hearing his voice made her heart beat stronger. She had no idea if it was due to what was happening at night or was it because she was simply glad he called.

"Hi, Jeff, what's up?"

"I'm good. Listen, I was wondering if you had any plans for today?"

"Not particularly, no. Why?" "I would love to ask you out for coffee somewhere around lunch time. What would you say?"

Evy smiled. That seemed like a great idea. She was pretty worried about their relationship after she had failed him the day before, but apparently everything was fine again.

"I'd love that! Where should we meet?"

"I've been thinking about that small café at Shawmut Avenue, do you know where it is?"

"The one near Hanson Street?"

"Yeah, exactly. Do you like that place?"

"I do, it's very cozy."

"Okay, so see you there. Is 1 p.m. fine with you?"

"It's perfect. See you."

She put the phone back on the table and smiled. So, apparently, Alyssa was using her charm on different levels. Great! Evy came back to her bedroom and looked at the mess she hadn't cleaned up yet. It no longer seemed that much disturbing.

64

Around 1:30 p.m. Evy entered the café. Jeff was already sitting by the table and waved to her. She waved back and went his direction. The place was very stylish and charming. The interior was wooden and the tables were dressed with purple cloths. Despite the fact that it was a sunny and warm day, all the windows had their shades stretched, giving shelter to the heat. Jeff picked a table next to an open window.

"Hi, sorry I'm late, the traffic was insane," said Evy.

"No problem, I'm glad you're here," Jeff said as he stood, pulling out her chair. *Yeah, it seems you're really good at being late, aren't you?* He heard a mean voice inside his head. Surprised by his own thoughts, Jeff made sure he did not say it out loud and helped Evy take her seat. A waitress named Rhonda came to them to take their order. Evy asked for a Crème Brule latte with cinnamon sprinkle and Jeff decided to try the café's double espresso with cream. On his way to the café, he considered telling her about Jake's sabotage. It felt personal for him and, truthfully, he wanted to wait until he resolved the whole misunderstanding.. On the other hand, Evy was his partner, so she had to know OMNIBUS was about to face some pretty nasty problems.

"So, how has your weekend been so far?" Evy asked and smiled.

"Pretty good. Actually, I'm worried I might be getting the flu or something because for the past couple of nights I have felt chills all over my body."

Yeah, I know what you mean. "Like shivers?" she asked.

"Exactly. They were pretty strange and then gone when the morning came. I have no idea what it was, but it was intense."

"Strange. I did not sleep well last night either." Evy looked at Jeff curious to see if there was any trace of him knowing what she was talking about, but she did not see anything.

"Why?"

"No idea. Sometimes I just can't fall asleep."

Rhonda brought their coffees. The pleasant smell of freshly ground beans filled the air around their table. Evy took a sip and Jeff couldn't resist looking at the tip of her nose decorated with foam. At first he thought she looked silly, in a cute sense, but a second later he realized she simply looked ridiculous. *What was she, five?*

Evy wiped her nose and looked at Jeff a bit embarrassed. He smiled at her, she smiled back, but couldn't resist the feeling that his smile was kind of forced.

"I need to tell you something. You're not going to like it."

"What is it?"

"Looks like things with OMNIBUS will not go as smoothly as we have planned."

"What happened?"

Jeff leaned on his chair and told Evy about the conversation he had with Abram. He told her about the so-called *anonymous* phone call to MODENA and how the printing house no longer had its arms opened to greet them and work for them. Evy was listening to him carefully hoping for a minute he was joking. He wasn't. He really wasn't.

"So it was Jake who called?"

"Mhm," he replied drinking coffee.

"You're entirely sure?"

"Mhm, yes."

"What are we going to do now?"

"I have a good friend who has been present in the paper business for a long time, he might know some people that could help me."

Evy sat quietly for a second. This was serious. There was a huge difference between being mean and boorish during board meetings and sabotage. *What a weasel. What a fucking weasel.* Suddenly, a thought appeared in her head.

"Do you sometimes log on to the Intranet?"

"No. I am a manager, I don't have the need to read some crap about me being a loser forcing people to work." Jeff laughed.

"Yeah, I hardly ever go there myself, but I was in the office yesterday."

"You were? Why?"

"Oh, I forgot to take something from my desk. Anyway, I logged to the Intranet, out of the blue, to see what was happening, and I saw a strange topic on the chat, saying that Jake was up to something, that he was going to sabotage your plans to take your position."

"When did that appear?"

"I am not sure, on Monday maybe?"

"And when did you see it?"

"On Thursday"

Jeff was looking at her very intensively. He couldn't believe what she was telling him.

"Jake called MODENA on Friday morning, before our meeting with the board. You knew since Thursday that Jake was probably planning sabotaging me. *Us.* How could you not immediately tell me about this? Evy, for the love of God! If you had told me about this the *moment* you read the posts, I could have printed them and confronted them with Jake and the board! Jesus!"

Evy was stunned. She had never seen Jeff so upset and it was all her fault. Again! Not even after the meeting did he look like that! She felt terrible! She remembered thinking she needed to tell him about all this, but then she got up late for the meeting, and then she forgot—oh God, she forgot because first she was focused on searching for something belonging to Jeff in his office and then she was busy having wild sex with a phantom Jeff-like lover. Oh my God!

She felt she was about to cry. Looking at his anger and disappointment, she wanted to run away.

"Jeff, I don't know what to say—I thought it was simply office gossip."

"I have no idea what is happening with you, Evelyn. I thought we were a team, but apparently it was only *my* point of view."

"No, please, we *are* a team. You know I have never failed you before! And I never will again!"

"You bet you won't!" Jeff got up and went out. Evy ran after him.

"Jeff, what are you saying?"

"I don't know, Evy. I need to think. Leave me alone," he replied and went to his car. Evy ran after him and was standing on the parking lot, completely shattered, looking at him getting into his car and driving away.

"Hey, lady! There's a check to pay!" she heard Rhonda shouting behind her.

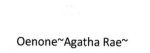

Oenone~Agatha Rae~

65

Jeff was furious. He had no idea what was going on with Evy and he did not really care to find out. Yesterday it turned out she was unprofessional, now it appeared she was also not loyal. Richards could not comprehend how it was possible she had changed so much within a few days. At the beginning of this week he decided to make her the manager of OMNIBUS and was hoping that once all this pandemonium was over, maybe it would be possible for them to be together. Today, right now, he felt he wouldn't want to see her again. But this, although painful, was not the biggest problem; Jake-motherfucker-Pinett was. Never in his life had Jeff wanted to beat someone up as much as he wanted to now. Fucking loser. *Fucking smirking loser.*

Jeff was so angry he decided to pull over and stop the car for a few minutes. He felt the blood buzzing inside his head, stampeding under his temples. He had to calm down and think what to do next. First of all he had to check the forum, hoping the posts were still there. Secondly, he had to speak to David, this had gone way too far; Garbinsky had to know what was going on in his own company. Besides, Jeff needed a backup and he also had to have a good reason to explain why MODENA changed its mind. It was quite possible Jake had already told him about Jeff's problems, proud of his own achievement, but Richards had always had David's support, hence, since the chairman hadn't told him anything yet, he most probably didn't know what was going on.

God damn it, Evy!

Jeff leaned on his chair, closed his eyes and sighed. What a nightmare. What a fucking nightmare. All those months of hard work, planning, calling, booking, searching, editing, the pressure of time limit, countless meetings, everything was now jeopardized and Evy *forgot* to tell him something *that* important. That was unreal. That was beyond any comprehension.

After a few minutes, when he was able to think clearly again, Jeff turned the engine on and headed toward the office.

Jake better not be there, or so help me God, he thought while getting into the gear.

Oenone~Agatha Rae~

~66~

"Come on, what's taking you so long?" laughed Laura, looking down at her husband struggling with steps leading towards the Vancouver Art Gallery. She was almost to the top and Bruce was moving at a snail's pace, barely reaching half of the distance. This was their second day in British Columbia and the first day in Vancouver. They were planning to spend two days there and visit some local attractions including Science World, Capilano and Gastown. The weather was fantastic.

The Levinsons were staying in a huge RV in Osoyoos. They enjoyed the lake and the beach during the day and spent a wonderful evening preparing and eating a delicious dinner and drinking wine from a local vineyard. Lying on the bed nestling, and listening to crickets' concert in the high grass around their RV; they both felt they were regenerating and resting after all those difficult months that had passed. The next day they rented a car and headed to Vancouver for two days.

Bruce was not feeling too well and Laura had been aware of that for some days now. He was often tired, and had visible problems walking long distances. Whenever Laura asked him what was wrong, he would just wave his hand in a "there's no problem" gesture, ignoring both her questions and his symptoms. He was assuring her (although Laura had a feeling he was rather assuring himself) that he had been running too much after the longer break and, apparently, strained his body and was now paying for it. She even asked him three days before their trip if they should postpone it.

"It's not a big deal, Laura, no worries, I'm fine," he told her and kissed the tip of her nose, which always made her smile. She believed him because in her worst nightmares she would never assume what was actually coming. Her husband was simply tired, exhausted by the struggle they both had faced. Period.

Today, apart from feeling weak, he was also pale. Before coming to Vancouver, Laura had asked him few times if he really wanted to go, after all, they could just stay in Osoyoos, enjoy the sunshine and water, but Bruce did not even want to hear about it. She had to admit that he did look better once they arrived in the city. After strolling down the downtown and stopping for lunch, they decided to visit the gallery. Seeing her husband struggling hopelessly to catch her up on the stone stairs, Laura felt fear piercing her heart. Something was wrong. She had no doubt about it.

"It's ok, Bruce, don't rush," she said walking down to him. He looked at her both hopelessly and surprised and sat down on the stairs. He took a bottle of water out of his backpack and was now thirstily drinking it. Laura sat next to him and put her hand on his back.

"What's wrong, honey?" she asked softly.

He looked at her, screwed the bottle cap on tight and shook his head.

"I don't know. I have no idea."

At that moment Laura felt she was on the verge of panicking. If her husband was confessing he did not feel good, it meant the situation was becoming serious. Normally, he would never admit anything was wrong with him, they often joked that if he had a finger cut off, he would try to convince everyone it was just a scratch and there was no need to bother any doctors. Now they were sitting in the middle of not too high steps and he looked as if he was about to have a heart attack. By the look on his face, Laura was able to see he couldn't comprehend what was happening.

"I can't catch my breath, Laura," he finally said with disbelief.

Laura was looking at him for a while, and for a second, she hoped he was joking. She was actually waiting for him to stop so they could both laugh together and she would tell him how dumb he was. However, Bruce was perfectly serious and it terrified her.

"You mean you're tired?"

"I mean I can't catch my breath," he replied a bit irritated. "I feel pretty weak."

"We don't have to go to the gallery if you don't feel like it."

"It's not that I don't like it, Laura. I *can't* go there. Those steps are going to kill me, I know it."

"Bruce, what is wrong? You're scaring me," she whispered.

He drank some more water and wiped his face with his palm. *Damn it, why did it have to be so hot there.*

"I haven't been feeling too well lately."

"What do you mean?"

"I mean exactly that. I've been having problems while running. I was unable to run the distance I used to have no problems with for some days now. At first, I thought it was because I had a break and that it was a matter of time until I was able to run like that again. But has gotten worse. The night before we left I wasn't able to run more than one mile. I—I have no idea what is happening."

"Why didn't you tell me?"

"Jesus, Laura, I don't know. I didn't want to worry you," he replied irritated again. All those questions were becoming annoying. There he was, admitting to being weak, sick probably, feeling terrible for spoiling such an important holiday for her, and she kept asking him those stupid questions. *Why and what all the time. Damn it.*

"Are you kidding me right now?"

"It's true! You've just gotten yourself out of your mess; what was I supposed to tell you? I don't even know what is wrong!"

Laura was very disturbed, but she only embraced her husband tightly. They were sitting there on the steps of Vancouver Art Gallery in complete silence. The sun was pouring down on them and people were walking up and down the stairs unaware of the drama the Levinsons were facing.

"Can you get up?" Laura asked.

"Yes."

"Then come on. We're going back."

"Going back where?"

"Home."

Oenone~Agatha Rae~

❧67❧

Jeff entered WORDS and immediately went to his office. He turned on the computer and walked to the break room to get something to drink. He opened the fridge and found a can of soda.

This will do, he thought and opened it. A quiet hissing sound and the sweet scent of coke filled his nostrils and Jeff got back to his office. He logged into the Intranet and swiftly found the board Evy mentioned. He searched the list of topics several times, but was unable to find anything Jake-related. He scrolled the screen up and down about a dozen of times and thought it was probably due to his emotions that he wasn't able to find it. Irritated, he left the room and started walking nervously around the office.

What the hell are you doing? he thought to himself, this was not him to be so unstable. This was not the way to get rid of Pinett. He had to be calm, he had to have a plan. Jeff sat on a chair behind one of the desks and sighed, drank some soda and leaned his back and head on its headrest and started looking pointlessly at the ceiling. He looked to the right and saw his office. It occurred to him he was sitting by Evy's desk.

Evy.

She made a terrible mistake by not telling him about the forum, but he was way too harsh for her. She was clearly devastated by his reaction. Her help had been invaluable and, truthfully, he had never asked her *why* she forgot to tell him about the forum, nor why she arrived unprepared for the meeting. Knowing her to be as reliable as she was, it could have occurred to him that perhaps there was a reason she hadn't been her usual fail-safe herself.

Jeff sighed again and got up. He sat by his computer again and, with a clearer mind started looking for the topic one more time. He read everything carefully, used the search field on the page for "scam", "Jake", "Pinett" and "printing house".

Nothing. For the sake of his mind he also typed "motherfucker" and "asshole". Surprisingly, still, nothing. Apparently the users of the Intranet did not know Pinett that well. Jeff smiled bitterly. Of course all the evidence that something was going on was gone. He searched for the admin information on the website, but the only thing he was able to find was that its name was WORDS and there was no other way of asking about anything than by filling out a form on the website. That was the only contact. Jeff looked at it for few seconds, considered using it, but he quickly dropped the idea. It was probably Jake who was the admin, after all, why would the posts accusing him of sabotage have disappeared so fast? It had only been two days since Evy had seen them.

Jeff turned the computer off and was sitting in his office in a complete silence. His thoughts started focusing on Evy again; he looked at the corner of his room, and recalled the moment when they were sitting there, discussing their trip to Westville. At that point, he started recalling the Written Word festival, especially the night they spent together in his room. He remembered the feeling that she was the person he wanted to be with. Now that they got to know each other so much better, she simply felt like home. She *was* home. Immediately Jeff recalled the next morning and the uncomfortable feeling instantly came back. He got up and started picking up his things to leave when his cell phone rang. It was Evy. Quite surprised, Jeff picked up.

"Hi, Evy," he said.

"Thank you for answering. I was afraid you wouldn't want to talk with me," Evy replied relieved.

"I was thinking about you." "You were?"

"I wanted to call you to apologize for my behavior in the café."

Evy was quiet for a minute. Sitting on the sofa in her apartment, she felt as if a major weight was lifted off her shoulders. She was afraid he would not want to speak to her, but the sense of guilt and the terrifying vision of losing his friendship, of losing *him* basically, pushed her to swallow her fear and to call him.

"I totally understand your reaction. I made a terrible mistake, and I am *really, really* sorry."

"I am in the office. I checked the Intranet, the board, but the posts are gone."

"I should have made screen shots; I am such an idiot."

"Well, what's done is done. I am sorry I have never given you a chance to explain to me why you forgot to tell me about all this. I understand something very important must have been occupying your mind lately."

Yeah, getting it on with you in apparently every room in my apartment, Evy thought. "That's okay, I'll tell you later, once it all is over."

"Sounds good. I hope it's nothing serious, though."

"So, what are we going to do with Jake?"

"I have an idea, but I need to wait until Monday."

"Isn't what he did a crime? I mean he is trying to discredit you, to shatter your reputation."

"I know. I think it is something that lawyers ought to take a closer look at, but first of all, I am only assuming it was him and secondly, right now, I just want to get him. At this stage, it's personal."

"Are you sure you know what you're doing?"

"Oh yes. I am."

"So, are we good? I really hope you're no longer mad at me."

"I am not, I promise," he said softly, but the tone of his voice was only to cover his true feelings; he was still quite angry, Evy had immensely complicated his life because of her mindlessness.

"We'll get him, Jeff. I know we will."

"Thanks. I will let you know as soon as I know anything, all right?"

"Sure, that would be great."

"And I hope I might count on another coffee with you, if you're not scared of me, that is," he said and smiled.

"I'd love that."

Oenone~Agatha Rae~

~68~

When the Levinsons got to their hotel, Bruce was feeling better, but he was still pretty pale. Laura gave him some water and he laid down on the bed. She lowered the blinds and the room felt pleasantly chill. She sat beside him and gently touched his forehead.

"You don't have fever," she said.

"I know I don't, I'm just very tired. And weak."

Laura went to the bathroom, took a towel from a shelf, turned on the faucet and poured cold water on it. She wrung it and got back to the bedroom. Bruce laid on his back, and Laura got him a pillow to rest his head on and put the moist towel on his forehead. Its soothing touch brought him relief. He closed his eyes and, for a minute, Laura thought he was asleep.

"I'm sorry I've spoilt this day," Bruce said quietly.

"Don't be silly," she replied softly, "I couldn't care less about that right now."

She laid beside her husband, put her arm around him and kissed him on the cheek. He smiled sadly and put his hand on her palm. Laura thought the moment they were sharing was more intimate than sex. They were quiet for some time and finally she said, "I think we should get back to Boston. You need to see a doctor."

Bruce opened his eyes and looked at her attentively.

"I will be fine in a minute. Or two."

"You can be fine in three seconds, that's not the point. The point is you're sick and you need to see a doctor."

He closed his eyes again and swallowed loudly.

"You're right, something is wrong with me."

Of all the things her husband could have ever told her, that was what would scare her most. After all the years they had spent together, there was nobody as close to her as Bruce. He was her best friend, her lover, her shelter. Now that he had once again admitted he did not feel good, she froze. Obviously it was something more serious, she could tell that by how weak he was, but his admitting to it felt awful.

"What is it, honey, what is happening?" she asked him, stroking gently his forehead.

"I've been having problems breathing for some time. Usually after some physical effort. That's pretty much it, but it's getting worse, the symptoms. I mean, I thought I would faint on that stairs.", He looked at her and the anxiety in his eyes terrified her.

She leaned toward him and kissed him. Bruce closed his eyes again.

"We're going home," Laura said.

"Honey, I'm sorry I messed up. This trip was supposed to celebrate your coming back to health and I couldn't feel worse spoiling it for you."

"Shh." She put her finger on his lips, "Don't even think like that. You're everything I have, Bruce, you're my entire world. I couldn't care less about that trip if it meant you being sick. I love you. I love you so much." She kissed him again and felt some tears falling down her cheeks.

"What's this?" he asked surprised.

She hid her face in the mattress and said, "I feel awful because we've been so focused on my problems that we might have missed something bad happening to you." She sobbed.

"Honey, don't even talk like that. Your life, your health are the most important things to me, and I cannot imagine *not* being focused on you during the past months."

She looked at him with both gratitude and love in her sight. He embraced her and she laid her head on his chest. He was instinctively stroking her hair and they dozed for some time after.

Bruce and Laura decided to go back to Boston the next morning. They checked out from the hotel and got back to Osoyoos, spent the evening sitting by the lake, watching a picturesque sunset. None of them wanted to say it out loud, but they were both afraid.

~69~

On Sunday afternoon Jeff looked at the screen of his ringing cell phone and smiled when he saw Neil Jackson's number on the display. He answered immediately.

"Hi, Neil, how are you?" he said friendly.

"Hi Jeff, I'm good, how are you doing?"

"I'm okay."

"That good, huh?" Neil laughed. Apparently Jeff did not sound too convincing.

"Yeah, what can I say, I'm having some trouble here."

"I must say I was suspecting something because I haven't heard of you for quite some time and suddenly there are two missed calls displaying on my phone. I thought something might be happening. What is it? Can I help you somehow?"

"Actually yes, I kind of hope you can. I am having business problems and I know you're still in the paper industry, which might help me a bit. I thought you could give me a hand."

"I'll be glad to do that, Jeff. However, I have no time to go to Boston. Listen, I'm going to be in Providence on Tuesday, I have some business to take care of there, maybe we could meet for lunch? Or would you prefer to talk on the phone?"

"No, no, meeting in Providence sounds great! Thanks so much, I'll be there. Just let me know when and where."

"Will do."

"Thanks, Neil."

"No problem. See you on Tuesday."

Neil hung up. He hadn't seen Jeff for nearly two years, but they called and e-mailed each other quite regularly. Their friendship became a bit loose once Neil moved to New York. He knew what a great manager Jeff was, very professional, easy-going and creative, so it was quite strange to hear he was having business-related problems. Richards was a good guy, they used to hang out a lot when Neil was still living in Boston, so he was eager to help him. Not to mention he was intrigued because Jeff was not the kind of guy who'd look for help without a good reason.

Oenone~Agatha Rae~

70

Evy was trying to call Laura, but her friend's phone was turned off. Apparently they were having a great time in Canada and did not want to be disturbed. She turned on the TV and discovered that apart from few pretty bad comedy series there was absolutely nothing to watch. Evy turned it off and looked at her desk. Another book was there waiting to be edited, but she couldn't force herself to even touch it. Being full of energy and having no idea what to do with herself, she figured she would go to the gym. The treadmill seemed to be a good idea. Laura and Evy liked calling it "dreadmill" or "threadmill". She smiled when she thought of it. It felt like ages since they had both been to the gym.

Evy took out her gym bag, put a towel, a shampoo and a bottle of water into it. She checked her mp3 player to see if it was charged and left her home.

Fifteen minutes later, she parked Bob in front of the fitness center and walked inside. It was almost 9 p.m. so there was hardly anyone there, but the fitness center was open until 11.30, so Evy still had some time to work out.

***

At the same time Bruce and Laura were on a plane flying home. Bruce looked much better, he was dozing with his head leaned on a pillow and she was sitting next to him, holding his hand. It occurred to her she had not let him go for a second since they got on the plane.

The flight was to take about five hours. Bruce had been sleeping for over an hour. There was some dumb comedy on the screen, but Laura was unable to focus on the plot. From time to time she would unintentionally glance at the monitor in front of her when she heard people laughing, but she was completely absent-minded.

Laura was thinking about what had been happening in her life for the past few months. The cancer was completely unexpected, but all the trouble she was in because of it, she had to admit it, was at least partly due to her own neglect. Would she have avoided the trouble if she took care of herself? Hard to say, but maybe her condition would have been less serious. It was over now, but she had to keep on reminding herself that she was now safe and sound; it was all so fresh and seemed fragile. As much as she could comprehend and rationalize her cancer, she was unable to understand how it was possible that five minutes after her problems were gone, Bruce was apparently becoming seriously sick. The lack of strength, paleness, weakness. She was suspecting heart. Perhaps a heart attack was getting near. Of course he might have simply been weak due to everything they both had been through, but a voice inside her head kept telling her the problem was much worse.

She gripped his hand more tightly. Whatever was about to happen, she would not let him go.

71

The workout was fantastic. Evy loved those moments in the gym when she could simply indulge in her thoughts, focus on her plans and loosen her muscles. It was like a purifying ritual which she was always looking forward to. Having headphones in her ears, she was running on a treadmill and going through everything that had happened. She was thinking about Jeff's problems and how she had magnified them, about Laura's miraculous healing, which was simply amazing, and, of course, about the two wild evenings in her apartment. Despite having problems figuring out what in fact had happened, she had to admit it, she was hoping for more of such blissful moments. Evy was preparing her plan of work for the next couple of days when her treadmill started beeping, informing her the workout was over. She slowed down and was marching for few more minutes, drinking water and drying her head and neck with a towel. Finally she finished and went to the changing room to undress and get ready for the sauna. Evy put her clothes into a bag, wrapped a towel around her body and slipped flip-flops on her feet. She entered the sauna chamber and realized there was nobody inside. Evy sat on a wooden shelf, turned an hourglass on the wall and laid down.

After about thirty minutes, Evy walked out of the sauna, sweaty and exhausted and headed toward the showers. The area was dark, only with some city lights illuminating the bathroom from the outside, she walked to the shower stall, put shampoo and gel on a top shelf on the wall and poured the water. Tepid drops were wetting her sticky hair and cooling her body. The feeling of single drops penetrating all the curves of her body and teasing her skin felt very pleasant. Evy closed her eyes and bent her head down allowing the water to bliss her neck. It felt wonderful and relaxing.

Jasmine. She could smell it again.

She reached up for the gel and suddenly a man's hand outdistanced her and took the plastic bottle first. Shocked, Evy wanted to scream at, but his right hand covered her mouth and she heard him whispering to her ear.

"It's okay, Evy, it's me, don't be scared," Jeff said directly to her ear. He was kissing her neck, her ear's petal and breathing in the smell of her wet hair. Evy closed her eyes and allowed him to distribute the gel all over her body. She felt the smoothness of his hands and the silky touch of foam, shamelessly covering her entirely. Evy leaned her neck back and put her head on his shoulder. When he reached to her hips she turned around and touched the wall with her back. He lifted her up and when she embraced him with her legs, he leaned her against it. The city lights were coquettishly dancing on the stall's curtain and Evy felt she was simply losing her mind. They were swinging and allowing the desire to take over. Evy loved his gentle dominance. Good God, how she wanted him…

***

Evy's cell phone was vibrating in her backpack in the locker. Laura was waiting for her to pick up.

***

She opened her eyes and she was lying on one of deckchairs outside the sauna, covered with her towel. Evy looked around and realized she was dry and clean. Apparently she took a shower. And apparently Jeff was gone again. It amazed her how powerful those fantasies had become and it made her realize that someone might have seen her. Alarmed she looked around the area, but there was nobody there. Evy stood up and walked toward her locker stunned, confused and worried that all those things that she had been experiencing were possible outside her apartment. Since she had no control over it and was unable to predict them, it seemed a quite unsettling discovery.

72

Jeff woke up on Monday morning just before 5 a.m. He lazily looked at the clock on his bedside table. He did not sleep well. He felt cold again and he kept thinking about Jake and all the mess that was happening with MODENA and OMNIBUS. He went to bed around 11 pm and then he started having the shivers again. He was getting really tired of that. It was already the third time and, as unexpectedly as they would appear, they would also be gone rapidly. He was more and more convinced it was some peculiar reaction for the business-related troubles he had been facing lately.

He walked to his kitchen, and put the radio on; "Morning Edition" was on air. Jeff switched on a coffee machine. He poured the hot, aromatic coffee into a mug, sat by the table, rubbed his tired and unshaved face and one more time thought of his plan for that day. He felt very tired, but it was obvious he would not sleep a minute longer; his thoughts were running through his head in a wild speed, not allowing him to rest. The morning was quite cool; it was the beginning of September, and the far less pleasant aura than in the previous months was announcing fall getting closer. The sun was just rising and so the air had not been warmed yet, Jeff got up off his chair and opened the window. Chilly air hit his face, but it felt good; he hoped that the strong coffee and the refreshing blow of air on his skin might be just what he needed to wake up effectively.

First of all, he needed to meet with David. He wanted to tell him about his suspicions, the forum and the whole MODENA situation. David needed to know what was going on, because if there was one thing Richards would want to avoid was letting the chairman down. Garbinsky had always stood beside him and supported him, so he had to know that Jeff's unexpected situation was a result of some nasty intrigues and not his incompetence.

David would appear in WORDS quite seldom. It was his privilege as a chairman that he would come to work unless a situation called for it. It would be for example a board meeting or some paramount announcement for the staff. One of the things that Jeff admired his boss for was that he would always show up in a conference room and deliver the news, no matter if it were good or bad, directly to his employees. He never allowed anybody else to do it for him. It built the sense of respect toward him, people knew he was one of them and that he considered himself to be a member of the staff.

Since David did not have any meetings scheduled for that day, as Jeff had checked in the office on Saturday, he decided to go to Garbinsky's home and tell him everything that had been bothering him about Jake. For a second, Jeff hesitated and started wondering if it would not look as if he was looking for a shelter after having his ass kicked by Pinett, but the need of letting David know what was happening in the company he brought to life was stronger. He was going to call him about 10 am and ask his for a meeting.

Richards was also glad that Neil had time to see him. It had been quite long since they talked and it seemed that Jackson was willing to help him. His experience could be priceless, not to mention that Jeff was simply happy he would see his good friend again.

He checked the clock. It was 6.30 a.m. and Jeff rubbed his face again. His eyes felt irritated as if there was sand in them. He needed to sleep some more; it was out of question. Jeff closed the window, took his mug, poured the coffee down the sink and came back to the bedroom. He laid down and tried to fall asleep.

***

Evy woke up around 9 o'clock, with a smile on her face, stretched and sat on her bed. After yesterday evening she had a great sleep and it was pretty obvious that the treadmill was not the only reason for that. She pulled up the blinds; it looked like it was going to be a rather cloudy day.

Evy went to the kitchen and opened the fridge.

"I need to go shopping," she said to herself, looking inside and taking the very last raspberry yogurt out. She took a spoon from the drawer and put the kettle on to make herself some coffee. While waiting for the water to boil, Evy took a newspaper from her doormat and sat by the kitchen table. The moment she opened the lid, the telephone rang. Surprised at who could be calling her at this time of the day, she walked toward the bedroom where the telephone was.

On her way there, Evy hesitated and stopped for a second, because she felt something very weird growing inside her body. At the same time the familiar scent of jasmine appeared around her. It felt very distracting. Deep down in her guts, she felt a very peculiar warmth, a warmth that was growing, becoming stronger and which was now filling up almost her entire body. Confused, Evy sat on the floor, unable to move. The telephone ringing sounded as if it was coming from another apartment, muffled, vague, all she could hear was her heart pounding and the blood thumping in her veins. Suddenly, the warmth she was experiencing, changed into bliss. She was no longer worried, instead she felt a gigantic wave of sexual pleasure appearing in her body, growing, becoming stronger. It was taking her senses into possession and finally, when Evy thought she would no longer stand the insane heart-beat, the tension changed into a gigantic orgasm. The spasm of delight shook her body from head to toe and she moaned with bliss.

At that moment, everything stopped. Evy was lying on the floor for few more minutes, trying to comprehend what had just happened. She felt the drops of sweat on her forehead, and her pulse slowly coming back to normal. Evy closed her eyes and swallowed. The impression was insanely real and intense. She was feeling dizzy.

A few minutes later, Evy got up and after unsuccessfully trying to recall why was she in the hallway in the first place, she returned to the kitchen. Whatever it was that happened to her was incredible, but also quite disturbing on the other hand.

***

Laura and Bruce got home on Sunday, late in the evening Eastern Time. Early morning on Monday, Bruce was admitted in emergency room and had tests performed. Laura was in a waiting room, nervously pressing a tissue in one hand and calling Evy. She was terrified and she needed to tell her friend what was happening. Unfortunately, Evy was not answering.

Laura was becoming fed up with frustration. It was not even a month yet since she was a patient, and the smell of the hospital was making her nauseous. All those doctors wearing scrubs, people with uncertainty and fear in their eyes waiting for test results or a diagnosis, pregnant women in labor, groanings of pain, needles, bottles, pills. She saw a victim of a car accident being brought to the ER, the woman had blood all over her face and t-shirt. For a second Laura thought she would throw up. She was so convinced all those things were now behind her and yet, there she was again, not as a patient this time, but if there was anything wrong with Bruce, and something *was* wrong, she knew it, then she was about to spend another part of her life in hospital surroundings.

Laura was sitting outside the room where Bruce was undergoing tests and she was fighting the tears appearing in her eyes. She felt hopeless, a feeling she had learned to detest when she was battling for her health. It had been two hours since they were admitted. All Laura was able to think about was that she had to be strong and support Bruce, just as he had supported her; unconditionally. The problem was that she was now a woman with a burden and the perspective of going through the similar fight again in such a short term seemed to be beyond her strength. What was she going to do?

The doors of the room opened and a young doctor asked her to come in. Laura got up, threw the tissue away, took a deep breath and walked inside.

David Garbinsky was at his home sitting in a study. That was the part of the house he enjoyed most and was most proud of. It had wooden oak floor, with a royal green carpet lying majestically in the middle of it, and wooden walls covered with shelves and bookcases. A heavy-looking leather sofa was standing by one of the walls and it was the only space in the office where there were no books; apart from that only wall, the books were basically everywhere. Some of them were behind doors made of glass, but most of them were standing on open shelves, tempting everyone who would come into the room with their neat hard-covers to touch them and at least page them through. Opposite the door was David's gigantic wooden desk, designed and made for him exclusively, and his beloved, massive and extremely comfortable armchair. Carol, his late wife, would often joke it was a throne rather than an armchair and that sitting on it was regularly and systematically pumping up David's ego.

The room was his asylum, his fortress. The window blinds had been constantly closed since he had started living alone. David preferred sitting in rather dark surroundings due to a slight photophobia he had been suffering from for three years since a cataract removal. He had to wear sunglasses most of the day, a feature that would put him, as he liked to joke, somewhere between Bono and Ray Charles. Under the desk he had a small drink cabinet with some whiskey and glasses.

Books were the love of his life. He had hundreds of them. Those in the office were only his favorite ones, the elite one might say. He was unable to imagine the world without books. From his point of view they were the only valuable and resistant to fashion sources of wisdom, knowledge and entertainment. David could recall all of the books he had read, never forgetting the names of the main characters and the plots. It was this hobby that led him to start a publishing house. For him, the ability of introducing new books and authors made him, well, similar to God. Every time he thought like that, he imagined Carol smiling, shaking her head in disbelief and making remarks about his ego. However, the truth was the comparison wasn't exactly baseless; he was making life better, he was giving people hope, emotions, fascinations, passions, knowledge and, from mundane point of view, jobs. WORDS was his creation. David believed there were no weak books or mediocre authors, because every book published was basically bound to find a reader. There were simply too many people around the country, around the *world*, for this not to happen. Also, David had great respect to anyone courageous enough to create a story and brave enough to show it to others and face their opinions. His point of view had led to a lot of tension between him and his editors, even the board of his own company, and he could totally understand the doubts and dilemmas. Nowadays, books were products, destined to be profitable, to earn money. David truly comprehended that, however, from time to time, he liked to remind his co-workers that a book was, first of all, a piece of a writer's soul that was laid in their hands and that nobody's talent ought to be wasted just because it would not reach hundreds of thousands of sold copies. After all, written word had had tremendous potential. It was because of written stories that we know so much about history, civilizations around the world, about the long-lost cultures. It was the written word that had given people religions, wars, ideologies, truces, exterminations, salvation. Who were they to tell if a book published now, perhaps even unappreciated at a given point in time, was not to be discovered as symbol of a zeitgeist, the era they were now living in. Books needed time. Books needed patience.

Because of his love for books, it was difficult for him to come to terms with on-line selling, e-books, audiobooks, etc. He knew Jeff's ideas were innovative and brought them a lot of money, but as far as David Garbinsky was concerned, electronic books were soulless. Or maybe he was simply getting older.

He was 59 years old. He had been a widower for over five years now. Carol died in a car accident. Even though some time had passed, there were days he missed her so much it hurt. Physically hurt. He had always thought such an expression was cliché, overdramatic, but it was true. They spent thirty-seven years together. They had one daughter, Tessa. She was now living in London with her husband and son, thus David did not see her too often, usually twice or three times a year. This year it was his turn to go there for Christmas. Even though it was only the beginning of September, he literally could not wait. He felt lonely.

Tessa had asked him numerous times to move to London. She wanted him to be near her, to see his grandson growing, but he was not able to even think about leaving the house where he and Carol spent the happiest moments of their lives. It was in this house that he made the first business plan for what was to become WORDS, it was in the living room that Carol told him she was pregnant, it was here that Tessa was getting ready for her prom, and finally it was here that he got a phone call from a hospital five years ago, informing him that he was never to be a completely happy man again. How was he supposed to leave this place? As much as it ached him that his daughter was thousands of miles away from him, he could not imagine moving anywhere.

David was looking through some invoices when his cell phone rang. He looked at the display and saw it was Jeff Richards calling him.

"Hi, Jeff, how are you?" he asked.

"Good, good, thanks, how are you, David?"

"Fine."

"Listen, David, I know you're not at work today, but I have a certain business matter I need to talk with you about."

"Can't it wait until Wednesday? I will be in my office then."

"No, I'm sorry. It's too delicate to talk about it at work." Richards could easily imagine Jake lurking and snuffing around the moment he would find out Jeff was having a one-to-one conversation with David. Fucking weasel.

"Oh?" David was vividly surprised. "Well then, if it's all right with you, maybe you could come to my home? I'm alone and have no plans for the rest of the day."

"That would be splendid. What time may I come?"

"An hour from now, would it be fine?"

"Absolutely. See you at ten, David. Thank you. Bye!"

"Bye."

David hung up. He was very curious what was going on.

Oenone~Agatha Rae~

～74～

Bruce had lung cancer. However, as the doctor, who still had acne, said "apart from this he was completely fine." It was surreal. He had never smoked, he was slim, there were no cases of any cancer in his family, and he loved sports, especially jogging. It was not even that they were both terrified, Laura and Bruce. They were simply stunned.

The young doctor explained to them, completely emotionlessly, where the cancer was located, and showed them an X-ray picture to prove he was right. He also told them that the good news was that it was an early stage, advanced enough to give symptoms, but small enough for "a little bit of radiotherapy" which ought to help. Once the treatment had been over, Bruce was bound to be as healthy as a horse. He asked them to fill out some papers and informed them that Mr. Levinson might already stay in hospital if he wanted because they checked his insurance policy and it included cancer-treatment. Looking at Laura's and Bruce's faces he simply put the papers and a pen (asking them not to lose it, as it was the hospital's property) on a small cabinet next to the bed and informed them he would be back in about thirty minutes.

When he left, Bruce looked at Laura. He had no idea what was happening.

"How is that possible, Laura?"

"I – I don't know." She grabbed his hand.

"But it's ridiculous! *Lung* cancer? How?"

"I don't know," she repeated quietly. She looked at him astutely. 'You heard what he said…"

"The Doogie Houser?"

"Yeah." She smiled. "It's an early stage and radiotherapy is enough."

"Yeah, I feel like buying a lottery ticket!" he said sarcastically.

"Bruce, listen to me. You'll be fine."

"Of course I *will* be fine. I still cannot believe this is happening! It's outrageous! Two days ago we were on vacation in Canada, planning to finally understand curling, and now *this*? It's some kind of a fucking joke. It's *gotta* be."

She looked at him and after few seconds and they both burst out laughing. They had been laughing for few minutes, provoked by the completely insane coincidence and the fact that, apparently, cancer was contagious. It all seemed so unreal, so unbelievable that they kept laughing, so hard they had tears in their eyes. After a while, Bruce calmed down, dried his eyes with his hand and looked at Laura seriously. Immediately she became solemn and sat by his bed.

"I have no idea what is happening, honey, but we'll get through this. I promise you." he said quietly.

"I know," she whispered, "I know. I just don't understand why it is happening to us. Again."

"We cannot waste energy on such thoughts, there's no point. We're having a problem and we need to deal with it."

She took him by the hand. He kissed her palm and she pressed his to her cheek with love and tenderness.

The doctor came back and quite superficially asked Bruce if he had signed the necessary papers and if he wanted to begin his treatment on that day or would he prefer to come back tomorrow.

Bruce looked at Laura, turned his head toward the doctor and said, "Let's do this."

Laura grabbed his hand harder and fought not to weep. "It sounds like a little bit of history repeating…" Laura heard Shirley Bassey's voice in her head. Until then she loved the song, at this point she knew she would hate it until the end of her days…

Jeff arrived at David's home few minutes after 10 a.m. He had been planning on what to tell him for some time, but he was still quite nervous about the meeting. To tell the truth, he was not used to admitting to failure and coming there to meet Garbinsky directly, seemed pretty much like it. Besides, he kind of felt as if he was asking dad to help to him get rid of the bullies. It felt desperate, but necessary. Also, he felt that David needed to know what was going on, to know about Jake's low intrigues and to be more alerted about him.

Jeff walked on the porch and rang the doorbell. David opened after a few seconds. He was dressed informally, smiled warmly and welcomed Richards. Beyond a doubt, he treated their meeting completely unofficially.

"Welcome, Jeff, how are you?" He smiled and opened the doors widely.

"Hi, David," Jeff walked inside and shook his manager's hand. "Good to see you."

"You, too," Garbinsky replied, closed the door and took off his sunglasses. "Would you like anything to drink?"

"Some orange juice maybe?"

"Ok, I'll bring it in a second. Take a seat." He invited Jeff to the living room and went to the kitchen. Jeff had never been in David's house before, so he was looking around curiously. The house seemed peaceful; that was the very first impression. The colors were reserved, some would call them dull, beige and brown mostly. There was a chandelier hanging from the ceiling, but, to Jeff's surprise, its lampshades were not white glass or ivy, as it would be most common, but brownish. They must have given rather dimmed light. Undoubtedly, the room was fit for the needs of a photophobic.

There were books everywhere, but the room did not seem to be messy. On the contrary, everything seemed to be in a very well thought-through order. Jeff spotted that the books were put in an alphabetical order and that there was absolutely no dust on them. All of them were put on shelves, standing behind glass doors. Jeff was walking around the room looking at David's collection admiring it.

Garbinsky came to the room carrying two glasses of cold orange juice. Ice cubes floating on the surface were making a pleasant clattering sound as Garbinsky was walking towards Jeff. He put the glasses on a coffee table and encouraged Jeff to sit on one of leather armchairs.

"So, Jeff, I must admit that the tone of your voice was intriguing, what is it?"

"I can imagine. I'm very sorry for coming here, practically unannounced, but the information I bring, well, I believe it is better to be discussed outside the office."

David looked at him curiously and drank some juice.

"Has it got anything to do with OMNIBUS?"

"Yes, precisely so."

David took a deep breath and leaned on the back of his armchair.

"Jeff, I really hope you're not coming here to ask me for more money or more time behind the board's back."

"It's not about that, not at all." He took his glass. "It's about Jake Pinett."

David sighed and was rubbing his eyes for few seconds then looked at Jeff visibly worried. 'What is it?'

Jeff felt he was getting nervous, Jake was, after all, a board member, a share owner and all he had against him were his assumptions and intuition; no concrete *proof* that Pinett was truly sabotaging him. He drank some of the juice and felt its pleasant coolness down his throat, put the glass back on the table, cleared his throat and sat on his armchair. There was nothing he could lose.

"I have a feeling, actually, I am almost certain, that Jake is sabotaging my project."

David was looking at him focused and intrigued.

"What the hell are you talking about?" he said, not angrily, but quite firmly.

"I have been thinking a lot about whether I should or shouldn't tell you about the whole thing, but, I believe that as my boss and the most important person in WORDS, you need to know about my suspicions."

"Go on, Jeff, I'm listening."

"Okay. It's nothing new that Jake is prejudiced toward me. He has been since I started working at WORDS and, frankly speaking, I have no idea what the basis of his aversion is. I never cared about it too much, I've been focused on my work for the company and since Jake's reluctance has not had any influence on it, I haven't paid too much of attention to it. Unfortunately, it seems that Pinett has decided to sabotage my work, and this is where I need to react."

"What do you mean 'sabotage'?"

Jeff took a deep breath.

"The whole idea with OMNIBUS has never been in Jake's favor."

"Yes, he's the one who wanted to give you the time limit."

"I've thought so. I've been suspecting that." Jeff stood up, put his hands in his pockets and walked first toward the curtained window and then stopped behind a sofa.

"This week I was about to sign a contract with MODENA," Jeff continued, "but on Friday I got a phone call from John Abram. He asked me to come to his office where he informed me that the printing house received an anonymous phone call from a man introducing himself as WORDS worker, warning MODENA against any collaboration with me."

"What?" David asked stunned.

"My reaction exactly. The informer told them my assets were dependable on WORDS permissions and restrictions, and that I was about to lose your support, which would automatically make me insolvent. So, MODENA decided to investigate the case, but kindly informed me that whatever happens, they were no longer interested in co-operation."

"And you're suspecting Jake to be behind this?"

"Yes."

"Based on what?"

"Well, Abram kind of hinted to me it was Pinett, he never said it straight, but he certainly made it obvious."

"Jeff, I'm afraid it's not enough."

"Of course it isn't. On Saturday Evy told me she found some posts on WORDS Intranet forum warning the company against Jake."

"Who posted it?"

"It was anonymous, but the message was clear: Jake is up to something and that I might be his victim."

"I am not a computer geek, but is should not be terribly difficult to track down the person who wrote it."

"Sure, except for the fact the posts are gone."

"But did you read them?"

"No, they had been removed before I had a chance."

"So, again, you're not sure it's Jake."

"No, but the pieces can be easily put together."

David took a glass into his hand, drank a bit and put it back on the table.

"I guess, I need to show you something," he finally said, stood up and walked out of the room. "Wait here!" he said.

Garbinsky came back after few minutes with a piece of paper in his hand. He gave it to Jeff and sat back. Jeff skimmed the text and his face expression changed from shocked to outrage while reading.

"What the *fuck?*" he finally said and threw the paper on the table. "What the hell is this?"

"I got this e-mail on Friday. It's from our building's owner."

"I can see that! He wants your guarantee that I have the money to hire the offices for OMNIBUS"!"

"Yeah. I called the man the moment I got it and asked him why was he doubting, and he told me, he received an e-mail from someone working for WORDS indicating that I no longer wanted to sponsor your undertakings. The landlord wanted me to guarantee I would not stop supporting you throughout the contract you had signed with him."

Jeff was simply speechless. He quietly sat down and drank the rest of his juice. It was all unbelievable.

"I *might* be wrong, but I would assume it was Jake informing the landlord about my potential problems," he finally said.

"You don't know that for sure."

"Okay, but I think it's obvious it must have been the same person who called MODENA."

"Most probably yes."

"So I am clearly being under attack here."

"Looks like it, Jeff." David agreed sadly, visibly worried.

"David. I came here to tell you all about it, because I wanted you to know I had been doing everything in my power to make OMNIBUS work in the time limit you had given me. If it hadn't been for that phone call, my books would have been printed as we speak."

"I know, it looks pretty bad. I agree, someone wants to discredit you."

"It's Jake."

"You don't know that."

"I can *feel* that."

"Jeff, I am not going to take any actions against Jake only because you have a *feeling*."

"David, do you realize that by discrediting me, he is also messing up with *your* reputation? It's the second time he undermined the deal you gave me, the deal I let all my contracting parties know about. Them doubting in *my* financial stability means they are actually doubting in *yours*."

"Jeff, I know that, I can see that, but I cannot, I *will* not take any actions unless I *know* it's Jake."

"Your help could be crucial for compromising him."

"Jeff, I'm sorry. He's my board member. I cannot walk around throwing accusations left and right, because you have a hunch."

"Well…," Jeff got up. "I was hoping you could help me."

"Let me put it this way. I am glad you came and told me about all this. Don't worry, the six-months ultimatum is not exactly binding I can guarantee you that; I cannot, however, do anything else for you at this point."

Jeff smiled bitterly. "I think it's time for me to go."

He walked to the door, David opened it for him.

"I'm sorry, Jeff," he said, putting his hand on his shoulder, "Give me proof that it is Jake and then you will have my full support. But right now, I can't help you." He patted Richards on the shoulder with such pity as if his manager was a scout who was laughed at by his friends for being scared of a spider at night and needed some courage to face everyone next morning.

Jeff looked at him and nodded with understanding. He actually did comprehend David's point of view, but had hoped to get some support, perhaps a little inside investigation, *anything* that would allow him to expose Pinett.

Jeff said goodbye to David and left his home. He felt disappointed and surprised. He had always thought that Garbinsky was more dynamic, that he had more courage to defend his company, that he would be the one to take an immediate action. It was what he came there for, and he was now leaving with his hands empty. Strange feeling, it seemed unsuitable. David was visibly reluctant. *Was he afraid of something? Was it possible that Jake had something to use against him?*

Jeff got into his car, and drove off. Now he needed to focus on his meeting with Neil. Jackson was his last hope for help.

David was observing Jeff driving away, and the moment his car disappeared on the hill he turned away from the window, took off his glasses and rubbed his forehead.

"Jesus, what a mess. What have you done, Jake," he whispered.

Oenone~Agatha Rae~

⁊76⸲

Laura got back home, threw car keys on the table in the hall and mechanically, she went upstairs to the bedroom. She opened the door, walked inside, opened the wardrobe's doors and took out a medium-sized suitcase. She put it on the bed and started packing Bruce's things. Underwear, a book he had been reading recently, his glasses and contact lens solution, and slippers. Laura looked at the half-full suitcase, and, finally, she fully understood what was happening. Bruce was sick. Just as she was, not more than two weeks ago.

"Oh my God," she whispered, and tears started flowing down her cheeks. Laura sat helplessly on the bed, weeping, and embraced herself, and felt she was shivering. It all seemed too much. *What a nightmare*. She laid on the bed and allowed all the fear to come out of her. What was she going to do if she lost him? What if it turned out she was not strong enough to support him as much as he had supported her? But the worst thing of all was the perspective of going through the same drama again. Cancer. *Again*. How was it possible? Could they have avoided it somehow? Was there something they missed?

"Oh God, what are we going to do?" she sobbed and hid her face in her palms. Laura laid huddled crying her eyes out. After few minutes, she sat on the bed, cleared her nose, dried her eyes and reached for her handbag. She dialed Evy's number and was waiting for her to pick up…

***

After the unusual morning Evy had serious problems focusing on her work; her mind kept coming back to whatever it was that had happened to her earlier. It was incredibly, *overwhelmingly* sensual, appeared out of nowhere and stopped as rapidly as it started. The shadow of the tremendous bliss kept haunting her and, she had to admit, she wanted it to happen again. She even longed for it. It was quite disturbing, she had to admit it, mostly because it was so unexpected and uncontrolled, but as the day continued, she was hoping for it all to repeat itself. She was *waiting* for it. After all, why not? Evy was not planning to go anywhere, she had no meetings scheduled, and she could simply stay at home and enjoy that mysterious experience that was driving her senses crazy again.

She was full of energy and in a great mood. The endorphins were buzzing in her blood, and as much as she wanted to work, it was impossible for her to resist eating sweets and listening to loud music. Evy went to the kitchen, reached for ice-cream and was dancing all around her apartment listening to Cream's "Sunshine of Your Love". It was not until early afternoon that she had noticed she was still wearing pajamas. Amused, she went to her bedroom to get some clothes and looked at her bed. It used to be a synonym of loneliness, she remembered sobbing at night, longing for the warmth and comfort of a man's shoulder around her. Now everything had changed. Perhaps it was not the most typical relationship what she had had, but at least her physical needs were satisfied. For a second, a thought appeared in her head, asking where it was all heading? How long was it all going to last? She swiftly let the uncomfortable thoughts go and got back to the kitchen and freshly-opened vanilla-cherry ice-cream box.

Evy calmed down later in the afternoon, and in the evening she was sitting by her computer, editing another book for OMNIBUS, feeling a bit nauseous after all the ice-cream she had eaten. At this point, seeing how much work she had to do, she felt angry for allowing herself to dance carelessly all around the place instead of catching up.

A telephone ring distracted her. Evy put down her glasses and looked at her watch. 9 p.m. Who could that be? She was looking for her cell phone for a minute and it finally occurred to her, she had not taken it out from her handbag since the day before. She walked to the hall, and took the phone out. "LAURA" it said on the display.

"Hi, Laura, how are you?" she cheerfully asked.

"What's the matter with you, Evy, I've been calling you all day, why aren't you picking up the phone?" she heard Laura's irritated voice. It felt quite confusing, hearing her talking like that.

"You have?" Evy asked surprised.

"Yes, I called your cell phone twice and in the morning I called on your home phone."

"Oh, yes, now I remember, there was a phone call in the morning, but I couldn't pick it up."

"Why not?"

"I was—busy." Evy closed her eyes and the memory of what had happened appeared in her mind again. She bit her lip.

"And the cell?"

"Laura, are you inquiring an investigation? Apparently I could not pick up the phone. Besides, don't you have other things to do during your holidays than stalking me?" she wanted it to sound funny and careless, but she was quite irritated with Laura's grudge.

"I'm not on holidays anymore," Laura said quietly, but firmly.

"What? You just left."

"And I just got back. We're back in Boston."

"What's happened?!" Evy asked genuinely worried.

"Could you come over here? I know it's quite late, but I need you, Evy, and I'm not sure I should drive tonight."

"What's going on?"

"Please, come."

"I'm coming. I'll be there in half an hour."

Oenone~Agatha Rae~

~77~

Evy parked Bob in front of Laura's house about forty minutes later and spotted that the only light that was on was in the bedroom. Usually Laura liked having the lights on in many rooms; she had been afraid of darkness since childhood, and she always felt safer when it was light inside. Seeing the whole place dark except for one room seemed strange, unusual.

Evy knocked on the door, but there was no answer. She knocked again, much louder. Still nothing. She stepped down from the porch and looked up at the bedroom window. It was slightly open, which made Evy's heart start beating faster. No lights in the room, opened window, God, what was going on? A robbery?

"Laura!" she shouted. "Laura!"

The window opened wider and there was Laura looking through it.

"Oh, Evy. Come on in," she said, visibly tipsy.

"I'd love to, but you need to open the door first."

"Oh, right, give me a second."

Laura closed the window and about a minute later a light appeared on the porch. She walked downstairs and unlocked the front door. She was a mess. Her eyes were swollen, her breath smelt of rum and her hair was completely undone.

"Hi, Evy, I'm glad you came."

"My God, Laura, what's happening?" Evy asked shocked.

"Actually? The usual stuff." Laura smiled bitterly. "Come in."

Evy walked inside.

"Why is it so dark? You always leave at least the night lamps on downstairs."

"I haven't thought of that, really. Yeah, you're right. Strange," said Laura looking around the living room. "Would you like a drink?" she asked after a few seconds.

"No thanks, I'm driving."

"Ah, yes, then what can I give you?"

"Water. I'd like some water."

277

Laura walked to the kitchen. For a few seconds, the room was lit by a cold, pale fridge light. She got a small bottle out of it and gave it to Evy.

"Thanks," Evy said. She couldn't take her eyes off Laura. She couldn't remember seeing her friend in such condition; she never looked that miserable, not even during her recent fight for life.

"Laura, what's going on? I can see something's wrong."

"Come on, I want to show something."

They both walked upstairs to the bedroom. Evy looked around. There was a mess all around. An open suitcase was on the bed and there were a lot of men clothes scattered all around it. There were also clothes on the floor.

"Oh my God, Laura, is Bruce moving out?" Evy asked in disbelief.

"No, no, that's not it."

"Look at me, Laura." Evy took her by the hand and forced her gently to sit on an armchair. She kneeled in front of her and looked her straight into eyes. "What is going on?"

Laura looked at her for few seconds and started crying. "He's sick, Evy. My Bruce is sick."

"What do you mean?" She put her hands on her friend's shoulders.

"He's got cancer."

"*What?!*"

Laura curled her legs and sat more comfortably on the armchair.

"He felt very weak. I had no idea what was happening, he never told me anything until those stairs." She was sobbing.

"Laura, I can't understand you. What stairs, what do you mean he felt weak?" She gave her the bottle of water. Laura drank few sips and sighed deeply. Evy put her palm on her forehead.

"It's okay, calm down and tell me exactly what has happened?"

Laura took a deep breath, drank a bit more of water and took some tissues from the night table. She cleared her nose and for the first time she looked at Evy clear-headed.

"We went on a trip to Vancouver. We wanted to go to the Art Gallery. There are steps you need to climb up to get inside, not too many steps to be honest."

"Yes, I know."

"And he couldn't climb them."

"What do you mean he couldn't climb them? It's not like they're a mile long."

"Exactly. And he couldn't climb them. In the middle of the stairs he sat down and told me he was unable to go up, that he felt too weak and too tired."

Laura drank some water.

"He felt really bad that day. We came back to our hotel and Bruce spent almost an entire day in bed. He told me he had been feeling like that for quite some time, but refused to tell me about it in order not to trouble me. He started running again, but, as it turned out, for the past couple of weeks he was not able to run anymore. It looks like those goddamn stairs triggered something horrible, something that probably would have come up anyway, sooner or later."

"So, what happened then?"

"Then I decided we needed to come back and go to hospital. When we got back to Boston, yesterday evening, I tried to reach you for the first time, then the second time from the hospital, in the morning."

"Oh God, Laura, I'm so sorry." Evy grabbed Laura's palm and kissed it.

"He's got lung cancer, Ev."

Evy was looking at Laura for few seconds and it seemed she did not fully understand what she had just been told.

"*Lung* cancer?"

"Yeah. He has never smoked, he's always taken care of himself, he's always been active, and there haven't been cases of *any* cancer in his family. I don't know, I reckon that maybe I passed it on in him, that maybe I infected him."

"Don't even think like that, Laura. It's nonsense."

"All this situation is one fucking nonsense, if you ask me."

"What's his prognosis?"

"Not bad. Actually, better than mine. The cancer is in its early stage, they're not even planning on cutting it out at this point. The doctors say that radiotherapy ought to be enough."

"That's great news, Laura! You need to focus on that!"

"I'm trying. I don't know, I mean, I've been thinking about all this mess. I have no idea what it is happening to us. Again." Laura sighed, "Maybe it's some kind of a payback?"

"Payback?"

"I don't know, I mean it's all pretty unusual. First me, then Bruce. It just doesn't make sense. *Statistically* it makes no sense at all."

'But what do you mean 'payback'?'

279

"I've been thinking that perhaps it's because I've never been a religious person."

"Oh, Laura, come on."

"I'm being completely serious! I've never prayed, I've never been to church, maybe this is what God does to the people who don't give a fuck about him?"

"Do you even listen to yourself?"

"What does your philosophy say about it?"

"Deism says that God created the world, but lets it live on its own. Laura, there's no such thing as divine intervention. God doesn't reward and doesn't punish. He only lets us be."

"Sounds pretty bad, because it means I can't even pray to him for Bruce's health."

"It also prevents from having any grudge against him if anything goes wrong. It limits the feeling of injustice. Laura, you can pray if it helps, my philosophy is just don't rely on it."

Evy got up and looked around the room.

"So, what's all this?"

"I'm packing Bruce's things. He's already staying at the hospital. He's going to spend a few days there as they need to perform some further tests and he's going to have his first radiation soon. I told him I would bring him some clothes and toiletries." She started sobbing again, "and something to read." She hid her face in her palms, "I can't do this, Ev, I have no idea what to pack, and just the thought of doing it makes me so depressed I literally find it hard to breathe."

Evy kneeled back in front of Laura and embraced her; she felt incredibly sorry for her friend with all she had been through, and now this. The coincidence was truly amazing, in the most terrifying way. They were swinging gently and they were both crying. Evy also felt terrible she was not around Laura the first moment she needed her so badly. She felt embarrassed that such a trivial distraction did not allow her to be there for her friend sooner.

"Laura, you need to be strong and support him, just like Bruce had supported you," she said softly, stroking her head. "You heard the doctors; his condition is not severe, I'm sure he's going to be fine."

"I know," Laura replied quietly, "I'm just scared, that's all. I need to get through this; I'll be stronger tomorrow."

"Of course you will. Do you want my help with the packing?"

"Yes."

They spent the next half an hour, in almost complete silence, packing Bruce's things. Finally, when they zipped the suitcase, Laura asked Evy to stay with her that night. Evy agreed without any hesitation and about an hour later they both went to sleep.

Oenone~Agatha Rae~

~78~

Jeff was waiting for Neil at Al Forno. Jackson called him the other day and instead of a lunch, he proposed going for dinner. He said he was going back to New York on Wednesday, so they could spend time in the city catching up. Jeff loved the perspective and thought that going away for two days could be exactly the break he needed from all the mess that was now going on around him.

He arrived in Providence around noon. He walked slowly through downtown, enjoying the Victorian architecture, Burnside Park, Westminster Street and the wonderful skyline. He had a quick lunch and strolled down the waterfront area. The day was wonderful; sunny but not too hot, with a very pleasant mild wind blowing from the bay. It all seemed like the last desperate puff of summer.

The time he spent alone, walking at a leisurely pace, was a wonderful occasion to think about OMNIBUS, David, and Jake. About Evy. It occurred to him that his mind was no longer that occupied with her as it used to be. He even felt he held a grudge against her for all those strange situations. So many things could have been solved by now if he had known. What truly hurt him about it was the fact he thought she cared for OMNIBUS, for him. Perhaps he was far more engaged in the project than she was. And if so, then maybe it was a mistake to plan to make her his partner? Evy had seemed distracted for some time now. She was late for the presentation, she was editing the books with a delay. It looked like it all had surpassed her abilities.

Now it was 7 p.m. and Jeff was waiting for Neil. He ordered himself a beer and was checking his e-mail when Neil arrived. The two hugged each other cordially.

"So good to see you, man!" Neil said.

"Likewise, Neil," Jeff replied smiling.

They took their seats and a waiter came to bring them menus.

"How long has it been?" Jeff asked.

"Almost two years. But I feel like I saw you yesterday."

"Yeah, totally."

It felt good to see him again.

***

They spent the next two hours eating, drinking, laughing, and recalling the anecdotes from the past and catching up on their lives. It turned out that Neil's business was doing great; he started a company, which was designing and selling special-occasion cards, business cards, as well as menus and stationaries and he had signed long-term contracts with many hotels, printing houses and offices in his area, making him the leader of the local market. Oh, and he got married.

"You got married? Seriously?" Jeff laughed.

"Yeah, I know, right? Who knew? Her name's Anna, and she's a therapist." Neil said.

"I mean congratulations, man, but how did *that* happen? I remember Neil the Everlasting Bachelor. You even *vowed* you would never get married."

"Yeah, back then on the beach, well, weren't we, accidentally drunk then, huh?"

"Oh man, that was amazing." Jeff smiled. "So many things have changed," he added a bit lost in his thoughts.

"Don't get me wrong, I myself have still problems believing It happened. We *met* only four months ago and got married three weeks ago, so," he rubbed his wedding ring, "I am still getting used to it. What about you? How's Rachel?"

"Yeah, you're not exactly in the loop my friend. We split up about—I don't know a year ago."

"No way! How come?"

"Well, she wanted to get married, and I was totally against that. Apparently, I need to move to New York and find myself a therapist to change my mind!" Jeff winked.

"You know, since I have already been there and done that, I can assure you, marriage doesn't hurt. In fact, I have no idea what made me so against it."

"Guess you were waiting for the right person."

"Yeah, looks like it. So, are you seeing someone?"

"It's complicated. I mean I do *see* her, quite often even, but we're not together as a couple. We work together."

"Difficult, but manageable."

"I'm her boss."

"Ouch. Much worse."

Jeff drank some more beer and told Neil about his flirting with Evy, about Westville and their morning conversation. He told him about the ultimatum, the new publishing house and how his co-operation with Evy used to be perfect, but now seemed to be heading toward a quite unsettling direction. And that, apparently, he might have developed some highly unprofessional feelings toward her. Something he was not exactly proud of, but was no longer able to deny it.

"Do you love her?" Neil asked quite suddenly.

"Wow, talking about cutting to the chase. I don't know. Probably. I know I *could*. I know there was a point I felt like it. But I don't know. Something about her has changed. I would really need to spend some time alone with her, I mean, you know, like a date, not like call her to tell her to edit a book and prepare a presentation kind of thing."

"Honestly, you're lucky she did not sue your ass after that one night stand."

"I was afraid she might do it. I mean I thought of it afterwards."

"That's how it usually goes." Neil laughed.

"Yeah, I've been kind of wondering why she never did that, really.'"

"She wanted it as well, obviously. Besides, it's not like she slept with you because you promised her a raise or a promotion."

Jeff did not say anything. He knew Neil was right. Two months ago, hell *some days* ago he was sure, that she was not indifferent to him as well. Now it did not seem that obvious. There were moments he would even find her … repulsive. Splits of seconds, but still. And there was no real reason for that, but he was sure it was not because of her recent mistakes. He had no idea where it came from, but there were times, that were simply overwhelming.

"I am thinking of giving her the position of OMNIBUS co-manager. That way we would have equal status and thus, any possible relationship would not cause a professional tension'"

"Yeah, because there are two popes in the world, every plane has two captains, and every restaurants has two chefs."

"What do you mean?"

"I mean that it might be risky to have a co-manager, Evy or not, I think every company ought to have one boss only. Somebody to say "steady as she goes" and makes decisions."

"But I've known her long enough to see she would be perfectly capable to co-operate with me."

"Will you be perfectly capable to co-operate with her?"

Jeff sighed and shrugged his shoulders in 'how should I know?' gesture. He finished his beer.

"Looks like they're closing," Neil said.

"Yeah." Jeff looked at his watch, it was half past 10. "Wanna go for a walk? I need to talk to you."

"There's more? My God, you can't complain about boredom in Boston, that's for sure." Neil laughed. "Let's go."

Half an hour later, they were walking along Waterplace Park. The evening was wonderful, and a delicate breeze from the water was a very pleasant addition to the warm September evening. Crickets were giving concerts in the grass and some people were passing by jogging or roller-skating. There were couples kissing on the benches near the water.

Jeff told Neil about his problems connected with Jake, the jeopardized contract with MODENA, the possible problems with renting offices in the building, and the forum. He also told Jackson about David's reserved behavior and how he felt he was alone in this battle, without any idea on how to expose Pinett.

"I understand... you are absolutely positive it was Jake?" asked Neil.

"Yes. I know I have no evidence, but he hates me, he has always been against me and I know he would do everything to either fire or *at least* humiliate me. It makes perfect sense that it's Jake."

"Why does he detest you so much?"

"I don't know. He's been against me ever since my first day of work at WORDS. He's always criticized all of my ideas, he has always voted against me if there was anything the board was to decide on."

"Maybe he was hoping to get your job?"

"I've thought about it. It would make sense, but being a member of a board means he has much more power than me as a Creative Manager. After all, *I* need to inform *them* about all my ideas and to report about the progress. Not to mention that my actions depend on their approval."

They sat on a bench. Neil reached for Altoids into his pocket, took one and handed the box to Jeff.

"Want some?"

"Sure." Jeff smiled and took one. "You've always had them with you."

"Yep, in every pocket of every coat, jacket, pants. It drives Anna crazy, you have no idea how many times she washed Altoids because I did not empty my pockets." Neil laughed.

"It feels good? The married life?"

"Can't complain." Neil smiled. They had been sitting for some time, looking ahead in a complete silence.

"Listen, Jeff. I will try to find out something about Jake. I think I might help you as far as MODENA is concerned. I know their CEO."

"You do?"

"Yeah. I mean, you know, it's a pretty big printing house. I play basketball together with him."

"What, a paper-business people league?" Jeff laughed.

"No, not exactly." Neil laughed, too. "There are some people I play with and one of them brought a friend few months ago. He turned out to be Owen Mack, MODENA's CEO. Abram as the printing house's Boston branch manager is his direct subordinate. We're not best friends or anything like that, but sometimes we hang out with the rest of the team, we go for a beer after a game, that sort of thing."

"Do you think you could ask him about who called?"

"I think so. I'm pretty sure he might tell John Abram to reveal the secret caller."

"That would be great, Neil. That really might help."

"I hope it does, because I don't think there's anything else I can do."

"I understand."

"Where do you sleep?"

"Oh, I have a room in a hotel on Dorrance Street. It's somewhere close." Jeff smiled, pointing toward the downtown area with his hand.

"Okay, well, I gotta get going, my hotel is outside downtown and I need to be back in New York before 9 a.m. tomorrow."

"Sure."

They got up, shook hands and embraced each other cordially.

"It was really great to see you again," Jeff said.

"Likewise, Richards, likewise. Listen, don't worry about that asshole. We'll get him. This is not how business should be made."

"Thanks, Neil. I really appreciate it."

Neil got a taxi and went back to his hotel. Jeff decided to stay by the water for a while. The only meeting he had scheduled for the next day was with Evy at half past ten, so there was no need for him to leave Providence earlier than 8 o'clock. He could easily stay up a little bit longer. Jeff laid down on the grass and was gazing at starts taking great delight in having his head finally empty of thoughts.

***

Evy was sleeping in the guest room when, at around midnight, she felt the very intense smell of jasmine. She woke up confused and felt the well-known tickles all over her body.

It was happening again.

Evy needed a few seconds to recall where she was as the room, at first seemed completely unfamiliar. The moment she realized she was at Laura's home, she only managed to think "God, that's inconvenient.", and to cover her face with a pillow. A few seconds later her body was shaken by an intensive climax, leaving her biting her lip and suppressing her voice. Just as suddenly as it all appeared, it was gone. She was lying in bed, sweaty and breathless. Once it was all over, Evy put the pillow aside and looked at her cell phone. She squinted her eyes when a bright light appeared in the room and saw it was few minutes to midnight.

She lay on her back and before falling asleep, she realized it was the second time when it all happened outside her home. A sting of anxiety appeared in her head again; it could happen anywhere, and, apparently, she was unable to control it. Is *this* was what she wanted?

***

Jeff felt the well-known chill all over his body. It was swift, but very intense and unpleasant. He thought it was time to go back to his hotel, apparently lying on the grass was not the best idea; he froze to the marrow.

Oenone~Agatha Rae~

⁓80⁓

Laura woke up fresh and optimistic. She needed to let it all go last night in order to breathe deeper in the morning. That was what her mom would always say to her whenever she felt down and wanted to cry—let it go, don't fight the sadness, you'll breathe deeper once you clean your soul, she would say.

She opened the curtains. The sky was overcast, there was no single ray of sunlight visible. Laura opened the window and felt cool air in her nostrils. Yes, she did breathe deeper. A burst of wind ran through her hair and at that moment her intuition was whispering to her ear, telling her everything was going to be fine. It felt comforting, no matter how irrational it was. Her husband was in hospital right now, experiencing his first radiotherapy session, but she was no longer worried. Laura *knew* she was going to stand by Bruce and help him no matter what. Maybe this was the world's strange way of giving her a chance to repay for his care.

She closed the window, put on a wrapper and walked downstairs with a plan to wake Evy up and make some fresh, intense coffee. To her amazement, the guest room bed was made and coffee was already in the mugs.

"Hi, Laura, how did you sleep?" she heard Evy's voice. Laura turned around and saw her friend in the kitchen, waiting for toasts to jump out.

"Actually, I slept really well. You?"

"Yeah, me, too," Evy answered. Apart from a small earthquake around midnight, she thought. "Want some coffee?"

"You bet," Laura replied and took a seat by the table. "Thanks for staying with me tonight."

"No problem. I'm glad I could help."

"Would you like to sit on the porch?"

"Sure. Just let me take my jersey."

A few minutes later, Laura and Evy were drinking coffee and sitting on a swinging bench outside the house. They were looking at the street, observing the cars passing by, people rushing here and there and spotted a school bus between the buildings, waiting for the kids.

"And life goes on, huh?" Laura said.

"Of course. And it always will."

"No matter what," Laura added drinking coffee.

"No matter what," Evy agreed. She looked at Laura and it struck her that her friend looked as if she was about ten years older than yesterday morning.

"What are you going to do, Laura?"

"I'm going to get dressed, take Bruce's suitcase, and drive to the hospital."

"Sounds like a good plan." Evy smiled.

"Yeah, the best one under those circumstances, I believe…What about your plans?"

"I need to go to OMNIBUS today. I was supposed to finish editing another book about, um, three days ago, but I haven't done that yet. Had no time."

"Oh? What made you so busy you couldn't finish on time? I can't remember you overstepping any deadline. Ever."

Evy thought about it for a minute. That was true. She had always been on time with her work, it was a matter of her professionalism. At first she wanted to tell Laura about all those erotic phenomena that had been going on around her, to explain to her the reason of her distraction, but she thought that Laura was now facing another painful moment in her life, and so it was not the best moment to mention her mystique sex life. *Mystic sex life, wow, sounds like a porn movie title*, Evy thought.

"I don't know, I think I need a break. I've been working very intensely on OMNIBUS projects and OMNIBUS itself; I guess I'm feeling a bit burnt out."

"You should talk to Jeff about it. Maybe he could give you few days off?"

"Maybe. Yeah, I guess that's a good idea. I just don't think he would let me go right now. Things are getting pretty intense with the schedule."

"Yeah, six-months limit. How much time do you have left?"

"About two months."

"It's not that much, maybe you could hold on to that for a bit longer, and then go for longer and well-deserved vacation?"

"Yeah."

"So, how's Alyssa's magic? Still working?" Laura asked and smiled.

Evy was very surprised by the question; she did not want to talk about it. Maybe it was because of what happened last night, which made her realize she had no control over "Alyssa's magic", but Evy felt there was nothing to boast about. It felt too intimate and too embarrassing.

"It's okay, I mean, you know, I have my moments of fun, but it's just like more realistic fantasies, that's all."

"So, it's working then?"

"I guess so."

"May I ask how much you paid her?"

"Well, she hasn't asked me about the money yet."

"Really? I got a text message from her with a bank account number the moment it turned out I was healthy."

"Well, I haven't had any contact with Alyssa for some weeks now. Also, she hasn't given me the amount of money she wants for her little help in cheering up my evenings."

"So, you have no idea how much money she may want you to pay?"

"No."

"Aren't you afraid the sum might be, you know, too big?"

"Well - I mean, the money you paid seemed rational, after all, she saved your life. Do you think she might charge me more for something which is nothing more but sexual experience?" Evy wanted to smile, hoping she would not sound worried, but Laura was right. What if Evy was unable to pay Alyssa? Oh God, she was so excited with the possibility of getting closer to Jeff, she completely lost her head. A thought even more alarming appeared in her head when Laura said she got a bank account number the moment she knew she was healthy. Since Evy hadn't received anything else, did that mean her situation was not over yet? And if not...what else was there to happen?

"Yeah, I guess you're right," said Laura unconvincingly and finished her coffee. "I need to change and I want to go to Bruce."

"Yeah, I gotta to go, too."

Oenone~Agatha Rae~

81

Evy was supposed to meet Jeff at 10.30 a.m. At first she wanted to go to the office straight from Laura's place, but decided to go back home and refresh herself. She was fully aware she might be late for the meeting, but, to her own surprise, she did not care about it too much. It was Jeff, a guy she had slept with, the one who kind of broke her heart, and now her partner at work so nothing wrong would happen if she got there a few minutes late. There was however a second voice inside of her head telling her she should act more reliably than usual, because she had already screwed up on so many levels, not to mention the book she had not edited yet. Well, too bad. He'll wait.

Jeff arrived at the OMNIBUS office a few minutes before 11 a.m., fully convinced Evy was waiting for him. He got there straight from Providence, tired after less than six hours of sleep and over two hours of driving, worried he would make Ev wait. Seeing she wasn't there in their office took him aback quite a bit. She was never late. One could simply set up a watch according to her sense of time. At first he glanced at his watch thinking he was so late she simply had decided not to wait for him any longer. It was 11.05.

Oh, come on, he thought. Jeff looked around, walked out to the corridor and was trying to find anyone on the floor to ask if they had seen Evy. There was nobody around. Then he thought that maybe something had happened, an accident or maybe she was mugged. The blood in his veins started running faster once the thought of Evy being in possible danger crossed his mind.

Jeff was coming back to his office with the intention to call her when he heard the elevator bell and it turned out she just got there. Wearing big sunglasses, with her hair freely falling down her shoulders and a lavender shirt temptingly unbuttoned just below the cleavage, she looked astonishing. She was walking down the corridor, saw him and took off her glasses.

If only you knew what we do at nights, she thought and smiled delicately.

Jeff, intrigued at first, was now looking at her attentively.

"You're late," he said quite formally once she got to him.

"Sorry," she said and walked inside the office.

He walked inside too and closed the door.

"I was in Providence yesterday."

"Oh, why?"

"I met with a friend there who perhaps might help us curbing down Jake's sabotage, the one I told you about on Saturday the one who used to be my client years ago. He knows a lot of people in paper industry. It turns out he might help compromising Pinett," he said

"Okay, so he will help us, great!"

"You mean will he help *me*?" he asked. "I'm the one that Jake is against, remember?"

Evy was quite surprised. "Well, as far as I remember, I was told I was to be your partner. So, I understand that if someone's sabotaging *you*, the person is automatically sabotaging *us*."

If you felt so sabotaged, why didn't you take any actions? Jeff thought and the bitter taste of disappointment and anger appeared in his mouth again. "Yeah, well, the important thing is that Neil is going to pull some strings in my cause. In *our* cause," he said.

"I'm glad to hear it."

"So, how's the book? Did you finish it?" he asked the question, knowing deep down she hadn't finished it yet. He was actually counting on it, because he was hoping for a chance to remind her who was the boss and who was to obey in their little business arrangement, as she seemed to have bigger and bigger problems understanding that.

"Yeah, about that," Evy looked down. "I- I haven't yet."

"What? You're joking!"

"No, I'm not, and I'm sorry, I did not have time."

"Yeah, Evy look, you see, as far as I remember, you were told, you were to be my partner. So, I understand that if you don't do your job as well as you should, we *both* face the consequences," Jeff said angrily.

"Don't be unfair. So far I have never screwed up!"

"Excuse me? You've been screwing up on a regular basis lately! You fucked up the meeting with the board, you acted irresponsibly not telling me about the forum, and you stopped editing books on time! I mean come on, Evy, I offered you working with me, because I thought you were professional, but now I am beginning to wonder if the position is not too much for you!" He had never talked to her like that. He was angry, and what he had felt in the café was nothing in comparison to the anger that was now pulsing under his skull.

"Oh my God, calm down, Jeff. Look at yourself!" She got up and leaned over the desk toward him. He stood and Evy looked him straight into eyes. For a split second he thought that not so long ago, being so close to her would have made erotic sparkles fly. To his own amazement, it occurred to him that those days seemed to be over.

"Seriously, Jeff, what are you doing?" she asked categorically. "Okay, fine, I screwed up, I'm sorry; I will have the book edited by Thursday, okay? But don't you dare talk to me like that again!"

"Or else what?"

"Or else you'll need to find yourself a new editor! Would you really want that? Especially now? I have always supported you, Jeff, and you goddamn know that!"

He was breathing heavily. Dark, heavy thoughts were buzzing in his head. Jeff had no idea what was happening. He had been managing people in different companies and under different circumstances for almost ten years. It always seemed to him he had a good approach to his employees, and he was truly ashamed of him being so nasty, so unprofessional to Evy. For God's sake, she really *had* been there for him all this time, editing, making phone calls, meeting with ad agencies, organizing the entire office. And he *knew* that!

"I'm sorry, okay?" he said still angrily, "but things aren't looking too good, all right? MODENA withdrew their contract with us. I met with David on Monday, he showed me a letter from our landlord asking Garbinsky to guarantee he was financing us, because he got a fucking anonymous e-mail informing him kindly that we were at the verge of bankruptcy. Jake wants to destroy us, he wants to destroy me. So stop telling me what a fine fucking team we are if you cannot do your job the way you're supposed to, because *that's* the kind of support I am hoping for, not patting me on the fucking shoulder!"

"So all I have been doing so far was patting you on the shoulder, huh?" Evy felt tears coming to her eyes. She was furious, he was so unfair that it physically hurt. "I've been working my fucking ass off here, okay!? Being a secretary, an editor…"

"Yeah, some editor, you haven't finished the book on time," Jeff said sarcastically.

"What's the point anyway since we don't have a contract with the printing house?"

He looked at her coldly and severely. She was right, he *knew* she was, but he was furious and it was impossible for him to calm down at this point.

"Has it ever occurred to you to ask me *why* I started screwing things up? Have you ever thought there might be a reason behind it?"

He was silent. He turned his eyes away from her, and was looking through the window. Of course the thought occurred to him, and he even wanted to ask her about it, but—apparently he forgot. He was standing with his hands in his pockets and had no idea what to say. Her argument surprised and embarrassed him, but he was still too angry to admit it.

"You know what? Why don't you call me once you regain clarity of thought and the puberty is over!" she finally said.

Evy took her bag and walked out of the office, slamming the door. She was shaking all over while rushing to the stairs. She did not want to call the elevator and risk waiting for it while Jeff would come out of the office and drag this craziness even a minute longer. What a jerk! How dare he talk to her like that! They had been working together for months, she was *always* on time, on schedule, reachable, accessible, devoted, and caring. And now what, a mistake or two and he allowed himself to treat her like some fucking doormat? Evy felt tears coming to her eyes again and this time she knew she had to let it go, let it all come out. She was walking down the staircase and stopped two floors down to use the bathroom. She locked herself in a stall and started sobbing. Confused and hopeless, she was sitting on the toilet seat, hiding her face in her palms, weeping loudly.

Jeff observed Evy storming out of his office with confusion and anger. He did not want her to go, the moment she disappeared behind the door, he wanted to run after her, stop her and apologize. He was sincerely sorry. Eve was right, she did screw up *this* time, but he had to admit, there had never been any doubt in his mind that Evy was completely devoted to OMNIBUS and, well, to him. At least till now. He had no idea what was going on, but everything that had just happened made him realize that something had changed in his relationship with Evy. As much as he had always loved being with her, as he had always looked forward to meeting her and was coming back in his thoughts to their night in Westville, he had to admit, that for some days now, he was finding her irritating. Annoying. The sarcasm in his head, the lack of any patience. And a complete loss of any physical attraction to her. It seemed it had vaporized. He was still able to think warmly of her, but only when she wasn't around. God, he used to dream of her, and now he was yelling at her for basically no reason. *What the hell was going on?*

Jeff grabbed his cell and was already searching for Evy's contact when he put it back on the desk. It was too soon. He would call her in the evening. Everyone should calm down.

He sat heavily on his chair and closed his eyes.

"Richards, you're such an idiot," he whispered.

Oenone~Agatha Rae~

82

Because Bruce's tumor was rather small and at least not malignant yet, the doctors had decided to treat him with RTH radiotherapy. As the young doctor had informed him, the treatment's basic role was to crash the tumor and, hopefully, to get rid of the problem in this way, without surgical intervention. It all depended on Bruce's body's reaction to the treatment. The really good news was that the tumor was not innervated, so once they would get rid of it, the problem should never reappear again. Bruce was to stay in hospital from Monday to Friday for three consecutive weeks to be treated on a daily basis.

Laura was sitting next to his bed as he was resting after the first radiotherapy session. He felt very well.

"So, I assume radiotherapy is less invasive than chemo?" asked Laura.

"Yes, far less invasive."

"What about side effects?"

"Well, I might feel quite weak, especially toward the end of the treatment, so they advised me to stay home and rest afterwards. But I can drive, it shouldn't affect…"

"You can, but you won't," said Laura quite firmly and kissed him on the cheek.

"Yeah. And you need to feed me well, woman. I should not lose weight." He smiled. "I might develop a cough during the treatment, but it ought to go away without any problems."

"What about your skin? I mean, you're going to be exposed to radiation."

"Oh, right. The doctor told me I would need to hide my chest away from sunlight, or at least use a highly protective sunscreen on it. It will get irritated."

"And the hair?"

"No, the hair is going to be fine. I might, however, lose the chest hair, at least for a while. Guess you won't have to persuade me to wax anymore, the problem will solve itself." Bruce laughed.

"Yeah, because that's *exactly* what I was counting on when I heard about the radiotherapy."

"Just saying," Bruce continued, "could be a nice experience afterwards."

"You're unbelievable. You look like you're on holiday rather than in the hospital."

"Well, do you expect me to cry and be depressed?"

"No, God, of course not, but a little bit of seriousness wouldn't hurt."

"Laura," he said as he took her hand and gripped it firmly, "You cannot look at my condition from the perspective of your experience. My cancer is incomparably less threatening and I have absolutely no doubt that I will be fine." He kissed her hand and she smiled. Laura bent over his bed and kissed him.

"I love you," she said.

"I love you more," he replied. They kissed again and embraced each other.

"Now, show me what you brought me in the suitcase," he said brushing her hair off her forehead.

❧83❧

Evy was sitting at home drinking wine. It was a late evening, and she was thinking of going to sleep, but kept on analyzing her quarrel with Jeff. The emotions were still buzzing in her head. For half of the day Evy considered leaving OMNIBUS, but in the end decided that it would be, despite anything, unfair. She had to stay until the ultimatum had finished, she had promised him that after all, then would reconsider her presence in the company. In case she wanted to leave, Jeff would write her great references. What was far worse than debating over having the job or not, was that she was so tremendously disappointed with Jeff. Maybe the image of him she had so far was simply distorted by her fascination. Evy was outraged by his behavior, and as for that moment she was unable to imagine ever seeing him again. Of course it was inevitable, but some time had to pass. She was planning on finishing the editing, but would rather send the text via a courier rather than delivering it by herself to his office. *His*, not *theirs*.

She drank the rest of the wine in the glass and was reaching for the bottle when she heard a door bell. Evy, surprised, looked at a clock. 11.15 p.m. It was funny, but for a second she was waiting for jasmine scent to fill out the room. She would surely need some lovin' that night.

Evy put the bottle back on the coffee table and went toward the door and heard a very quiet knocking. The singularity of this situation, the fact she was not expecting anyone and the late hour made her blood run faster. Who was it? She looked through the peephole and saw Jeff standing in front of her doors with a piece of paper saying "I'M SORRY". Evy smiled at first, relieved it was nobody to be scared of, but she immediately felt anger growing in her guts.

She opened the door, only a little bit, just to see him, but not to invite him inside.

"Evy, I'm so, so sorry," he said softly.

"Are you insane, do you know what time it is?"

"I know, I know, I hope I did not wake you."

"No, you did not, but I have nothing to say to you, so you've wasted your time. Goodnight."

She wanted to close the door, but he slipped his hand between it and the wall.

"Please hear me out."

"What, you want to tell me again how disloyal I am? How I constantly screw things up? No, thank you, I've had enough."

"I know. I can't tell you how sorry I am. But I need to talk to you."

"What if I'm editing now and you're distracting me? Will you handle slowing down my work?"

"Well, it's not like we have a contract with a printing house, so…" he said looking at her.

God knew she wanted to smile and let him in, but she felt that something burst inside of her that day.

"Jeff, I'm really tired. Go home."

"Evy, I won't be able to look at myself if I don't talk to you about what had happened. Let me in for the sake of my peace."

"Did you think about my peace when you were yelling at me today? I don't think so."

"You're right."

"Goodnight."

Evy closed the door and turned the key. She leaned on the doors and sat on the floor. This was the right thing to do, there was no doubt about it; she really did not want to see him. Suddenly she realized what this thing she was going through the entire day. The thought was illuminating. Everything was now in the right place—she realized she had been living in her own fantasy, waiting for God knows what, and imagining Jeff to be someone entirely different and that morning finally made it all clear.

"Looks like it's just you and me," she said sadly looking at a half-empty bottle of Porto. She got up, walked towards the table and took it in her hand. For a second she was considering pouring the wine into a glass, but who needed that. What was the point of the convention when she was all alone? Evy uncorked the bottle and drank straight from it. When she finished, she put it down, sobbed quietly and went to the bedroom.

***

The sunlight on her cheek was intense enough to wake her up. Sleepy, she turned from her belly on her back, lazily opened her eyes and stretched. She got up and went to the bathroom to get a wrapper. It was few minutes past 9 o'clock.

Evy was on her way to kitchen when she heard the doorbell.

What the…? She thought and looked through the peephole *(Groundhog Day, I swear to God,* she thought) and saw her neighbor, Ms.

Kenneth looking at her door. Ms. Kenneth was the oldest person living in the apartment block and a woman who usurped the title of the wisest person in the world. She was also exceptionally nosy, a gossipy and, what was the worst, the head of the apartment community. Any unexpected interest from her was an equivalent of trouble.

Ms. Kenneth rang the doorbell again. *What do you want?* Evy thought and, unwillingly, opened slightly.

"Good morning, Ms. Kenneth, what can I do for you?"

"Good morning," the woman replied roughly and looked at her in a judging manner. "Ms. Dax, whatever you do in your own apartment is your own business."

"Yes, I'm glad we're on the same page."

"But I believe *this* is too much. I strongly suggest you do something about *it*, and fast, or the housing community will have to do something about it. And about *you!*"

"Excuse me?" Evy said loudly and opened the door wide. Feeling something heavy falling on her feet, she immediately looked down and saw Jeff lying on the floor. Apparently he had just awakened as he was looking up at Evy, but he clearly had no idea where he was nor what was happening.

"What the hell, Jeff?" she asked him and immediately looked at Ms. Kenneth who gave her the usual evil eye and wagged her finger at her.

One day I need to tell her I'm not in high school anymore.

"Good morning, Evy," said Jeff smiling.

"What are you doing? Get up."

He stood up and walked inside her apartment.

"How long have you been here?"

"All night."

"All night?! Are you *insane?*"

"I told you I needed to talk to you. I was hoping you might want to hear me out in the morning."

"Yeah, you *are* insane." She looked at him and had to admit he impressed her. "Prepare two coffees and I'll be right back. You can also make breakfast," Evy said in a decisive tone and went to the bathroom.

"You got it!" Jeff smiled.

Evy closed the bathroom door and smiled.

***

Twenty minutes later, they were sitting by the kitchen table eating pancakes with maple syrup. Evy noticed that Jeff was wearing the same clothes as in the office.

"Did you come here straight from OMNIBUS?"

"Not really, but I haven't been home for, let's see, three days."

"Providence."

"Providence."

"So, you told me yesterday, before you went berserk, that you met with David. What was that about?"

"I did. I went to see him on Monday. I wanted to tell him about Jake, how I suspect him of sabotaging our project."

"*Our* project, who knew," she replied quite sarcastically.

He looked at her, waiting to see her smile, but she didn't. She was completely serious.

"And what did David say?"

"He told me that since I only assume Jake is against us, his hands are tied."

"Bullshit. He's the chairman, and he should *at least* check what his Creative Manager is suspecting."

"That's what I was hoping for," said Jeff pouring syrup on his third pancake. "But he was clearly reluctant to give us any help."

"Maybe he had a reason."

"Maybe. Anyway, I am waiting for information from Neil. Perhaps he could help us."

They were silence for a moment when they were busy with eating and drinking. When Evy finished her breakfast, she put the plate into the sink and sat back on her chair, looking at Jeff. It was kind of sweet to see him eating the most important meal of the day at her place. God only knew how many times she had dreamed of this and how much she had hoped for it. If only the circumstances were different, then she would actually enjoy it.

"So, I'm waiting to know what was so important you had to treat me like a doormat yesterday."

Jeff put away his fork and looked at her very seriously.

"Okay. First of all, I am very, *very* sorry for what happened yesterday. There's no excuse for my behavior, for what I said. The truth is, I need you, Evy; you're the only person I know I can make it with OMNIBUS, and I fully appreciate your help and commitment. I know I would never, *ever* have made it to the point where I am—where we are, if it wasn't for your devotion and help."

Evy finally smiled.

"Thanks. But truthfully, I don't think I will be able to forget about what happened yesterday any time soon."

"I know. And I understand. I deserve it. But you have known me for some time now, and I hope you do realize that such behavior is not really my thing."

He was right. He had never acted like that, she had never heard any stories of him going berserk, and if he did have at least one episode like that, it was more than obvious that the employees of WORDS would talk about it few minutes later.

"So what, is the conflict with Jake stressing you out so much you're losing control once in a while?"

"Maybe, but I've given it a lot of thought and I think it's something else. Or at least that it's more than that. May I be honest with you, Evy?"

"Sure."

"It has something to do with you. At least partly."

"Me?"

Jeff got up from the table, put his hands in his pockets and leaned on the work surface.

"You know I like you, a lot. The thing is, though, something has changed recently. I mean, I have been far too nervous lately, and far too often you were the victim of my deteriorating behavior. But the worst thing of all is that, from my perspective, it looks like *you* are the source of my irritation."

"What?"

"It's insane... trust me, I know, but um... like on Saturday. I called you and asked you out for a coffee, and God knows I wanted to spend a nice afternoon with you, and for once not to talk about work, projects, books."

"Well, you had the right to be angry with me then because..."

"I know, but it started a moment earlier. I felt irritated the moment you *walked* in. When you told me about the board, it only enhanced my anger, I think."

Evy was looking at him and was literally waiting for him to burst out laughing, but a few seconds later she understood he was...serious.

"Oh my God, you really mean it!"

"Yes," he replied worried.

"Are you now trying to offend me?"

"No!"

307

"You come here, practically *force* me to let you in, and tell me that you find me irritating. So what, now you're gonna tell me it was actually *me* to blame for your behavior?"

"No, damn it, Evy, listen to me!"

"What, irritated already?"

Jeff sat back on his chair and looked at her firmly. What the hell, he came here to be honest, so he would be.

"Evy, until recently, there wasn't a day that I wouldn't think about you, that I wouldn't imagine being with you, that I wouldn't recall our night in Westville and feel guilty about running away from you like that," he suspended his voice, swallowed and looked at her searching for some kind of reaction, waiting for a smile. Nothing happened, she was listening to him attentively, but that was it. He could tell, however, that she was very focused on him.

Evy, at the same time, was very much surprised that Jeff's words did not trigger absolutely *any* reaction from her side. Perhaps if it wasn't for what had happened the day before, she would be thrilled hearing it all, however, his recent behavior made her distanced towards him. He showed her a countenance she was completely unaware of.

"But the truth is that, without any reason, something has changed," Jeff continued.

"What do you mean?"

"I mean that it's gone. That I no longer have those feelings, that, I don't know why, but there are moments I find you *repulsive*. And as much as I hate it, I can't control it, and, I mean, you saw me yesterday."

"So, you're saying that you've grown some kind of allergy towards me?"

"I don't know, it is actually a very good way of putting it. I've also noticed that it all started, more or less, when I started feeling cold."

"Cold?"

"Yes. There are nights that I feel very cold, freezing, without any reason. I used to get up, check to see if the windows were closed, make myself some hot milk or look for a blanket to cover myself up. Now I don't do it anymore because I've learned it usually passes as unexpectedly as it appears. I thought I was getting sick, but I'm fine. Apart from the freezing."

Evy was listening to it all in horror. *Oh my God...could this be possible...*

"When was the last time you felt it?"

"Two nights ago, in Providence. But actually, that one is explainable. I was lying on the grass, it was evening, which must have been the reason I felt cold."

Damn! So, whenever I feel jasmine, he - he feels cold? Is that it?

"Have you considered going to a doctor?"

"But what type of a doctor? A psychiatrist or a general practitioner?"

"Maybe both?" she smiled back.

"Please believe me, Ev."

She sighed. She believed him and was terrified.

"So why aren't you angry at me now? You're not finding me irritating after pancakes?" she asked a bit sarcastically.

"No. I guess I've run out of steam for a while."

"That's comforting."

He smiled bitterly. "I don't want to act like that, I - I'm afraid I'm losing my mind," he said and covered his face in his palms.

He looked so weak, so hopeless that Evy couldn't help but feel deeply sorry for Jeff. She walked toward him and embraced him. He hid himself in her arms, closed his eyes and for a moment nobody said anything. Evy was thinking about what he had said. As much as she loved the part about him thinking of her, she was terrified that perhaps, due to her actions, it all was lost now and, what was more, he was now convinced he was going insane. She couldn't tell for sure if it actually was her fault, but there were far too many weird coincidences.

"You know, I was thinking about quitting working for OMNIBUS. After the six months are over, that is."

"I understand that, but, Evy, please give this decision a second thought. I can't imagine this company without you. I need you, Ev." He opened his eyes and looked up at her.

"I know, Jeff, I know. We'll figure it out. It's just that for the time being, I'm not sure if I want to work with a boss who has anger management issues towards me."

Jeff sighed.

"I can promise you that I will leave the room whenever I start feeling uncomfortable around you."

"Okay. But please, check it out, look for a therapist, allow someone to help you."

"I'll think about it."

"Jeff?"

"Yeah?"

"You've got maple syrup on your chin."
They both burst out laughing.

~84~

Jeff went home around noon. They agreed on limiting their contact until his condition had improved and hugged each other as friends before he went out. They both looked visibly relieved after their breakfast and sincere conversation. Jeff was glad he managed to explain his behavior, no matter how crazy it sounded. He wasn't even sure if she believed him, hell, he wasn't sure *he* would believe if he was told such a story. Evy was relieved she reconciled with him, however, she was very much worried about his confession, because it evidently lead to Alyssa. From what he said, the sudden senses of cold, and the aggression towards her started more or less simultaneously to her sexual…disturbances. And this whole lack of any physical interest toward her? Could it be because of that?

"What have I done?" Evy whispered in disbelief wandering around her apartment. She had to talk to Laura about it.

***

Laura spent the night next to Bruce. In the morning, her husband asked her to go home and get some rest. He insisted he was feeling fine, which was later on confirmed by the newest test results. He kept on saying he did not want her to spend so much time in the hospital with him, claiming it was way too soon after her own hospitalization.

"Laura, I'd hate myself if you had to spend another day here because of me. Like I said yesterday, my condition cannot be comparable to yours. I will be fine."

When Bruce's doctors found out she had had cancer herself not too long ago they strongly advised her to limit her visits. They were concerned her body had not fully regenerated after the chemotherapy and she might easily get an infection. Finally Laura gave up, and kissed Bruce goodbye. They agreed on him calling her in the evening.

The moment she got back home, Evy called and insisted on seeing her. She claimed it was urgent and that they needed to talk. Laura told her she would come to see her during lunchtime.

While waiting for her to arrive, Evy was still putting pieces together, and was strongly fighting with the sudden urge to smoke. She quit five years ago, but during any very stressful moments, she craved nicotine, and this was, by far, one of the most stressful things that had happened to her for many, many years. If all of it turned out to be true, how would she supposed to live with the awareness that she had allowed Jeff to be so manipulated? And that it was because of her he was thinking he was going insane.

Evy was coming back from the grocery store next to her home, after having bought a supply of nicotine chewing gum, stunned there was even a carrot flavor these days, when Laura parked her car next to her. Evy stopped, popped the gum out from its container and was waiting for her friend to come.

"You want to smoke again?" Laura asked surprised to smell the scent of the gum.

"More than you can imagine."

"What happened?"

"Not sure if *anything* really happened. But if it did, I can't even imagine *not* smoking."

Intrigued, Laura entered the staircase with Evy without a word. They were also completely silent in the elevator. Laura was looking at her best friend lit by the pale ceiling light. Something was different about her. She seemed distanced, absent. Evy was chewing the gum intensely, visibly focused on something, not willing to chat with her. Something really must have happened.

"I bought us some lunch. Do you feel like having a tuna salad with me?" Laura asked when they entered the apartment.

"Yeah, sure. You know where the plates are," Evy said while throwing away her gum. The crap was disgusting.

Laura took out the plates and cutlery, put them on a table and placed the salad on them. Evy was walking around the room for some time and when the lunch was ready, she sat on her chair and looked at Laura.

"Will you finally tell me what is bugging you?"

"Laura, how did you find Alyssa?"

Laura looked at her for few seconds, expecting there might be something additional to this question, but Evy was silent, she was only looking at her.

"I found her brochures in the clinic. There was a telephone number and a website address on it."

"What did it say exactly?"

"That she was healing souls."

"And you called her when you were in the middle of the chemotherapy, right?"

"Yes."

"Why then? Why not at the beginning?"

"Because I found her brochure after one of the sessions, not at the beginning. Also, it said she was healing souls and I was getting more and more depressed by the cancer."

"And you thought a soul-healer would be a good idea?"

"Evy, I'd go to any Shaman, an herbalist, a goddamn voodoo master if they would promise me help. Why are you asking all this anyway? You know it all, how I found her and why I went to her."

"Have you ever experienced any side effects of her healing you?"

"What? No! Where did you get that idea from? Evy, what the hell is going on?"

"I think it's possible we've opened a fucking Pandora's Box."

Evy told Laura about Jeff's recent behavior, about the jasmine-flavored sexual experience that was becoming more and more omnipresent in her life and how, at the same time, Jeff started having his chills, and how his attraction to Evy had vaporized.

"And you think it's all Alyssa's fault?" Laura asked, although she had to admit, Evy's arguments were suspiciously cohesive.

"Yes, that's exactly what I think. There's just far too many coincidences here. And it's not just the sex stuff. Laura, I've started screwing up left and right since it all began. The meeting with the board— I got late and I was unprepared."

"It can happen to anyone, for God's sake."

"Yeah, but two days before it, I knew Jeff was counting on me and I was perfectly ready for it. Then I got late and I forgot very important stuff; he was furious with me, and I was unbelievably embarrassed. Then I did not tell him about the forum, and if I had, he might have caught Jake in the act and the story with him sabotaging us would have been over. Then I failed you."

"Me? How?"

"I did hear the phone when you were calling me after you came back from Canada, but the moment I was walking toward the bedroom, this whole thing started again and I was lying on the floor, focusing on how great it felt, and totally forgot about calling you back. I guess I was high on endorphins, but at that point, to tell the truth, I wouldn't care if it was God himself calling. And you had a very important message for me. And because of the same thing, I did not manage to finish editing the book, which made Jeff so furious."

"Oh come on, I am also the reason why you did not finish it on time. I asked you to stay at my home."

"Laura, I should have finished editing this book about a week ago. That's what I would normally do, just not when I am busy having unreal sexual intercourses or waiting for them. I'm telling you, it's destroying my life, piece by piece. God, I am actually hoping it doesn't happen as we speak."

"You think it might?"

"I don't know. It happens almost every day and the last time it took place was at your home."

"At my home?"

"Yes. I'm not proud of it, trust me."

"So, what's your theory?"

"I know it sounds crazy and all, but I think, I mean I *suspect* that Alyssa, somehow, took all this sexual tension from Jeff, she personified it and passed it on me."

"Giving him the feeling of cold and lack of patience for you?"

"Rather leaving him with the feeling of cold and repulsiveness toward me."

"But he was here, you talked this morning, I suppose he wasn't repulsed then?"

"No. He thinks it's because of yesterday's total burst of emotions. He thinks it allowed him to calm down for a while. Laura, he thinks he's losing senses. And it's *my* fault."

"Oh for heaven's sake, Evy, are you listening to yourself? It's totally bonkers! How would Alyssa do that?"

"How would she heal you?"

Laura went silent. She looked at Evy carefully, and Evy could tell her friend was getting angrier with every second. Nevertheless, she continued.

"I mean, come on, Laura, you *know* Alyssa's not a human! Have you paid any attention to her eyes? And I am not talking about the color, I mean, they're completely empty, soulless if you will. And you told me her apartment was white and calm, and when I got there, two days later, it was bloody-red, with candles and erotic paintings on the walls."

"She redecorated it." "So drastically? In what a couple of days? Even *Extreme Makeovers* people need more time! Laura, think about it! She gave you the sense of peace and gave me the sense of erotica! These were exactly the reasons why we went to her!"

"Okay, fine, let's assume you're right. There's just one thing missing. I'm fine and nothing wrong has been happening to me."

"No? You're sure?"

Laura was completely flabbergasted.

"Stop. Stop it right now."

"Think about it, Laura! Your cancer at least had some basis, it runs in your family. Bruce has no genetic burden."

"People get cancer, Evy, okay? They do! That's it, it just fucking happens!"

"Right after yours? *Statistically* speaking, how much do you think it's possible for spouses to face cancer weeks between?"

"Do you realize that if your way of thinking is correct, I probably attracted a possibly fatal disease on my very own husband? Are you out of your mind?"

"I've never said you did it deliberately—"

"I DIDN'T DO IT! God!" Laura started crying hysterically. "Oh God, oh my God, it's not true, God, please, it's not possible!"

Evy went to the sink and poured her some water. She came to Laura, gave her the glass and touched her shoulder. Laura emptied it in one gulp, turned around to Evy and said, "You know, you were dreaming of screwing Jeff, and that's the thing. It was simply shallow and *dumb*, so you got punished. That's it."

"Laura!"

"You have been punished for being superficial. And for being coward. You'd probably be with him without *any* outside help, but you were too impatient, you wanted him there and then. So there you go. You got what you wanted. How's my theory work for you?"

"Look, you may want to hurt me, but if I'm right, think about it, maybe if we find her, talk to her, Bruce could be fine?"

"He WILL be fine. He IS fine. He's in far better condition than I was. No, Ev, you've crossed the line. Suggesting I put this all on him—"

"I haven't said anything like that!"

"I mean, Evy, compare your case and mine! I was fighting for my *life*, looking for help to survive! All you wanted was to bang him!"

"Get out!" Evy shouted.

Laura went silent. They were standing in the middle of the living room, looking at each other, both having no idea what was happening.

"I mean it, Laura, get out from my home," Evy repeated and went to the hall to open the door. She had had enough. Laura was panicking, it was obvious, but what she said, and the way she said it, hurt her deeply.

"I'm sorry, Evy, I didn't mean to."

315

"You did, you meant it. It's time for you to go."

"I'll—I'll call you," Laura replied and left the apartment.

"What the hell is happening?" Evy whispered when the doors closed.

She smelled jasmine and only managed to think *Oh God, not again.* She wept silently, sat on the armchair and closed her eyes waiting for it to be over.

"Hi, Neil, how you're doing?" Jeff answered the phone.

"Hi, Jeff, got a minute?"

"Sure."

"I have something that I think will be interesting for you."

"I'm all ears," said Jeff and sat down comfortably on his office armchair. He put his legs on the desk and truly hoped that the news was going to be juicy.

"I thought the issue we had been talking about was too important for you, I have decided not to wait for our next basketball meeting and I just called Owen Mack."

"You did? So, did he say anything?"

"Well, I told him your story. He seemed genuinely concerned and promised me to check it all out."

"That's great, thanks, Neil! I really appreciate."

"No problem, I was wondering if you wanted to hear what he found out?"

"He called you back already?"

"Yeah, twenty minutes ago."

"Sure, what did he say?"

"He told me he spoke to Abram and asked him to disclose who called him. Abram said that at first the man did not want to say his name, but when John informed him his warnings were not to be taken seriously unless he had revealed his identity, the guy said his name was Ted Gardner."

"Ted? Are you sure?" That was *very* surprising.

"That's what Owen told me. He also asked John to fax him a signed statement in which he would confirm it was Ted who called."

"That's fantastic! Okay, thank you, Neil, you've helped me a lot."

"Listen, you should sue that guy. I mean he's just deliberately screwed up months of your hard work, and he cannot walk around throwing allegations."

"I know. I only need him to confess in front of David."

"I can come on Tuesday if you want. I'd love to be there when you are going to disclose the fucker to Garbinsky."

"That would be great. I will arrange a meeting with David then and will let you know about the details."

"Great. I am really stirred by this story. Such people like Jake and Ted, they ruin the idea of business. If they are capable of such actions, then it's better for everyone to move them away from any decision-making positions."

"I'll call you the minute I know when the meeting with David is to take place."

"I'm waiting. We'll get him. We *already* did. Let's just watch him crawl."

"Can't wait, my friend, can't wait," replied Jeff and hung up. He couldn't help but smile.

~86~

Two days passed and Laura still hadn't called her. There were times Evy wanted to make the first step and at least send her a text, just to break the unusual and awful silence between them, but it did not seem to be a good idea. Evy told her what she was convinced was true because it all creepily added up and made sense. And Laura panicked. She thought Evy was accusing her of putting Bruce's life in danger. Maybe it was a mistake, but she had the right to know about Evy's suspicions. On the other hand, she could not believe she had not predicted Laura's reaction. She knew how petrified she was with Bruce's condition, so it should have been obvious she would react like that.

During those two days, Evy had no idea what to do with herself. As much as she was pushing the thought away, she had to admit the whole sexual disturbance was slowly terrorizing her. She was simply afraid of leaving her own apartment as she was worried "it" might happen everywhere, at every time and moment. Evy was sure she wouldn't be able to handle the embarrassment. This was no way to live. Supposedly, the sensation would not go away, what would she do? Ban herself for life from leaving her home? The disturbances were happening quite often, and Evy knew she simply *had to* break free, otherwise her life would become a complete mess. Not to mention she felt she owed Jeff, bringing his own life back; his current problems were undoubtedly her fault.

On the third day of Evy's forced imprisonment the weather was awful. She made some on-line grocery shopping and was waiting for the supplies to be delivered. It was the beginning of the third week of September and it seemed like fall was on its way. A storm just finished and it was raining, and a chilly wind was blowing. Evy convinced herself that she would have stayed home anyway. Once the shopping arrived, she cleaned her apartment, made herself some spaghetti for lunch and sat by her desk to, once more, analyze what she knew and what was happening. Looking at Alyssa's eyes, at her behavior, Evy knew deep down she was *not* a human being. She was very enigmatic, etheric even, and there was no doubt she *did* have some kind of power inside of her.

It was quite alarming that Evy still hadn't received any payment notice. Laura got the bank account number immediately after she had found out she was healthy. Apparently, it meant that Alyssa's plans toward Evy hadn't finished yet. The thought brought chills down her spine. What more should she expect? It seemed that there was no hope for her problem to finish soon. She had to stop and the sooner the better.

Evy turned on her laptop and started looking for Alyssa's website. She was Googling for over half an hour, but could not find absolutely any information about the healer. No official website, although Laura claimed this was her source of information, no profile registered at any social or career network, no posts about her on any boards, no clips.

Nothing.

There was simply not a word about Alyssa. Evy thought about the common saying that if you can't be found on-line, you probably don't exist. Was that it? Alyssa did not exist?

"My God, why hadn't I checked her out before I got myself into this whole mess?" Evy asked herself, knowing the entire time it was because she trusted Laura; and Laura believed in her.

She kept on searching, but she was unable to dig out any of Alyssa's patients. There were no statements proving her healing powers, no evidence she had ever helped anyone. No telephone numbers, no P.O. Box, no registered business. She even entered Femina's website, since the clinic was allowing the brochures to be distributed there, it was possible they would mention her.

Again, nothing.

It was simply creepy.

Since, at least in the internet reality, Alyssa did not exist, then perhaps, Evy was looking for her using the wrong name. Maybe Alyssa simply was not Alyssa, maybe she was someone (or something) else? Evy got up from her chair and went to the kitchen to make some tea. The rain was now calming down and there were big, heavy drops drumming against the window panes. Evy sighed deeply. When she was waiting for the water to boil, she was focusing on the memory of Alyssa's non-human-like features. The eyes, the healing powers, the fact she knew so much about her. Was she a witch? A demon? Just the thought made Evy nauseous, but she knew she had to check that lead. But how? It was doubtful there would be a devil labor union with registered members. She got back in front of the computer, opened the search engine and she started writing entries:

MIRACULOUS HEALER—26,500,000 results.

"Jesus. No, I need to narrow the parameters."

HEALING DEVILS—countless discussion boards entries. Quite surprising, since the juxtaposition of the two words seemed obviously oxymoronic for Evy.

She skimmed about fifteen forums only to find one peculiar post, stating that the devil cannot be a healer as Christ described him as a 'murderer and a 'liar and the father of lies'. There was even a passage given, John 8:44. Evy checked the bible online and it turned out the forum user was right. Even though, it did not explain anything really, because being 'the father of all lies', it was kind of possible the devil would heal Laura just to have fun watching her lose her husband. Or giving Evy the physical pleasure just to see Jeff losing his senses. She added the board to the bookmarks and thought about other entries. *Actually, who said Alyssa would need to have anything in common with the Bible and Christianity? There are so many religions and, mythologies around the world, who said Alyssa would be the devil?* What other creatures had been known for healing people? Sadler was defining herself as an herbalist, a Shaman. Maybe it was a clue; perhaps she was a nature-power believer?

Evy wrote SHAMAN'S HEALING POWERS—1, 500, 000 results. She scrolled few pages of forums and boards, but these were mostly books and publications concerning the phenomenon. There were also spells given, but it wasn't what she was looking for. She thought about it for a minute and wrote:

PAGAN HEALER—1,820,000 results.

"This is hopeless." She scrolled five pages of results and there was one sentence that drew her attention.

"Earth-centered people, aka *Pagans*, are ritualistic in their *healing* practices."

She clicked on the link and skimmed a few posts. Pagans liked to describe themselves as people who associated their religion strictly with nature. They obeyed her laws, prayed to her and all of their rituals were strictly succumbed to the circle of life she had created. One of the people mentioned that she had become a neo-druid because of the idea of promoting harmony and worshiping nature and because of her fascination with mythological nymphs.

Nymphs. Something struck Evy. She went to the study corner of her living room and started looking for a book on Greek Mythology. As a child, she used to love reading all this stuff. All those dramatic stories intertwining, all those gods, titans, wars, romance, betrayal, cruelty, passion, it was purely fascinating.

Evy brought herself a chair from the kitchen to seek the higher volumes on the bookshelf. Weren't Nymphs ancient healers? Some of them for sure!

She finally found a huge anthology. It was very old, she got it from her grandmother, but it did not matter, it wasn't like the stories told there would change in time. The book was covered with dust and looked pretty wasted, but it was ready to serve its purpose. Evy put it down on a coffee table, sat down on the sofa and carefully looked at the back of it in the search of appendix.

NYMPHS, pages 52, 75, 164-178, 219, 340, 412, 510.

Evy opened the book on each of those pages and finally found a description of the creatures. The books stated that nymphs were divine creatures, yet different from gods. They were beautiful maidens, who did not get old once they reached adulthood, they loved to dance and sing. They would reside in mountains, live in rivers and lakes, but also among tree tops. They were not immortal, but were capable of giving birth to immortal offspring if conceived with a god. Most of them were rather harmless to people, but some of them were powerful enough to have a direct influence on the mortals' lives.

All this information did not bring Evy closer to solving the mystery of who Alyssa was; however, she found a classification of Nymphs according to their type of dwelling. Apart from their environment, the book gave examples of Nymphs and some basic information about each of them. The categories were: celestial, with Asteriae, the daughter of Atlas, responsible for stars, Hyades, who could send rain on earth, Nephleae responsible for clouds activity and Maia, Zeus' lover, the mother of Hermes.

Among land, Nymphs there were Leimonides, who kept her eye on meadows and Oreads responsible for mountains. There were wood and plant Nymphs, with maidens to take care of flowers, trees, ivy, woods, water Nymphs—. Wait. Evy put her index finger up few lines. Where was it, where—oh! Land Nymphs.

Oenone—a Nymph living on Mount Ida in Phrygia.

Known for healing powers.

"This could be a lead!"

Evy searched the appendix looking for Oenone, but it was all the information she found. She came back to the computer and searched for her name.

Bingo! "This is interesting. *Really* interesting."

≈87≈

Oenone was the wife of King Priam's son, Paris. The exact same one who later started the Trojan War when he fell in love with Helen, the most beautiful woman in the world. Paris left Oenone and their son Corythus as he wanted to live with Helen in Troy. Oenone, betrayed and devastated, was looking for retaliation.

In one of the versions of the myth, she used their son to drive a tiff between Paris and Helen. Paris did not recognize Corythus and, filled with anger, killed his own son. Oenone did not cry a single tear as she was only focused on avenging her own humiliation and pain.

Evy was not able to find a lot of information about the Nymph, she was clearly a minor character in the whole mythology, but surfing the Internet, she found a narration stating that wounded Paris was brought to her straight from a battlefield. He was mortally wounded and Oenone was known for her power of healing.

The power of healing. Evy kept on reading.

Paris begged her to heal him, but her heart was still hurt and she ordered his soldiers to escort him away from her. Finally, overcome with remorse, Oenone decided to help her husband, but by the time she got to Helen's bed where he was lying, it turned out he had died. Mad with pain, she threw herself onto his burning funeral pyre and died embracing his body and crying. Other sources claimed she hanged herself, or threw herself from the cliff. Evy also found a poem "The Death of Oenone", by Alfred Lord Tennyson, but it seemed only to repeat what she had already read. She printed the notes she had found and added the websites to the bookmarks.

Evy felt her eyes hurt. She rubbed them and her forehead with her hands. She was both tired and hungry. As shocking as it may have seemed, it turned out she had spent almost four hours researching Alyssa. And she did not even know for sure if it was actually her that she had managed to find.

Evy went to the kitchen and got milk out of the fridge.

Really, a Nymph? A Nymph residing in Boston, messing with people's minds? But was it that silly to be surprised? There was no doubt something out of this world had entered her and Laura's lives. So, why not

323

a Nymph? It could have been much, much worse, Evy supposed. *God, where are Mulder and Scully when you really need them?*

She ate some flakes with milk and decided she was far too tired to search for anything more that night. Half an hour later, Evy was in her bed, falling asleep. Despite all the revelations, all the research and possible supernatural encounter, she felt calm and steady. She closed her eyes, took a deep breath and felt she was floating toward Morpheus' arms. Mythologically speaking.

A telephone. A telephone was ringing. Evy lifted her head, looked around, checked the alarm clock on her night table. 03:17 a.m.

"What the fuck?" She turned on the lamp. The brightness made her squint her eyes, so she covered them with one hand and she reached for the phone partially blind.

"This better be good, it's the middle of the night!" she said irritated.

"Bruce's in a coma!" Laura cried into her ear. Evy immediately woke up.

"What?! When did this happen?"

"Two hours ago. They called me from the hospital, told me he collapsed, they fixed it, but now he's in coma. I don't know what to do, Evy, oh God!"

"Calm down, Laura, please. Are you in the hospital?"

"Yeah. I'm waiting for further information."

"Do you want me to come?"

"Yes," Laura whispered, it was clear she was crying and had problems keeping her voice on the same level, "I *need* you to come here."

"Okay, give me half an hour."

"Evy?"

"Yes?"

"I called Alyssa. For help."

Evy was silent, she had no idea what to say. It was probably the worst thing Laura could have done, but it was understandable, she was desperate.

"And?" she finally asked.

"Nobody answered."

"Well, it's 3 a.m., Saturday night. Maybe it's not the best moment for any unwise conclusions?"

"Maybe. Please come."

"I'm coming."

She got out of bed and put the papers she printed out in the evening in her handbag.

Could be handy.

Oenone~Agatha Rae~

88

Evy was on her way to the hospital. It was still heavily raining so the driving conditions were quite difficult. The streets were empty, only some single police vehicles here and there. It was also very dark as the part of the city she was driving through had some kind of power damage, probably due to the rain and the storm.

She was in the middle of her way when she smelled jasmine.

"Oh no, not now, please!" she cried, but it was useless. The once-pleasurable feeling of warmth growing down her belly, was intensifying, and the last thing that came to her mind was to pull over and wait until it was over.

She was lucky it was the middle of the night; she might have caused some accident if the street was crowded. When the wave was overcoming her, the only thing she was able to think about was not to cause the police suspicion. Evy did not think she would take it, being questioned about pulling over without any visible reason, right in the middle of her distraction. A few minutes later, breathless and angry, she turned the keys again.

"This has to stop. I can't live like this!"

She arrived at the hospital about twenty minutes later. Laura was sitting nervously on a chair in the corridor.

"Hey!" Evy said. Laura did not respond, she just embraced her. They were standing there in the middle of the hall hugging and crying.

"I'm so sorry for what I've done," Evy said.

"I deserved it. I'm sorry for what I've said," Laura replied.

"I don't even remember a word from it anymore."

They sat down.

"What's happening, Laura?"

"Well, nothing new. Bruce's in coma. Nobody knows why he had collapsed; nobody understands why he's unconscious. Everything was fine until tonight."

"Could it be some kind of a side effect of the radiotherapy?"

"No, the doctors excluded this option entirely."

"How long can it last? The coma?"

"Nobody knows, especially since the cause is unknown. All they're telling me is that they're performing tests."

"Did you see him?"

"Not yet. I was told they would let me know if I could."

"I'm so sorry, Laura, you must be terrified." Evy hugged her again.

"I am, Evy, I am. It's so unexpected. The cancer, the coma. I have no idea what is happening. It's so confusing. I feel totally hopeless." She was weeping.

They kept on hugging when Evy asked, "So, Alyssa hasn't answered yet, huh?"

"No. I think that if there is anyone who can take my husband out of this mess, it is her. I need to go to her and beg her for help."

She's probably the one who got your husband into the mess. "Listen, could I come with you?"

"Even though you don't trust her?"

"Yeah, I mean, it's bugging me I still haven't gotten any information about the payment. Also, I want to ask her to take that whole crap off of me, I've had enough."

"If you want. I'm going there as soon as possible. I hope she doesn't sleep at 8 a.m., because that's when I'm going to her."

"May I stay with you here until then?"

"Yes. I need you here with me."

"I'm here, Laura. I'm here." She hugged her again. "It's going to be all right."

"You can't be sure."

Evy did not reply. She wasn't.

❧89❧

The hospital staff took Laura to a break room where she could sleep a bit on a coach. Evy spent the night dozing on chairs with her jacket bundled under her head. A smell of fresh coffee woke her up. It was Laura, she looked quite rested. She brought Evy a cup and handed it to her after waking her up.

"Come on, Ev, it's 8.30."

Evy took the cup and looked around. She needed a few seconds to recall why she was in the hospital in the first place.

"How's Bruce?" she asked, taking a sip.

"Nothing new. Still in coma."

"But he's not getting worse; that's good news, I suppose."

"Yeah, you might look at it that way, I guess."

"What's wrong?"

"Apart from my husband's coma?"

"You know what I mean. You're different."

"Alyssa's not answering. I'm going there."

"Like I said, I want to go with you."

"Let's go then. The sooner I talk to her, the better."

Or not. Evy checked if she had the papers in her handbag.

They agreed to go to Alyssa separately. Laura already drove off when Evy was in the bathroom, washing her face. She was truly intrigued with what they were going to find out. She did not have a shade of doubt that Alyssa not answering was not a coincidence. However, because of her previous conversation with Laura, she decided to keep her mouth shut and let her friend discover on her own who they were both dealing with.

Fifteen minutes later Evy parked Bob by Archstone Avenir. The closer she was to Alyssa's place, the more nervous she was becoming. After taking a deep breath, she got out and walked toward the building. Laura was already waiting for her by the door.

"It's 9.15 a.m. Sunday. Most of people are usually home at this time, am I right?" she asked.

It struck Evy to see how her friend had changed. The experience of her own cancer and what was now going on with Bruce were visible on her face. It was hard to explain, but there seemed to be a permanent shadow cast on her countenance. It pierced Evy's heart, because she was not able to tell when that burden reflected itself; whether it was already there when she was sick or if it appeared later on when Bruce was diagnosed. She would risk to say it was the latter, which made her feel even worse, as she was so absorbed by her own problems, which at this moment seemed simply shallow and selfish; she didn't see that earlier. Laura had changed. The way she gave her coffee that morning…she was determined, focused and ready to fight for Bruce. It looked as if the times of despair had finished; it was now time for action.

"Yeah, I'd say so. Did you buzz her?"

"I did. Nobody's answering."

Evy pushed the button herself. Silence.

"Listen, Laura, I think I may have found out—" she started, but at this point the door opened.

They walked inside to the staircase and called the elevator. It seemed awkward, kind of haunting to be there again. Evy felt how her pulse was increasing. To tell the truth, she wasn't sure if she truly wanted to see Alyssa again, but there was no other way to get rid of her problem. She kind of hoped that maybe it was all happening to her because she still hadn't paid and hoped she would get a bank account number and settle the whole thing.

Laura knocked firmly on the door; Evy was standing right next to her.

"Who are you?" a woman with a baby on her hands, confused to see two women, opened the door.

Laura was completely taken aback, and Evy immediately looked at the number on the door.

"Yes?" the woman asked again. She was a short blond wearing a sleeveless shirt and shorts. Her feet were bare and there was a biting scent of cigarette smoke coming out of the apartment. The baby in her arms was drinking milk from a bottle and there was a TV on in one of the rooms, which was way too loud. Two other kids were running in the corridor.

"Um, hi, we're looking for Alyssa."

"Who?"

"Alyssa."

"Does Alyssa have a last name?" the woman asked.

"Sadler," Evy said. "We're looking for Alyssa Sadler who lives here, in, um, this particular apartment."

The women put the baby down and sent it with a gesture to one of the rooms. She walked toward Laura and Evy and closed the door a bit.

"You must have gotten the wrong address; nobody named Alyssa lives here."

"How long have you lived here?" Laura asked.

"Three years."

Evy and Laura had no idea what to say.

"Look, you obviously have the wrong address, I'm telling you."

"Maybe it's the wrong floor. Do you know if any Alyssa lives here in this building?"

"No, I have never heard of anyone named Alyssa Sadler. Sorry."

The woman closed the door and Evy and Laura were standing by the elevator, trying to understand anything.

"How the *fuck* is it possible?" Laura finally asked.

"I—I don't know," Evy said. She was stunned. What were they going to do now?

They walked out of the building in complete silence. Once outside, heading toward their cars, Laura stopped and asked, "So, we've been tricked, right?"

"Apparently," Evy admitted.

They went silent again. Neither had any idea what to say.

"Do you now believe me that Alyssa is, by far, not an ordinary person?" Evy finally said.

"I still think it sounds ridiculous—"

"Oh come on, Laura! Check the facts! Am I supposed to list them again? And even if you don't believe me, then maybe you should go back to the apartment and talk to the woman again? You *heard* her. Alyssa never lived there, unless three years have passed since we both visited her."

"Okay, fine, I believe you, all right? I do! So who is she? What is she? A devil? A ghost? A fucking alien?"

"I've done some research, and I think I have a clue on what she might be."

"What have you found out?"

"Come on, let's have some breakfast first."

They went to a small restaurant nearby. Since the weather was clearing up, they decided to buy takeout and have it at Rose Kennedy Greenway Park.

While they were sitting on a bench eating their sandwiches, Evy took out the printed papers from her handbag and gave them to Laura. She was studying them for a few minutes, and it was obvious the material was simply fascinating for her.

"Oh my God, is *that* what Alyssa is? A Nymph?"

"I don't know, but the description surely fits."

"You mean the healing powers?"

"That and also being a mean bitch. And, what day did you visit her?"

"It was June, around the 25th."

"Midsummer period. The time in ancient Greek when people would drink wine, celebrate the beginning of summer and commune with gods and nature. The time when gods were the closest to humans. Perhaps this was the time of her most intense activity."

"But why would she do all of that to us?"

"I have no idea, but I don't believe she would do it *only* to us. Maybe that's her game; maybe messing up with people's lives makes her happy?"

"How did you come up with that?"

Evy told her all stages of her research. Laura was listening carefully, but did not seem to be too convinced.

"What, you're not buying it, are you?"

"It seems very probable, no matter how *improbable* it sounds. And that's really scary. However, you could have simply found a fitting character and thus it influenced your opinion."

"Maybe. Maybe not. When I went to see her, to ask her for help with Jeff, she told me she was unable to control human emotions, only primal instincts, thus the whole sexual experience. She told me that sex had always been about procreation and pleasure and that the emotional aspect of it is something new in the history of mankind and artificially created."

"And?"

"'Nymphs were very sexual creatures. I have found countless descriptions of them searching for men to have intercourse. Unsatisfied, always wanting more, and very violent once a demand was not fulfilled. This could explain the intensity of my disturbances."

"You call it disturbances?"

"What else am I supposed to call it? I loved it at first, it was all very romantic, mysterious and incredibly erotic. But quite soon, everything started changing. First of all, it turned out it could happen anywhere, anytime!"

"Anytime?"

"Yes. And it wouldn't be that bad if it happened only in my apartment. But I've experienced it at the gym, at your place, finally last night when I was driving to the hospital."

"I can't think how uncomfortable that must be."

"It is. And it's no longer romantic; it's awful. I feel it coming, can't stop it, can't control it, it's only physical, you know what I mean? It appears for five, maybe ten seconds and disappears. Actually, I spent last two days at home, because I am becoming afraid of going out anywhere and being humiliated. I mean imagine it happening to me while being in a supermarket for example. It simply makes me want to cry. I feel enslaved to it."

"Can you predict it somehow?"

"I smell jasmine a few seconds before it starts. But I cannot stop it, I only know it's coming. Thanks to the smell, I managed to pull over before it got me. I have no idea what would have happened if it happened while driving and traffic was normal."

"It's that intense?"

"It is, and all the physical aspect is there as well. I get tensed, I close my eyes, I get relaxed; you know, the chill that happens just after that. And then I get immensely angry and frustrated it happened again."

Laura hugged Evy.

"How is it possible that I have gotten us both into such mess involving a Nymph, cancer and compulsive sexual needs, I have no idea," she said and it sounded so ridiculous they both started laughing.

"So, a Nymph, huh?" Laura finally said. "Guess they're not little creatures with wings jumping from one flower to another after all, are they?"

"Guess not," replied Evy. "So, what are we going to do?"

"We need to find her, ask her to take all this away from us."

"How?"

"I don't know yet. May I stay at your place for a while?"

"Sure."

"I don't want to be in an empty house. I don't want to be alone. Plus, you live closer to the hospital."

"So, do you want to go now?"

"Yeah, I guess there's nothing else we can do here. You go and I will come to you in the afternoon. I need to get some things from home."

"Okay."

Oenone~Agatha Rae~

❧90❧

Laura came to Evy in the late afternoon while she was watching a "Friends" re-run on TV. It was one of her favorite episodes, the one in which the girls and the boys changed their flats. A doorbell distracted her in the middle of a scene in which nobody could tell what Chandler's job was. Evy got up, put away a jar with chocolate sandwich spread and went to open the door.

"Hi, sorry it took me so long." Laura walked inside.

"Hi, no problem, I managed to clean a bit."

"What are you watching?" she asked and looked at the TV. "Oh! I love this episode!"

"Me, too." Evy laughed.

"They called me from the hospital. Bruce's stable, but they still don't know what happened."

"I'm sorry."

"'Me, too, but I hope that he wakes up as unexpectedly as he went into the coma."

"So, what's in the bags?" Evy asked, looking at three huge paper bags Laura put on the kitchen table.

"Well, two of the bags contain some grocery stuff. I figured that since you're afraid of going out of home, you may be missing few things."

"That is so kind of you; thank you!" Laura really was a great friend.

"No problem. So, I got you tea, some cookies, some vegetables and bread."

"You're so sweet." Evy kissed Laura. "But what's in the third bag?"

"Well, I did some research myself. You see, the reason why I came this late is that I've been searching for some information on how to summon a Nymph."

"What?"

"What, do you think you have the monopoly on finding supernatural content on the internet?" Laura smiled and went to the hall to hang her jacket.

"Um, no."

"So, I did some research and found out that the most common way of summoning a Nymph is setting out candles in all four directions of the world and send out the thoughts of welcome. It supposedly helps if you sprinkle the candles with a bit of ginger. We should light the candles and after that sit and focus on her to come."

"Laura, listen to yourself, this is nonsense!"

"Maybe it is, maybe it isn't," she replied and took four thick, long candles, a compass, ginger and matches from the third bag.

"Whoa! Have you ever done this? Because I surely haven't!"

"Yeah, Evs, I summon Nymphs every second weekend."

"That's my point, how do you know if it works?"

"If we don't try, we won't know, will we?"

"But don't you think we need someone experienced to do this?"

"The description said that only the people wanting something from the Nymph should summon her, otherwise they never show up as they do not like to be invoked."

Laura took the candles and the compass and walked to Evy's living room. She stood by an armchair and started moving it toward the wall.

"Are you gonna help me?" she asked.

"Laura, it's crazy, I mean look at us! Twenty-four hours ago we had no idea Nymphs even existed and now you want to summon one?"

"Are you afraid it might not work?"

"On the contrary, I am terrified it might! What are we going to do then? How do we *unsummon* her? And what if it's not Alyssa that comes?"

"That is why we need to focus on her. *Precisely* on her. That's what I've found out on Google."

Evy looked at Laura completely unconvinced.

"Oh come on, as if you didn't start your own research like that, *please*. The description I just told you was the most common one. Then I went to the city library and searched a lot, trust me, *a lot* of books and files on the Nymph tradition and magic it involves. So, are you helping me or not?"

"This scares me, Laura. That's the truth. We really don't know what we're dealing with."

Laura sat on the armchair and looked at her seriously.

"We should have been scared in the first place, but we were both too focused on achieving our goals. And on achieving them in the easiest and fastest way possible."

"What do you mean? You had cancer, for God's sake."

"I did. But nobody told me it was a fatal case. I never managed till the end of the chemotherapy, maybe I gave up too soon. All I know is that if I had known that this would have caused Bruce's illness, I would have never, *ever*, gone for it."

"How do you know? Maybe the will of life would have been stronger?"

"And what, you think I'd consider living with the burden of killing my own husband to achieve that?"

Evy said nothing. She knew Laura was right.

"Evy, you want to regain your previous life back as well. What, are you going to tell me that you want to spend the rest of your days trapped in your own apartment?"

"No, of course not."

"Then come on. Let's try, that's the least we can do."

"Shouldn't we wait for full moon?"

"Don't patronize this, Ev. I am scared, too, but I will do whatever it takes to save Bruce."

Evy helped Laura move the furniture and put the candles on the floor, according to what the instruction said. They sprinkled them with ginger and started lighting them, one by one. Once they were burning, they sat face to face in the middle of them and grabbed each other's hands.

"This is it, Ev. Anything might happen now. I just want you to know I feel totally sorry for bringing you to Alyssa and involving you in this whole mess."

"I went there because I wanted to. It's not your fault, I've never even thought like that."

"I love you."

"I love you, too."

They closed their eyes and focused on Alyssa, calling her to come, to talk to them, to take the spells away.

***

They had no idea how much time they spent summoning her. The entire time they thought of the Nymph. Evy finally opened her eyes when she realized the candles were no longer burning and the smell of fuse smoke filled the room. She looked at Laura and spotted her friend was crying.

"Laura, what is it? Did you feel anything?"

"No, I did not. I made a fool of myself, with all this summoning, didn't I?"

"No, not at all! No, Laura! You're searching, *we're* searching for help! And my problem is nothing in comparison to what you've been going through for months. I totally understand you need to check all possible solutions."

"But it was all naive. Dumb."

"It was what we've had so far. Please don't cry, we're going to look for other ways of contacting her."

"Like what?"

"I don't know yet, but we'll figure it out."

"Will we?"

"Don't we always?" Evy asked and Laura smiled at her.

"Come on, we need to open the window, the scent of smoke is pretty intense."

"Maybe we did something wrong. Did you concentrate well?"

"Of course. Did you?"

"Yeah. I don't know what might have gone wrong," Laura said.

"Maybe it's just that we're amateurs? Maybe we need to find a medium or something?"

"Would you ever imagine us talking about things like that? Medium or nymphs?"

Evy looked at her for a second and finally said, "Come on, help me put the armchair back on its place."

"I really hoped it would work."

"I know, Laura, I know," Evy replied softly.

When they put the furniture back in its place, they agreed they were both very tired. Maybe it was because of the physical effort, maybe the long-lasting focus on Alyssa, or maybe the fact they both almost did not sleep at all the other night, but they felt exhausted. Laura went to the bathroom and Evy made the bed. She sat on it and yawned, knowing it was way past time to rest.

Laura came back from the bathroom and Evy took her place. After about fifteen minutes, they were both lying in bed, falling asleep.

"Evy, if the distraction comes, please don't molest me," Laura joked.

"I promise I won't; I'm pretty self-sufficient then," Evy replied smiling.

Laura woke up rapidly, as she was dreaming she was falling. She hated the feeling, the sudden stress and the thrill overcoming one's body. She opened her eyes and, to her amazement, it turned out she was lying on the grass. Moist, early-morning grass, cold and unpleasant. She was wearing her pajamas, but did not feel cold. Laura stood and looked around.

She was standing in the middle of a meadow, surrounded by a thick forest. The meadow was covered with delicate fog, hanging lazily above the grass. Single rays of sunlight were bashfully tearing the dark sky, bringing the very first symptoms of the upcoming morning. Birds were singing amongst the trees and everything was very peaceful.

"Laura!"

She turned around and saw Evy. She was also wearing her pajamas.

"Evy!" she ran toward her. "It looks like we're having the same dream!"

"I know! It's crazy! Where do you think we are?"

"I have no idea, but it all feels very real. I mean I can breathe this air and it feels so clean, so fresh."

"It is real," a third voice shouted.

They turned around.

"Alyssa!" Laura whispered. The Nymph was walking toward them, only it seemed that she was gliding, just above the ground surface. She no longer looked like the Alyssa they met. Her skin was very pale, it had the color of milk and it was so thin it was almost possible to see through her. Her hair was clipped, but single locks were gently touching her cheeks. She was dressed in ethereal purple robes. The only thing that was the same were her green eyes, which were glowing and it looked both fascinating and scary.

"I am impressed. You are the first people in centuries who have discovered who I am," she said. Her voice seemed out of this world; it sounded pearly and soft. It was hard to see if her lips were moving.

"So you are Oenone, aren't you?" Evy asked and walked a bit closer to her.

"I am."

"We called you."

"I know, and I heard. It truly amused me, the ritual, but I have decided to see you anyway. Like I said, I am impressed with your research. Hardly anyone has made such an attempt. And trust me, I've dealt with a lot of people."

"So, is this what you do? Pretend to help people and actually destroy them?" Laura asked.

"I don't like the tone of your voice, Laura. As far as I remember, I cured you."

"Only to pass the cancer on to my husband."

"Side effects," the Nymph said smiling.

An angry grimace appeared on Laura's face and she moved closer to Oenone.

"Take it back from him. I demand it!"

The Nymph started laughing in disbelief and amusement.

"You can't be serious. Nobody talks to me like that," she added firmly.

"Why did you do that? Why did you put the misery on us?" asked Evy.

"And why not? That's my nature, that's what I do."

"But you're a *healer*! You cure people!"

"And I did! Laura is healthy."

"You never said the *side effect* would be my husband's coma and sickness. That's lying!"

"Have you ever asked me about the consequences? Also, both of you, deep down, felt uncomfortable around me, I knew it, I felt it. But the temptation was stronger than your intuition."

"You made it clear all you wanted was money in return, how was I supposed to know you also required such prey?" shouted Laura.

"Oenone, you made a mistake not helping your husband, why would you impose a similar drama on other people?" Evy asked.

"Be quiet! You know nothing about my husband!" the Nymph said angrily. "My husband betrayed me, allowed Helen to seduce him; I lost *everything* once he decided to leave me!"

"I understand that he hurt you, unimaginably, but my husband has always been faithful to me, there's no need to punish him!"

"*Him*? It's all about you, Laura!"

Laura was standing in front of Oenone, who seemed to be very tall from such close perspective, and she had no idea what to say. She was breathing heavily and realized she was feeling dizzy.

"W- Why? What have I ever done to you?" she asked.

"Remember when you came to me for the first time? You said you wanted my help because it wasn't your time yet. It always puzzles me when people say so, because, who is to decide when someone's time is coming to an end or not. To manipulate with the lifeline?"

"But I was in the middle of chemotherapy when I came to you, I was already manipulating with the lifeline, so what's the difference?"

"This *is* different! When you were being cured in the hospital, you were fighting, it was a battle. And as long as two parties fight, the outcome is never obvious. That was honorable; that was fair. The cancer attacked you and you were struggling with it. Coming to me was the sign of weakness. I *hate* weakness. My husband was *weak*! His *weakness* caused my, our family, my child, and Paris himself. I detest weakness!" Oenone's eyes became visibly darker. "Don't think you were so special, Laura. It wasn't only you, remember you found the information about me in the hospital. That is the place where weakness takes advantage of people. I only test those who succumb to it."

"I only wanted to live; isn't it the most basic instinct of all?" Laura asked and she felt tears coming to her eyes.

"It is, but, you see, I am a Nymph. Humans have always served as entertainment for us. Feasting, satisfying sexual needs among people has always been natural, but your moral compass is something completely strange to us. People are fun. Nothing more."

"You enjoy tormenting people?"

"A bit." Oenone smiled and her eyes were glowing normally again.

"So you must love what you've done to me. I bet you're having great fun," Evy said.

"You got what you wanted, too. You wanted physical closeness, that's exactly what I gave you."

"It's destroying my life. I need it to end."

"Sorry. I never take back what I do."

"So how am I supposed to live?"

"Your situation was so trivial. All you had to do was confess, tell the man how you felt, but you came to me. You've decided to use non-human power just for the sake of experiencing bodily pleasure with a man you wanted. Compare this to Laura's problem. You—you've insulted me by *asking* for my help," Oenone added with disdain in her voice.

"So you're punishing us for being naive and wanting our lives to change for the better easily, and you think you have the moral right to use us for your entertainment?" Evy said.

"Yes."

"What am I supposed to do to make you change your mind and take it all back?" Laura asked.

"There's *nothing* you can do. I've been around for millennia, I've seen everything there has ever been to see and there's nothing you can do to make me change my mind. People are weak, selfish and have no dignity when it comes to satisfying their needs or making their dreams come true. They are an abomination."

"So what, you're going to leave us like this?" Evy asked. She was too stupefied with what she was hearing she had a feeling it was impossible to be really happening.

The sun finally appeared on the sky in its full grandeur, shining strongly and chasing away the clouds and the haze crawling around their ankles. In the sunlight, Oenone looked almost transparent. She turned around and started walking away from them.

"Wait, what are you going to do with us now? Where are you going?" Evy shouted. "I asked you a question!"

"I heard that. I don't know yet. You're not too much fun knowing who I am. It spoils the pleasure."

"When will we see you again?"

"You won't."

"I want the cancer back!" Laura shouted.

"What?!" Evy replied.

Oenone stopped and turned around. She looked confused.

"Go on," she said, intrigued.

"I want the cancer back, but Bruce's health in return."

"Laura, what the hell are you doing?" Evy shouted.

"So, you want to face your illness again to save your husband?"

"Yes."

"Are you sure?"

"I've never been surer of anything in my life."

A thunder ripped the sky. There was no single cloud visible, but suddenly a torrential rain started. All three of them were standing in the middle of the meadow, soaking.

"I want to sacrifice myself, my health and my well-being for my husband's life. I understand you've been hurt, Oenone, but I love Bruce and I will never bear a thought that I live peacefully at his expense. Seeing him suffering breaks my heart; he's my best friend, and he's my soul mate. If one of us should die, I want to be that person."

Oenone was standing there stirred. Laura surprised her. Laura was the first person ever to sacrifice her greatest desire, to overcome the fear or the crave that was obscuring the rational thinking, the first one who had ever deliberately demanded Oenone's spell to be broken for the sake of someone else. And she did that out of the purest intentions.

There was another thunder, but now also a wind appeared. The Nymph was looking at Laura in silence, her eyes were again darker. Evy wasn't sure, but she had a feeling a tear fell on Oenone's cheek. Although, it could have been a raindrop. At this point the wind became unbearable and both Evy and Laura fell down. The last thing they saw among grass and sand flying around them was the Nymph looking at them with purely muted eyes and they both heard a telephone ringing.

Laura woke up first. It was her cell phone.

"Hello? Yes, it's Laura Levinson. Oh my God! He did? I'll be right there! Thank you so much for calling!"

She sat on the bed and looked at Evy who just opened her eyes.

"What happened?"

"Bruce woke up. I'm going to the hospital."

"It's, it's wonderful!" Evy replied in a sleepy voice and immediately spotted her hair was moist. The sheets were, too. The whole bed was.

She heard Laura bustling about, changing her clothes and packing the car keys to her handbag.

"I'm leaving, I'll call you from the hospital!" she shouted and closed the door.

"Oh my God," Evy whispered and sat on the bed. "We did it. We summoned her."

Oenone~Agatha Rae~

$\approx$92$\approx$

Bruce was fine. He had woken up an hour before Laura got to the hospital. She walked inside his room when the doctors were finishing the examination.

"So, am I healthy?" Bruce asked.

"Well, the coma did not damage your brain, and you have no problems with memory and impulses. But, frankly speaking, what made the biggest impression on me is this," the doctor said and pointed to Bruce's chest. There was no sign of radiation-caused damage on the skin.

"What does it mean?" Laura asked.

"Perhaps due to the break in radiation sessions Bruce's skin healed itself. It's quite remarkable, because it's been only three days since the last dose; I've never seen skin healing so swiftly."

Laura froze. She knew what it might have meant. Miraculous recovering, no signs of treatment's side effects. Oh my God, she did it. She cured him. Laura felt her heart pounding. Bruce was safe and sound, she was absolutely sure of it.

"So, now what?" she asked the doctor.

"We're going to run some tests. Typical ones, nothing to be worried about. We're completing the first week of treatment, and want to see how Bruce's organism is doing, how it is handling it."

"Sure," Bruce replied.

"Okay, I'm going to leave you now, we'll see each other in about three hours," doctor said and left the room.

Laura looked at her husband and she embraced him dramatically. She was stroking his head and was crying. He embraced her back and for few seconds neither said anything. After a while, she looked at him.

"I was so scared," she said.

"I know, and I'm sorry," he replied and kissed her.

After a few minutes, a nurse came to transport Bruce to his previous room. Laura walked right by his wheelchair, they were holding hands. He asked her to bring him some carrot juice from the canteen. When they were alone again, with Laura sitting on Bruce's bed, he opened the bottle, drank a few sips and looked at her. He was very serious.

"I need to tell you something."

"What is it?"

"It may sound weird, but I've always been wondering if people in a coma dream. If they are conscious to dream, to *remember* the dreams. How long was I asleep?"

"Nearly three days."

"Because I had a dream. It felt as if it was few seconds long, but, it was very clear, I remember it vividly."

"What was it?"

"I dreamed that a woman came to me. I was helpless, powerless, lying on the grass, with rain dropping on me—" he stopped to drink some juice. It was obvious that the reminiscent of the dream was emotional for him. Laura was listening to him carefully and she had a feeling her heart was about to jump out of her chest. She knew who came to him. But what was her message?

"So, that woman came to me. She looked so dreamlike. She wasn't a human, that's for sure. Her eyes were glowing green, they were petrifying and fascinating at the same time. She reached out to me; her hand seemed transparent, but she was strong. She picked me up and I had no idea what she wanted from me. She spoke, with such an unusual voice, if only you could hear her…"

I did.

"She told me, I mean I heard her in my head, she did not move her lips, "It's time for you to wake up. You have someone waiting for you there." I asked her if she meant you. She nodded. "She loves you. She deserves you. Go back to her. You need to live. Good days are coming"'. Laura gripped his shoulder, but he just looked at her and added, "She told me she knew you. She told me you were ready to sacrifice yourself for me in return for my health…Laura, was it Alyssa?"

"Yes. It was her." Laura nodded.

"Who the hell is she? I know it was a dream, but I am also sure it happened for real!"

"Bruce." She touched his cheeks with her open palms forcing him to look at her, "I think she cured you. I think you're healthy, the cancer is gone."

"Is this how it works? Is this how she made your cancer go away?"

"No, in my case it was all physical, I mean I met her, I spoke to her, and she looked completely different."

"But what is she? She—she's not human, right? Is she an angel?"

"No."

Laura sat on his bed and told him everything.

Oenone~Agatha Rae~

"How is he doing?" asked Evy. She was in the bathroom applying hair conditioner. Being very disappointed and depressed that Oenone did not break her spell and since her plan for the nearest future did not include going out anywhere, (God only knows for how long), she decided to relax and provide herself some comfort by creating a private spa. Evy took a really long, hot bath with aromatic oils and soaps, rubbed moisturizing lotion on her body and was now sitting at the edge of her tub waving her feet to speed up the toenails to dry after polishing them.

"He's fine. Ev, I think she cured him. Alyssa."

"Oenone."

"Yeah. He told me she came to him while he was dreaming, when he was in a coma. He described her exactly in the same way we saw her. And it looks like he was in the same place that we were; he remembers the grass, the dew, the summer smell of the air."

"My God, that's simply beyond any explanation. It's remarkable."

"I know. Remarkable *and* scary."

"So she came to him and what?"

"She told him he needs to go back, that there was someone waiting for him who loves him."

"Jesus—"

"Yeah," Laura sighed. "So, I told him what we did. He was astonished, but believed everything. Apparently, Oenone's charm is unquestionable."

"So, is the cancer gone?"

"We don't know yet. The truth is, he awoke without any traces of radiotherapy on his skin. Because you know, he had a bit irritated chest, due to the treatment."

At this point Evy felt a bitter pinch in her heart. It looked like she was Oenone's toy. It must have been really funny for her, bringing such anguish. Who knew, maybe she was even the one who controlled when the distractions would happen. The Nymph helped Laura, she helped Bruce, but apparently there was no hope for Ev, who was too dumb to ask a man out. That did not seem fair. Evy felt the jealousy arousing inside of her.

"But how are you going to ask the doctors to re-diagnose him? Because he had a dream?"

"He was taken about fifteen minutes ago for routine tests since the first part of radiotherapy was over. They want to check if everything is fine, if his body's reacting to the treatment. Anyway, how are you holding up, Ev?"

"Not too well. I am tired, I haven't left my home for three days, I am trying to make it up to myself somehow, but, I won't lie to you, I am pretty disappointed Oenone screwed me like that."

"Maybe she thought your problem wasn't as serious."

"Oh come on, Laura, give me a break. Let me repeat I haven't left my home for three days. Oenone's funny little trick turned my life upside-down. I mean, I know I'm not sick, but what am I supposed to think, that I am stuck in this crap forever? I'm not even sure if I won't need to finish our conversation any minute because *it* might appear."

"I'm sorry, I didn't want it to sound like I'm patronizing the whole thing. Of course I understand your frustration. I don't know why she didn't help you."

"Maybe because she thinks I'm selfish, so I don't deserve the spell to be broken. I mean I have no husband to back me up."

"Evs, I'm sorry it's all happening like that, but I will *not* be sorry she saved Bruce."

Evy sighed. "Of course that's not what I meant. I'm just bitter. And I feel hopeless; I don't know what to do."

They were both silent for few seconds and Laura finally said, "Tell him."

"Who? What?"

"Tell Jeff what you did."

"What?"

"I mean, Oenone told you all you had to do was to take the first step, maybe it was a hint; perhaps she wanted your need to confess?"

"Well, it does look like she wants something in return. In your case it was taking the cancer back."

"In yours it could be admitting to what you've done. Under those circumstances it can be quite difficult; I mean, it's not like you deleted an important e-mail or something like that."

"Yeah, maybe. Who knows? I can't think of anything else anyway."

"We can always try to summon her again?"

"No. No, no, no. I am not doing that again! Ever! I guess talking to Jeff might help. At least he will know he is not going crazy, he'll know it's my fault he feels like this."

They went silent again.

"Laura? Do you think you might get cancer now again?"

"I don't know. It's possible."

"Did you tell that to Bruce?"

"No, of course not. I don't even know if it's going to happen. There's no need to bother him. But you know what?"

"Hmm?"

"I know I will take care of myself now. I guess I will always be on guard now, but I think it's good. I've learned my lesson."

"The hard way."

"Almost the hardest way possible. Okay, Ev, I need to go. Talk to Jeff, please. You owe him that; you've messed his life up pretty badly."

"I know. I'll call him later on."

"Bye."

"Let me know what Bruce's tests show."

"Will do."

Oenone~Agatha Rae~

❧94❧

Jeff was waiting for Neil at his office. He could barely sleep at night due to the excitement. It was very possible that it was the day that Jake's game would be over. Richards booked a meeting with David, who seemed quite reluctant when he found out that Jake was to be the subject of it, and it turned out to be pretty convenient as Garbinsky had some office hours scheduled for that day anyway. Their meeting was supposed to start at 10.

It was now 9:50 a.m. and Jeff saw Neil parking his car through the window. A moment later, Jackson was shaking his hand in the office.

"How was the trip?"

"Excellent. The traffic was fine. I had a very nice breakfast on the way."

"Great."

"So, where's David?"

"One floor up. Let's go, he's waiting for us."

At ten o'clock sharp Jeff and Neil shook David's hand and sat opposite of him by his desk.

"I understand you have some serious issues you want to talk about, Jeff," David started.

"I do."

"Gentlemen, would you like some coffee?"

"Yes, I'd like some, thank you," Neil said. Jeff asked for water instead. He was getting really excited and nervous about this whole thing. He could clearly see David felt uncomfortable because of their visit, a thing that made him both disappointed and angry.

David pored Jeff some water and asked Donna to prepare some coffee for him and Jackson and looked at them seriously.

"So, Jeff, by the phone you told me you had some news about Jake and his possible sabotage."

"Yes, you see my friend Neil has found out something."

"I've been contacting Mr. Owen Mack, MODENA's CEO, recently about that mysterious anonymous phone call that the printing house got concerning Jeff's questionable financial situation."

Neil stopped for a minute, hoping to see some interest in David's eyes, but Garbinsky was only listening.

"Well, I thought you might find it intriguing that the phone call wasn't so anonymous at all."

"Was it Jake?"

"No. It was Ted Gardner."

"Ted?" David asked, surprised. "Are you sure?"

"Yes. John Abram, the manager of MODENA's Boston branch said it was Ted who called him and he even faxed his statement in which he claims it was Gardner. We also have a phone number which was used during that conversation, but it's most probably a phone booth."

"David, is Ted at work today?" asked Jeff

"Yes."

"May we speak to him?"

"Certainly. It all looks unbelievable." Jeff couldn't help but notice that David calmed down. He finally seemed concerned. "So it wasn't Jake after all."

"Looks like it." Jeff nodded.

David asked the assistant to call Ted and now they were waiting. Finally Gardner arrived. He walked in confidently, but stopped in the middle of the office once he saw Jeff in the room.

"Hi, Ted," Richards said.

"Hi, Jeff. David, you wanted to see me."

"Yes, please sit down. I'd like you to listen to what these two gentlemen have to say. It's very interesting."

Ted rubbed his thighs nervously and sat down on a chair next to Neil.

"Ted, this is Neil Jackson, my friend from New York."

"How do you do?" said Neil and reached his hand to Ted.

"Hi," Ted responded while shaking hands.

"So, Neil is good friends with Owen Mack, do you know him?"

"No. Who's that?"

"He's MODENA's CEO, from the company headquarters in New York," Neil added.

Ted's face became a bit red. He was getting very nervous and Jeff had to admit he loved looking at Ted's discomfort. *This should be fun.*

"So, I met Neil a few days ago in Providence, and we were catching up and started talking about our work, businesses, that sort of thing, and I told him what an ugly thing happened to me, how MODENA dropped the contract and what problems it had caused, all because of some irrational anonymous phone call."

Ted's face got stiff. He was listening carefully, and Jeff actually spotted sweat on Gardner's forehead.

"Yeah, I got upset, because I am a businessman myself and I thought that such a move was simply low. I contacted Owen Mack to ask him if there was any way he might find out who *exactly* called John and said all this anonymous bullshit."

"And?" Ted asked.

"And it turned out it was you, Ted," said David.

"What! You can't be fucking serious!"

"Oh, trust me, *Ted*, we're all *very* fucking serious," said Jeff firmly.

Ted got up rapidly. "This is some dirty game you're all playing. I'll have my lawyer look into it!"

"Sit down, Ted," Jeff said in a tone that did not take no for an answer.

Ted sat back on his chair.

"I have a statement here, signed by John Abram that it was you calling, that you introduced yourself when he demanded the name of the person who would make such nasty allegations. He signed it. He also gave us the number of the phone which displayed while you were calling."

"You can't prove it's mine."

"Of course it could be any pre-paid one, or maybe you were just calling from a phone booth, doesn't matter, it's not up to us to find out, but it could be quite interesting for the police."

"The police? Are you fucking kidding me?"

"No, Ted, we're not," Jeff replied.

"What is all this, Ted? Why did you do that?" David asked.

Ted was breathing heavily. For a moment Jeff thought Gardner was going to have a heart attack, and, for a split of a second, he was wondering what they all would do if it really happened.

"Are you really going to call the police?"

"Yes," Neil said.

"Ted, you either start talking about what happened or I'll need to—"

"Okay, fine. I've had enough of this. It's just not worth it."

"What are you talking about?" asked Jeff.

"Could I get some water?" Ted asked.

~95~

Ted downed a glass of water in one gulp and poured himself another one. He put it aside, sat comfortably on an armchair, stretching his back and unbuttoned his jacket.

"Yes, it was me. I called MODENA and told them Jeff was facing serious financial problems."

"Why did you do that?" David asked.

"Because Jake Pinett forced me to."

Jeff couldn't resist smiling. He knew it! He knew it right from the start!

"So it was Jake after all!" Jeff said and looked at David.

"What do you mean David *forced* you?" Garbinsky said outraged.

"Look, there's no point for me to carry on this farce. Jake's number one priority is to take Jeff down and he's been using me for this purpose for quite some time now."

"What has Jeff ever done to him?" asked Neil.

"He *is*. That's it. Jake's hated him since the first day Jeff started his work for WORDS. All his successes, his ideas, David's respect, all of it only made him hate you, Jeff," answered Ted, resigned.

David looked at Jeff. Richards was very focused, intrigued by this whole revelation, but it was obvious he was going to dig this whole thing deeper.

"I'm sorry, Jeff. I've never had anything against you, but Jake—"

"No, hold on a minute," David said. "What do you mean Jake *hates* Jeff?"

"He does, I don't know why, but he detests him."

"And the letter I got, the one from the owner of the building, demanding my assurance that WORDS co-finance OMNIBUS...did you send the letter, too?"

"No, that was Jake's idea and he did it. What he was forcing me to do was keeping his side during all the board meetings and always voting against Jeff and then there was that phone call. I guess he felt sending a letter was *more* anonymous, and thus *less* risky, so he decided to do it on his own."

"And the forum? Was it you who posted warnings against Jake?" Jeff asked.

"Yes, it was me. He discovered it very soon and removed my posts."

"Wait!" David said. "How can he have such power over you? How the hell is it possible?"

"He's been blackmailing me for some time now, David. It's actually my own fault."

"What does he have against you?" Neil asked.

Ted drank some more of water, sighed deeply and rubbed his forehead.

"When I became a board member of WORDS, Jake and I hung out a lot. We went to see the Bruins, went to clubs together, or he would invite me to his home for some really crazy parties… And apparently during one of such nights, Jake spotted my weakness, he recorded it and now he's got me."

"What weakness?" Jeff asked.

Ted licked his lips nervously and reached for the glass.

"I like to party…hard. What can I say?"

"Drugs?" Neil asked.

"About a year ago Jake organized a major birthday party at his home. There were about a hundred people, music was pounding, limitless alcohol. It was wild. And yes, there were also drugs, mostly pot. The atmosphere was great, too great, and pretty soon I found myself stoned and surrounded by some nice, hot women. Things got out of control and it turned out Jake was recording everything. Later on, I passed out and woke up around noon. I had a major hangover. I remembered vaguely seeing him recording me, but wasn't sure if it actually happened."

David got up and started walking nervously around the office with his hands behind his back. He looked very uncomfortable.

"So, I understand he started using the recording to blackmail you."

"Yeah, fucking weasel. I didn't want any of this to come out because I was afraid of losing my job and about four months after the party I met a girl and we've been in a really nice relationship since."

"When did the blackmail start?" Neil asked.

"When Jeff came to work. I think Jake is jealous of his position."

"Oh come on, he has much more power as a member of the board than as a Creative Manager," Jeff said.

"I meant he is jealous of David's respect. Jake always lacked it."

"So he decided to crash me and used the party clip to make you help him."

"Yes. I'm really sorry, Jeff. You need to understand that as long as it was all only some sort of personal animosity, I felt uncomfortable about it, but was willing to co-operate with him. But the letter, the phone call…it was too much; it became dirty. I could have supported him in the board with voting against you." He looked at Richards and put his palm on his chest in an assuring gesture. "But he is really out of control now."

"And yet you haven't said a word or refused to make the phone call."

"I was afraid. We're talking about the possibility of me losing my reputation. Technically, what I do at work and what I do in my own free time are two separate things."

"Provided they do not intertwine," said Jeff looking at Garbinsky.

"They don't, trust me. However, we all know how it works. Such things as drug-and-alcohol-ignited sexual behavior is able to destroy everyone's career. Not to mention a relationship. I mean you must have seen "The Cable Guy", right?"

"I think now I might get that coffee, David," said Jeff.

"So, what are you going to do now?" asked Ted.

"Will you testify against Jake?" Neil asked.

"Yes."

"Even though it will more than likely mean revealing your sex-tape?"

"I've had enough of this crap; it's been a year. Jake needs to go down."

"What? You're not seriously thinking of informing the police about all this, are you?" David asked.

Everyone turned around and looked at him in awe.

"You're saying Jake should not be punished for an attempt to destroy my work, for sabotaging my business, for blackmailing Ted? David, what the hell?"

"I'm just saying that notifying the police is a very serious step and that well, basically, nothing bad happened, everything was revealed in time."

"David, you've always defended Jake, no matter how irrationally, hysterically and irresponsibly he has behaved. I've noticed it many times, and it had always puzzled me. But I must say it's no longer puzzling, it's fucking crazy. What is going on, why are you protecting his sorry ass?" Jeff shouted.

"Because he's my son, okay? Jake Pinett is my son!"

There was a complete silence in the room.

359

Oenone~Agatha Rae~

❧96❧

"Hi, Ev, I've been trying to call you for some time. I hope you're fine and just went for a walk or to the gym. Listen, Bruce's test results came back. He's as healthy as a horse. No signs of cancer. Nothing. The doctors couldn't believe it at first, but it's a fact. My husband is fine. The doctors told me they had never seen such quick a reaction to radiotherapy, but the three of us know what really happened. Anyway, they're letting Bruce home today, and we're planning on going back to Canada to finish our holidays. Please call me back or I'll get worried. I'll come to see you tonight, okay? Hugs!" Laura said as she recorded a massage on Evy's voice mail.

Oenone~Agatha Rae~

~97~

"Carol and I were together for thirty-seven years. God knows I loved my wife all this time, but around our fifth year of marriage we were going through a rough patch. It was quite soon after Laura was born, we were not handling things too well. Carol had postpartum depression, I was in the middle of getting WORDS going and our relationship was pretty tense. To tell the truth, I was simply escaping from home, from the always-crying Tessa, always-irritated and depressed Carol. I was entirely focused on work.

I would often visit a bar in the evenings, before coming back home and this was where I met Catherine. She was fascinating. Long legs, beautiful, dark hair, mysterious smile. She looked like a film star from the 50s. Classy, gorgeous. And she was as lonely as I was. I hadn't even noticed when we started seeing each other regularly, first in the bar, then we were meeting in the evenings at WORDS' first building. We would drink wine, talk until late at night and have sex. We both knew it was only for a moment, that it was just temporary, neither of us were thinking of creating a relationship, we were just comforting each other. Two lonely people seeking warmth. It lasted about three months. I don't know if Carol suspected anything, I assumed she did but never said anything.

Anyway, my marriage started getting back on the right track and I felt I no longer needed Catherine. On the night when I was supposed to tell her it was over, she told me she was pregnant. She was crying, asking me what to do, and my mind went completely blank. She was considering abortion, but I convinced her not to do that. I assured her I would support her financially, but I was rebuilding my marriage, so I would not be present in the child's life. Catherine was supposed to think it over and two days later she informed me she was moving to her aunt's place in Rhode Island. We made a deal I would send her money until Jake was eighteen years old and she would never say anything to Carol. I got a letter from her seven months later that Jake was born. I was sending her money every month. I paid for Jake's summer camps, school. I was lucky, WORDS was really successful so it was easy for me to hide the money from Carol."

"So how did Jake become a board member?" asked Jeff.

"First of all, Catherine never kept my fatherhood in secret from Jake. Even though I first saw him when he was twenty-eight, four years ago, he knew exactly who his father was. The problem started when Jake did not get in to college. He had been rejected three times as a candidate and he managed to graduate from some minor business school, but was unable to find a steady job. His mother contacted me then, for the first time after almost thirty years, and demanded my help. She threatened she would inform my daughter that she had a brother out of wedlock. It turned out she knew exactly where Tessa lived and I would never stand the notion of her finding out about that particular episode in my life.

Catherine said Jake deserved my help for spending his whole life without a father. So, I hired Jake as my assistant. He spent almost three years in that position, but he wanted, as he claimed, a more serious one, something allowing him to make decisions. He wanted to become Creative Manager, but I was absolutely against it.

Quite soon I discovered that Jake was unable to fulfill any duties. He loved partying, he would often come to work hangover, and I can't even tell you how many meetings he missed because of his poor organization skills. Sometimes I wonder if he is really worthless, or if he is just trying to pay me back after all those years of my absence in his life. Anyway, I decided that a Creative Managerial position was everything my son should never have and I gave him a board-member status. It was a mistake, but at least he doesn't have the majority and all I need to handle are his irrational arguments, but he's harmless." He paused, "Or so I thought until today."

"So, he really wants my job," said Jeff.

"Only now he wants it because he's jealous of my respect and good rapport with you."

"Yeah, suddenly he's lacking his daddy," added Ted, making David twitch.

"Jeff, please, let's not make any rash decisions here; I mean we *know* what he did. We can stop him now, and there's no need to get the police involved."

"David, are you kidding?"

"No, by all means, no. Listen to me, I can degrade him, I can fire him, but I cannot send him to prison. I was absent in his life for over thirty years. He got here in search of help and now I am supposed to watch him face charges?"

"With all due respect, David. Your complicated family situation is not my problem. I have been working my ass off for your company, and for the last six months I have been building a new publishing house in order to increase your profit. Jake has undermined my authority as a manager, he caused me the loss of a very important contract and is one obsessed lunatic who would not step back until he gets what he wants—need an example? Look at Ted."

"But I've been protecting you, Jeff! I cleared up landlord's doubts, I was the one who pushed the idea of giving you the six months' time to start OMNIBUS, Jake wanted me to fire you right away."

"David, I appreciate that, but if you feel any remorse because you were absent in your son's life, then why don't you catch up that time by giving him the very first example of father-to-son practical wisdom—that one needs to take responsibility for his actions."

"Jeff—"

"End of story, David. Come on, Neil, let's go."

They left David's office and in complete silence went downstairs to Jeff's. David sat behind the desk, took his glasses off and rubbed his face with a gesture of a tired and resigned man. He looked at Ted who was still sitting in his chair.

"I'm so sorry, Ted. I really am," Garbinsky said calmly.

Ted shrugged his shoulders and shook his head. "What a mess," he said finally, finished his water, put the glass back on the desk and left.

Once Jeff and Neil were inside Richards' office, they closed the door and sat on the sofa.

"This is all unbelievable," Neil said.

"This, my friend, calls for a nice drink," Jeff replied and got up to a mini bar.

"At 11.10 in the morning?"

"I could make a toast for getting rid of Jake Pinett at 5.30 in the morning. Without hesitation."

"Okay, you're right." Neil laughed.

Jeff poured some whiskey into the glasses and threw a few cubes of ice into each of them. He handed one to Neil.

"So, I guess the whole battle begins once we notify the police, right?" Jeff asked.

"Yeah. Sabotage, blackmail. It all sounds pretty severe to me."

"What if Ted decides not to testify? I mean he's in a combative mood now, but who knows? He might think things through and decide he won't do it."

Neil reached into an inside pocket of his jacket and took out a small digital voice recorder. "I don't think he will have a choice."

"That is simply beautiful," Jeff said as he laughed out loud. They rapped the glasses and drank the whiskey.

Jeff and Neil had lunch together and Jackson went back to New York. Richards was wandering around downtown for some time, enjoying the wonderful feeling a person had once something was taken off one's chest and thought of Evy. It felt quite embarrassing that he hadn't thought of her earlier, after all she was in the middle of the whole Jake pandemonium and needed to know what happened. Besides, it had been several days since he saw and talked to her; they had never had such a long break. He missed her, what could he say. She wasn't at work since the day they had had that fight at his office, and she hadn't sent the book she was editing either. It did not seem like her. Suddenly, a very uncomfortable thought appeared in his head, pinching his conscience that maybe something bad had happened.

He called her cell phone six times in a row. Nothing. It seemed odd at first, but he thought she might have gone out or maybe she was seeing Laura. He kept calling her, though, and when she still wasn't answering, something inside of him told him he should go and see her.

Jeff parked his car outside Evy's apartment block and walked inside to the staircase. He pushed the elevator button, but the anxiety inside of him aroused so much, he decided not to wait for it and walked upstairs instead. Jeff knocked on the door, but Evy didn't open. He rang the bell once, twice, three times, but nothing happened. He took his phone out and called her one more time, but she still wasn't answering.

Finally, he knocked more aggressively and spotted the door was slightly ajar. Now, he was truly worried. Jeff entered the apartment slowly and silently, carefully closed the door and looked around. Everything seemed to be in perfect order. Not knowing what, or who—his first suspicion was that the apartment was being robbed—to expect, he looked around the corridor took an umbrella which was resting next to the wall, and, pointing its sharp end ahead of him, ready to stake whomever or whatever would come out at him, he gently moved forward.

"Evy?"

He walked into the kitchen and the living room. The TV was silently on and the coffee table was knocked over. There was a horrible mess all around the place; dirty plates in the sink, cups filled with unfinished tea, crumbles all over the kitchen top. Closed windows did not allow any fresh air in, indicating that the garbage was not taken for some days.

"Evy!" he finally shouted.

"Go away, Jeff," he heard her. She was in the bedroom. He walked toward it silently, unsure of what to expect and cautiously opened the door. What he saw was petrifying.

The smell in the bedroom was awful. The air was musty, filled with a scent of sweat, apparently Evy did not open windows for a few days. The blinds were half-closed, so it was quite dark inside. Flabbergasted, he put the umbrella on the floor and walked further inside. Evy was on her bed, tired, completely run down. She was half naked, her sheets were partly torn and the whole room felt stuffy. She was exhausted, sweaty strands of hair were sticking to her cheeks and her swollen eyes made it clear she was crying. Evy seemed to be only partly aware of what was going on, but she spotted him. Her eyes widened.

"Go away, Jeff, don't look at me," she said sadly, closed her eyes and turned away from him. A few tears fell down her cheeks.

"Oh my God," he whispered. "What's happened? What is going on?"

Jeff walked toward her, took off his jacket and covered her up. He helped her to sit down, sat next to her and she put her head on his shoulder. He embraced her tight.

"What's going on, Ev?" he asked quietly.

"I -I need help, Jeff. Please take me out from here."

"Of course."

He lifted her up and helped her walk to the living room. She sat on the sofa and curled up her legs. Jeff went to the kitchen annex, opened the window and fetched her a glass of water. Evy drank a few sips, swept her hair off her face and looked at him.

"I need to tell you something. You'll probably hate me even more for that, but I don't care. I even think I deserve it."

He sat closely to her. "What is it?"

"Those waves of cold you've been experiencing, the anger you feel toward me, it's—it's my fault," she said and started crying.

"What are you talking about?"

"I fell in love with you, Jeff, I really did, but I was afraid of asking you out because you're my boss. Then we had this weekend in Westville and I'll be honest, I really thought we could make it, but the next thing you know it, you made the decision, for both of us, that we were not to be together." She sniffed, and reached for a box of handkerchiefs, "I thought

I was fine, but it wasn't true, I was lying to myself. So, Laura found this brochure of Alyssa, a healer…"

"Calm down, Evy, we have lots of time," he said and stroked her hair.

Evy took a deep breath. "I'd be calmer if you brought me a t-shirt."

"Sure." Jeff stood up. "Where would I be if I were a t-shirt?"

"In the wardrobe, on the left."

Evy told Jeff everything. About Laura finding Alyssa, the distractions, how she enjoyed them at first and how soon they became the source of frustration, how they affected her work and how she had spent days in her apartment, afraid of going out. Evy was crying all the time she was confessing it all to him and Jeff was standing by the kitchen top, listening carefully to what she was saying. When she finished, she drank some of the water again and looked at him miserably. Her eyes were swollen and her face was red. She covered herself with a blanket. A few strands of hair stuck to her cheeks and forehead again. Jeff thought she kind of looked as if she had the flu. She was waiting for him to say something, or to just walk out and was sure that if he kept quiet and motionless for another minute or two, she would simply go insane.

"So, that Alyssa, she really helped Laura?" he finally asked.

Surprised that his very first question concerned Laura, Evy nodded positively.

"So, you decided to mess up my life *after* you have checked that the healer worked."

"Jeff—"

"No, that's a bit comforting, because at least it wasn't a pure experiment. I mean, I should be glad and thankful I only have those waves of cold, and occasionally lose my temper like a madman. After all, who knows, I could have had my skin changed into scales or start changing into a wolf at night."

He laughed bitterly, looked down and started nodding his head in disbelief. Evy had no idea what to say. He was right. God only knows what kind of side effects her little wish might have had. Oenone did seem unpredictable.

"If it wasn't for my own strange behavior I would have problems believing you. Because, you know," Jeff continued, "Apparently those cold waves, it must be some kind of substitute for the feelings I had for you. As well as the anger. Honestly, Ev, I think Alyssa, must have replaced my emotions with anger and cold. That would make sense."

"Then why aren't you angry now?"

"I don't know."

"So, Oenone finally healed Bruce, he doesn't have the cancer anymore. Of course Laura is now ready to hear she has her own back. Jesus, it's like a vicious circle." She curled her legs again and covered her face with her hands.

"You know, most of it all is actually my fault."

"What do you mean?" She looked at him.

"The truth is," he walked toward Evy and sat down next to her, "I've had feelings for you from the first day I saw you, from our very first lunch we had in a break room. But I was too dumb to admit it. I mean, practically weeks before I had split up with Rachel and afterwards, I had all this 'I am free, I want some fun' attitude in my head, and I kept pushing away the emotions which were growing inside of me. When we were in Westville, God, I never wanted to use you, it's not like that. It's just that, I wanted to be with you with every cell of my body. I dreamed of spending a night with you and did not want to resist it any longer. In the morning I realized how complicated things could have become, and made up that stupid talk about not promising you anything. I felt like a total jerk. I knew I was hurting you, but I was too afraid to act any different. And then OMNIBUS started and we were both insanely busy…The truth is, I have never wanted to go to work so much as then because I knew that half of the day I would get to spend with you. And I was still too dumb to confess my feelings. So, I really think I only have myself to blame for this whole crap that had started. You were the one who took action. Desperate, bizarre and *seriously* fucked up, I'll admit, but at least you did something. I think I kind of deserved it all."

She hugged him, spontaneously and honestly. Evy was sure he would condemn her, that he would shout, walk out shutting doors. And here he was, calm, and regretting. And he forgave her.

"Jeff, I don't know how to take it back."

"We'll figure it out. I…I just want my love for you to come back. I can't stand pushing you away like that, it breaks my heart."

For the first time since Westville he kissed her. It was a gentle and smooth kiss, but it had more emotions and was far more dramatic than Evy thought she could handle. There was everything in that kiss; apologies, forgiveness, confession, honesty, hope. Their hearts were pounding, they felt dizzy and, suddenly, the nightmare was over. She knew it. He looked at her and they were both completely silent. He knew it, too. They both finally knew how precious they were for each other. They grew up. It was a great relief.

"How about trying that again?" he whispered.

"I'd love that," she nodded smiling.

"Would you like to have lunch with me tomorrow?"

"No."

"No?"

"No, Jeff. I'd like to have dinner with you. Tonight."

He smiled, kissed and embraced her again.

"I'll pick you up at seven."

"I'll be waiting."

Oenone~Agatha Rae~

～99～

About two hours later, Evy walked into her bedroom. What a sorry view it all was. She took the sheets off her bed. They reminded her of her own enslavement, weakness and misery. She went to the kitchen, took one gigantic trash bag and pushed them inside of it. She tied it and put it next to the door to throw it away. She would burn it if she could. Next, Evy opened the window and aired the room. She took her cell phone out of her handbag, went to the living room and called Laura.

"Hi, Laura!"

"Ev, thank God! I've been calling you all day!"

"I know, I heard the phone, but I couldn't pick it up."

"Because of —*this*?"

"Yes."

"Oh, I'm so, so sorry."

"So, I got your message, and I'm thrilled, Laura! Bruce's fine, you're fine—"

"It's been only two days, so it's hard to say if I'm fine."

"You will be, Laura, I have no doubts about it. Just, take care of yourself this time, okay? Remember about prevention."

"I swear I will. It's been crazy time, and I've learned my lesson. Evy, you sound different."

"I sure hope so," she said as she smiled.

"What happened?"

"Jeff was here today. I explained everything, and I think *they're* gone. The distractions. I can't explain it in anyway, but I'm pretty sure it won't happen again."

"Oh my God, that's so wonderful! Ev! So that was it! You had to be honest with him!"

"I think so. And, he was honest with me, too, I think we're finally on the same page, Jeff and I."

"Wait, don't tell me more, I'll bring some wine in the evening and you'll tell me all about it." Laura laughed.

"Umm, no, here's the thing, I'm busy in the evening. I'm having a date."

"With who?"

"Santa Claus, Laura!" Evy laughed. "Jeff's picking me up at seven."

"Finally! So, he admitted it? He finally told you've never been just a co-worker?"

"Yes."

"I'm so happy for you, Ev, oh my God, you have no idea."

"And I'm so happy for you, too."

"It's scary, but I kind of think Oenone helped us a lot. Even though she did make a lot of mess in our lives."

"But we did learn something, didn't we? I think I can finally see it now."

"We did, that's true."

"So, Laura, when are you going back to Canada?"

"The day after tomorrow. Bruce's totally fine, there's no sign he had ever had any health problems, so we don't need to see the doctors anymore or ask their permission. We're just going. And when we come back, I am planning to send my resume and apply for a position of a senior editor at OMNIBUS. What do you think, do I have a chance?"

"Well, I'll back you up in case the manager had any doubts," said Evy smiling.

"Okay, I gotta go, we're about to leave the hospital. I love you Ev."

"I love you, too. Thanks Laura."

"For what?"

"For everything."

At half past seven, Jeff and Evy were sitting in an Italian restaurant on Columbus Avenue, drinking red wine and waiting for their chicken and shrimp pastas. They were having a great time laughing and joking. Jeff told her how he and Neil compromised Ted and Jake and Evy couldn't believe that suddenly she was rediscovering not only her long-time boss, David Garbinsky, but also Ted, whom she thought she knew quite well.

"I mean you know, we used to talk a lot during Christmas parties and at work, so I thought he was a nice guy. Who knew?"

"Right? I had the same feeling. That is why I was really taken aback when Neil told me it was Ted who had called. All in all, you have no idea how glad I am to have it off my chest."

"Believe me, I kind of *have* a feeling."

"True. So, David called me about two hours ago and offered me Jake's position as a member of the board. I think he feels pretty bad about what happened."

"I think you should take it. You deserve this."

"I think so, too." He winked. "But I declined. I want to focus on OMNIBUS now. I want to make it strong enough to be independent from WORDS one day, and then I will have my own board. What do you think about that?"

"Sounds great."

"Listen, tell me more about that Oenone. How did you manage to find out who she was?"

Evy told him in detail how she found out Alyssa was a Nymph and how they summoned her, and about Bruce's dream. She thought Jeff would laugh at some point, after all, the story seemed somewhat crazy and unrealistic to *her*, even though she had experienced it. He didn't do that and, instead, he was listening to Eve very attentively.

"You must think, it all sounds like a scenario for a pretty bad fantasy movie," she said in the end.

"On the contrary. After all, I have experienced it all myself. And, although meeting a Nymph sounds reality-challenging." They laughed. "I have always believed that there are some strange creatures *in* this world or *out* of this world. And that it's better to stay away from them."

"I wish I had such knowledge before."

"Sometimes knowledge kills the intuition." Jeff took her hand and kissed it.

"So, I talked to Laura today. She is going to Canada with Bruce to finish their holidays and asked me if there was any chance for her to work for OMNIBUS as a senior editor, what do you think?"

"I have absolutely nothing against that, but you need to ask the co-manager."

"Co-manager? Who?"

"The lovely Ms. Evelyn Dax, of course."

Evy laughed and they raised their glasses.

"To OMNIBUS, to honesty and, to us," Jeff said. They tapped the glasses and kissed.

About the Author

Agatha Rae (Joanna Bogusławska) is an author and a college teacher from Gdynia, Poland. She has published a book for the teachers of English "Teaching English Through Culture, Teaching Culture Through English" (co-written with Agata Mioduszewska) as well as an anthology of essays analyzing popular culture "Popkultura – pop czy kultura?" (Eng. "Popular culture – pop or culture?"). Her articles written both in English and Polish have been published in magazines Forum For The World Literature Studies, The Teacher, Kino, Top Guitar and Perkusista, she also collaborated with http://www.stephen-moyer.net website, published a dozen of film reviews there and she runs a blog on one of Poland's biggest opinion-forming portals www.natemat.pl. She is a PhD student at the University of Gdansk. Among her favorite authors are Stephen King, Billy Bryson, Tennessee Williams, The Beat Generation authors and Charles Bukowski.

Oenone~Agatha Rae~

Made in the USA
San Bernardino, CA
04 September 2013